Floating on Air . . .

"So who were you talking to before?" Jake asked.

"John and Elizabeth."

"Your sorority sister?"

"Not really. I guess you could call them angels." Lilly grinned as she moved past him, leaning in just so, letting her shoulder brush against his arm. She wanted to lift up on her toes and kiss him, but other than dancing with him three years ago, it was really like they'd only just met yesterday. She should be happy with her progress so far; she had him right where she wanted him.

Ah, the heck with it. As soon as he slid in behind the wheel, she scooted over and, turning his face toward hers, she softly pressed her lips where she'd been dying to all night.

Oh heavens! She'd had no idea what she was getting into here. What started as a brief, gentle kiss quickly turned wicked, heating up areas that hadn't been heated in, well, maybe never.

"What was that for?" he whispered hoarsely.

"Thanks for saving my life."

JENNA McNIGHT

A Date on Cloud Nine

AVON BOOKS

An Imprint of HarperCollins*Publishers*

AVON BOOKS
An Imprint of HarperCollins*Publishers*
10 East 53rd Street
New York, New York 10022-5299

Copyright © 2004 by Ginny Schweiss
ISBN: 0-7394-4601-0

For Julie Beard, Eileen Dreyer,
Shirl Henke, Carol Monk,
and Karyn Witmer-Gow,
who have more good ideas
on how to steer a plot
than any other gals I know.
Thanks for Thursdays!

And for Charlotte Nations,
who eagerly answered my call for a reader
at the last minute.
Thanks again!

1

Lilly Marquette couldn't believe she was parked in front of Cloud Nine. Sure, she'd promised her best friend anything she wanted for her birthday, but she hadn't figured on a shop with a red-lettered notice on the glass door that said: ADULTS ONLY. MUST BE EIGHTEEN OR OLDER TO ENTER. NO EXCEPTIONS.

She snuggled deeper—meaning *lower*—into the limo's heated leather seat and turned her fur collar up on her neck. If she scrunched low enough, she could disappear, safe from the eyes of anyone driving by. The only witness to this fiasco so far was her driver, and he'd forget anything for a pound of Godiva.

"I'll wait here," she said.

"You can't," Betsy argued.

"It's okay, I like to watch it snow."

"It's freezing."

"Then don't hold the door open when you get out."

Betsy put on the same persuasive little pout that had

gotten Lilly into lots of trouble over the years. Once they'd reached puberty, it usually revolved around the opposite sex.

"Go by yourself," Lilly insisted. "I wouldn't be caught dead in there."

Still the pout. "But you said you'd buy me whatever I want for my birthday."

"Yeah, a purse. Or a scarf. Not . . ." She trailed off, waving a hand toward the red ADULTS ONLY sign. "I'll get it off the Internet."

"But my birthday's today. What's your problem?"

"Gee, I don't know. Maybe watching you sort through vibrators might be embarrassing."

"Well it shouldn't be. Brady's been gone five months now. I'm sorry, sweetie, but it's a fact. And here's another one. If you ever expect to have those kids you want so bad?—you need to start getting out. You should come in and practice making doe eyes at the clerk."

"*Doe eyes?*" Lilly snickered. "You've been buying your novels here, too, haven't you?"

"Don't knock it. Whatever you want to call it, it's set more men drooling over you than I can count."

"Flattery won't work. But feel free to keep it up."

Betsy grimaced. "Ooh, a word of caution. When you go in there, you might not want to say anything with the words 'keep it up' in it."

"No problem, I'm not—"

"And it's not flattery." Betsy slumped against her door. "Shit, it's not fair. Men *think* they want blue-eyed blondes until they see you. You know what Brian said you remind him of?"

"Probably nothing nice." Because Brian was ancient

history, before Brady, a two-and-a-half-year marriage, and widowhood.

"Whiskey," Betsy answered, as if Lilly were interested, which she definitely wasn't. "Let's see, how'd he put it? Something like you're 'a tall glass of prime liquor, with a golden spark in your eyes that sets a man on fire.'"

"Oh puh-lease."

"There was more about burning a fire in his insides on the way down."

Lilly hooted, prodding Betsy with her foot. "You want to step out in a dignified manner, or do I have to open that door and shove you out?"

"You have to come in to pay anyway."

"I don't have enough cash."

"They take charges."

"Oh yeah, I want my accountant to think I shop at Cloud Nine."

"Come on, it'll give you a chance to meet the clerk. I promise, the man oozes pure sex. Swear to God, he's got enough charisma to jump-start a dead woman's heart. Though," she admitted, knowing it mattered, "I doubt he has a dime to his name."

Lilly slid a meaningful glance at the storefront. "Hence where he works. I'd like to think I'm more discriminating."

"Well, you should enjoy this then: I tried to pick him up last time I was here, and as much as it pains me to admit this"—she lowered her voice—"I failed."

"No!"

Betsy bobbed her head in silent confirmation.

"Well now I have to go in." To see the man who'd turned Betsy down, Lilly'd brave both cold and embarrassment. "Hand me that hat, would you?"

The only other car in the lot was a yellow taxi, with two bright red, heart-shaped balloons dancing at the end of their tether, tied to the antenna. It also had an inch of snow covering the hood, so it'd been there a good long while which meant there'd be no other customers to get embarrassed in front of. Lilly followed Betsy inside, pulling up short as soon as the door swung shut behind them.

"You go ahead," she said, suddenly wondering how she could make a graceful exit without appearing majorly intimidated by a few racks of wispy, next-to-nothing lingerie. She butted the door open, making excuses as she backed out. "I hear my phone. I think it's my broker."

Betsy hauled her back in. "Funny. You know that gadget in your purse you're so connected to? It's not ringing."

"It's on vibrate." She winced as soon as she said it, her gaze darting around to make sure no one was paying them any undue attention. So far, so good.

"I won't be long," Betsy promised. "Stay."

"Okay. I'll, uh, just hang around here, you know, by the door."

She felt conspicuous and stupid standing still, so she brushed snow off her hat, tucked a few stray dark wisps of hair back underneath, then stamped slush off her leather boots, all the while surreptitiously checking out the store to make sure there'd be no witnesses to their folly.

Surprisingly, once she allowed herself to really look, the inside of the store itself wasn't too bad. Instead of the sleazy, dirty, dimly lit, smoke-filled area she'd imagined from the condition of the neighborhood in general and the strip mall specifically, it looked like a place someone took pride in: well lit and tidy. Even the carpet was clean enough to pick up a wayward nickel and pocket it.

Betsy groaned, as if being with someone who'd pick up a stray coin was somehow ten times more embarrassing than being in a sex shop. "Tell me you didn't."

"What? It's a nickel."

"I swear, all your money and you'd still stop on a highway if you saw a dime. I'm moving now. I'll be over there."

The interior was nicely organized, with clothing to the left and shelves straight ahead. To the right were racks of gadgets, with—*Wouldn't you know?*—three women standing in a loose group, discussing a package they passed back and forth, and they weren't exactly whispering. Lilly looked away to give them their privacy; but shoot, this was the twenty-first century, and if they were in here buying vibrators together, secrecy sure as heck wasn't an issue. They looked perfectly normal and average; they probably carpooled all week, got together on Friday nights to play Bunko, and took the kids to church on Sunday.

God, wouldn't that be great? Well, not the average part, but she'd give anything to be a mom. She wouldn't shuffle her children off to nannies and boarding school, either, no way. She'd be what she'd never had: a loving mother who'd bandage her kids' scrapes, read them stories, and hug them to pieces without notice.

A faint odor abruptly caught her attention, and she sniffed the air to place it. "I think I smell gas. Hey, Betsy—"

A big guy in a navy T-shirt popped into view for a split second, to her right, behind a counter piled high with stacks of inventory.

"Sorry about that," he said. "I thought I had it all aired out."

Sooo . . .

His voice was promising, a nice, deep timbre with a sexy rumble that made her think she'd be willing to forgive him anything, just as long as he kept talking.

"Furnace is on the blink," he explained, ducking out from behind the boxes and passing behind a tall rack on his way to the door.

Lilly took her own inventory. Thick black hair—she could see that over the rack, so he was tall. Long legs, no holes in his jeans, leather boots instead of ratty tennis shoes. This was getting better by the second. He might be worth a couple dates down the road, when she was ready again. Large hands. Muscular arms that could have taken the door off its hinges without tools if it hadn't cooperated. A quick check of his ring finger as he worked at propping the door open was inconclusive. What she really needed was for him to turn around.

Please, God, let nothing on his face be pierced.

The three women perked up and drifted in his direction. They all took off their hats, fluffed their hair, and unbuttoned their coats. One swiped on fresh lip gloss.

"The repairman's working on it now. I hope it's not too cold in here for you. Better move away from the door. Wander around, let me know if you need help."

He was the kind of big that a man gets partly from genes, partly from working hard. Her gaze boldly roamed over impressively wide shoulders stretching his navy T-shirt to its limits, a trim waist, a nicely rounded butt, and well-muscled thighs. With that much virility to look at, she didn't care how cold it was. Maybe not even where she was.

He breezed behind the rack again, not lumbering like many big men, but exhibiting an easy grace as he headed straight back behind the counter and all those darned boxes. "See anything you like, let me know."

Politely helpful—or had she been caught staring?

The boldest of the three zeroed in on him. "I need to pick up a video for my neighbor. Can you recommend something?"

"Sure, be right there."

Lilly drifted away from the frigid air, staying to the left and center of the store, not lingering too long on any one thing. Was he single? Was he watching her thumb through crotchless panties, curious as to whom she'd wear them for?

Was he straight? She touched a pair of fuzzy handcuffs to see if they were as soft as they looked. Better move on; he'd think she was kinky.

Was he in a relationship? She picked up a key chain, thinking that looked safe enough to handle, until she noticed it was a miniature glow-in-the-dark penis.

Well, who could be without one of those?

She started to read the front of a box, but it was a game for lovers only. *Move on before he thinks I have one.* All the time thinking, *Come out, come out, wherever you are*, and wondering what was a safe question to ask that would bring him into full view. Try as she might, she couldn't find one non-sex-related item to ask about.

"Hey, Lilly, I think I found what I want," Betsy announced loud and clear.

He started ringing up purchases for the three women, and politely said, "Well . . . thank you," to the one who was writing her phone number across his hand as Lilly strolled by. She still hadn't gotten a look at his face by the time she joined Betsy, her attention only half-there and half-listening to the rest of the conversation by the register, trying to pick up any personal information he offered. Something like *My wife likes this one* would be a real clue.

"What do you think of this?" Betsy thrust a package into Lilly's hands.

It was wrapped in clear plastic so the consumer could check out what she was getting before she paid for it. No way Lilly could pretend she was holding some normal massage therapy gadget.

"Or this?"

Now she had two. *Please, God, keep him way over there a little while longer.*

"We're having a buy-one-get-one-half-off special," he announced across the store. She probably could see his face now if she turned, but geez, she could just imagine what he was thinking.

"Great idea!" Betsy said. "Why don't you get one while you're here, Lill? You know I'm going to love this, and then you'll be jealous and just have to come back for your own. Then you'll miss the sale, and you know how you get when something costs you extra."

"Pick one," Lilly gritted through clenched teeth, low and threatening.

"No wait, I know. You love to read in the limo. Let's get you a book."

From *here*?

"*The Kind of Sex Men Really Want* sounds good. And look, pictures."

"*Betsy.*"

"All right, don't get huffy. Geez, how long's it been since you got naked with a man in the backseat anyway?"

"I don't get naked in the—"

"Well what good's having a limo if you don't utilize it?"

Lilly caught the dangerous glimmer in Betsy's eyes that said she knew exactly where Lilly's mind was, how it worked, and how to tease her.

Betsy held up several packages and, loud enough to be heard three blocks away, asked, "What do you think? Red, blue, or green? Or there's natural."

Lilly's pithy retort died a dry, lumpy death in her throat as Sexy Rumble strode toward them.

"There's a sampler pack here," he said, snagging it off a nearby rack on his way. "Different colors, different textures. Better price."

"Oh," Betsy purred. "A beginner's set. Look, Lilly."

She tried not to. She tried darting a glance up at him beneath lowered lashes whenever she thought he wouldn't notice, but that just meant she still couldn't see his face, and she so wanted to know whether it went with the rest of him. If nothing ridiculous was pierced, she wanted to chat him up a few minutes and see where that went, maybe ask for his number—strictly for future reference—but then how would she answer the question that inevitably would come up down the road: So, how did you two meet?

In a dildo shop. Now there was one to tell the grand-children.

"Or there's this one." He handed Betsy another package. "My ex-girlfriend said this big boy can do anything a man can do *and* it doesn't snore."

He tipped his head just so, just enough to indicate that he knew he should be embarrassed to talk to women so frankly, but hell, he was so damned sexy, he could get away with it.

Geez, this guy could sell a sex toy to St. Peter.

It'd be better to drive by someday when he was locking up, then "bump" into him somewhere else like, say, the grocery store. Then she could talk to him a few minutes, see if there was mutual interest—Yeah, that was a plan. In the meantime, so he wouldn't recognize her later, she pulled her hat down to her eyebrows.

Betsy grinned up at him, way up. "You say she left you for one of these?"

"That's not exactly what—"

"Want a second opinion?"

"Oh-kay." Desperate to stop this before they made out in front of her, Lilly made a show of pushing up her sleeve and checking her watch. "Say, did I mention I have a twelve o'clock appointment? It's almost twelve now. We should go."

"You want this one then?" he asked.

Betsy even made "Uh-huh" sound sexy.

"You want one, too?" he asked over his shoulder, heading toward the register with a second package in hand.

"Uh, no thanks."

"Did you decide on a book?"

Great, he'd heard that. "No thanks."

Following him past a rack of Velcroed pants, Lilly pictured him in a pair, the kind he could rip off with one deft maneuver during a striptease. She wondered why he worked in a place like this, what he got out of it, and what he thought of the women who came in here. Too bad she couldn't strike up a conversation with him, ascertaining whether he had a brain to go with the body and was worth her time, or whether he was several IQ points short of desirable.

Hmm, did that make her a dildo shop snob?

"That'll be thirty-seven twenty-two."

Still mesmerized by his voice, which rumbled even more close-up, and putting up a pretense of searching through her purse for something so she could keep her face averted, Lilly automatically handed over her charge card.

And then snatched it back. "Uh, sorry," she said, laughing self-consciously. "I need to get some change, so can you break a, uh, twenty? Two twenties, I mean?"

He probably was rolling on the floor inside, knowing exactly why she was paying cash and why she was buying a toy for her friend.

Shit, he'll think we're a couple!

Good thing she wasn't trying to pick him up here and now; he'd think she wanted a threesome. She rooted through her purse for more of a disguise. Lipstick; no help. Tissues—she could blow her nose. Not attractive; he'd look away. Good. She blew.

"Don't feel bad," he said. She could just hear the grin in his voice. "It used to be impossible to find a virgin over the age of eighteen. Now it's hard to find a woman who doesn't have her own toys."

Sunglasses!—thank you, God. She shoved them on.

"Your change is two seventy-eight."

The coins he dropped in her palm were warm, far too toasty to have come from a register in a store where the furnace wasn't working. He'd probably been holding them in his hot hand while he eavesdropped. Lord, the things he must hear in here! He added the dollar bills next, which she should have been able to hold on to, but she was so caught up in the study of the inside of her purse that a breeze from the front door plucked them up and sent them fluttering across the floor.

"Oh, sorry," he said. "I'll get—"

But she was already off after them, bounding across the carpet, diving under the rack of red and pink crotchless panties on sale for Valentine's Day.

"Let her do it," Betsy said dryly. "When it comes to money, it doesn't get away from Lilly."

A heart-splattered Merry Widow caught on Lilly's fur hat and flopped over her face.

"Hey, Lill, maybe that's a sign," Betsy said. "You should buy it."

"Get real."

It'd be a long time before she wore a Merry Widow for anyone. She'd need a decent amount of time before she started dating again—because she'd like a loving and devoted husband, too—add to that the months it'd take to weed out the losers, then add months more to establish a deep relationship, get engaged . . . Geez, at that rate, it'd be *years* before she had a baby.

She caught both wayward bills and stared at them. Money was important, sure, but she'd give up all of hers to have a baby a whole lot sooner.

There was a crash in the back of the store, followed by

a curse, and Sexy Rumble pulled up short. "Everything okay back there?"

A shout followed. "Everybody out! Now!"

The ensuing explosion was the last thing Lilly heard before something hit her in the head, hard. She went down. Just before she blacked out completely, her last thought was of her parents reading the world's worst headline: DILDO SHOP DETONATES, ONE DEAD.

2

Lilly thought she'd heard quiet before, until now.

Suddenly there was nothing. *Nada.* Not even her own heartbeat. Total blackness. Total silence, like . . .

She couldn't even say what it was like. But it was eerie. *Am I deaf?*

No sooner had she given life to that thought than she began to hear things again. Fire crackling, voices shouting—one a deep rumble, the other, Betsy.

No matter how hard Lilly tried to hang on to the voices, on to the brief, fleeting comfort they provided, they started to fade about the same time she saw a pinpoint of light overhead. Glowing steadily, it grew larger, brighter, closer. She sensed movement. She saw others all around her in a tunnel of nothingness, though they were different, more energy fields than bodies.

This couldn't be right.

"No, wait!"

Her voice echoed back, mocking her.

She stopped traveling before she reached the bright light, involuntarily pausing in a place that was boundary-less, yet somehow peaceful. She waited a moment, but nothing significant changed.

"Hello? Anybody here?"

She'd read everything she could get her hands on about dying, a few months ago. She'd been curious why her husband, Brady, had died with such a peaceful expression on his face when his leaving her had been so sudden, so unexpected. He was only thirty-three, played racquetball twice a week, and actually enjoyed the healthy meals their chef prepared. One minute he was smiling tenderly at her across the table, sharing a private joke, and the next—*bam!*—he was on the floor at her feet, no heart-beat, and nothing she did helped.

She knew about going toward the light.

"Hey, I think there's been a mistake."

She began to move again, but not straight ahead.

Uh-oh, this doesn't look good.

She was traveling off to the right, not exactly away from the light, yet not toward it either, finally coming to rest in front of a less-intense beam. Still, there was that bright spot off to the left, holding her attention. So much so that she hardly noticed the . . . *beings* in front of her until they morphed into two human forms in flowing white robes.

"Welcome," the taller one said. His hair and beard were white, and he spoke the single word without emo-tion, his attention riveted on the electronic clipboard in his hands.

"You're early," the woman standing next to him added

gently. Her hair was the whitest blond Lilly'd ever seen, her long tresses flowing over her shoulders and halfway down her robe. Under any other circumstances, her beatific smile would have been reassuring. "We didn't expect you this soon."

"Good, because I think I don't want to be here this soon."

So much for saving for a rainy day. She'd amassed a nice-sized nest egg because, when her father's investments had all gone bust, she'd learned firsthand what it was like to go from the haves to the have-nots. There wasn't anything wrong with wanting the best for your kids. She was determined that hers would have the best of everything, with no worries about necessities and tuition. Or . . . they *would* have.

"Where am I?"

"Transition," he said, evidently not one to waste words.

"Think of it as a holding room," the blonde added more gently.

This can't be good.

"Who are you guys?"

"I'm Elizabeth." Smiling warmly, she added, "In your incarnation, I was your grandmother."

"Really? I never met—"

"I know, dear. That was one of my biggest regrets, that I didn't live long enough to teach your mother that she could be both strong *and* nurturing. Now I know you have a thousand questions, but I think John's ready to explain everything."

"Okay, I see what happened this time." John kept stabbing the clipboard with his index finger as he perused whatever information it held. "Welcome back, Lilly."

"I've, uh, been here before?"

"That's right." He sounded so neutral, she couldn't pick up on which way this was going to go.

"More than once," Elizabeth added. Her voice was soft and sweet, like the good witch of Oz. "You can't seem to learn your lesson, so you've been diverted here again."

Oh great, Judgment Day, and I get the tag team.

Elizabeth laughed lightly, the way you'd expect an angel to. John barely smiled. Maybe it was a grimace.

"Oh, God," Lilly groaned. "You know what I'm thinking, don't you?"

"There are no secrets here," John said. "Your life, everything you've done, every thought you've had, it's all an open book. Now, let's get down to business."

"About being in that store—I can explain. See—"

"Please. Don't." He held up a hand to forestall any conversation on her part, so she didn't mention that crack about St. Peter either. "You weren't supposed to die quite so soon. If you hadn't dashed across the floor after that money, you would've been in the clear along with everyone else." His sigh was eloquent. "And we had such high hopes for your son."

"My—What son?" She'd suffered through a miscarriage two years ago, and after that Brady hadn't cooperated, but these guys knew that.

"The one you were supposed to have before your next birthday." Elizabeth's tone was gentle, as if she understood how close this was to Lilly's heart.

"Really? That soon?"

Lilly's hands closed protectively over her flat belly, wondering, *dreaming* as she had many times, what it would be like to feel a tiny flutter there, to give life to another person. *Oh*, she'd be such a great mother. He'd be her first, and she'd nurture him and teach him to be a great big brother, to love all the little ones who'd follow. No nanny. No boarding school. No last-minute, long-distance birthday wishes from Tahiti or Paris.

But . . . she was here. She'd died.

"He was destined to do such important things." Even though John's tone was still neutral, his choice of words alone indicated lament, and something more.

They were *blaming* her? The hell with that.

"Well," she snapped, "maybe if my husband *hadn't* die . . ."

Elizabeth sighed. "If only you'd picked the right one."

"Yes," John agreed. "Then your son would've had all the right genes. All the right memories."

"Did you mean what you said, Lilly?" Elizabeth asked. "Would you give anything to go back and have your baby?"

"Yes!" Lilly said quickly, knowing whatever she had to give up would be worth it.

"Now, Elizabeth, remember we have to stick to the rules," John said. "We can only send people back who gain new insight. I don't think that applies in this case."

Lilly felt as if she'd been slapped.

"Do you have new insight?" John demanded.

Think fast.

"Uh, if I smell gas, get the heck out of the building?"

John was polite enough not to shake his head, but Lilly could tell he wanted to. Elizabeth, on the other hand, arched her eyebrows and rubbed the tips of her fingers against her thumb.

"Money? Oh!" What had John said? She was early because she'd been in the wrong place, because she was chasing two dollars across the floor. That was it. "Money's bad?"

No way!

"New insight?" Elizabeth prompted.

"Oh. Bad, bad, bad. I'll go back, and I'll never chase money again."

John hung his head. Elizabeth, though, shot looks of encouragement her way. So, recalling the nickel she'd pocketed and that she had to give up something, Lilly took another stab at it.

"I'll pick it up and give it to the nearest person? Yeah, that's what I'll do. I'll give it away."

John shook his head. "I'm afraid this is a waste of time."

"But—"

"How much money did you give to charity last year?" he demanded.

"You mean to the nearest penny?"

"Yes."

"Uh . . ."

"Zero! And how much do you have?"

"To the nearest—"

"As of yesterday, your net worth was eighteen million dollars."

Great! Lilly thought with a rush of pride. *Except for that "was" part.*

"And you're still hoarding nickels—"

Oh. Not great.

"—and chasing small bills across the floor!"

"Okay, okay, I get it. You want me to tithe. Five percent."

"You can do better."

"Ten percent?" It hurt just thinking about it, but still, it'd be worth it.

"Ten times better."

"*All* of it?" If she weren't dead, the shock would've killed her.

"All of it! And not just the money. The house and cars, too. The airplane. Jewelry, antiques, everything."

"Jesus!"

"No"—John smiled—"but maybe next visit, *if* you're lucky." He punched some buttons on the clipboard.

It took several moments for Lilly to work past the shock. "So, let me get this straight. If I learn my lesson, gain new insight—" She thought using their terminology was a nice touch; it showed she'd been listening. "Then go back and get pregnant—"

John glanced at Elizabeth. "Did you remember the deadline?"

"Oh, that's right." Elizabeth, who appeared to be less seasoned at Transition, turned back to Lilly with a chagrined smile. "I can't believe I forgot to tell you. You have to give everything away and have the baby by your next birthday."

Lilly counted months on her fingers. "That only gives me a few weeks, and I'm not even *dating* anyone . . . Wouldn't it be easier if you just handled this like you did with Mary? You know, send an angel and *bam*, I'm pregnant?"

"It's not as if you'll be carrying the Son of God," John said dryly.

"Which brings up another point. Giving away all my

money really doesn't make sense from a logical perspective, you understand, because then we won't have anything to live on."

Elizabeth cleared her throat gently, warningly, and mouthed, "Have faith."

Lilly sighed. "Okay, strike that last part." But already her mind was spinning through ideas of how to sock some money away.

"I think we need to give her some guidelines, John."

Yeah. Guidelines. Giving away everything was so foreign a concept, there was no way she could undertake it on her own.

"It's a test. She needs to gain this insight on her own," John said.

"Well, it hasn't worked the last two lifetimes. We should give her a little help."

John checked his clipboard again. "Hm, I'm already overbooked. Do you have time?"

"I have a few minutes."

"Okay, then. Congratulations, Lilly, it looks like you'll be going back immediately."

Good, she'd have time to work on a loophole.

"Not in this lifetime," John said, grinning, then sobered again. "I'll just say my piece and then turn you over to Elizabeth. Remember, Lilly, you have to prove you're capable of change from the get-go, or you'll be back here before you know it."

"I'll work on it, I promise."

"As a matter of fact, you might want to rethink the whole thing right now." John's tone turned ominous. "Because if you take this second chance and fail in *any* way, there will be repercussions."

Lilly swallowed before she asked, "You mean . . . ?" She didn't want to suggest hell.

John's grin was devilish. "Not exactly."

He moved off, a light receding into darkness, with no definite beginning and no definite end, leaving Elizabeth and Lilly to finish up.

"What'd he mean?"

Elizabeth held out her hand. "I can show you."

Lilly stepped forward and reached out, expecting to feel nothing. Instead, Elizabeth's hand was solid and warm in hers, as comforting as a grandmother's should be.

"Close your eyes. Good, now clear your mind."

"Okay."

Elizabeth sighed. "Really, Lilly, if you don't stop thinking about money, you're going to fail miserably."

"Sorry."

"And I stress the word *miserable*."

Lilly cleared her mind as best she could and saw what Elizabeth meant. She didn't want to say she had a vision, but she did feel as though she were looking down on a scene.

There, standing by a large, ornate gate was St. Peter. He was positioned to one side, greeting new arrivals, shaking their hands, welcoming them in. To the other side, a line of very bored-looking people stretched to infinity.

Lilly didn't do lines.

"Notice anything?" Elizabeth asked.

"They're all dressed differently."

Men and women, rich and poor, wore a wide variety of garb: pantaloons, bustles, cowboy boots, suits of armor, peasant rags, loincloths, ruffled collars, crowns, and powdered wigs, among others. She couldn't view the whole line, yet she knew every time and place and class was represented.

"Some people have been in line a long, long time," Elizabeth warned, and Lilly understood this would be her fate if she failed.

"Pretty darned close to hell, if you ask me."

"You were pretty quick to agree to go back. Want to change your mind and stay?"

Lilly realized she wouldn't be going right in; otherwise she wouldn't be in Transition now. She'd be in line with everyone else.

"Not so far back, though," Elizabeth said.

"You know I'd never give up the chance to have a baby."

She saw St. Peter's smiling face as he welcomed the next new arrival, and she knew she wanted that, too, a *Go directly to heaven* pass.

"Good choice." Elizabeth released Lilly's hand and broke the connection to her dubious future. "You've got your work cut out for you, I'm afraid. To carry a baby full term, you have at most a few weeks to complete the first step. After that, well, John's been in charge of Transitions for several centuries now. He demands—let's see, how can I put this?—a high level of change."

"In other words . . ."

"Clean up your act, girl."

"Um, can you be more specific?"

"Well, for one, you can't go throwing money away. You can't hand it all over to your friends. In fact, you can't give any of it to your friends. You must ensure that it all goes where it will do good. The more, the better."

"I could give it to the Church, I guess."

"May I make a suggestion?"

"Please!"

"Spread it out. Reach more people, and I mean on a personal level. Don't just write a bunch of checks and drop them in the mail. Go see where it's needed, meet those who need it. Give just what's warranted in each situation. Nothing extra. Make every dollar count. You're good at that, and John will expect you to put it to good use."

"Whew, that could take a while." She'd look up Mr. Sexy Rumble in her spare time. But that raised a big question. "So how will I find the right man right away?"

"I can't tell you that."

"Not even a hint?"

Elizabeth leaned close and whispered, "It's someone you already know."

"That's the best you can do?"

"There'll be perks," she said with an enticing wink.

"Other than having a baby, the only perk I can think of is—" Lilly felt her cheeks burn hell-hot. "It's not so bad that you know everything I've ever said, but do you have to know every thought I've ever had, too?"

"It's pretty universal, really. Every woman wants one night of lusty, heart-pounding passion." Elizabeth sighed. "The multiple-orgasms-until-you-think-you'll-pass-out type."

"Yeah, I wouldn't mind trying that." In light of Elizabeth's glow, it was impossible to be embarrassed.

"You'll do fine if you just keep the rules in mind. Break any of them, though, and *pfft*, you're right back here, and you'll be dealing with John, instead of me."

"Will I remember this? Well, I guess I will, if I'm going to be writing my net worth down to zero. Otherwise my friends'll have me committed."

"If you're comfortable, you can share some of what you saw and felt. You know, the usual near-death-experience stories." Elizabeth's voice began to fade. "But I just want to caution you against telling anyone *why* you're doing what you're going back to do. That never works out. Oh, and since you were early, everyone's already booked, but I'll see if I can find a mentor to get you through the next few months. Wouldn't want you to go astray again."

"Will I—Hey, wait!" At first she thought Elizabeth was fading, but then she realized it was she herself who was moving away from the light.

Elizabeth's parting words were, "Whatever you do, don't take it off."

"What? Don't take what off? Wait. How will I know who my mentor is? Elizabeth!"

3

Jake Murdoch didn't mind the snowstorm. He'd grown up in St. Louis and was used to its unpredictable weather. Fifty degrees one day, six inches of snow the next. Big deal.

Nor did he mind filling in for Tom at Cloud Nine, especially in bad weather; in fact, he insisted on it. His neighbor was elderly, had broken his hip last year, and shouldn't be out in the snow and ice. Jake could make up lost time in his taxi later, when more people were out and about.

And he could handle the minor—ha!—gas leak in the store. Call a repairman ASAP, open the doors, bad air out, good air in. Should've been a piece of cake.

But he was really pissed off with the outcome: explosion, dense smoke, missing customer. The other woman—her friend—ended up in the same corner as he, so it was a simple matter to grab her by the arm and propel her through the gaping hole that used to be the front door. Now she was standing outside next to him, crying, screaming at the store, at him, at the world in general, he guessed. He never thought he'd be grateful to have his ears ring so loudly that he couldn't hear someone, but if the view of her tonsils was any indication, she was shrieking loud enough to be heard by everyone else in the state.

He shook her by the shoulders until he had her attention, then mimed the hand signal for telephone, thumb to ear, pinky to mouth, and yelled, "Nine one one!" in her face so she couldn't miss it. Understanding dawned. When she pulled a cell phone out of her coat pocket, he turned away, ready to deal with more important matters.

Smoke poured out of the store's every gaping wound. It was dense from the burning plastics—the shop was full of them—and probably toxic. Continually fed by the flames beneath, it rose into the gray sky.

Without hesitation, Jake grabbed his leather bomber jacket out of his taxi and draped it over his head. He dragged in deep gulps of frigid air and charged headlong into the building, knowing he had a customer to find, a woman in danger.

The floor was uneven, strewn with products, packages, chunks of wood, and drywall. Negotiating his way across all that without actually being able to see any of it was like walking on a rocky beach at night, every step hampered, every lump testing his balance, using up precious time, precious oxygen.

Still, he pressed on.

Two engineering degrees hadn't prepared him for this, but knowing where the missing woman had been and the approximate trajectory of the blast by where he'd been thrown, Jake hoped logic worked. He'd pray for it, but he wasn't a praying man.

He stumbled toward the wall where he thought she'd most likely be, moving as quickly as he could. The leather jacket stayed draped over his head, and he kept both hands down low, rooting through everything on the floor, skimming over the hottest stuff if it was too small to be a body.

Along the far wall, his path was blocked by a metal clothing rack. It leaned on an angle, forming a canopy of flaming panties and bras. Quickly running out of oxygen, he had to make a decision. Go out and come back, or keep going.

Flinging the rack out of his path, the toe of his boot encountered something—some*one*—soft.

He scooped the limp body into his arms. Hunched over, partially to shield her from more injury, partially to smother the fire singeing her fur—not that he gave a damn about the coat, but he didn't know how deep it was burning—he got them the hell out of there.

In the parking lot, he dragged in huge, lung-clearing breaths and laid her gently on a bed of snow. That'd take care of any burns on her back. He flung his smoky jacket aside and patted her down, starting at her head, putting out any lingering embers. She'd lost her hat, and the ends of her hair were singed. Her face was smudged, a little red, but not burned. It was also vaguely familiar.

The coat was a total loss. And her purse? Surprisingly, she still had it clutched in one hand in a death grip.

He kept working downward, patting everywhere, knowing it would be a long time before he'd forget the stink of burning fur.

Recognition suddenly dawned—in this case, about as welcome as the damned explosion—and his gaze locked on her face. With a handful of snow, he wiped away sooty smudges for a better look.

Son of a bitch, Lilly Marquette.

Just who he needed to make this, without a doubt, the day from hell.

His devilish side screamed, *What a perfect opportunity to get even. Let her burn.*

He put her out anyway.

After every ember had been smothered, he cooled his hands in the snow. Then, peeling open her coat to assess the damage, he found the fire hadn't burned through the backing. Too bad. A little, lingering discomfort—say a couple weeks of not being able to stand the feel of clothing against her skin—wouldn't be too severe a sentence for her, for what she'd done to him. Yeah, that'd be fair. He'd like that.

How could he have missed recognizing her earlier?

Of course—she'd been acting funny in the store. He was so used to customers playing low-key, trying to be inconspicuous, to remain incognito, that he'd thought nothing of it when she'd tugged her hat down to her eyebrows and donned sunglasses.

The first time he'd seen her was almost three years ago, on her wedding day. Two years and eleven months, to be exact.

As best man, he'd been more than happy to pose with her for a formal picture before the ceremony. He'd dangled his arm around her shoulders and said something cute and complimentary about Brady—his best friend and partner, her groom—keeping him so busy on the West Coast because Brady was afraid he'd steal her away. She'd laughed, just as he'd meant her to, and when she'd smiled up at him, up close like that, it hit him. All those photos Brady'd shown him, Jake had thought it was the camera that did an outstanding job of catching the light in her hazel eyes. But it hadn't been the camera at all. She really did have gold flecks that caught the light, that made her eyes dance and mesmerize him. So much so that he missed the photographer's next order, until Lilly obediently snuggled up next to his side and turned toward him, just so.

"A little more . . . A little more . . ." the photographer said.

That's when he'd really gotten into trouble. Her breast pressed against his side, feeling fuller and fuller as she turned a little more, a little more, practically rolling it across his rib cage, and he suddenly felt so goddamned hot. Since when was a woman in a wedding dress a turn-on? And why the hell the bride of his best friend?

Fortunately his tux jacket covered for him. But there were other things to worry about, like the stupid impulse to take her by the hand and drag her off behind a locked door and make love to her until she forgot that Brady even existed. Nothing like personal and professional suicide all tied up in one neat package.

It wasn't very creative—but then his brain wasn't getting much blood—but he saved himself by staging an awful coughing fit right after that pose, then excusing himself. He and Brady had been friends since the summer between junior and senior year in high school, when they'd worked the same construction site. Sure, Brady was the boss's son, but he didn't act like it then, and he didn't act like it years later when Jake went on a drunken binge and tore another site apart over Angie, his college sweetheart.

He and Angie had been inseparable, the perfect couple according to friends. They wanted a short engagement, but Angie's mother begged for a big, traditional wedding, so they figured why not and, together, kept a lid on the planning.

Then one day, out of the blue, Angie stopped returning his calls. She changed her phone number and her locks. Her mother, in tears, said she couldn't tell him anything, but when she hugged him, he could tell it was final on her end. Still, he didn't give up. He camped out on Angie's doorstep, showed up at her work, haunted every place they'd ever gone together, but he never saw her again. Within a week, she left St. Louis. No forwarding address. No phone message. None of her friends would talk.

He'd drowned his pain in hard liquor until Brady found him, dried him out, gave him an alibi that cleared him of all damages at the construction site he'd ripped apart, and provided the money to start the tech company in Silicon Valley.

Nobody had to remind Jake how much he owed Brady; lusting after his bride certainly was out of bounds. He avoided Lilly as much as possible the rest of the day, giving her one chaste kiss after the ceremony and dancing one obligatory dance with her at the reception.

And then he'd gotten the hell out of town before anyone discovered he'd just fallen head-over-heels for his best friend's wife.

The second and last time he'd seen her was at Brady's

funeral. He'd only just approached Lilly and swallowed her in a big how-could-he-die-and-leave-us? hug when Brady's brother dragged him away to discuss something of little importance. Try as he might, he'd been unable to contact Lilly for the next month. Then he found out she wanted nothing to do with him. And why.

He couldn't believe he'd just saved her life.

"Jake?" Lilly said, hoarse from the smoke. She'd been quietly muttering to herself for a minute, but until she said his name, her words had been too garbled to decipher.

"Don't talk." He didn't mean to growl at her; it came naturally. "And quit moving around."

She lifted her head from the snowy parking lot.

"Hold still," he cautioned, gently placing his hand on her forehead.

Big mistake, touching her like that. Protective feelings welled up inside his chest, unbidden, urging him to throw her into the taxi and race through the icy streets to the nearest hospital. That was the side of him that still—

But no, he couldn't still love her. He'd never been a man who let his heart dictate his life. So what if it was family tradition? He was only in *danger* of falling head-over-heels again, and if he was careful, *very* careful, he could overcome that. It helped to remember that he'd learned the hard way what she was capable of.

"You'll be okay if you don't move."

Yeah, so okay that she'd probably go straight to her attorney's lavish suite of offices and initiate a lawsuit against him for negligently allowing her into the store in the first place when there was a slight gas odor. Just what he needed. He couldn't afford a lawyer. He'd had one once, over that whole life insurance fiasco, where *supposedly* his and Brady's tech company would be protected financially if something happened to either of them. *Ha*! If she sued him now, he'd spend so much time in depositions and court, he wouldn't have time to work. He'd never get back on his feet.

She'd fucked him over five months ago. Might as well give her the keys to the house and taxi right then and let her finish the job.

He left the scorched coat on her to keep her warm until EMS arrived. He owed it to Brady to protect the woman he'd loved and married, even if he *was* still pissed. Jake covered Lilly's legs with his jacket, the leather scarred now, looking as though a few thousand cigarettes had been ground out on it. Then he sat in the snow and, resigned to his fate, cradled her head in his lap.

Brady had died five months ago. That's when the real trouble had started. Oh, Lilly didn't have anything to do with Brady's death, Jake was sure of that.

But she sure as hell stole his three million dollars.

Caught off guard, Jake couldn't stop Lilly when she suddenly jackknifed upward and scurried to her feet. He rose more slowly, watching as she pulled up short, mouth agape, in awe of the whole blackened scene before them. She circled her limo slowly, staring at it, laying her hands on it. Probably praying over the damned thing, which was undoubtedly insured to the hilt. People like Lilly didn't take chances on losing their possessions without full compensation.

And sometimes people like her got more than they deserved.

Ankle-deep snow cratered around her boots as she pivoted in a tight circle, taking in the entire surrounding area. She was talking to herself, too, probably calculating property values so she'd know how much she could realistically get when she sued the owner.

It was below freezing, but you wouldn't know it to watch her. Shit, if she slipped and fell . . .

He moved closer. "Call me crazy, but I'm pretty sure you're not supposed to be on your feet after you've been blown up."

"I'm fine."

"*Sit down*." His sisters said he was intimidating—to others, not them—when he ordered people around.

But Lilly just grinned up at him and said, "Stop being so bossy."

"Oh what the hell, you just survived an explosion. No need to worry about a little fall doing you in."

"Exactly. Betsy looks all right. Was anybody else hurt?"

He preferred to think she was the type who wouldn't care. Made it easier to dislike her. But she hadn't forgotten there were others involved, including her friend, who was tending to the chauffeur.

"The repairman made it out the back door in time. Your limo caught a lot of the blast, and your driver looked as if his arm was broken. So you'll be needing a new one. Driver, I mean. Well, both actually."

Either tell her what you really want to say or shut up, stupid.

But he couldn't, not yet. After Brady's death, their tech company had folded fast and furious, leaving serious debts. Jake's dad had volunteered his house and masonry business as collateral on a private note to pay them off. That note was held by none other than the man with whom Murdoch Masons had done decades of business—Frank Marquette, Lilly's father-in-law. Contract negotiations were currently under way. No way he was pissing off a Marquette right now. No way he'd be responsible for his parents losing their home and everything else they'd worked for.

He was never so glad to see EMS arrive and take someone away.

Three hours later, Lilly'd been poked and prodded and thoroughly checked out by a gorgeous doctor who should've made her blood race, but didn't. She could hear better now. Before Betsy had left, she'd gone on and on about how manly Jake was, how knight-in-shining-armor of him to run into a burning building and search for her. How strong he must be to carry her out when he must have run out of oxygen by then.

"They're letting you go?"

Jake. When she'd opened her eyes on the parking lot, he'd stared at her with a gaze so intense, so penetrating, as if she were the only other person on the planet and he was looking into her soul. Shame on her for not recognizing his voice in the shop. His deep rumble was very distinctive, but it *had* been almost three years since they'd said more than hello. She'd had other things on her mind that day, though she'd picked right up on the fact that her heart shouldn't be pounding when her groom's best man whispered in her ear.

"Don't you have a concussion or something?" he said.

They were standing just inside the ER entrance, where

she'd been staring out the wall of glass at the falling snow, marveling at how well she felt, considering what she'd just survived. Her hair and nails had suffered, but there wasn't a scratch on her.

Jake wasn't so lucky.

"Oh my God," she said.

Both of his hands were bandaged. She touched his wrist gently, hoping the damage wasn't extensive. He made his living with his fingers, delicate strokes on a keyboard or wiring small connectors. If he'd sustained permanent injury for her . . .

"You're hurt. How bad is it?"

"I'll live."

There was a small gauze square above his right eye, which made his hair look blacker and drew her attention to his extraordinary blue eyes. How did one man get all that? A deep voice that growled one instant, and rumbled and oozed pure sex appeal the next. Dark blue bedroom eyes, sending out currents that made her hormones sit up and take notice. A body sculpted and filled out by years of manual labor. And according to Brady, a brain that wouldn't quit. Her husband had been no slouch in that department, and Jake had amazed *him*.

"Your friend getting the car?" he asked.

"No, she had to leave about an hour ago."

"Family coming?"

"I'm waiting for a taxi." She sighed. "Have been for thirty minutes."

It was her first reminder that unless she got busy, things could be worse; she could be waiting in the hereafter line that stretched ad infinitum.

"Snow's keeping them busy."

"I guess. There's one parked out there, though. I'm hoping if I stand here long enough, the driver'll show up and take pity on me. I'm really sorry about your hands. Do they hurt much?"

"Nah, they're tough from years of laying stone."

He shrugged noncommittally, though there was a twitch along his jaw that made Lilly suspect he was holding back, refusing to say more. She couldn't tell if he was really in no pain or just acting brave. He looked tough, in the best of ways; years of laying brick and stone had really paid off. She remembered there were long-standing professional ties between his family, Murdoch Masons, and her in-laws, Marquette Construction.

A gray-haired man shuffled by, his body as worn and weary as the shabby coat hanging on him. "Hey, man," he said, patting Jake on the shoulder. "Thanks again for the coffee."

Jake didn't explain, and Lilly wasn't surprised. After charging into a burning building for her, what was a cup of coffee for a stranger?

"You should sit down."

"I'm a little fuzzy on the details at the store," Lilly said softly. "Did I thank you?"

"You were a little confused."

"Well then, thank you. Really. It was crazy, you pulling me out of a burning building. And your hands—you won't be able to work for a while. I feel so guilty."

Instantly, a frown puckered his brow. "Why would you say that?"

"Because if I hadn't been running after my change, I would've been in the clear with you and Betsy."

"True."

He met her eyes unwaveringly. If he'd fixed that very intense gaze on the ER's female staff, he must have dates lined up through March.

"I hope you remember that," he said, "when your attorney hears about this and suggests suing me."

Startled, she said, "I wouldn't sue you."

"No?"

"No way. In fact I expect you to send me a bill for your time off until your hands heal. Ow—"

A sharp pinch bit into her right arm, making her jump. Baffled, she looked around to see if she'd bumped into a tiny nail sticking out of a wall, only there wasn't a wall close enough.

"You okay?"

"Yeah."

He pointed toward a row of vacant chairs. "Sit down."

"I can't watch the taxi from there. Where was I? Oh I remember. Let me know anything your insurance doesn't cover, okay? I mean it. Workman's Comp or whatever you have, whatever they don't cover."

An even sharper prick zapped her directly on the wrist. She jumped again, praying no one on staff noticed, afraid they'd welcome the chance to poke and prod her some more.

"You sure you're okay?" Jake asked.

"Yes I'm sure," she hissed. "Keep it down, would you?" She shook her arm out, noticing an attractive—though obviously costume—charm bracelet she'd never seen before, but its being on her arm was just too weird to investigate with Jake studying her like a bug under a microscope. "It's probably just a bruised nerve or something."

"Because I can walk you back to the desk and have them take another look at you."

"Only if you have a death wish."

He grinned. "Didn't like all those tests and exams, huh?"

"It beats getting blown up—"

"Yeah."

"—but not by much."

"Go sit down."

"God, you're bossy. First on the parking lot and now . . ." *Oh*. He hadn't been bossy at the wedding. "*You're* my mentor?"

"That does it. I'm getting a doctor."

"Wait." She laid her hand on his arm.

He stopped in his tracks. She couldn't blame him for thinking she was confused. She was the one who'd been to heaven and back, and nothing was crystal clear to her either. Didn't he know how much it had hurt when they didn't find time to talk at the funeral?

"I missed you after the service," she said. "I tried calling you later. I was so lonely. I needed to talk to . . . someone." But his number had been disconnected.

Jake offered no explanation of any kind. He was sole owner of the tech business in Silicon Valley, yet he was here in St. Louis, working in a sex shop.

Lilly pressed on. "Elizabeth said she'd send someone to help me. But you live in California, so . . . Why were you working in Cloud Nine?"

He glanced away abruptly, but not before she saw anger spark in his eyes.

Cautiously—because if he was her mentor, she didn't

want to start off on the wrong foot—she inquired, "Did something happen to the company?"

He glowered at her, said, "Get your own damn doctor," and turned toward the door so quickly, you'd think she'd just insulted his mother. Okay, so business was a forbidden topic, but if he was her mentor, she needed him right away. So shouldn't he be hanging around?

If they were to spend any time together, it looked as if it was all up to her.

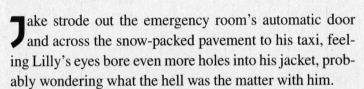

4

Jake strode out the emergency room's automatic door and across the snow-packed pavement to his taxi, feeling Lilly's eyes bore even more holes into his jacket, probably wondering what the hell was the matter with him.

No way he could stand there and chat with her like two old friends. Not even like two people who'd shared a traumatic experience and found they had a little bit in common. He'd called his dad from the treatment room and was warned to stay away from Lilly Marquette. Until the custom-home contracts were signed, they didn't need anybody—meaning *him*—pissing off any Marquettes—meaning *her*. Even if she had stolen his money.

Once she saw he was the taxi driver she'd been hoping for, would she run after him and beg for a ride? Demand one? He slid behind the wheel, fumbling with bandaged hands, a thin key and its tiny target, the ignition. He checked his rearview mirror.

Ah, yes, here she comes now.

From the looks of her short, angry steps, he prepared to get chewed out. Not that he'd take it from her, of course. But he'd let her get started, then simply push the button—if he could isolate the stupid little thing from all the others, damn it. He'd slide the window up and let *that* do his talking for him.

Yes, there, he got it down and rested his finger on it. He was ready.

"What are you doing?" she demanded.

It was silly really, how a five-foot-three wisp, shivering in the cold, could cross her arms over her chest and think she was formidable.

"Where the hell's your coat?" Jake asked before he could stop himself.

"In the trash."

"You can't stand out here without a coat."

"Me? Let's worry about you. You can't drive with your hands like that. It's not safe." She grabbed the door handle. He stabbed around to find the lock button, but before he could push it, she opened his door. "Slide over. I'll take you home and catch a cab from there."

"You can't drive my car."

"Oh, don't sound so horrified." She perched her hip on the edge of the seat, lined her sweet thigh up against his, and nudged him. "How hard can it be?"

Damn, if she kept bumping against him like that, they'd both find out.

"My insurance won't cover you, and even if it did, how long's it been since you've driven in snow?" He knew he'd regret this later. "Get in back, and I'll take you home."

"Oh yeah, I want to be blown up *and* crash in the same

day. No thank you." She shoved harder. "Come on, I fly an airplane. How hard can a car be?"

"You don't drive *at all*?"

She laughed sweetly at his panic, and he realized she was teasing him. It'd be a hell of a lot easier to stay mad at her if she'd quit being nice.

"Just a little pilot humor. What are you doing?"

"Taking off some of these bandages so I can drive."

"Geez, and you're supposed to be looking out for me? Stop that."

She grabbed his wrist, and suddenly neither of them was talking or teasing. He found himself staring into delicious hazel pools, mesmerized by the sparkling flecks of different colors and how they were all mixed up and at the same time perfectly blended to create warmth, humor and—suddenly—sexual heat. She must have felt it, too, because without another word, she abruptly unperched herself and got in back.

He knew where she lived. The sooner he got her out of his taxi, out of his sight, out of his smell, for chrissakes, the sooner he could go back to blaming her for everything that had gone wrong with his life in the last five months. Just so he wouldn't let his guard down again, he reached up to the bandage on his forehead and ripped it off. Nothing like a little pain to keep a man's mind straight.

He reversed out of the slot, then shifted into DRIVE, at which time the androgynous, computerized spiel began. "Sit back and relax. There's a seat belt for your comfort and safety."

"What the heck is that?"

Upon detecting her voice, it paused automatically.

"Just a little something I've been working on."

"It's not going to give me seat belt fastening instructions, is it?"

"Let's listen and see." He didn't want to talk to her. Talking to her was dangerous and weakened his position that he was the injured party here, and she owed him big-time.

"Let's not. Shut it off, will you?"

The last thing he wanted was to take orders from her, but he punched the button anyway.

"Thanks. Gosh, I can't believe I didn't recognize you in the store."

"I think you were more concerned with my not recognizing you."

Glancing at her in the rearview mirror as he drove, he noticed incredibly smooth skin. Heard her every time she moved or batted the red balloons aside. Remembered every photograph Brady had shown off when he came to the coast.

Jake had committed every one of them to memory, knowing it was all he'd ever have of Lilly. He'd listened to Brady's stories about how she'd said this or that, or surprised him with breakfast in bed on his birthday, or an Easter egg "hunt" in the closet, or a turkey day "feast" on the kitchen table. To hear Brady tell it, they'd humped like rabbits.

"I don't think this is the way," she said.

"Aren't you still in the same house?"

"I want to swing by Cloud Nine."

"Nothing's left. Let's not." Try as he did to resist the temptation, he glanced at her via the rearview mirror. Bad move. Even the reflection of her eyes danced. He had it under control, though. He had to. "Did you want to buy something? Because I can check through what I salvaged in the trunk and see if I have what you need."

"See, it's assumptions like that I'm trying to avoid."

He chuckled, in spite of himself. "Oh, don't worry about it. I've been pretty much desensitized by my neighbors."

"Don't tell me they all shop there."

"Not while I'm there, they don't. Well, Ruby did once. You have to understand, she's old enough to be my grandmother. I can't help it, it weirds me out to see a sex manual on one of their coffee tables—with a bookmark sticking out of it, no less. I feel like a damn Peeping Tom or something. Anyway, after sweet little Ruby came in for a board game, I made it a rule that from then on neighbors can't shop when I'm filling in."

Now, if only it were as easy to get rid of Lilly.

She was blessedly silent while he drove, but it might've been better if she'd talked his ear off. Then he wouldn't have had time to be at war with himself, on one hand surprisingly pleased to see her again, on the other, royally pissed off.

What really burned him, though, was how she acted as though she hadn't a clue that she ought to stay clear of him, that she shouldn't talk to him as if they'd be on friendly terms. In fact, she acted so innocent and totally unconcerned that he began to doubt what he knew to be true.

"So," Lilly muttered to Elizabeth. She felt a connection there that she needed to hang on to, like a lifeline, because this was all so unreal, and if she forgot what *was* real, she might forget to do what she'd promised. "He's my mentor, huh? Just pluck him right out of California and set him down in St. Louis?"

The smoke hadn't hurt his sexy voice at all, and for the first time ever, she thought about trying out the backseat and wondered whether it was doable. The taxi was frigid at the moment, but they could warm it up fast.

"Ooh, is he supposed to be the father-to-be?" *Yum.*

"You talking to me?"

"Um, I said, so, you drive a taxi now." If he didn't bite her head off this time, she'd find out if this was as much a surprise to him as it was to her.

"Yeah." He turned up the heater, which had to be solely for her, because he cracked his window and shrugged out of his jacket. "My uncle's in Arizona for the winter, I lease it from him, we both make money."

"You've been back in St. Louis a while then?"

He didn't reply. She thought for a moment he was going to turn the preprogrammed message back on, but it remained blessedly silent, *Thank you, God.*

Now *there* was a previously unconscious thought that suddenly took on new meaning. Given her recent experience, she'd make an effort to use the Lord's name more judiciously in the future.

"Should the meter be running?"

"No, we just put 'em in for decoration."

Well, well. He even had the appropriate surly attitude that came from owning a successful business one day and being a driver-for-hire the next. Had Elizabeth really made that happen? And how? Lilly was dying to know— well, okay, maybe not *dying*—but he'd already walked away once when she'd asked. Maybe in a few days when he'd had time to recuperate.

Back to the meter. "It seems high." She felt a sharp pain in her arm—the second one since she'd been in the backseat—but she couldn't find anything sharp there, either. "Maybe the explosion knocked it out of whack."

"Tell you what, I'll have it checked. If I overcharge you today, I'll send you a full refund."

"Really?"

"Hey, it's only money."

Uh-oh, money again.

She'd been out of the hospital for what, five minutes tops, and she was already trying to save it instead of give it away. Seems there was going to be more to her current life lesson than writing a few hundred checks and getting pregnant within a month.

"Sorry," she whispered. "I'll do better."

They drove through a neighborhood that was neglected, peeling, uncared for, a place to drive through to get to a good shopping area, into the city, or out to the county malls. Surely there were people here who needed money, but how did she go about finding out who, and since she wasn't allowed to give more than necessary, how much?

She was totally out of her league. She could sink the whole lot right here and not make a dent, and once it was gone, it was too late if John said she'd done it wrong. Good thing Elizabeth had sent Jake.

"Want me to lock the doors?" he asked, making fleeting eye contact as he drove.

"What?" The three tassels swinging from the mirror distracted her. Were they from his uncle's childrens' graduations, or were they his? Jake had at least two degrees that she knew of.

"I noticed you looking around. Neighborhood's not

what you're used to, I guess." He engaged all the locks.

"That's an understatement." If Elizabeth was responsible for putting him here to mentor her—Lilly wasn't sure about that, but she *was* sure she'd better cover all bases—then it was time for him to be useful. She leaned forward and said, "Do you know this area?"

"Yeah, sure."

"I don't want to go home just yet." She connected with his reflection, noting that it did nothing to diminish the sexy heat in his bedroom blues. "Are you okay to drive me around a while?"

"Sure. Clayton? Ladue?"

"Here. Downtown. The Projects. Do we have Projects?"

"My, you want to do some serious slumming."

Within minutes, she realized she wouldn't accomplish much without some narrative. "Talk to me like a tourist," she said. "And not that darned recording."

He scratched his head, rubbed the side of his nose, and finally said, "Say, how 'bout them Rams?"

He made her smile; that was good. On a day like today, that was very good. "Wait. Pull over."

"Here?" Buildings on both sides of the wide street were boarded up.

"I want to ride in front."

"Nope. Fares ride in the—"

"Stop, or I'm climbing over the seat."

"You can't do that."

She tossed her purse onto the front seat.

"You just got out of the emergency room!"

"A very good reason not to mess with me."

"All right, all right. Give me a minute."

He stalled by making a big show of checking for other

vehicles; there were none. At the next stop sign, she took the decision out of his hands, unlocked the back door, and hopped out. He immediately popped the rest of the locks and didn't wait for her to buckle up before moving on. The only concession he made was to pull a clipboard, an expensive camera, and a half-empty pan of fudge out of her way.

"Mm, fudge," she said.

He set it on the family-photo-laminated dash, as far to his side as possible.

"I'm starving."

"I'll stop at the next drive thru."

She pouted, but it didn't help.

All the photos on the dash were of children. Babies in swings, toddlers in a wading pool, kids in snowsuits and Halloween costumes, teenagers in prom attire. School plays, music recitals, camping trips.

"I know, I know, it's a terrible thing to do to a car, right?"

"I like it."

He gave her a funny look, as if he suspected she was lying to him. "Nobody else does."

"They're so sweet. Aw, look at this little girl. I wonder why she's crying?"

"Because *he* got stuck in a hand-me-down snowsuit."

Lilly grinned as realization hit. "But you're adorable in it."

"I'm an only boy."

"And how old—?"

"Five."

"At five, you were already gender conscious?"

"It was *pink*. I got even, though. When I passed Julie

up, I insisted on a black one so she'd get stuck with it the next year."

Hearing past the words, Lilly discerned a lot of affection between Jake and his sister.

"So these are all your family?"

"It's Uncle Paul's collage, so there's kids from Aunt Joanne's side, too."

He was driving, so pointing out the different children was hit-and-miss, along the lines of, "The one hanging upside down on the swing set is my sister Jodie." By the time Lilly'd located the upside-down little girl, Jake was on to another. After oohing and ahhing over several more children who'd been lucky enough to grow up in a normal family, Lilly turned her attention back to the streets. Few people were out. Those who were walked quickly through the falling snow, heads down into the wind as if they had a definite destination in mind, though none of the storefronts looked ready for any business, ever. Most were barred.

Jake fumbled with his tiny phone, made a quick call, and assured someone he was fine. "Really, I swear. Hardly a scratch on me." When he signed off, it was with a warm, "Yeah, let everyone else know, okay? Love you, too."

"Your mom?" she guessed.

"Sister." He grinned then. "The Murdoch brigade worries about me. Since I got through on call waiting, and they both have speed dial, everyone'll know in ten seconds flat."

Lilly was thinking how nice it must be to have such close siblings when, down a side street, a small group of people caught her eye. Loosely congregated in a ragged line, they appeared to be waiting for something.

"What's that?"

"Where?"

"Back at the corner, down that street."

"Food kitchen."

People in need! "Go back."

"What? No way. I'm not taking you to some food kitchen."

"Why not?"

"Well, for one thing, it's for poor people. Homeless folk." He continued driving away.

"Fine." She settled back and pulled her cell phone out of her purse. "I'll call another cab and give someone else a big tip. I'd go by myself, but *someone* blew up my limo."

"And that makes you poor enough to take food out of their mouths?"

She shuddered. "I don't want to eat there. I want to give them money."

He stared at her.

"Watch the road."

"I have great peripheral vision."

"Fine, use it on me, but watch the road."

"A few minutes ago you were worried about my meter cheating you and now you want to stop at a food kitchen and give away money?"

"It's a charity, right?"

"Yes."

"They do good, right?"

His second "yes" came slower, as if he was trying to figure out her angle.

"I want to write them a check." She dug through her purse to make sure—Yes, there it was. Her checkbook; her ticket to having a son.

He looked as if he wanted to argue some more, but finally made a right and circled back, parking in front of an

old brick church. It was squeezed in by a neighborhood
that had once been actively growing and encroaching, but
now seemed little more than deserted.

"You really going in there?" he asked when she unlocked her door.

"Yes."

He reached over and opened the glove box, bumping
her knee with the back of his hand as he did so, which
sent her traitorous libido off on a tangent. He said something to her, but none of his words registered. She preferred to blame it on the drugs they'd given her at the
hospital, but she didn't think they'd given her anything
that would account for this. Still, if he noticed anything
amiss, that's exactly what she'd claim.

"Take it off."

Startled, she dared ask, "What?"

He leaned back in the corner where his seat met the
door and stretched his right arm along the back between
them.

"It'll be safe in here, really. Don't look at me like I've got
two heads. Most of these people are all right, they're just
here for a little help, but why tempt the one who doesn't
care that he can hock your diamond for only twenty bucks?
To him, it's that much closer to his next fix."

"Oh, my ring! I thought you said my, uh, my drink, and
of course I don't have one."

"Actually, I said 'jewelry.' "

She stuck her finger in her ear and wiggled it. "Darned
explosion. I still can't hear right."

When she started to remove the one gold earring that
hadn't been lost in the blast, he leaned toward her and
brushed her hand down. "Don't make a show of it." His

gaze darted around, checking their surroundings.

"What?" Her gaze followed the path of his. "You're expecting an onslaught of eagle-eyed homeless people to storm the car?"

"Go on, make fun of me if you want, but they have pride, just like anyone else. They don't need rich people flashing their gold jewelry in front of them."

"Oh." She really did need a mentor.

"Take it off."

She surreptitiously removed her earring and dropped it into the glove box, followed by her rings.

"The bracelet, too."

"I don't have a—"

He stared pointedly at her right arm, so she did, too.

Oh yeah, *that*. It had two gold tone chains. One held three oval charms, each engraved with a single word: *Serenity*, *Courage*, and *Wisdom*. Dangling from the other were small stars, shiny, some embellished with a single rhinestone, the rest punch-cut with numerals one to eighteen. It didn't take a genius to figure out who was responsible.

"Whatever you do, don't take it off."

She heard it as clearly as if Elizabeth were sitting beside her, which Lilly knew she wasn't, because she looked. She turned around and checked the backseat, too, and just outside the car, in case she'd traded in her long white robe for a dirty, threadbare overcoat.

"Meter's running."

That got her moving. And when she realized her actions were motivated by money—*again*—she started to chide herself, but then gave herself a break because she'd been blown sky-high today, literally, and she'd do better tomorrow. Besides which, she'd been around and around this darned bracelet half a dozen times, with no luck.

"There's no clasp."

He leaned back in his corner again, a picture of patience. "Well, how'd you get it on?"

"Elizabeth did it."

"The same Elizabeth you think sent me." It sounded more like an assessment of her sanity than a question.

Maybe he didn't know Elizabeth sent him. Maybe he was just the type of person she needed, so *voilà*, here he was. She hoped when she got back to heaven that someone up there gave her a comment card to fill out. She had a thing or two to say regarding their procedures.

Jake seemed to be waiting for an answer. Or an explanation.

"You believe in heaven, right?" she asked.

A quick release of breath revealed his cynicism. "Not anymore. It ranks right up there with tarot cards and that channeling shit."

Okay, she wouldn't be sharing any pertinent details with him. Funny that Elizabeth would pick a nonbeliever, but it'd undoubtedly make sense if one knew all the facts. This called for wisdom—in this case, relying on Elizabeth's.

To explain the claspless bracelet, Lilly blurted out the first thing that came to mind. "Actually, it's a sorority thing."

"Uh-huh."

" 'Sisters forever' and all that. Eternal, get it? No end?"

"You didn't wear it at your wedding."

She grinned, stupidly, irrationally happy to hear that he'd paid attention that day, so she hadn't been the only one. "Taking inventory, were you?"

"We danced together."

"Just once."

"I would've noticed it."

"Where *did* you spend the rest of the evening?"

It was his turn to grin. "Taking inventory, were you?"

Touché.

She'd chalked it up to prewedding jitters, the very unbridely thoughts she'd had when he'd draped his strong arm across her shoulders and pulled her close. She didn't know much about Jake at that point, just that he'd laid stone for years before he and Brady formed their partnership. He certainly had the muscles from it.

Unable to stop herself, she glanced at his arm on the back of the seat, bridging the gap between them.

Oh yeah. Still has 'em was quickly followed by *Concentrate. Get pregnant.*

"What?" He glanced at his arm as if she'd seen a bug crawling along his skin.

"Uh . . . nothing." She jabbed the charm bracelet up under her sweater. It fell right back down.

"Here."

He grabbed a rubberband off the gearshift lever, helped himself to her hand, slid it on until it and the chains were wrapped around each other, then shoved both up as far as they'd go. Then instead of dropping her hand, he commenced with briskly rubbing it between his own.

"Why didn't you tell me you were still cold? I could've turned the heat up more."

You just did.

Lilly tugged gently, trying to pull free, but Jake's strong hands kept rubbing and rubbing and holding on. If they'd been sitting closer, she imagined he'd tuck it between his thighs while he rubbed the other one to warm it, too. And heavens, what she could do with it once it was there.

Shoot. She suddenly remembered that John could read minds, so she threw her door open and bolted through the slush to the snow-covered sidewalk.

Jake caught up, grasping her arm just above the elbow. "In a hurry?"

Her tenth-grade English teacher had taken points off a short story assignment once because she said you couldn't hear a person smirk. Lilly begged to differ. She didn't dare look at Jake, but she definitely heard a smirk in that question.

"Here, put this on."

He held his ruined jacket open, and rather than tell him he'd toasted her to a crisp in the car, she slipped into it, relishing the touch of his fingers on her skin as he lifted what was left of her hair free from the collar.

"And you forgot this." He held out her purse.

She might have taken it, if he didn't still sound so smug. She knew how to deal with smug.

"Aren't cab drivers supposed to carry bags?"

"Generally it's our option."

"I'm afraid I need both hands free in the snow."

"Fine." Still smug, he tucked it beneath his arm as if it belonged there.

"Cute. A clutch suits you."

"You don't think it makes my butt look big?"

"Oh, absolutely."

5

St. Matthew & Mark's food kitchen was going to be a revelation to Ms. Leather-Bound, Gold-Initialed Checkbook.

Jake couldn't wait for the fallout. She'd march up those steps in her designer boots, open the door, and get hit with a composite odor derived from years of cheap cooking, unwashed bodies, and disinfectant. She'd reel out of there so fast . . .

Being the nice guy he was, he of course followed behind, ready to catch Lilly before she catapulted down the steps and broke her neck.

Not to mention that he was also the guy she'd gypped out of millions, and it wouldn't give him any great heartache to watch her humiliate herself. Shouldn't take more than five seconds. Ten tops. Then they'd leave, and he'd try really hard not to let on how much he'd enjoyed it.

He started a countdown as Lilly pulled open the heavy, turn-of-the-century door. One . . .

She paused briefly, letting her eyes adjust to the dimmer light. Two . . .

She marched right up to the scruffy, grizzled man cleaning the otherwise deserted steam table, as if she did this every day—*must not have inhaled yet*—and politely said hello and asked to see the director. Three . . .

That guy didn't appear much better off than the people loitering outside, but he took one look at her, no gold, no diamonds, no fur in sight, a lot of singed hair, and jerked his chin over his shoulder.

"Back there." Four . . .

"Thank you." She smiled sweetly.

"Can't miss 'im. Name's Kellerman."

Jake was so caught off guard by the extra information that he let Lilly get several steps ahead of him, which was a big mistake, because then he couldn't pull his gaze away from how the bottom of his bomber jacket brushed back and forth across her hips. Repeatedly.

Forget counting. She must have breathed in by now and still, there she went, moving ever forward on a determined course.

Give them money, indeed. What? Twenty-five dollars? Fifty? Sure, every little bit helped—he dropped a five into the donation box at the door—but that was chump change to her.

He was further taken aback when she marched right up to the director, pulled out her checkbook and a thousand-dollar pen and, in a very businesslike tone, asked how much his annual operating budget was and what the shortfall for the past three years had been.

Kellerman was salivating as he took in the checkbook and the pen, politely, avariciously ignoring his benefactor's damaged hair and the three sculptured nails she had left, which were painted a tasteful, elegant, brownish pink. Jake supposed there was a name for that, like mauve or something, but he knew his way around electronics and quarried stone, not colors of nail polish.

Kellerman stuttered out a reply, then swallowed his spit and stood by mutely as Lilly started filling in zeroes. She paused right before the last one, as if thinking it over. But then she nearly leaped out of her shoes and dashed off the rest of the check as if her life depended on it, matching Kellerman's amount to the last digit.

With my *money!*

Kellerman, poor bastard, didn't know what to do with his hands, alternately holding them behind his back so as not to appear too eager, then letting them flutter out there in midair, ready to snatch the check into his possession.

Jake felt a similar reaction coming on.

"Thank you." Kellerman read the name on the check. "Mrs. Marquette, I . . . I don't know what to say."

Neither did Jake, but he was working on it. If she was pulling some modern-day, quasi–Robin Hood stunt, she sure as hell could write him a big one right now.

"Just say you'll put it to good use. Maybe add something extra for any children who come in."

"Oh, I will. I will!"

"Good."

Lilly tilted her head back and stared at the ceiling, long enough that he and Kellerman finally both looked up, too. There was nothing there but peeling paint.

"See something?" All Jake could see was red.

"Sh, I think she's praying."

She turned briskly and headed toward the door, muttering something that sounded like, "I can't believe I just did that."

Neither could he.

Kellerman leaned close, waggling the check. "Is this for real?"

Jake could grab it and make a run for it, but it wasn't enough, and it wasn't his style.

"She's got it," he said grudgingly. "But she was in an explosion earlier today, so if I were you, I'd get that in the bank before she claims brain damage."

"I heard that."

"Sorry, Reverend, gotta go."

He caught up to her on the icy steps, and remembering his obligation to take care of Brady's wife the same way Brady would if he were here, he grasped Lilly's arm in a very secure hold. She didn't seem to mind. She didn't even seem to notice. But he did, and his body's unwanted yet predictable reaction dragged his mind off in a direction best left unexplored—at least until she paid him back.

"Slow down, damn it, it's slippery here," he said, determined to focus on what was important.

"It's bad form to cuss this close to a church."

He knew he shouldn't bring this up, but if he could just feel her out a little bit . . . "About that money—"

"One down and a bunch to go. It hurt, but not as bad as I thought it would."

He narrowed his eyes and took a closer look at her. "You feeling okay?"

"I'm fine. Do you know other places like this?"

"Sure, but—"

"Can you drive me to them?"

"Let's talk money first."

"Of course. How much do you make in a week?"

"What?"

"I need a driver and a car." She spoke slowly, as if she thought *he* might be the one with a head injury. "You're a driver. You have a car. Hence, I'd like to hire you to drive me."

"To more food kitchens?"

"Any charitable organizations you can think of that need money."

"Huh." Beyond that, he was at a loss for words.

"What?"

"Nothing."

"No really, what?"

"Well, it's just that Brady always said you were tighter with a dollar than he was. And the way you took off after your change this morning, well I'm just surprised you're giving money away, that's all."

"Nothing stays the same forever."

"Huh. Get in the car before you catch your death, then we'll talk."

She shuddered. "I wish you wouldn't use that expression."

Not half as much as he wished he could stop worrying about doing what was best for her.

"What?" he groused. "Get in the car?"

" 'Catch your death.' "

"Oh, sorry." It was thoughtless of him, and her admonishment caught him up short. Of course she was still sensitive. Brady's death had been totally unexpected. No one had known about his heart problem until it was too late. No one had had time to prepare. "But get in."

She faced off with him over the door. Could the woman not follow *any* directions?

"You know, with your hands like that, you'd have a heck of a time making change. Or keyboarding. If you drive for me, you won't have to. How many stops could we make in a day? Four?"

"I'm not driving you around." Imagine spending eight to ten hours every day in the close confines of the cab with her rambling on about no-cussing zones and who-knows-what else between stints at giving away his money. No way.

"Maybe five?"

"You talk to yourself."

"I'll stop."

"I've got regulars. People who *count* on me," he said, trying not to growl at her, but really, she was exasperating. Brady'd never mentioned that.

"Well, we don't have to go out every day, and I'm perfectly willing to share cab space when we do. I'll even help make change. Tell you what . . ." Standing in the cold in what was left of *his* jacket, she rooted through her purse again. With a flick of her wrist, the pen and checkbook were open and ready. "Do you spell Murdoch with a 'k' or an—Oh shit."

"Generally not the 'oh shit'—you know, being this close to a church and all."

"My pen won't work."

"Yeah, right."

"No, really." She scratched it across the check to prove it. "And there's nothing sacrilegious about saying shit."

"It's still cussing, so get in the *goddam* car."

She did so, saying, "Well I don't know if I want a grouchy driver."

And he didn't want a bossy passenger, but he couldn't let his best friend's widow travel into questionable areas of the city with an unknown driver who wouldn't look after her the way he would. Besides, if she was in the mood to give away money, he wanted what was his.

Leaning down between her and the open door, he said, "I'll work on it."

"Good. How's fifteen hundred a week?"

He coughed to cover his surprise. "It's okay."

She grinned, not fooled at all. "And I promise not to claim head injury on payday."

"You won't make me late for my regulars?"

"Wouldn't dream of it."

"And you won't treat my car like your own personal trash can?"

"Why would I—"

"People do, and I have to keep it clean, you know. Nobody does it for me."

"No talking to myself, no making you late, no trash in the car. Got it."

"In advance, then." He shut her door, sealing the deal.

This would give him time to work things through and pick the best approach while he waited for his dad to conclude his business deal with Lilly's father-in-law. He'd already tried attorneys—forget that. Hers were bigger than his. He'd tried the direct approach, calling her house and writing her after the funeral, only to be deflected by Brady's brother's threats against his dad's business and house. He'd deemed it wise to back off until further notice.

Well, further notice was on the way! If she had second thoughts later, no way he was letting her back out of it. By the time he slid behind the wheel, he was also thinking he'd agreed too soon. If she'd offered fifteen hundred, she would've gone higher. It didn't have enough zeroes in it, of course, but it was a start.

"Plus expenses," he said. "Gas, oil, lease, mileage—"

"*That* seems a little redundant."

"You want me or not?"

She smiled wickedly. "Well, if you put it that way."

She's hitting on me?

There was only one thing he could think of to protect himself, because while his brain knew what she'd done, how devious she was, his body—and maybe even his heart—was in danger of writing it off. Fortunately, his brain was back in control.

"Make a pass at me, lady, and you ride in the back."

"Hm, I hadn't counted on that," Elizabeth said. She was looking in on Lilly's progress from her higher vantage point, her robe swirling around her legs as she paced in tight, agitated turns and waited for John.

This had to go better if she was going to save Lilly *and* get what she, herself, wanted—more freedom to help others in the future. John was a by-the-book kind of guy, and much too strict, in her opinion. People were weak and needed a gentle, guiding hand.

Three million dollars hanging between Lilly and Jake— boy, what a test. She'd worked with John when he'd sent others back, but Lilly was the first one to reap the benefits of Elizabeth's persuasive talents. Lilly could turn over a new leaf and get right into heaven upon her return; she just needed a little guidance.

"Be sure it's only a little," John said when he arrived.

The two of them gazed down at Lilly, who was drooling over Jake's pan of fudge and trying to get him to share, and Jake, who was chomping at the bit to confront Lilly about his money.

"It won't be long before he tells her," Elizabeth said, "and then she's going to feel obligated to pay him back."

"One would hope so."

"But according to the rules, she can't give her money to friends. Well, we just need to bend them a little bit, that's all there is to it."

"No."

"But Lilly's a good person at heart. She'll see to it that the rest of the money—"

"Elizabeth, Elizabeth," John said, shaking his head. "Haven't you noticed people's tendency to slide by? Give them an inch, and all that? No, I guess you haven't been doing this long enough. I'm sorry, but without rules to follow, Lilly would simply reimburse Jake, dash off a few thousand checks to charities, produce a child, and think she's home free."

"But you don't know—"

"I *do* know that there are many good reasons we have apprenticeships at this job, and so will you, in time."

"But we're angels. We're forgiving. We're understanding. Or we should be."

"Ah, Elizabeth. I see Lilly isn't the only one who must have faith. People have to help themselves. They have to struggle"—his arms spread and rose theatrically—"defy all odds, surmount all obstacles."

Elizabeth, who'd stopped pacing long enough to watch, yawned at the display.

"A test must equal the gift of going back," John said, "and it's no different in Lilly's case. We cannot make exceptions."

Elizabeth gnawed the inside of her cheek. How was Lilly supposed to resist the claims of a strapping big hunk like Jake? How was she going to spend every day with him, giving money away left and right, then hold out over the life insurance money she'd inherited in his stead? As a man, he was irresistible enough to be persuasive. Scratch that, as a man, he was downright, drop-dead irresistible.

"He won't do anything illegal, will he?"

"You mean like forging a check? Well, one thing I've learned from watching people—"

"Yes?"

"You just never know."

"He could get close to her and steal all her money, thinking he can use it to start his business again. Then she wouldn't be able to follow the rules. Then what?"

"I hope she's wearing comfortable shoes."

"But, John, she hates lines. Making Lilly stand in line is like making an artist live in the dark."

"Fortunately for her, Jake's always had her best interests at heart."

Elizabeth breathed a sigh of relief, knowing that was true. Jake had left town to keep his feelings for Lilly hidden, so no one would think she'd encouraged him in any way.

"Although . . . he is pretty mad at her," John mused. "Who knows what he might do? Money is a great temptation."

"But that wouldn't be fair!"

"Hey, life's not fair. Besides, Jake has life lessons to learn, too."

"He's mastered patience."

"So far." John shrugged. "Maybe it's been too easy. So he lost a little insurance money. Big deal."

"Ah, so Lilly's there to try his patience. Well, it's a good thing for her sake that I took out a little insurance of my own."

John's eyes narrowed. "What do you mean?"

"You'll see. Maybe I'm working with you for a totally different reason than you think. Maybe I need to learn to fight for what *I* believe in."

"Lord, woman, what have you done?"

At home that evening, Lilly took stock. She wanted to talk to Elizabeth—in fact, she did talk to her, quite a bit, but no reply was forthcoming.

She wasn't sure if she should continue.

"I mean, come *on*," she said heavenward. No way she could give away eighteen million dollars. "I must have been in shock. You're not really real. I never really talked to you. You're a figment of my imagination. Aren't you?"

She could prove it. She'd call the bank first thing and put a stop on the check.

"Ye-ow."

Damn, but that hurt.

"Okay, so you're real," she muttered, shaking her arm

out. When the phone rang, she hoped it was a new avenue of communication with Elizabeth. Boy, how she'd like to give her a piece of her mind!

But it was only her weekly, after-dark, heavy breather. Shortly after Brady's death, the nuisance calls had begun with silence on the other end of the line, which frightened her at first. Changing her number hadn't worked. She couldn't screen every call, because she wasn't always in the same room with the answering machine or caller ID. About the time she got used to the silent harassment, it escalated to heavy breathing. Blowing a shrill whistle into the receiver hadn't worked, though she'd spent one night laughing and hugging herself at the thought of the scumbag writhing on the floor in pain.

She spent hours in her glass-roofed atrium. Tending the exotic trees and plants and feeding the koi usually relaxed her, but tonight, thinking back over her day with Jake turned out to be an exercise in frustration. She wasn't quite certain what to make of him. Sometimes friendly and polite, sometimes a chip on his shoulder. Moody? Or contemplative?

It didn't matter which, really. She had to complete a mission, as it were. A few weeks to get pregnant, at most. With her irregular cycle, no telling when the key dates were.

She'd confessed she hadn't any prospects, and then *bam*, Jake had shown up. No doubt about it; had to be him. And he wasn't just a tool, a sperm donor. That would be impersonal and unfair. She felt they had a real connection. Sure, it wasn't much yet. It needed to grow and be nurtured. She needed to get to the bottom of why he was driving a taxi and seemed to have abandoned any profession his degrees had prepared him for. As long as she got pregnant soon, they'd have a lifetime for all that and more. Hadn't Elizabeth said to have faith?

At ten o'clock, Lilly started packing up odds and ends that she didn't want sitting around when she marketed the house, which, as part of her net worth, had to be liquidated. Everything of any monetary value had to be converted to cash. If she gave it all away too soon, she'd be destitute. She needed a legal arrangement that would allow her to sell the house but stay on until whatever else she was supposed to take on faith happened. That would take a unique buyer.

"Elizabeth, if you can hear me, I need some one-on-one time. You know, down here? Face-to-face?"

Unfortunately, she couldn't shut her mind down while filling bags for the next Salvation Army pick up.

Why *was* Jake in her every thought? What had he done to make her hormones sit up and take notice, other than exchanging a few words and—oh yeah—touching her arm? That might do it. The fact that she hadn't had sex in the whole last year of her marriage probably had a lot to do with it, too.

He couldn't be serious about her not making passes! If he was *the right one*, he'd just have to get over that and get down to at least one night of the heated passion and endless lovemaking she knew she'd get with him. Too bad getting pregnant might take, oh, thirty or so such nights.

To hell—*excuse me, God, I'll try to do better*—with John. He could close his eyes or his ears or not read whatever page of her life story that'd be on.

She called Betsy. "Abstinence sucks."

"Hold on," Betsy whispered, which meant there was an overnight guest in her bed. She picked up in another room, chuckling. "So it's finally gotten to you, huh? I knew it would eventually."

"Don't sound so smug, missy. You were the one begging for a vibrator this morning."

"Not anymore."

"Yeah? Who is he?"

"That cute paramedic from this morning, and *wow*, does he know a thing or two. But back to you. You want me to fix you up with one of his friends?"

"Can you just tell me how to make a pass at a man who's told me not to?"

"Why bother? Unless it's a doctor. Ooh, I'll bet there was a cute one at the hospital."

"No, not a doctor."

"Well, who else? Andrew?"

"Oh c'mon, he's my brother-in-law."

"*Was.* I've seen those exquisite bouquets he sends you."

"He's being nice."

"Yeah, a hundred bucks a week's pretty nice. I read the last card. 'To my favorite Lilly of all. Love, Andrew.' "

"He doesn't mean it like that."

Betsy gasped audibly. "Oh, wait a minute! You don't mean the store clerk?"

"His name's Jake, and you should've remembered him from the wedding. He was Brady's best man."

"Well," she said, drawing the single word out very suggestively. "And you want to seduce him?"

"In a word, yes."

"Way to go, girl. Invite him to dinner."

"My chef quit, remember? I do takeout now."

"Gotta do better than that. I know, have a caterer deliver something yummy, and then disappear. Let's see, you'll need candlelight, soft music, sheer blouse, perfume on the pulse points. What's his favorite hobby?"

He designed computerized home control systems, but Lilly didn't know if that counted as recreation. "Selling sex toys?"

"Hm, I was going to say whatever his hobby is, leave a book on it lying around, as if you're interested, too? But I doubt that counts unless he designs them."

"Oh yuck." Lilly had a less-than-pretty mental picture of someone bent over his workbench, fashioning the next-generation vibrator.

"Hey, somebody has to do it."

"Let's say it's not him."

"Okay. So next time you see him, find out his hobby. If you don't know anything about it, act interested. If you know something—Hey, wait a minute, didn't you ever seduce your husband?"

Lilly sighed. "I don't think I was very good at it."

Brady'd had a little trouble in that department, and the more Lilly tried to help him through it, the more distance he'd put between them. He wasn't the kind of man who asked for help. He certainly wasn't about to accept any, either. Eventually he'd changed bedrooms.

"Did you wear red?"

"I don't know. Sometimes."

"Can't go wrong with red. It sends a subliminal message."

"I thought it was a power color."

"Mm-hm, makes 'em feel more *man*ly, if you know what I mean."

"I don't know, Betsy. Maybe it was me."

"Don't be ridiculous. I'll take you shopping, and we'll buy lots of sexy red stuff."

"Yeah, let's not," she said with a short laugh. "I can't stand to get blown up again."

After the phone call, she sorted boxes, one for her mother-in-law, one for Jake, if he wanted it, seven for a charity, and one she wasn't quite sure what to do with. She left a message for Andrew that she had a box of his brother's things he might want to go through.

The phone rang at eleven, undoubtedly Betsy with more good advice to impart. Hopefully not along the lines of crotchless panties.

"Lilly?"

Ah, now there was the voice of the man she might consider wearing them for.

"Oh. Jake, hi." If only he were after her instead of throwing out ride-in-the-back ultimatums.

"Good, it doesn't sound as if I woke you."

"I wish. But I've been on this cleaning frenzy." *Don't babble.* "What's up?"

"We forgot to set a time."

"No we didn't. Eight o'clock tomorrow morning."

"Huh. Oh yeah, now I remember."

Maybe this was his subtle way of hitting on her. Smiling to herself, she sank down on the carpet and leaned against the bed, getting comfortable, feeling cozy. "You're checking up on me, aren't you?"

"It's the least I can do. You know, for Brady."

"Really."

"Yeah, I owe him."

Gee, thanks. "So, you want to check me out, Doctor? Ask me what year it is and who's president?"

"Nah, you sound fine. Call me if you need somebody, okay?"

Now that sounded better. "Promise."

"Good. See you at eight."

Suddenly she didn't feel like cleaning anymore. She leaned her head against the comforter and replayed their conversation, not for the words, but to hear Jake's deep sexy rumble, to relish how nice it was to have a man care enough to call.

But she didn't need nice. She needed horny. And potent. Very, very potent.

6

Lilly was up again at 6:00 A.M. She'd chosen red silk pajamas last night, hoping they'd give her concrete ideas for successfully seducing Jake. No such luck, but they'd felt unexpectedly decadent against her skin. Between Jake's heated touch and the sumptuous silk, she recognized a pattern of at least one heightened sense.

She'd learned some valuable lessons in the five months since Brady's death, and she reviewed them while she fed the koi and lovebirds and strolled through the atrium at a leisurely pace, checking everything from the tiniest primrose to the tallest tree.

Who knew beforehand what happened when their time was up, what they were supposed to have learned? She did.

Most people weren't prepared. She would be next time.

They didn't know what to expect. Again, she did.

Her mother-in-law had given her a framed copy of the Serenity prayer after Brady's funeral, and she'd carried the words engraved on her consciousness for months now. *Grant me the serenity to accept the things I cannot change, courage to change the things I can, and wisdom to know the difference.*

Thanks to Elizabeth, she was practically wearing it on her arm, too.

So far Lilly had just about mastered the serene part. She couldn't change Brady's death; she'd moved beyond that. Now John and Elizabeth had thrown this whole go-back-but-you-have-a-deadline issue at her, which pretty much blew serenity out of the water.

As for the courage part, well, she could change how she lived. She would. It'd take a lot of courage to give away *every blasted cent.* Think about it. What if she ended up on the street, dependent on the charity of others? How ironic. That could be her standing in line outside a food kitchen, eight-and-a-half-months pregnant and hungry.

It would also take a lot of courage to chase a man until he got her pregnant. How much time could she invest in Jake before cutting her losses if he wouldn't cooperate? With only a few weeks, there really was no room for failure. The dashboard photos spoke in his favor, showing her that he'd had the rollicking, boisterous childhood she'd always dreamed of, the very same childhood she wanted for her kids—no way she wanted a man who wasn't close to his family. If she had half a chance with him, she had to go for it.

Jake popped into mind again, full of life and vigor and not many clothes.

With a renewed burst of energy, Lilly searched for

something in the kitchen to scrub. Eventually she stumbled upon the tub of miniature Snickers bars in the refrigerator, left over from Halloween. Stuffing one into her mouth, she closed her eyes and savored the sweetness.

God, chocolate had always been her favorite—and a chilled Snickers was hard enough to break teeth, that's why she kept them that way, to slow her down—but since when did one taste this heavenly?

Oh yeah, since I got blown up. As soon as it was chewable, she consumed it and stuffed in another.

The doorbell bonged promptly at eight o'clock.

Lilly's hands flew to her hair, her face, her pajamas. She didn't need a mirror to see what a mess she was. Lopsided hair. Eye makeup that hadn't quite all come off the night before. Wrinkled pajamas, far too silky to disguise anything beneath them, which she thought might be a little too blatant to hit her target with so early in the morning. She hadn't even brushed her teeth yet.

"I'll unlock the door," she said into the intercom. "But I'm not dressed, so count to ten before you come in."

Once Jake stepped through the leaded-glass front door into the cavernous marble foyer, he could rest easy that Lilly hadn't changed her mind about hiring him. While the salary she was paying was a pittance compared to what she owed him and what he needed to get his family out of debt, it was more than he'd clear picking up fares.

And it gave him an additional reason to be with Lilly, one he could rationalize as to how their togetherness was potentially beneficial and not detrimental to his objectives.

He thoroughly enjoyed watching her race back up the

gently curving staircase. In this weather, sleeping alone, he would've pegged her for flannel pajamas sprinkled with delicate little violets. Certainly not that silky, red-hot set that skimmed over her skin as she topped the stairs and turned the corner. Damn, Brady had been a lucky man.

Well, maybe not. Brady was dead.

And I'm here.

He felt just the tiniest bit of elation over that.

He could be here all right, as in *with Lilly*. He got hard just thinking about the possibilities, distracting him from what his conscience was telling him. If he didn't mind being a gigolo, the whole money issue would be moot. But no damn way he was going there. He owed Brady life and loyalty, and guilt edged its way in and settled in his gut.

He wouldn't have been surprised if Lilly'd reneged on the job and refused to open the front door this morning, but she hadn't. So it looked as though they were poised for a day playing give away—with *his* money. Remembering that ought to keep his head clear and in control, as if he were on a tightrope that required constant balance and careful steps.

Strolling through the house, which he'd been in plenty before he'd moved away, he noted the changes since Brady'd gotten married. It was still a gorgeous, three-story, stone-and-glass affair, but now that he'd glimpsed Lilly running through it in red silk, it seemed warmer, more intimate, as if she brought pure sexual energy to everything. Marble foyer and stairs, two-story entrance, soaring glass windows, arched doorways—in the space of seconds, it had all been transformed. Yes, softer now. More inviting.

Unsettled with that introspection, he retreated to Brady's office, where he could count on the familiar, lingering aroma of cigars past.

Only he couldn't, because the smell was gone, and it nagged at him because it was part of their history—his and Brady's—and he'd counted on that being there forever. It was like losing him all over again.

No problem, Jake knew where the good ones were stored. He'd right this soon enough. It was a tough job, but somebody had to do it.

"What the heck are you doing?" Lilly demanded, before he was halfway through a truly fine cigar.

Sprawled in Brady's leather recliner, totally vegged out and at peace with the world, he turned his head toward the door. There stood Lilly, feet planted, arms akimbo, fire in her eyes, one button too few buttoned on her red blouse, and the whole thing pulled taut across her breasts. Instantly hard again, he couldn't help but imagine—

Shit! Remembering Brady's hot recounting of this very chair, a bottle of wine, and Lilly in a sheer black teddy, Jake vaulted out of the recliner, damned near damaging himself as he tripped and scrambled to his feet.

"Sorry, didn't think you'd mind."

She yanked the cigar out of his teeth.

"I, uh, missed the smell in here."

"And you obviously have no idea how tough it was to get it out."

He dogged her heels to the kitchen sink and watched helplessly as she drowned the poor thing. He must have looked heartbroken, because she said, "Aw, poor baby," and offered the rest of them to him, as long as he promised to smoke them far, far away.

"You need to update your alarm system," he said as they left.

"My father-in-law sent a company out to look into that after Brady died. They said they'd never seen anything this high-tech."

Jake didn't mind taking a little pride in that, since he'd designed it. "Well sure, but that's *them*."

"Ah."

He also didn't mind the way Lilly glanced up at him, her single word laced with acknowledgment of his superiority.

"I could upgrade it in an afternoon."

"Thanks, but I'm selling, so there's really no need. Oh, here, I don't want to forget." She handed him his first week's check with a cheeky grin. "Wouldn't want you telling people I'm not good for it."

She got into the front seat instead of the rear, just as he'd figured she would. Good thing, because he had Mooch set up in the back, curled up in a nest of blanket, his tail wrapped tightly around him. The cat wasn't in a good mood. One long, low, mournful yowl from him had Lilly whipping around to see what it came from. Jake swiped her checkbook out of her purse and tucked it in the crack beside the seat before she glanced from the cat to him.

"One of your regulars?"

"He lives here. Mooch, Lilly. Lilly, Mooch."

Mooch was a huge mixed-breed feline who looked as if he'd been tumbled in a dryer with several shades of earth-tone paints, then plugged into an electrical outlet. And his attitude was a prickly *Yeah, what of it?*

"He lives in the car?"

"Yep. I came out one morning, there he was, sitting right where you are. Refused to get out. I tried to pick him up and put him out, but let me tell you, he has all his claws and knows how to use them. So beware. Tomorrow, he'll probably want his spot back."

"Day *and* night?"

"Well, he's started coming into the house with me in the evenings. And he gets out to do his business. Boy, does he hate the snow."

"He wasn't here yesterday."

"He was at the v-e-t getting f-i-x-e-d."

She snickered. "You're *spelling*?"

"Hey, animals understand more than you know."

"You don't believe in heaven, but you think he knows he was fixed?"

Mooch hissed, showing off a full set of pointy teeth.

Jake started the car. "Try not to rile him too much. I'm supposed to keep him from jumping around for the first twenty-four hours."

He thought Lilly looked at him a little differently after that, but she kept her thoughts to herself. They could have been anything from *What a nice guy to take in a big, ugly stray* to *What kind of demented nut lets a cat ride around all day in his taxi?*

Within half an hour, they were headed into the city, all three of them munching on their respective drive-thru sandwiches. Jake was having a damned hard time getting rid of the image of her in the recliner, on top—yeah, definitely on top—wearing a sheer black teddy and tousled hair.

"You sure that's okay?" He indicated her sandwich with a tip of his head.

It was a dumb question, especially since she'd hummed over the first bites as if they were a five-star dinner. But if she talked to him, he'd have to focus on her, here and now, and see that she'd put a nice, thick winter coat on over her snug blouse.

"Mm," she said. "It's delicious."

When her cell phone rang, she flipped it open with a smooth skill that could only come from lots of practice. Why hadn't Brady asked him for a decent phone for Lilly? That standard retail model was okay for everyone who didn't know better, but a piece of shit for someone like her. He'd fix that tomorrow.

In the meantime, he was good at tuning people out. You had to be, sometimes, when you drove a taxi. Some people ran on at the mouth and said absolutely nothing of interest, or gabbed about personal stuff he really didn't want to hear. Fights with boyfriends, girlfriends, wives, husbands, bosses, employees. Sex problems with all the above. Money woes. Nothing he could fix, so he took Uncle Paul's advice and didn't try.

He picked up on Lilly talking to someone about selling her house—*Oh, wait'll Brady's mother hears about this.* He told her so when she hung up.

"That house has been in the family for years," he warned, surprising himself with a hint of censure in his voice. "I know, because my dad did the stonework on it."

"Is that why you're being proprietary?"

He swallowed his last bite. "I'm not."

"But you don't want me to sell it."

"I'm just explaining that Brady's dad had it built special. Same as having my grandfather do the stonework on his parents' house. I'm just saying they won't want to let it go to strangers."

"Is that how you and Brady met? Family friends?"

"I wouldn't go that far. I worked Marquette Construction every summer. Brady's dad thought it would be good for him to understand how the other half lived, and he just happened to be put to work on the same site as me. We carried hod, we talked, we went out afterward for beer. Good times."

"He missed you, you know. He knew you had to be in California, but he missed you."

"Yeah, me too."

"And he worried about you."

No way he was going there. He bagged up their cups and empty wrappers. "I'm just saying you might offer it to his mom first."

"Oh, good idea," she said, making him feel stupidly pleased for helping.

"I don't know how you'd agree on a price, though."

"Betsy's in real estate. She'll make sure I get what it's worth."

He promptly drove into a branch of her bank and cashed his first week's check. Just in case.

Then Lilly called a broker about selling an airplane. From the way the conversation went, it seemed it was hers. Brady had piloted it on his trips to the coast, but Jake doubted he would've known all the answers Lilly was handing out, rattling off statistics without second-guessing herself.

"The plane's yours?" he asked when she was finished.

"Yeah, I used to fly private charters."

"Really?"

"Mm-hmm."

"*Really?*"

"Don't be sexist."

"Bear with me, I want to get this straight. You'd fly other people around, take them where they wanted to go, cater to their every whim—"

"Make your point."

"—then come home and get into a chauffeur-driven limo?"

She laughed lightly. He hadn't meant her to, but it sounded so nice, he might try it intentionally later. When he got over being pissed at her, which would be about the same time she gave him a seven-digit check and called off her in-laws.

"Wait a minute, I thought you grew up rich. Why were you flying charters?"

"Temporary reversal of fortune," she said. "You've heard of the domino effect? Well, so did my dad's investments. He lost a lot of his brother's money, too, but my uncle managed to hold on to his plane and his charter business. He's the one who taught me to fly and took me on as a partner. That's how I met Brady, you know. Oh, maybe you don't. He hired me to fly him to Silicon Valley a couple times. To see you. After we got married, *then* I hired a chauffeur and eventually quit doing charters, for most of those reasons you just mentioned. Boy, people can be so bossy."

"Stingy, too."

"And *rude*, oh my gosh, you can't believe how—"

"Sure I can. Did they tell you stories you didn't want to hear?"

"Are you kidding? They curled my hair!" She turned

in her seat, facing him, caught up in the moment they shared.

She was so beautiful, she took his breath away. Sure, some people might say her eyes were too big or her hair too singed. Not he.

"Makes me shudder, just remembering," she said.

Jake quickly withdrew, afraid to think they had anything in common. If they were going to spend a lot of time together until he got the all clear from his dad and demanded the fortune she owed him, it would be better to maintain a professional distance. Easier on him anyway.

"And the men! What is it about men that I no sooner get the wheels up, and they say, 'Let's see how this baby handles'?"

Try as he did to resist, he grinned at her testosterone-laden imitation. No wonder Brady'd bragged about Lilly. Most women would freak out over their burned hair or mismatched fingernails. She'd taken one look at his sore fingers and unwrapped his breakfast sandwich for him, and then Mooch's, too. She even cooed at the cat while she took care of him. It was hard to be mad at a woman who liked his ugly, mean-tempered cat.

"Anyway, I leased out the plane with the stipulation that I could fly it often enough to keep up my license, and when he got his, Brady could borrow it."

"To come see me?"

"Yeah."

Lilly's voice trailed off, and Jake wondered if she was thinking along the same lines as he—what might've been if they'd met at the airport on one of those days? Would it have been *their* third wedding anniversary coming up?

"Anyway, you can bet I was always nice to my chauffeur. Which reminds me." She flipped open her phone and speed-dialed him three pounds of Godiva chocolates. *On account.*

He'd had a lot of customers, but he'd never seen that before. One button to nirvana for the chauffeur.

He also noticed that during the two-minute call, Lilly dropped her phone three times, fumbling it like a hot potato, banging it off the window, the dash, and finally the steering wheel. Mooch gave one long mournful moan, then hoisted himself to his feet and poked his nose in Lilly's hair. Jake watched him closely, because he wasn't used to the moaning, and he wanted to be sure Mooch wasn't anti-Lilly and out for a bite of her neck, but he settled back down shortly thereafter.

"Maybe you should have that arm x-rayed if it's still bothering you," he said when she finally corralled her phone and flipped it shut.

"It's nothing." She glanced at him through lowered lashes. "Nothing that'll stop me, anyway."

Jake didn't like the predatory way Lilly looked at him when she said it, but it wasn't obvious enough to call her on it. Even so, he felt a little bit like a lab rat. Or a guinea pig.

7

The first thing Lilly did after breakfast was restore her appearance. As her stylist trimmed away the singed hair, he started listing options ranging from pixie to sophisticated.

Lilly interrupted. "I want seductive."

He'd known her for years. He knew she was recently widowed. "How seductive?" he asked tentatively.

"Well, I don't want you shaving letters on my scalp, but otherwise, in-his-face."

"Oh-kay," he said, pausing to reflect. He studied her features and toyed with her hair, measuring bounce and wave and whatnot. "I know just the thing. You want color, too?"

"You're a man, what do you think?"

"Personally, I like highlights. But once you take your clothes off, he won't be looking at the color."

"Okay, just the cut then, and if that doesn't work, I'll be back for stage two."

She ended up with a sexy little bob. Now that it was shorter, it had a natural kink, lending her a naughty look, she thought. Very much a *Come open the package and see what's inside* invitation. She finished the morning by getting her nails resculptured in the same salon.

"Red," she decided.

The nail artist winked at Lilly and held up three tiny bottles. "So I heard. I've got Ravishing Red, Seductive Scarlet, and Kick-Ass Claret."

"Seductive Scarlet."

"Yeah, that'd be my choice, too. Don't want to overwhelm the guy. If you come back for highlights, we'll switch to Kick-Ass."

As Sandi worked on one hand, Lilly called her mother-in-law and offered her first option on the house.

"I knew it, that house is way too big for you. We have plenty of room here, if that wouldn't make you too uncomfortable." Donna made the same offer at least once every week.

"Actually, I'd like to stay in the house a few months."

"But you want to sell it now?"

"I know it sounds strange, but I just feel a real need to get everything in order, you know?"

Donna was too polite to say she didn't. "Of course, dear. I suppose it's only natural, with Brady dying so suddenly. Maybe you should talk to someone."

Lilly chuckled, knowing exactly how to change *that* topic. "I did. She's a Realtor. Are you interested?"

"Let me get back to you."

When Lilly's nails were finished, she carefully used just the very tips of her fingers to pull her wallet out of her purse. Everything was going fine until she reached for her credit card. That damn bruised nerve zapped her again, making her squeak, sending her wallet flying across the room, turning her moments-ago Seductive Scarlets into Scarred Scarlets.

Jake materialized by her shoulder. "Again?"

"A little bit," was all she'd admit to.

"Let's see, first time, you were telling me to send you a bill. Second time, you were ordering chocolate for your chauffeur. Now, you're charging something. Damn, Brady said you were tight with a buck. He didn't say it actually hurt you to part with money."

"Don't be silly."

She frowned heavenward, wondering whether Jake had hit on something. Maybe he had a point, but she had to pay her bills. She hadn't been zapped when she'd paid him to be her full-time chauffeur, so there had to be some leeway. John and Elizabeth couldn't expect *all* her money to go to charity.

"Consider this an investment in sedu—uh, in *securing* my 'future,' " she said through gritted teeth.

"What?"

"Not now, Jake."

"Weren't you talking to me? I could've sworn you were, because the cashier's on the phone, and I'm the only one, you know, *listening*." He eyed her suspiciously. "You get hit in the head yesterday?"

"Probably. What's your point?"

"I'm just wondering how long it takes for a head injury to show up."

After signing the receipt and having her nails touched

up, she found Jake in the freshly plowed parking lot, leaning into the trunk of his taxi. She peeked in, too, only to find a jumbled mess of packages from Cloud Nine.

"Looking for a good time?"

"What? Oh." He grinned. "No, just inventorying what I was able to salvage from the store. The owner wants a complete list. Got your phone on you?"

"Yeah, why?"

He pulled a small box out of the trunk and extracted a tiny cell phone. "This one's better. It's yours if you want it."

"Really?" Fascinated by its minuscule size, Lilly took it gingerly and, careful of her nails, gave it a once-over. "I've never seen one like this."

"Well"—he grinned boyishly—"they're not exactly retail. I programmed it with your number, and if you like, I'll transfer your phone book this evening."

"Well sure. Thanks."

He shrugged as if it were nothing, which maybe it was to him, but she was touched that he'd thought of her. Being on his mind meant she was closer to getting him in bed.

Then again, the frizzy, homeless cat was on his mind, too. He'd actually ordered a to-go cup of water for Mooch and lifted him out of the taxi so he could go potty without jumping down and hurting himself—wouldn't he make a good dad?—so maybe being on Jake's mind didn't mean anything of the sort.

"Brady should've changed the phone out for you. I'm just doing it for him."

Hoping that wasn't his sole reason, she moved closer and peeked into the open trunk. "What other high-tech stuff do you have in there?"

"Unless you consider vibrating dildos high-tech, nothing."

The box in the rear corner didn't hold adult toy items, but umbrellas, purses, a briefcase, a sweater, and a pair of white underpants that were bagged in a Ziploc— silky-looking, but way too tame for a self-proclaimed pleasure shop.

"Interesting stuff you carry around."

"Customers left all that in the backseat. No ID's, not even in the purses. I keep it handy, hoping I'll pick up somebody again who'll ask me if I found something they can identify."

"*Underpants?*"

He chuckled. "What, nobody left those in your air-plane?"

"I had a couple try it once." She winked. "We hit a bit of turbulence, and they got very ill."

"Too bad taxis don't have wings."

"I'd throw them away."

"I did that once." His lips twisted in a grim line, and he rubbed the back of his head as if it were sore. "I found out why Uncle Paul said to wait six months. How was I sup-posed to know she'd track me down for a pair of twenty-dollar Victoria's Secrets?" He closed the trunk lid. "So who were you talking to before? You know, in the salon."

"John and Elizabeth."

"Your sorority sister?"

She gave him points for remembering and decided it'd be better—and in the long run simpler—to be honest. "Not really. I guess you could call them angels."

"Not me. Here, better let me get the door so you don't mess up your nails again."

Lilly grinned as she moved past him, leaning in just so, letting her shoulder brush against his arm. She didn't know whether it got his attention, but it sure felt fine to her.

"Oh yeah, you of the 'tarot cards and channeling shit.'"

"Damn straight. Give me scientific facts and hard data, then we'll talk."

She wanted so badly to lift up on her toes and kiss him, but other than dancing with him three years ago and a brief hug at the funeral, it was really like they'd only just met yesterday. She should be happy with her progress so far; she had him right where she wanted him—confined in the front seat, not two feet away from her, scheduled to be there day after day. Red blouse, naughty haircut, scarlet nails—he couldn't help but notice she was available.

Ah, the heck with it. As soon as he slid in behind the wheel, she scooted over, and turning his face toward hers with a hand on his cheek, she softly pressed her lips where she'd been dying to all night.

At first he did nothing, didn't even kiss her back. At least he didn't jump out of the car. But just when she was about to give up, his lips softened ever so slightly against hers, then more, and finally he angled his head for a better fit.

Oh heavens! She'd had no idea what she was getting into. For what started out as a brief, gentle kiss, it quickly turned wicked, hitting awfully hard deep inside, heating up areas that hadn't been heated in, well, maybe never.

When she dragged her lips away from his and put a mere breath of space between them, he whispered—hoarsely, she was pleased to notice—"What was that for?"

She cleared her throat so she wouldn't strangle on whatever popped out of her mouth, which was not eloquent—

who could be eloquent when she'd just had her insides sautéed?—but instead, was very simple.

"Thanks for saving my life."

"You're sure?"

"Heck yes."

"No, I mean you're sure that's all it is. Because if not, I still have half a backseat open."

Instead of being offended, she smiled and nuzzled his lips again, teasing him, but not daring to taste him with the tip of her tongue the way she was dying to.

"You kissed me back."

"I'm a man. You put a beautiful woman in my lap, I'm not responsible."

"Is that so?"

She grinned against his mouth, gave him one last light-as-a-butterfly kiss, and backed off. For now.

He was pond scum, pure, unadulterated pond scum. No, what was lower than that? Whatever it was, that was him.

His best friend was dead only a few months, and at a tragically young age. Poor guy hadn't even passed on his genes.

And what the hell was he—Jake—doing? Messing with his best friend's wife. His *widow*, for chrissakes, and not all that long at it. Stoking the fire that had begun three years ago and couldn't burn itself out naturally.

But technically, *she* was messing with *him*. He'd kept his hands to himself, for which he should get a medal. He hadn't dragged Lilly up against his body. He hadn't slipped his tongue past her lips and tasted her the way he'd wanted. The way his body had *demanded*.

But that didn't make him a saint, because the pure,

undiluted fact was, he'd wanted to. If her lips had—
Damn, they were so soft. Not a chapped spot on them. If
they had remained on his another second, he wouldn't
have been responsible for where his body would lead
them. Not his brain—his body—because his brain hadn't
gotten any blood from the instant she'd slid across that
seat.

Speaking of which, the seat was wide, flat, plenty of
people had sex in cars. The steering wheel could be a
problem, he supposed.

Hell, how was he supposed to drive now?

He looked around, shocked to see that he *was* driving.
He'd gone at least a mile, somehow starting the car, putting it in gear, missing other vehicles. Shit, he needed a
night out with the guys. They'd set him straight. They'd
tell him to stay away from Lilly. They'd remind him to
keep networking with the guys out in Silicon Valley, to
stay focused on the big picture until he could seize opportunity and reestablish himself as a technological wizard.
If he didn't wreck the car first.

He buckled his seat belt—the only thing he knew he'd
forgotten. Not that there might not be something else,
like respect for the dead.

Or like his *brain.*

Lilly wasn't able to get her lips near Jake's again all
week.

Fairly certain she couldn't get pregnant right away,
she'd been willing to go slowly, set the stage, get off on
the right foot, so to speak. Talk a lot, laugh together, trade
life stories, that kind of thing, all while driving around
and giving money to needy causes.

She'd taken to signing the checks at the various charity offices with her eyes closed. Elizabeth's "have faith" was easier said than done. It just plain hurt to see her own name below so many zeroes.

"I'd like to do something different today," she said one morning as she slid into the taxi. "At least one thing."

"What do have in mind?"

"Writing checks is really boring. I mean, how many hands can I shake and how many framed photos of volunteers on the wall do I have to stare at before I go stark raving mad? They thank me real nice, and they tell me where my money's going to go, but I don't *see* it." She sighed. "Do you think it's possible for me to help people?"

"You're helping lots of people."

"I mean personally. For *me* to make a difference *personally*. With individuals."

Jake studied her for a moment, a curious look on his face. "You're serious about this?"

"Yes."

He put the taxi in DRIVE. "Hold that thought, I know just the place."

Half an hour later, they drove between brick pillars that were flanked by twin guards—one snowwoman, one snowman, just about all that was left of the big Valentine's Day storm.

Lilly peered through the windshield at the huge complex. "What is this?"

"It's a club for boys and girls. A safe place for them to go after school and on weekends. Summers, too."

"There's more here than just a safe place."

"That's what I want to show you." He opened his door. "I take care of their computer needs, but they also have a health clinic, performing arts, athletic teams—"

"Must cost a fortune to run."

He grinned and said, "That's where you come in. Come on, I'll introduce you to Ollie first."

They found the director in a fairly tidy office, with his door open wide and a big bowl of candy on the desk. He was about thirty, skinny except for the pooch right behind his belt, already balding, and he had the soft eyes of an angel.

"Dang, Jake," Ollie said, crossing the room quickly to shake hands with him. "If I'd known you knew a beautiful woman, I'd drop by for a beer more often."

"We just met a few days ago. Ollie, Lilly. Lilly, Ollie."

Ollie shook her hand warmly. "Nice to meet you, Lilly. Usually he just brings that mean-tempered cat of his."

Lilly's jaw dropped as she turned to Jake. "You *don't*."

"Hey, Mooch gets along fine with the kids. I'd bring him in today, Ollie, but he had surgery recently. So, how about I show Lilly around—"

"How about you go do whatever magic you do in the computer lab and *I'll* show Lilly around." It wasn't a question, and Ollie took Lilly by the elbow and ushered her out the door.

"Computers are all fine," Jake said, tagging along.

"You haven't even checked."

"I can check from home."

"Talk about Big Brother. Hey, you'd better not be able to tap into the confidential files."

"Not to worry."

"He says that, but I don't believe him," Ollie murmured to Lilly. "He was like that in college, too. Hands in everything. Have you seen his house? He makes inanimate objects do things that inanimate objects shouldn't do." He shuddered, but she could tell Ollie'd been the class clown.

A dozen boys and girls greeted Jake by name as Ollie led Lilly on a tour of the facility, which could only rightfully be called a complex, and explained how much good they did in the community, keeping kids off the streets, teaching them character, leadership, and skills everyone needed.

Ollie introduced her to several of the children, and she carefully considered each boy's name as a possibility for her son. The weird, artistic names were just out, period; if her child was destined to do something great, he could use a strong name for starters. She was looking for something powerful, yet distinctive. Names were supposed to be important in one's destiny.

"Who's the little guy following us?" Lilly whispered, as they finished up an hour later.

The small boy had been trailing them for fifteen minutes, ten paces back, stopping when they stopped, peeking around corners and doors to make sure they didn't get too far away.

Ollie knew who Lilly meant without looking. "Reggie's kind of shy, doesn't talk much," he said softly. "We try to get him involved a little more every day, but then he backs off. He prefers just to hang out until his grandmother picks him up."

Her heart went out to Reggie, whose shyness got in the way of his obvious need to connect.

Reggie. Reginald. Nope, way too different.

"He talks to Mooch," Jake said.

"He'll come around. Some of these kids don't get much interaction at home. Single parents, two jobs, that kind of thing."

"I'd better explain why Mooch isn't here today." As they passed through a community area, Jake took a chair and waited for Reggie to inch by. Lilly knew instinctively that Jake sat so he wouldn't loom over the child.

"He does seem to like Jake's cat," Ollie admitted.

"You two known each other long?"

"Since college. We were on the same floor in the dorm."

"It's nice you've stayed in touch."

"Well, that's mostly Jake's doing," Ollie admitted. "But then, that's Jake. He's real close to his family, and that spills over into his friendships. You okay?"

"Oh." She'd been watching Reggie. "He reminds me of myself at that age. I want to just go up and hug him—"

Ollie cleared his throat, ready to issue a warning.

"—but I know he wouldn't welcome it." She'd been stuck in a boarding school twenty-four/seven, no one to go home to at night. Sad thing was, she missed her nanny the most because she'd been closest to her.

They returned to the office, where Lilly got down to the business of a charitable donation.

"You've seen everything," Ollie said. "Is there one particular area you'd like this to go to?"

Well, that was a nice change, unlike the usual obsequious handshake and "I look forward to seeing you again next year."

"Can I get back to you on that?" Out the window, she watched Jake and Reggie at the car, the back door standing open.

"Sure, stop by anytime. If you want, we can always use volunteers."

One thing she'd learned from her many stops—volunteers were the backbone of charities. She wondered if they were ever given their due.

She strolled outside and huddled alone on a nearby bench to give Reggie extra time with Jake and Mooch. After asking Jake a myriad of questions about Mooch's surgery and what it was for and if it hurt, Reggie gave the cat a gentle pat and sauntered away.

Lilly headed for the warmth of the car. She was in her seat, rubbing her hands together in front of the vent when she noticed Jake sitting sideways, studying her.

"What?"

"Nothing. I just noticed you freezing over there on the bench, that's all."

"I didn't want to scare Reggie off."

"Huh."

"What?"

"Just surprised, that's all."

The next day, Lilly set about concentrating on the other half of her mission—getting past Jake's defenses. From here on in, she could ovulate at any time. She could track her temperature, of course, but what was the point if she couldn't even *kiss* him?

Betsy was sitting at the tile-topped table in Lilly's atrium, having rushed over in response to a plea for help. And she had a whole different objective. "Tell me again why you're giving money away."

"I saw the light."

"At the end of the tunnel," Betsy repeated.

"Yes!" Lilly said, with all the exasperation that had built up over the last half hour of repeatedly explaining the concept, all the while puttering about her plants and feeding healthy treats to the bonded pair of lovebirds who ruled the atrium during daylight hours.

Jake, too, had asked one day why she was suddenly so benevolent and did it have anything to do with nearly dying. She'd started to explain about the angels, and he'd said, "Fine, if you don't want to tell me, don't," and that was the last she'd heard about it from him.

Betsy should be so easy.

It was time to move upstairs and find something to wear. Either Betsy would get this or she wouldn't, but there was nothing else Lilly could tell her to make it happen.

"He's going to be here in a few minutes, and I'd really rather discuss how to get him into bed—*soon*—if you don't mind."

"What makes you think I'd know?"

"Exactly how many hours did it take you to get that cute paramedic into bed?"

"He went back to work first. Do I have to count that?"

"I rest my case."

Upstairs, Betsy sat on the bed while Lilly dug deep in her closet, searching for more red.

"Tell me again how you looked back on your life and saw you hadn't been generous enough."

"No." Lilly poked through a lot of stuff she hadn't seen, much less worn, in years. She really should start boxing some of it up for the women's shelter.

"But, Lill, you've been doing this all week, and you're selling your house and your airplane. I'm worried about you. I mean, this is a complete turnaround. It's not like you at all, and I think you should talk to someone."

"I'm fine."

"You're not fine. You're giving away money as an excuse to ride around every day with Jake."

"That's not why—"

"Stop right there."

Maybe if she retreated far enough into the back of the closet, she wouldn't have to listen.

"Now, I'm not criticizing you—"

Nope, wasn't working.

"I'm telling you it's okay to chase the man. You can tie him to the bed and tear his clothes off and have your way with him for all I care—"

When Betsy paused, Lilly figured she was dabbing off a little drool at the corner of her mouth, because that's exactly the effect the image was having on her. Especially after that kiss. Oh my God, what had she been thinking? That kissing Jake for the first time would be like kissing a husband for the thousandth time when he came home from work? Although—whew!—wouldn't that be the kind of husband to have.

Shoot, Brady'd never kissed her like that. She hadn't known *any*one kissed the way Jake did. It just reinforced her belief that there was definitely more out there that she'd never experienced, that she should've experienced at least once a week in years and years of making love.

Hm, she was going to have to downgrade that from lovemaking to sex. Ho-hum sex, she was pretty sure now.

Betsy was still talking. Lilly had no idea how much she'd missed, but unless it was a detailed, itemized list of what she had to do to get Jake into bed, it probably wasn't all that important.

"It's not okay to feel so guilty about it that you have to rationalize a cockamamie reason like giving away a whole bunch of money just to be with him. And another thing . . ."

Blah blah blah . . .

Lilly found herself measuring time not by the amount of dollars flowing out of her accounts, not by how much slower Mooch vacated his favorite seat every morning, but by the number of red items she'd gone through in her quest to get Jake's attention. Blouses, sweaters, jackets— she had run out of solids within days and started dredging up anything with any little spot of red in it. At the end of a week, the pickings were mighty slim.

She held up a black dress and red belt, interrupting Betsy in midsentence to ask her opinion. "Will this get him hot?"

"Black? Lill, if the man has any sense of decency, it'll just make him think you're still mourning his best friend."

"Oh my gosh! I wore a black skirt with my red jacket yesterday. And black pants the day before that. *That*'s why I'm not getting anywhere with him?"

"Du-uh."

She'd been in an increasingly uncomfortable state of carnal desire all week, with no end in sight. How dumb could she be? Brady'd been Jake's best friend. Of course he respected her grief. Shoot, how was she supposed to get around that before she ran out of time?

"Darn it, Betsy, it would've been nice if you'd mentioned that instead of telling me I couldn't fail in red, so I would've known there's nothing wrong with *me*."

"That remains to be seen."

Laughing with relief, Lilly tore through her closet for anything not black, selecting a royal blue dress instead. It'd been tight across her breasts last time she wore it, but that would only help her quest, not hurt it.

Maybe once she slept with Jake, the dreams would stop. They were driving her crazy, replaying each unproductive day with him over and over, each version a little different, so that by the time she woke up, she wasn't clear on exactly where or why she'd struck out.

They also hit her right in her conscience, plaguing her with feelings of guilt that she sublimated during waking hours. It boiled down to pursuing Jake for procreation purposes without cluing him in to the outcome. Awake, she could rationalize it, having a baby at last, the gift of life, for the greater good and all that. Asleep, she couldn't.

"Really, Lill, I'm worried about you."

Lilly slipped into the dress and twirled for inspection. "Good?"

"You need more red than just a belt. Got anything else? A scarf maybe?"

"Tights?"

"Oh, please no. I'd say throw them out, but," Betsy suggested with a wicked smile, "they make great ropes."

"Ooh, you're making me hot." Lilly fanned herself theatrically and tucked the tights under her pillow just in case. "See, that's the kind of stuff I need to know. What else?"

"Earrings."

"No, not earrings," she whined. "Can you not *focus* on what I need?"

"Sure. And your red shoes."

Lilly gave up. Maybe it was time for stage two.

The doorbell rang. "If I don't make serious lip contact with Jake by the end of the day, I'll try your bedpost thing."

"Girl, if you don't make serious lip contact, I doubt you'll be able to tie him to the bed. It's kind of a prerequisite."

Betsy held a red purse out like a flag. Lilly nabbed it on her way out the bedroom door, checking to make sure her checkbook was in it on her way down the stairs. The darned thing was never where it was supposed to be, slowing her down like a series of speed bumps in her path to the poorhouse. Once she'd even found it under Mooch; you'd think it was his the way he'd hissed at her for taking it back.

Minutes later, she slid into the front of Jake's taxi, nudging Mooch over toward the center. He gave a mournful, threatening moan or yowl or whatever the heck you called that terrible sound that droned on and on until he felt he'd said enough and hopped disdainfully into the back.

She said, "Morning," in a voice that she meant to be provocative, but it just sounded chipper to her.

Her straight hem rode up on her thighs, though, exposing enough skin to get any man's engine revved. She didn't tug it down. In fact she wiggled her butt on the seat, as innocently as if she were trying to get comfortable, purposely letting it ride higher.

Surprisingly enough, the inexpensive jewelry she was wearing didn't detract from the whole picture. These days, she left the gold and the diamonds at home. Day before yesterday, when she'd written her net worth down to seventeen million, the "18" charm fell off Elizabeth's bracelet. It bounced off the desk in a local bird sanctuary, hit the floor, and vanished. Since it wasn't real gold, Lilly didn't search very hard for it. Too bad it didn't have monetary value, because then by not searching endlessly, she'd be offering proof that she wasn't so accumulation-oriented anymore. She needed the extra proof, because the rate she kept mislaying her checkbook surely made her life-altering transformation appear less than complete to Elizabeth.

Besides, she thought, glancing over at Jake behind the wheel, she had some*one* a whole lot more interesting to pursue. Should she scoot over there and lay one on him now, or wait a little while?

Jake twisted in his seat, stretching out nicely, reaching into the back, scratching Mooch behind the ears, giving Lilly a nice hint of how he'd look stretched out on her bed—with or without ropes. He didn't have bandages on his hands anymore, so she didn't have to worry about hurting him. As he settled back in place, he tossed an unwrapped package onto the seat between them.

Well, looky there. A vibrator.

"I thought we'd try something different today."

He must like her in blue.

No, that couldn't be. He'd already had the package in the car before she came outside. Maybe seven days of red had finally screamed *Sex here! Get some sex here!* loud enough to reach him. Maybe he'd made peace with the idea of sleeping with his best friend's widow.

Maybe who the heck cared.

When she thought she could speak without squeaking,

she said, "Oh, all right," in what could only be interpreted as ridiculously, high-school-virgin perky.

A *vibrator.* Their first time together, and he wanted to bring along a toy? She'd never done a pseudo-threesome before. She wasn't sure whether to be offended or excited.

Excitement won, hands down.

8

Jake grew increasingly uneasy on his side of the car. All week, Lilly'd been well behaved.

Well, other than that one pass she'd made at him—if something that hot could be labeled a simple pass. He didn't think she'd meant it to be so passionate, but it had been, and he was damned glad she hadn't made another, at least not one blatant enough to call her on.

Some of those looks she was shooting his way now, though, sure were flaming, and he steeled himself for the worst.

He cracked his window to cool himself off. Her, too. Maybe she'd get cold and tug her skirt down. Not that he wanted her to—what man in his right mind would want her to hide those killer legs?—but it would make life in the small confines of the front seat a whole lot easier.

Distract her, he ordered himself. Remember your best friend and how much you owe him. Deal. With. This.

"I think that's the vibrator you bought for your girl-friend," he said. "Why *did* you buy her one, anyway?"

"I promised her anything she wanted for her birthday."

"Oh. Nice. Do you see her pretty often?"

"Yeah." She sounded puzzled.

Good. "Would you give it to her, then? Because it's all paid for and everything, and it's only right she gets it."

Lilly picked up the box and held it between them. "This is for Betsy?"

"Yeah. Would you mind?" He tried to pay attention to traffic and watch her legs at the same time.

"This. For Betsy."

Damn. It'd finally gotten so they could talk easily, on and off, all day, every day. To a reasonable degree, he'd learned to shelve the passion he'd felt for her on the day they'd met and nearly every day thereafter and just con-centrate on the platonic part. It was a struggle, but he kept thinking of Brady, how much he owed him, how Lilly was his wife—that usually did it. For about five minutes, then he'd have to start over.

From the wistful way she studied the photo-laminated dash every day, he could tell she longed to be part of a family as close-knit as his—he'd have to be blind not to see that—but that sassy banter of hers continually said just the opposite. It revealed intelligence and wit, sure, but still it was classic, protective, keep-people-at-a-distance repartee. And just in case all that wasn't enough to confuse him, there were those hot looks she sent skit-tering his way.

Damn.

Talk wasn't coming easy this morning. Lilly wasn't

making sense, which set off warning bells. If she came scootin' across that seat again, he'd—Well, he sure as hell couldn't jump out the door into traffic, but he'd resist. He would.

"You want me . . . to give this . . . to Betsy."

"Ye-ah."

"Ha!"

Sounded angry to him, which wasn't fair, because he was only angry with her when he remembered that she'd stolen his money.

No, not her; *someone*. He could no longer believe she was responsible; it just wasn't possible. Instead of a cold-hearted bitch, all he'd seen every day was a kind woman with a sympathetic heart.

The first full day they'd gone out together, she carried miniature Snickers bars in her purse and handed them out to any kids she saw. Didn't matter if they were shy or pushy, clean or dirty, homeless or standing in line at Taco Bell with their mom. He learned fast that Lilly hated lines. She always told him what to order for her, then she went off and cooed over somebody's baby. She had a way about her that didn't intimidate kids.

The second day, she switched from candy to little boxes of raisins because they were healthier. Quarters weighed her down in the morning and were gone by afternoon. He'd lost count of the number of times she'd made him stop so she could stock up on more of both. Once a day at least.

It wasn't just children she had a big heart for. Whenever a dog crossed the street in front of his taxi, her hand lifted automatically in silent warning, like a crossing guard for stray canines. He'd had a devil of a time on Tuesday convincing her she couldn't run after a black-and-tan Rottweiler mix, check its tags, and if it didn't have any, give it to Reggie.

"If he could have a dog, it'd be Benjie, not Cujo," he said, both surprised and touched that she was still thinking about the reclusive little boy.

"That's what doggie foster homes are for, to check them out first."

"His grandmother's allergic to dogs. And cats."

"Hm. Rabbits?"

"Probably. Or maybe she just doesn't want animals in the house."

"Ah."

It'd gotten so bad, she had the local animal control on speed dial—the one that rehabbed strays into decent pets and found them homes.

He wouldn't undignify all she did every day by thinking she'd stolen *anything*, much less three million dollars. Brady was a shrewd businessman; he must have had good reason to change the beneficiary.

In spite of the fact that Jake's dad had called last night with the all clear—the contracts were signed—Jake no longer needed to bring it up. It was done. *Move on.* He still swiped her checkbook from time to time; at the rate she was writing checks, someone had to look out for her or she wouldn't have anything left to live on. Brady'd roll over in his grave.

Ordinarily, every time Jake saw a loose pet before Lilly did, he distracted her with an interesting (or not) building and turned the nearest corner in the opposite direction.

Sometimes he did it just to prolong the intervals between her philanthropic endeavors.

But not today. Today she'd been in the car five minutes max and was talking in riddles and exposing enough leg to make a Victoria's Secret photographer sit up and take notice. He didn't need this kind of distraction. Bring on the dogs and cats and jackasses for all he cared. Bring on *anything* to distract her.

He could have closed his eyes and still felt her gaze roaming him head to toe, heating him up way past where he wanted to be. Hell, he hoped she couldn't make out a hard-on from that angle. It might spur her on.

It wasn't as if he didn't understand where she was coming from. If he'd had sex with someone special every night, sometimes twice, for three years running, the kind of spontaneous, up-against-the-wall, out-and-out fucking that Brady always bragged about, then *nothing* for the last five months—Shit, he'd be stark raving mad from withdrawal. A real lunatic.

Yes, Lilly'd been really well behaved for someone with justifiable cause. Couldn't let her fall off the wagon now. He needed a diversion—for *her*.

"I thought we'd take Susannah grocery shopping today," he said.

Nothing like a chaperone.

Susannah was a sweet, Southern hoot. She sashayed up the walk to her back door ahead of Jake, who was carrying three plastic grocery bags in each hand.

Lilly, with one bag in each, enjoyed the play of muscles in Jake's arms, then admired his long legs as he took the porch steps two at a time. She'd followed him around the grocery store for over an hour, irrevocably charmed by the magnitude of his patience with Susannah, who inspected every ingredient label and advised him on what he should and should not buy when he shopped for himself. If Lilly weren't already primed to get seriously naked with him, his kind, gentle manner with the geriatric belle would've won her over.

Susannah's house was near the end of a quiet, dead-end street, a two-story brick house in an older neighborhood of pleasantly varied architecture, three-quarter-acre lawns, and towering oak trees.

"Open, Sesame," Susannah drawled at her back door when they delivered her home.

To Lilly's amazement, the door unlatched and swung open *by itself*. She stared at it on the way in, then as it swung itself shut and the lock clicked in place, she backed away as if it were possessed.

"Jake did that for me," Susannah boasted. "Isn't it just wonderful? I have to go outside to get to my basement, to do laundry, you know, and now I can go back and forth without having to set anything down. Isn't he just the grandest?"

Jake tipped his head ever so slightly to the side and grinned at the older woman as if she were his favorite doting grandmother.

Susannah didn't seem to notice. "My, you should've seen his house in the Bay Area. It practically knew what I was thinking every time I walked into a room. Why Bill Gates didn't snap him up is beyond me. You just wait, though. He'll get his business up and running again in no time. Now Jake, sugar, you just set those little ol' bags there on the table, and the two of you run along." Susannah winked at Lilly. "I know you have more important things to do."

Yes, Lilly was liking her better by the minute.

"Oh," Susannah said, "I almost forgot to tell you. Irene gave me her recipe for orgasms, so if you don't get enough—"

Lilly dropped one bag and fumbled the other.

Jake's long stride brought him instantly to her side, hovering protectively. "Is it your arm again? I knew those bags were too heavy for you. Here, give them to me."

She tried to answer, but he'd wrapped one big, muscular arm around her—it was the closest he'd dared get all week—and heaven help her, it felt *good*.

And here she'd thought she was flunking seducing him. He was just a sucker for a woman in distress, that's all.

If eyes didn't lie, and she believed they didn't, Jake was concerned about her, and in more than an impartial, *The stranger fainted at my feet, what was I supposed to do?* kind of way.

Instead, he had a penetrating, *Talk to me, I'm not listening to anyone but you* gaze. A long, fixed look that took her breath away in anticipation, not of sex, not of passion—

Well, yes, passion, but not the sexual kind. Passion from the heart, from caring for someone so deeply that he wanted only to be in tune with her, to know her every thought, her every feeling. She'd gotten glimpses of it all week, but whenever she'd thought she'd seen it, it had skittered away elusively. Now it was there, heating up between them.

"You all right?" he asked.

She managed a jerky little nod.

"Here it is." Susannah returned with a recipe card, and even her presence didn't break the tension between them. "Now remember, sugar, capital T's are tablespoons, lower case t's are teaspoons."

As he tucked it into his shirt pocket, a slow, wicked smile pulled at Jake's lips. "Wait'll you try Irene's Chocolate Orgasms," he said.

Lilly licked her lips.

As he plucked a few cans off the floor, Jake's gaze blazed back and forth between Lilly's eyes and her lips. "Decadent," he said, and she wasn't sure if he was talking chocolate or her.

"Best fudge you'll ever taste," Susannah said.

"Fudge?" Lilly hated sounding surprised. Might as well open mouth, insert foot.

"Yeah." Jake's deep rumble was laced with a little chuckle, and the tension between them was undeniably sexual. "What'd you think it was?"

"Oh, I don't know. Could be anything. Brownies, cookies, ice cream . . ." Then she remembered. "Not that fudge you had in the car last week." She'd filched a few bites when he wasn't looking.

"Yep."

"Some people say they're better than sex"—Susannah winked—"but that's not the way I remember it."

If real orgasms got better than that fudge, Lilly thought, she'd greatly underestimated the vastness of her deprivation.

Susannah aimed two folded greenbacks at Jake's pocket, finally diverting his attention, but not before leaving Lilly in a state of sensual mush.

"Now, Susannah, you can't keep doing this." He gently pushed her hand away. "I mean it this time."

Lilly, after a moment to regain her wits, retrieved the rest of the groceries she'd dropped and stacked the cans on the counter.

"Don't be silly, sugar." To Lilly, she said, "He never lets me tip him. I keep telling him it's not fair. If he was out picking up strangers, he'd be making money, so he should let me give him some. Lilly agrees with me, don't you, Lilly?"

"I'm on salary now. I wouldn't be earning extra out on the streets, so you keep your money."

"Nonsense. You've earned it, and I know how much being in debt bothers you."

Except for when he was swatting at Susannah's attempt to pay him, Jake stood with his feet spread, hands on hips, equally determined to win the argument. Lilly was afraid the standoff could last for hours, and now that she'd felt his arm around her again and seen the flame of passion smoldering deep inside, now that she knew his weak spot, she wasn't willing to wait all day.

"I bet he'd take another pan of fudge instead."

"Oh, I don't know. We've been gone an hour and a half. Seems to me his time's worth more than—"

"I'd love some more fudge."

"Well, that's just fine, then." Susannah beamed proudly. "You two youngsters go next door—Jake, sugar, show her all those electronic gizmos you have at your place—and by the time you're ready to leave, I'll have a pan ready."

"Yeah, Jake," Lilly said wickedly, wondering what kind of woman-in-distress scenario she could play out.

She'd never been that type. "Let's go to your place and you can show me your gizmos."

"That was a brilliant idea. The fudge," Jake said, as he and Lilly cut across the dormant lawn, side by side.

"Need I mention my small, fifty percent, fudge brokerage fee?"

"Oh, goes without saying."

The ground was mushy from the thaw, but the area between the houses was sunny and the zoysia thick enough that they didn't sink as long as they kept moving. There wasn't a slice of slippery ice anywhere, so he couldn't ever-so-innocently take her by the arm; he knew, because he looked.

Lilly sighed wistfully. "I'll bet Susannah's a great mother-in-law."

"You in the market for a new one?"

"Eventually. Right now I just want the one I have to stop criticizing."

"I know Donna," he said. "Tell me about it, maybe I can help."

Lilly picked her words carefully. "Some of the people I've seen in the past week, well, they called her and told her what a wonderful thing it is that the 'Marquette family is so civic-minded.' "

"Doesn't sound so bad."

"They also mentioned 'that nice young man' driving me around."

"Ooh."

"Yeah. What'd you do to get on her bad side? Other than, you know, where you were working."

"She didn't like where I was working?"

"I didn't think 'pervert' sounded very complimentary."

"Huh."

" 'Pervert shop' were her exact words."

"That's better than just straight out calling me one, I guess."

"Oh, she covered that, too."

"Well then," he said, sure he was grinning pretty goofy for a man whose reputation was in tatters.

On the back porch, Lilly paused to admire the stonework on his parents' three-story.

"Dad built it before I was born. He and Grandpa and Uncle Paul."

"Gorgeous. Neat—the garage looks like an old carriage house."

He unlocked the back door with a simple touch on the small thumb pad. It swung open smoothly, flawlessly, better than anything the Marquettes had.

"What? No retinal scan?"

"Cute, I'll have to remember that for the cat door. Mom's got arthritis real bad in her hands, and she doesn't trust a voice-activated lock like Susannah's— she's afraid it'll open by mistake during a thunderclap or something and let a *real* pervert in—so I whipped up a fingerprint identification system."

"Just whipped it up, huh?"

"Sure. Welcome to the pervert's house. Come on in, take your coat off, make yourself at home."

"Wow."

Lilly inched inside, her gaze raptly taking in everything. Jake was so accustomed to it all that he forgot the impact it had on visitors the first time, until he had to drag her in so he could close the door. He held her hand longer than necessary and squeezed it lightly before he released it, thinking it was a good first step toward letting her know that he knew he'd been wrong about her. That didn't change the fact that he owed Brady to keep his hands off her, but there was no reason they couldn't be friends.

Lilly was absorbed by the kitchen. The two most notable elements were the tall wood cabinets, fronted with leaded-glass doors that had been rescued from a turn-of-the-last-century building slated for demolition, and a massive stone fireplace, topped with a cherrywood mantel that had been carved out of a single piece of wood. Most people didn't get past those until the second visit, when they started noticing hand-painted Italian tiles and other small embellishments that his mom had selected. It wasn't the Marquette mansion, but it was home.

"You live here with your mom?"

"Nah, when she and Dad get back, I'll live over the garage."

Knowing he should keep his hands to himself, Jake still couldn't resist helping Lilly with her coat, letting his knuckles brush along the length of her arm as she slipped out of it.

"They're spending the winter in the Southwest," he said. "Phoenix."

"Oh. Mine too. They winter in Death Valley every year. Great big RV park. You should see a picture of it. It's like this huge parking lot, only people live there for months at a time until it gets too hot."

He could tell by the little shudder in her voice that it wasn't where she'd choose to spend any time.

"It's not the retirement they'd planned, but what can you do? Shit happens."

"Maybe they like it."

She gave him a surprised look. "That's what they said when I tried to give them money, that they're the happiest they've ever been! I can't believe it."

"Yet you're giving away an awful lot."

"Hey, I've seen the light. They haven't."

"How do you know they haven't? Maybe we all see 'the light' differently."

"Yeah? Have you?"

He shrugged, starting to pass it off, then changed his mind. "Maybe. Yes. I don't know."

She was studying him thoughtfully. "But I thought you didn't believe in heaven."

"Maybe one person sees heaven and another sees something else entirely. Maybe we each see what we need to see." He hadn't spoken so philosophically to a woman outside his immediate family since Angie had deserted him. But it felt right. Lilly appeared to be giving his opinion due consideration, while his attention wanted to wander to sexier topics.

"If I believe in heaven and my seeing the light involves heaven," she asked, "what would your light be?"

"I believe in hard data, so I guess it'd have to be something irrefutable. Objective. You know . . . measurable." Her coat was warm and toasty in his hands; he reluctantly tossed it onto a chair. "Ready for a tour?"

"Sure."

"This is the kitchen," he said, knowing that was dumb and stupidly boring, but safe territory. It was also his favorite room, all sunshine, homemade bread, and fresh, cinnamon-laced cookies. "It's probably a little rustic for your taste, but we like it."

"Hey, a stove's a stove."

"Yeah, I guess you haven't met one you couldn't cook on."

The kitchen only reminded him of Brady's "my wife" dinner party story about the quickie he'd copped between courses. His description of Lilly on the edge of the granite counter, her thighs spread, no panties beneath . . .

Damn, other than his taxi, was no place safe?

Of course Brady hadn't gone into any more specifics than that. The jerk just let him imagine the rest. It hadn't occurred to Jake at the time, but now that he looked back, it was as though Brady was trying to compete with him. As if he'd been jealous.

"Frankly," Lilly said, "I haven't met a stove I'd *want* to cook on."

Jake thought he said, "What?" but he couldn't be sure.

"I don't cook."

"You can fly a plane, but you can't cook?"

"I hate it," she clarified.

"No."

"Uh, *ye-es*."

"But Brady told me you're a gourmet cook."

Ah, there it was again, that sweet, fun laugh that was all joy and light, all Lilly, with no artifice behind it, no games. He'd heard it once or twice early in the week, then increasingly often as the days passed. It was never enough.

"A gourmet deli shopper, maybe."

"Really?"

"One day I was a rich girl in boarding school, the next I was poor and flipping burgers and chicken patties in a drive thru. Ugh, never again."

What the hell? He couldn't be more confused if Brady was standing here now, relating how *my wife makes the best blank*—insert name of any exotic dish or bar drink.

"Hm, and here I was figuring you knew how long it'd take Susannah to make that fudge."

She laughed again—*yes!*

"I remember it tasted like it'll take all day," she said, licking her lips.

Damn, but it was a mighty fine line between basking in the light of her laugh and cowering in a corner, scared to death that she was coming on to him, because if she was, they had to get out of here. *Now.*

"Cool!" Lilly started playing with the automatic water spout at the kitchen sink, which had no faucet handles. "Hm, perfect temperature. No chance I can burn myself, huh?"

"Only if you say 'water, hotter' enough times. Detergent dispenser's automatic, too."

"I should talk to it?"

"Not that I wouldn't like to see that, but all you have to do is pass your hand under the tip."

She tested it, looked around, then while holding her wet hand over the sink, finally turned to him. "And the dryer is . . ."

"A little rudimentary." He retrieved a dish towel out of the top drawer and held one end while she dried.

"Prehistoric. I like it."

This was working out nicely. Lilly was distracted, back to friendly banter instead of sexy moves. Couldn't last long, though, unless he kept her busy.

"Come on, I'll take you on a tour. Susannah'll be expecting feedback."

The next hour passed quickly. Lilly was a delight to watch, like a kid in a candy store.

Family pictures were sprinkled throughout the house, mixed in with artsy collections of shelves, pottery, and sculptures. Mostly action shots instead of posed; family football on a leaf-strewn lawn, synchronized swimming, father and son versus mother and four daughters in a muddy tug-of-war.

"Terrific photos." It was impossible to miss the longing in her voice, the way she lingered over each one.

"They're Mom's. I got the bug from her."

"What's this one?"

He peered closely. "Mom volunteers at the community center. That's from the thirty-years-of-service party we gave her."

"Your family?"

"Yeah."

"Well, what did the community center give her?"

He shrugged. "Maybe a pin?"

She *hmph*ed.

Once she knew about the voice-activated stereo system, Lilly picked something different for every room. "Music, Mozart" in the living room. "Music, Brahms" in the dining room. A classic freak; who knew.

"TV on," she ventured in the family room, then whooped in delight when she discovered channel surfing without a remote.

Whatever agenda she'd had coming over here, she'd moved on. She tried everything, and what she couldn't try, she wanted demonstrated or explained. Like the furnace.

"You mean if your heart rate goes up, the room sensor detects that and automatically lowers the heat?"

"Right. So when my folks are sleeping at night and their heart rates slow naturally, the house cools down."

"But then it's cold when they get up."

"That's the one time the system's overridden. It warms up at six-thirty. If they want it warmer, they just say—"

"Don't tell me. Heat, up."

"Sure, for Mom."

"And your dad?"

"Anything along the lines of 'damn it's cold in here' will work. The humidifier's automatic, but responds to voice control, too. It's all computerized in a home control network. Along with adjusting the drapes and blinds when the temperature strays too far from optimum."

"Hm, must be interesting living with someone who thinks of everything."

"Well, Mom likes me around." He resisted taking pride in Lilly's compliments; they shouldn't matter to him. But damn it, they did.

"Show me."

"What?"

"Run in place or do jumping jacks or something so I can hear the furnace shut off."

"Right."

"No really, I'm serious."

"Okay, let's go to the gym."

"You have a gym?"

"We have a closet we call a gym."

He ran on the treadmill for her, which was a really big mistake, because all there was for her to do was stand there and watch him. Thinking about her thinking about him sent his pulse soaring, and sure enough, the blower shut off way sooner than called for.

"Now leave the room," she said.

"I'll be in the kitchen getting ice water."

She followed a few minutes later. "I don't get it, Jake. Why are you driving a taxi when you can do stuff like this?" Her arms spread wide, indicating everything in the house. "You could be making millions."

It wasn't an off-the-cuff remark. Because she seemed really interested, he pulled two chairs out from the table. "Let's talk." When they were seated, he opened with, "Well, for one thing, it takes time to start over. Lots of networking. Capital."

She sipped a glass of water while he laid the facts out quickly and clearly, the agreement he and Brady had entered into as old, trusted friends, one rich, the other talented.

"For two smart men, you'd think one of you would've thought of insurance."

"We each had a policy payable to the company."

She cocked her head to the side. "Not big enough?"

"Three million."

"Then what happened to—Wait. *Three* million? But that's exactly what I got from the insurance company. And this is why you're in St. Louis, driving a taxi?"

He shrugged. "I didn't want to file for bankruptcy. My dad put up his business and his house, Uncle Paul helped out, and I was able to pay everyone off, but now, of course

I need to repay them. I network, I do some consulting, develop new programs—doesn't pay much, but it beats wiring intercoms in new subdivisions. Shit, where's the challenge in that?"

"But I don't understand. If it was payable to the company . . ."

"Andrew said Brady changed the beneficiary."

"He did, huh?" She thought a moment, then shook her head. "Doesn't sound like Brady."

"That's what I thought at first." Jake was elated by Lilly's objective assessment of Brady's character when she easily could have said it was the dead guy and thrown all suspicion from herself—not that he suspected her any more, but she couldn't know that.

"Well, who . . . ? Wait, you don't think I—"

He waved her denial off. "Not since I've gotten to know you."

She grinned slowly. "But you did at first, didn't you?"

"Can't deny that."

"I'm surprised you didn't throw me back into the fire."

"I didn't think about actually *throwing* you back in," he said with a chuckle. "But I debated all of a second or two on not putting you out."

"Any regrets?"

Her eyes never left his, and he had no trouble saying exactly what he felt. "No regrets. And I mean that sincerely."

"Hm, well," she said. "I think I can fix this."

"There's no need."

"Brady would want me to, I'm sure. Where's my checkbook?"

For once, he was sorry he'd diverted it again, because

when she jumped to her feet to find it, he lost the precious connection with her.

"I'll just run out to the car and—*Ye-ow!*"

Startled, it took him a moment to realize what she was doing, but the way she was cradling her arm and dancing around the kitchen left no doubt that she'd swear Elizabeth or somebody wouldn't allow it. He was hugely disappointed in her—and in himself, because he'd thought they'd finally broken through her arm's-length barriers and were having a serious discussion. Apparently he was way off the mark.

"Oh, for Pete's sake. This again?" Aggravated, he surged to his feet, his chair legs scraping across the floor in protest. He started to pace off his annoyance, but quickly collided with her as she stopped abruptly and shook her arm out. He took hold of her shoulders, faced off with her, stared her right in the eyes, and promptly felt his anger ebb.

"I can't, uh, write this right now," she said, gritting her teeth. "But somehow, Jake, I promise you, somehow I'll see that you get it back."

Damn this fooling around with his feelings, swearing he deserved the money but *pretending* she couldn't give it to him. If this is how she was going to be, she could damn well keep her own self company. Fine, it'd make it that much easier to keep his hands to himself. He strode out onto the back porch and slammed the door behind him.

Lilly wasn't sure what just happened. One minute they were talking, chatting, having a good time. The next, Elizabeth darned near had her laid out on the kitchen floor.

"Elizabeth!"

She was suddenly there, lighting up the kitchen with an aura that Lilly hadn't noticed in Transition.

"You couldn't *tell* me I owe him three million dollars!"

"The money is irrelevant, Lilly."

"*Irrelevant*? One minute we're connecting, and the next you're zapping me in the arm. I can't get him in bed like that."

"Hm, I see you're having trouble with serenity."

"You're damned right—"

"Oh my, and you're not using wisdom either. Please, Lilly, you must have faith. You must continue. It'll all work out if you put your mind to it."

Lilly took a deep breath, though she couldn't say it was very calming.

"Now, let's see. What was it I needed to tell you?"

"John's your supervisor, right?" Lilly demanded. "I want to talk to him."

Elizabeth didn't do earthly things, like tugging on her sleeve or examining her fingernails or chewing her lip. She just gazed off into space, then said, "Shoot, I wonder what it was. Well, maybe later." She started to fade.

"Hey, wait a minute!"

"I'm not supposed to be here," wafted back to Lilly. "If only I could remember . . ."

It threw Lilly off-balance to find herself suddenly addressing a kitchen cabinet. "I must continue," she muttered Elizabeth's words with a sarcastic bent. "It'll all work out. Yeah, sure, maybe when I talk to John."

She'd been doing pretty well so far. Jake had quit hugging the car door, quit doing his best to avoid her touch. He even seemed to enjoy giving her a tour of all the automated controls he'd installed in his parents' house. But after this fiasco, well, there was always stage two. She flipped her cell phone open and got lucky; someone had just canceled their appointment for tomorrow. Lilly nabbed the spot.

She called Betsy next and left a voice mail. "Mayday, Mayday. Meet me at Victoria's Secret."

"Tell me again why I need thongs?" Lilly asked.

Jake had come around after a few minutes of fussing and fuming on the back porch, almost as if he'd decided that getting mad at her had been propitious. He'd dropped her off at Galleria Mall, and she and Betsy were presently studying a wall hung with scores of colorful, minuscule panties.

"I mean, it's not as if he'll know," she rationalized. "By the time he sees it, sex is pretty much a foregone conclusion, if you know what I mean."

"Because you'll feel different."

"Yeah, like pulling ribbon out of my butt every two minutes."

"Trust me, after the first day, you won't even notice. But you'll feel sexier, and if you feel sexier, girl, you *are* sexier. That's what he'll notice."

Resigned to putting herself in Betsy's hands because she had more experience, Lilly sighed and said, "Okay."

"Along with no visible panty lines."

"I can get that with panty hose."

"Oh yeah, ditch those, too."

"Oh, I'm so looking forward to going outside in a skirt and a bare behind."

"I have two words. Garter. Belt."

"Me too. Frostbitten. Ass."

In spite of Lilly's objections, Betsy thrust two red thongs at her, one lace, one satin. "Try those on for size." She snagged matching red bras off the wall. "These too."

"The cups're only half here and, my God, look at all the padding. I'll fall out of them."

Betsy winked, added a red garter belt, and summoned a salesclerk to unlock a dressing room. Five minutes later, she expected a report. "How do they fit?"

Fit? The bra Lilly had on was more like a shallow shelf with a high peekaboo quotient. The thong covered as much as a child's plastic bandage, and was about as comfortable as one would be in the same place. The garter belt was actually okay.

"How about I go with just the garter belt and a sign around my neck?"

"Let me see."

"Over my dead body!" Which, come to think of it, had already happened. "Oh, okay."

Betsy slipped inside the dressing room, took one look, and nodded approvingly. "If that doesn't do the trick, there's something wrong with him."

Lilly doubted there was a thing wrong with Jake. She should know; she'd kissed him. More importantly, he'd kissed her back. While he'd been tentative at first—poor guy'd probably been shocked out of his boots—he hadn't let it end that way. Nosirree. Just remembering how his lips had taken possession of all her senses made her hot. Now, if she could only repeat the experience.

"Okay, now we shop for skirts, blouses, shoes . . ."

"I have plenty—"

"Trust me."

By the time they were done three hours later, Lilly had some killer clothes. She ran into two friends from the country club who exclaimed over her new hairdo, how fabulous she looked, and how it was great to see her out and about. Seems word was out that she'd been blasted to Kansas, never to be seen again.

"I just knew what I heard couldn't be right," Helen said.

Hannah agreed. "Of course not. Whoever heard of someone getting killed by a flying dildo?"

Lilly just smiled and said no, she was still here.

"Mrs. Therringer's been asking after you." She was Lilly's former nanny, who'd gone back to college and now worked at the club.

"I'll give her a call," Lilly promised, then asked after their adorable little boys. They invited her to attend a bridal shower at the club in April, then went their own way.

"Isn't that your brother-in-law coming this way?" Betsy said.

"Andrew? Where?"

At first glance, Lilly felt a pang in her heart, but it wasn't just because he looked so much like Brady, which he did, with his trim physique, brown eyes, and impeccably styled blond hair. It was simply because he reminded her of Brady when they'd been in love, how his eyes used to light up whenever he saw her, and the slow smiles they'd shared over special moments. But that had been so long ago.

"Hello, ladies." Andrew smoothly hugged Lilly and bussed her cheek, and she couldn't help noticing that he smelled delicious.

"Hi, Drew. I don't know if you remember Betsy?"

"Yes, hi." He smiled politely and shook Betsy's hand, then quickly turned his attention back to Lilly, nodding toward all the pricey shopping bags. "Going on a vacation?"

"Betsy thinks I need new clothes."

"I'm trying to get her circulating again."

Andrew gave Lilly the once-over, and then the once again. He smiled slowly. "You look fine to me."

"Those are the old clothes," Betsy said.

"Like I said . . ."

Lilly shot an *I told you so* glance at Betsy and a *You're so sweet* at Andrew.

"I just got back in town and heard about your accident. Are you really as okay as you look?"

"Yeah, we were really lucky. Only my limo's a total loss, and my chauffeur has a broken arm."

Drew scooped his cell phone out of its holster. "I can help you find a new one."

"That's okay, I've already hired someone."

As he reholstered his phone, Drew winked in admiration. "You always were the capable one. I'm glad I ran into you. How about dinner this weekend?"

"Oh, that'd be nice. Sunday at your mom's?"

Betsy groaned.

Andrew smiled charmingly and said, "No, I mean just the two of us, out somewhere Friday or Saturday evening. Unless you'd like to come over to my place. We could put on some quiet music, open a bottle of wine, watch a movie . . ."

Ohhhh. "You mean like a date?"

She must've sounded pretty alarmed, because he backpedaled and said, "Just as friends"—He grinned engagingly—"and then we'll see. No pressure."

It occurred to her that this was a zillion times easier than getting near Jake. In five seconds, her lips had been closer to Andrew's than they had been to Jake's all week.

Uh-oh.

Had she targeted the wrong man again? Had Elizabeth meant she'd picked the wrong *brother*, not the wrong *partner*? Shouldn't it be this easy to catch the right man, since she was destined to have a baby who'd grow up to do something special—kind of a fail-safe child?

"Lilly?"

"What? Oh sorry, Drew, yes, I think I'd like that." She made herself smile and, even though she wasn't committing herself, said, "Can I call you?"

"I look forward to it." He tipped his head slightly and drew back, a silent good-bye.

"Oh, wait, do you have another minute?" Lilly asked.

"For you, sure."

Betsy excused herself in favor of a storewide shoe sale.

"I feel kind of funny asking this, but what do you know about Jake Murdoch getting gypped out of Brady's life insurance?"

Andrew scowled. "Is he bothering you with that?"

His hint of temper caught Lilly by surprise. "He just . . . mentioned it."

"I don't like him bothering you with that. It's not right.

Brady changed the beneficiary on his policy—legally, mind you—about a year ago, because their company was doing extremely well, and they had plenty in reserve. I'll have another talk with him."

Andrew's heated response unsettled Lilly. She didn't doubt Brady'd done it legally, but he should have explained everything to Jake. The fact that he hadn't just reinforced Lilly's belief that the money rightfully should go to him, in spite of word to the contrary via Elizabeth's home shock therapy bracelet.

"No, please don't say anything to him." She didn't need Jake even more reluctant to get into bed. He already had three million reasons.

"Well . . ."

"Really, Drew, please don't."

"You promise to let me know if he bothers you?"

"Absolutely."

He smiled, all hint of temper gone. "Okay then." He held up his cell phone to remind her to call, then strolled away.

"He's shorter than I remember," Betsy said, as she and Lilly hooked up. They buttoned their coats against the wind and walked out to her car.

"*He* didn't need to see me in a red ribbon."

Betsy grinned. "I saw him looking at a certain pink-striped lingerie bag."

"I'm sure that had nothing to do with it."

"Well, we know he wants you, but you don't want *him*, do you?"

"You don't like him?"

"Silly girl—while you're off chasing Jake, who do you think's gonna mend Drew's broken heart this weekend?"

Lilly grinned. "Oh, so I'm out of the picture already?"

"Once Jake gets a look at you tomorrow, you're gonna be too busy to see anything outside his bedroom."

Lilly buckled up. "So help me, if I see one woman on a street corner wearing any of what I bought, I'm burning it all."

"Just so Jake sees it first."

The first thing Lilly did at home alone that evening was open a bag of gourmet mixed greens, pour a really large glass of wine, sit in her atrium, and try to figure out how Brady could have erred in judgment.

He was a smart man; he had to have known Jake would need the money to keep the company going.

He was a loyal friend; he would have wanted Jake to have it.

He was an honorable man. Had he somehow known he was going to die and made the change out of a misguided attempt to give her all the security she'd ever dreamed of?

She lost her appetite, for food anyway, and refilled her glass.

It was only right that she clear up old business. The insurance money, in her opinion, amounted to a debt, and therefore was not part of her charity-bound net worth. She slapped her palm on the inlaid-tile table, satisfied that she'd worked the dilemma through. She'd been allowed to pay other debts and expenses. Armed with this conclusion, she opened her purse and started to date a check, but no sooner had she touched pen to paper than she got another zap in her right arm.

Stubbornly, righteously, she picked up the pen and tried again. And again. Always with the same result. She knew who was responsible.

"It's Jake's!" she shouted heavenward. "Brady was wrong to change it."

No reply. Of course. Angry, she threw the checkbook across the atrium, gulped her wine, and refilled her glass.

"I'll give away all *my* money, just like I agreed. *After* I pay Jake back."

The next morning, she didn't need an alarm clock to wake her out of a heavy, wine-induced sleep in time to make her first appointment. No, she had a frickin' bracelet for that. One second she was dreaming about how wonderful Jake's arms felt, holding her against him on the parking lot with the snow falling all around them, and the next she was on her feet, wondering how she got there. As soon as she tried to lie back down, another sharp jolt hit her and didn't let up until she aimed herself toward the closet.

Okay, so she'd give some money away today. But until she found a solution, she'd sure as heck go about it slower.

At Lilly's request, Jake drove her back to the kids' club a few days later. He wasn't really surprised, because she'd mentioned the children several times since her first visit, like wanting to give that stray dog to Reggie.

It was four o'clock, and the complex bubbled with children of all ages and colors, excited to be out of school after a long day. Just outside Ollie's office, Jake was tackled by a six-year-old girl in cornrows who wanted a ride on his shoulders. She climbed aboard with a big smile and securely clamped her hands to his forehead.

"I'm Kissee," she informed Lilly from her perch. "What's your name?"

"I'm Lilly. Kissee's a cute name." She was grinning up at both them, and Jake could tell from the merriment in her eyes that she was struggling not to laugh out loud. "Have you been finger painting, Kissee?"

"Uh-huh. I was painting a school bus."

Jake closed his eyes and hung his head. "Is it bad? Tell me I don't look like I have a schoolbus on my head."

She snickered. "Not to worry. It just looks like a bad case of jaundice." She knocked on Ollie's doorframe on her way into his office.

Ollie immediately handed Jake a package of wet wipes, all the while beaming at Lilly. "Couldn't stay away, huh?"

"I keep thinking about Reggie and how he comes out of his shell around Mooch."

"You should see him, it's like he's a different child."

"I know, I heard him talking to Jake and Mooch before we left last time. I couldn't stop thinking, wow, wouldn't it be wonderful if he had a cat he could pet and talk to and take care of? Wouldn't that help to boost his confidence. But Jake says his grandmother's allergic, so he can't have one at home?"

"That's right."

"And then I wondered if there are other kids like him here?"

"You mean introverted?" Ollie nodded. "Sure, a couple, though he's the shiest."

She gazed out the window at the complex beyond, some of which was still under construction. "Well, I was wondering, would you have room for a pet area here? You know, one where Reggie could 'help out' and interact with other kids like him?"

"We've thought about it, but we just couldn't justify it. Though if someone, say you"—Ollie grinned—"were to earmark part of her donation specifically for a 'pet therapy' room, well then, we'd have to include one, wouldn't we?"

Jake saw Lilly's smile and knew he'd been right to bring her here. She'd wanted more involvement, and just look how happy she was when she said, "Then consider it earmarked."

"I have to warn you, though, nothing happens overnight."

"The weather should warm up soon. How about a field trip to the Children's Zoo? It'd be therapeutic. Educational."

"Hey, you don't have to convince me." Ollie got that speculative look in his eye that made him a natural at soliciting. "But it would require special funding."

Lilly laughed and pulled out her checkbook.

Jake was torn between, *Well, there goes more of Brady's money* and *A week and a half ago, who would've guessed she had it in her?* He had to hand it to her, she'd stuck with it. Not that he'd wanted her to, because she was going overboard at it. But shoot, he had to admire what she was accomplishing.

Over the next week, Lilly learned a few things in her new clothes, stage two highlights and Kick-Ass Claret nail polish.

One, women reacted negatively. She suspected her dangling earrings and plunging necklines had a lot to do with their attitude, putting them off, making them cool until she handed them a check made out to their organization. That usually thawed them, though she suspected uppity Mrs. Dawson wondered just what Lilly'd done to "earn" a hundred thousand disposable dollars.

Two, men didn't take her seriously. And there she suspected not only all of the above, but also the amount of skin displayed between her hem and strappy, high-heeled sandals. Admittedly, she had a disproportionate number of doors held for her, both by men to whom she handed checks and any other male within twenty feet. She started carrying a scarf in her coat pocket, and whenever she went into offices of charitable organizations, she draped it around her neck so when she unbuttoned her coat, their attention didn't immediately plummet to her chest.

Three, little kids, bless their hearts, didn't notice or care what she had on. Just as before, some hung back out of shyness, others rested sticky hands on her skirt and begged for another box of raisins.

Four, Jake went through several stages. Hot glances. Stammered half sentences, then silence. Shorter than usual phone conversations with his sisters, on whom he normally doted. Distracted driving. A few times, he actually lowered his window and insulted other drivers, until he noticed the male ones stare at her, then he gave that up and sulked for a day.

"Is he sweating?" Betsy asked during one of their evening phone calls. Progress reports, they laughingly called them, although Lilly wasn't laughing nearly as much as she would've been, had she not been carrying a heavy burden of guilt. She still hadn't figured out how to get Jake the money she owed him.

"He lowers his window a lot."

"It's freezing outside, so that's good. It means he's hot, and you've almost got him. You're brushing up against him a lot, aren't you?"

"Well, maybe not a lot."

"Why not?" she demanded.

"Because he's already asked me twice if I've been drinking."

Betsy laughed.

"Yeah, it might've been funny, if we weren't standing in front of a *bishop* at the time."

"Whoa, you're moving up in the world."

"Yeah, between being a Marquette and giving away almost a million dollars a week, the word's spreading. I don't have to hunt for charities anymore, they're starting to call me."

She wasn't explaining to anyone the significance of losing the "17" charm on the bracelet; two million down, sixteen to go.

Her philanthropy had been somewhat hindered, of late, when the recipients noticed Jake's furrowed brow, so Lilly'd banished him to the taxi. Now each time she returned thousands of dollars lighter, she generally found him engrossed in his work, either smoothing kinks out of software for new-and-improved home control systems, networking by cell phone, or photographing something that caught his eye. Sometimes he was chatting by phone with one of his sisters or their kids.

Each day wasn't all about her. She also accompanied him on calls regarding a consulting job he was working on, until he said he couldn't stand seeing her bored and likewise banished her to the sidewalk or a nearby mall. She had to make do with window shopping, because of course she couldn't buy anything frivolous for herself. She was doing a pretty thorough job of turning over a new leaf—until she spotted the three-carat, antique-cushion-cut canary diamond ring across a store. It was impeccably set in platinum, nestled between two side trillions, and really did belong on *her* hand, because the woman wearing it was about two years behind on manicures. It didn't take much imagination to hear Elizabeth *tsk*ing at this selfish impulse. John was undoubtedly shaking his head.

"Sorry," she mumbled heavenward. She walked outside and handed a bag lady ten bucks.

On Thursday, she stopped by the country club to show Mrs. Therringer that she was, indeed, fine—and to ask her advice on something. Mrs. T. rushed from behind her desk to embrace Lilly in a hug that only served to remind her how much she missed the childhood closeness she'd had with her former nanny, how suddenly it had been taken from her the day she'd been sent off to boarding school.

"You look just fine," Mrs. T. said, holding her at arm's length, inspecting her for damage from head to toe. "I'm so relieved."

"Me? What about you? I never get over your transformation."

"Ugh, I sure don't miss the uniforms and sensible shoes." She favored peach dresses that showed off her pretty face and pumps that put a nice curve in her calves. "Are you here for lunch?"

"Actually, I wanted to run something by you."

"Okay." She indicated two chairs angled toward each other, next to the window.

Lilly sat on the edge of hers and smoothed her skirt. "I keep running into the fact that there are a lot of organizations in this city that run on volunteers. I mean, they put in a lot of hours, and while some of them are recognized for it, the majority aren't. I'd like to do something for them."

Mrs. T. beamed at her.

"What?" Lilly asked warily.

"You've grown into quite a woman." Mrs. T. popped to

her feet. "Just let me get a file and we'll get started on something."

On Friday morning outside a small shelter-cum–training center, Lilly returned to find Jake sketching out the mechanics of what he called a totally off-the-wall idea.

"How many degrees do you have?"

His pencil paused midstroke.

"I only ask because I've just given a hundred thousand dollars to a pompous ass." She checked her watch. "In thirty minutes, I couldn't find one reason his own mother'd be proud of him. Shoot, if I were her, I wouldn't even claim him."

"Being a little hard on the guy, don't you think?"

"Please. He had his diplomas enlarged and framed on the wall behind his chair, right over his head."

"You find that intimidating?"

"They were from high school and one of those schools that advertises on TV."

He snickered. "You're kidding."

"Nope. People go in there to see about vocational training for some low-level job, and he sits there all high-and-mighty—"

"You *saw* that?"

"Didn't have to. So how many, Mr. Low Profile?"

"Gee, you're putting me on the spot here."

"Give. It's no time for modesty."

He sighed. "You mean other than information technology, electrical, and mechanical engineering?"

"Never mind."

He grinned and said, "None."

Lilly's insides responded to his teasing with a mixture that was part heat, part completion. "Just those three, huh?"

"Yeah, that's all I had time for. Once Brady and I decided to start the company, I quit school."

"Dropout."

All week she'd wanted to reassure him about the money, but what could she say? *Look, I'm trying to get a one-on-one with an angel's supervisor so I can pay you back?* He'd kick her out of his taxi for sure, and then where would she be? No driver. No Jake. No baby.

The taxi suddenly seemed overly warm. Lilly unbuttoned her coat and stuck her scarf in her pocket. Jake's gaze dropped to the low V of her blouse—red, of course—for a second before he dragged it away. Pretty reluctantly, she thought.

Their last stop of the day was a grocery store. Lilly might hate to cook, but she liked salad bars and fresh fruit. Jake quickly commandeered the cart, as if he should be in charge of anything with four wheels.

"All this food," she said. "It amazes me that people actually like to prepare it."

"What do you like with your salad?" he asked.

"Dressing."

"You know, I could've predicted you were going to say that."

"Then why'd you ask?" She gave her total attention to a pile of plums so he wouldn't see how much she enjoyed sparring with him.

"Oh, my mother's going to love you."

Startled was a mild description of how she felt to discover he was thinking of her and his mother in the same sentence, the same thought. Already?

"Hey, you know plums don't bounce?"

She looked down at the floor and discovered she'd in-

advertently knocked several off the pile. She quickly
bagged them.

"They're bruised."

"They're more tender that way."

A small girl darted between them and reached up for a
plum. Before she could pull out a bottom one and set the
whole pile rolling, Jake intervened the way only a veteran
uncle could. He plucked a nearby orange off a display.

"She wants a plum," Lilly said.

"Nah, it'll be mush before she's out of Produce." He
tempted the four-year-old with it until she couldn't help
but decide an orange was definitely better.

"Where's your mommy, sweetheart?" Lilly asked.

The little girl plucked the orange out of Jake's hand
and ran off, knowing exactly where she was going.

"Cute kid," Jake said.

"How many nieces and nephews do you have?"

"Twelve and a half." He returned to following her
aimless path. "When I asked what you like with your
salad, I was thinking along the lines of cooking a steak
and a baked potato."

"Really? You cook when it's just you?" Oh man, he
cooked, too. Now she really had to catch him.

He sighed audibly. "Actually, I was thinking maybe
you'd like a home-cooked meal for a change."

She stopped in her tracks and figuratively shot a victo-
rious fist overhead. *Yes!* He finally wanted to follow her
beyond the driveway and *through* the front door. For her
purposes, it didn't matter why. But to her heart, it did.

She didn't have to call Betsy for advice. She knew
what it would be: Ply him with wine, lower his defenses,
then seduce him. Apply red tights as necessary.

10

Jake selected a medium-priced red wine, then thought about where the evening was headed and added a second bottle to the cart. Maybe a little libation would dull that anticheckwriting pain in Lilly's arm long enough to get his family back in the black. She didn't owe him, but hell, as long as she was giving it away . . .

He realized the trap in his plan as soon as he followed her into her kitchen, spotted the dark granite counter—the very one of Brady's *"my wife" and a between-courses quickie* fame—and remembered how disloyal it was to lust after his best friend's widow.

"Maybe we should do this at my house." He cradled the bags in his arms and wouldn't set them down.

"Don't be silly, we're already here." She took one from him, set it on the island, and started unpacking it. "I might avoid cooking at all costs, but everything works. Don't be shy, there's lots of room."

As if demonstrating that fact, she slid her palm across

the wide granite top. Jake broke out in a sweat.

"What can I do?" she asked.

"Hm. Uh . . ."

"You know, to help?

"Wash the potatoes?"

She rolled up the sleeves of her silky red blouse, which shouldn't have been a turn-on, but it was just that much more skin darting around in front of him as she washed potatoes and put groceries away. It got worse when she reached around him to open cabinet doors and brushed against him while getting into the drawers. Between that and the *click-click-click* of her sexy high-heeled sandals on the wood floor, he damn near lit a fire in the island's grill without turning any knobs.

"You're going to ruin your clothes," he said, not meaning to sound so gruff, so he got a grip on himself and softened his tone. "If you want to go change into sweats or something, you've got time." *Please, make 'em thick and baggy.*

"I'm fine."

She opened a lower cabinet and bent at the waist. Her short skirt rode up the backs of her thighs. Nice. Very nice.

No, bad, very bad. He was supposed to be getting her tipsy so she'd share the wealth, not her body.

"Where's the corkscrew?"

Instead of just telling him where it was, she stretched across him to pull open a drawer. She smelled nice. Sweet, like hyacinths. He'd planted scores of them for his mother, and their coming up always signaled the end of winter and the promise of better things ahead. Oh, he could only wish.

No! his brain yelled.

Yes! his body screamed.

"Darn." Lilly leaned closer, her breast grazing his arm. "I know it's in here somewhere."

He leaned with her, as if helping her look, when he was really just enjoying how their bodies melded, how she suddenly swayed, giving him the perfect excuse to circle his arm around her and pull her close. As if he needed an excuse to appease the rational side of his brain because the emotional side had just seized control.

Her voice was breathy and inviting as she turned her face toward his.

"Jake?"

"Hm?"

The tip of her tongue darted out, moistening her lips, brightening the new shade of red she was wearing. Who- ever'd invented that color should be arrested for the way it outlined the twin peaks at the center of her top lip. He hadn't been able to keep his mind on his driving all week.

He thought she was going to say something like *I can't find it with you all over me like that*, but instead she smiled softly, and her body melted against him. In the blink of an eye, her arms wound around his neck, her fin- gers dived into his hair, and he was lost, lost with his lips locked to hers, his arms around her body, his hands roam- ing up and down her back, touching her hair, grazing over her rear, and rubbing, squeezing, caressing every inch in between.

His left brain made one last attempt to remind him that this wasn't how things were supposed to play out, but testosterone overrode that with even greater logic. Hell, even Brady wouldn't blame him for this. No man could be faced with this woman and be held responsible for what happened next.

He dragged Lilly up against his chest, ground his hips against her, let her feel how hard he was, how badly he wanted her. She moaned against his mouth, a deep, throaty sound that told him she was as lost in the moment as he, as willing as he, *wanting it* as much as he.

Spanning her waist with his hands, he lifted her onto the island, dragging her body up his ever so slowly. The hell with Brady's "my wife" story. He'd only gotten her onto the counter. Jake had the whole damned island at his disposal. She could lie back if she wanted, open herself to him—

Hot damn, she was wearing a garter belt. He didn't know women wore them except on dates, and this was no date. How the hell would he drive her around next week knowing she was wearing a garter belt and stockings every day, with soft, creamy skin between the tops of her hose and the bottom of her—

Oh damn, no bottom; a *thong*.

He felt her hand patting his shoulder.

"You want it here?" Would she like him to remove it, rip it, or just pull it aside?

She patted him again. What the hell did that mean?

He slipped between her open thighs, spreading them around his hips, anchoring them there as he bent over her and eased her onto her back.

"Jake . . ." She could barely talk.

"Hm?"

"The doorbell."

"Forget it."

"Who could it—"

"Who the hell cares?"

He tasted all of her mouth with his lips, his tongue. His hand inched into the front of her thong, prolonging the moment for her as much as he was able to in this state, until he discovered few enough curls that he knew she'd had a bikini wax. After that, all he noticed was that she was wet and ready.

Her fingers dug into his back, his shoulders—

And then he heard it. Footsteps echoing on the wooden deck, advancing toward the back door. A man's voice.

"Lilly? It's me."

Warning bells rang, and Jake knew what he had to do above all else: *Protect Lilly.*

He scooped her against his chest, her legs and arms wrapped around him like a baby chimp, and he sprinted across the kitchen, into the dining room, where he pressed her up against the wall and struggled to catch his breath. His hands slowed. His kisses grew lighter, but nothing ended his ragged breathing or his erection.

"Ooh, I've never done it against the wall," she said breathily, then plundered his mouth, tilted her pelvis and squeezed her thighs around him.

Sweet Jesus.

"Lilly? Everything okay in there?"

"Who the hell is that?" Jake growled.

"Lilly? It's me."

"Oh God." Her groaning near his ear didn't help him cool down any. "It's Andrew."

"It's all right." Jake crooned sweet reassurances against her temple while wondering how to keep her exactly where she was and undo his jeans at the same time. "It's dark, he can't see us in here."

"He has a key."

Her breath was hot in his ear. So hot.

"We all have keys and alarm codes to each other's houses," she seemed compelled to explain. "You know, just in case." She unwrapped her legs from his hips.

Jake felt cold, deserted, and too pissed off at the interruption to be grateful that things hadn't gotten out of hand, hadn't gone too far when they shouldn't have gone anywhere at all in the first place.

"I have to, uh—"

He felt her hands between them, checking her buttons, tucking the tail of her blouse in, smoothing her skirt. Reluctantly, he gave her room. Then she giggled.

At least she wasn't mad at him.

"What?" he whispered, thankful it was dark and she couldn't see him grinning like a sex-starved fool.

"One stocking's down around my ankle. Where's the other one?"

"It's gone?"

"Yeah."

"You lost your shoe?"

"Apparently. Shoot, I hope they're not in the middle of the kitchen floor." *Visible from the window.*

"Here, I'll take that." He balled up the stocking she swept off, and for lack of a better place, tucked it inside the waistband of his jeans. Then he followed her into the kitchen.

"Andrew, hi," she said upon opening the door.

The bottle of champagne in Andrew's hand made Jake suspicious. Then Andrew kissed Lilly's cheek pretty damn slow and pretty damn close to the corner of her lips for a brother-in-law.

"Well, Jake, it's been a long time."

Andrew stepped forward and grasped his hand as if they were old friends, which they weren't. Especially not since Brady had died. Jake squeezed tightly, but he had to hand it to Andrew. The guy barely winced and didn't fall to his knees, which would have been so lovely. It wasn't as if Jake could punch the guy out in Lilly's kitchen.

"I hope I'm not interrupting," Andrew said.

Lilly started to reply, but Jake painted a clear picture with a few well-chosen words, managing to sound casual and pretty much at home here when he said, "Oh, I haven't put the steaks on yet."

Andrew tilted his head toward the driveway. "That isn't your uncle's taxi, is it?"

"Yeah." If one were critical, it could be taken as meaning, *What of it?*

"I thought he was out West somewhere. Oh, wait a minute—*You're* not Lilly's chauffeur, are you?" If one were critical, his tone could be considered mocking.

Lilly stood ever so slightly off to the side, almost between them but not quite, probably debating whether this was normal behavior or if fists would fly.

"Surely you've got better things to do than drive our Lilly around all day, every day."

Our Lilly. Hell.

"Just until five o'clock." It was seven now, so let the jerk infer whatever he wanted from that.

"And here I thought your job was in that sex shop. Oh, that's right, it blew up or burned down or something, didn't it?"

"Jake ran back into the building for me," Lilly said. "If it hadn't been for him, I wouldn't be here."

"Well then, well done." Andrew smiled broadly and clapped him on the shoulder.

How do you like that? Spend two weeks watching out for an old friend's wife—shit, he'd let that get out of hand—and then the brother-in-law comes charging in with insincere praise and a bottle of champagne. Instead of being grateful that Andrew's arrival had stopped him from making a serious mistake, Jake wanted to yank the bottle out of his hand and hit him over the head.

"Can I take that for you?"

"Oh." Andrew looked from the bottle to Lilly, then smiled. "I brought it to celebrate the sale of your house."

"It sold? Betsy didn't call me."

"We haven't told her yet. But you know Mother's affiliated with the university, of course. Well, when she heard you wanted to sell, she contacted the president right away. Seems they have a professor, well, two actually, they're married. They moved here at the beginning of the semester with their children, and the housing they're in just isn't adequate. So mother said she'd buy your house and lease it to them. She wants to know if you'll sell it fully furnished."

"Yes!" Lilly looked as if she'd just won a lottery.

"They need it immediately. I hope that's not a problem."

"How soon?"

"Next week."

Lilly's jaw dropped.

"If it's a problem, I'd be happy to have you move in with me for as long as you like."

Ah-hah. So that was the reason behind the champagne.

The little twerp. Once he got her behind closed doors, he'd bend her ear until she agreed to a new driver, then Jake'd never see her again.

Suddenly, it hurt to breathe. He needed damage control.

"Oh, sweetheart, here it is." Jake pulled her lace-topped stocking out of his jeans, slowly stretching it full length. He draped it over her shoulder. He could've stuffed it in her mouth, her jaw had dropped so low. "Actually, Drew ol' buddy, it makes more sense if Lilly moves in with me." He smiled suggestively at her. "That way we don't have to get up as early."

He held his breath, not sure whether she'd sock him one. Not sure whether it'd come now or later. Not sure whether he'd lost his mind.

How the hell would he stay out of her clutches under the same roof?

11

Lilly was a little dizzy from the speed with which events unfolded, but she realized what she was faced with: two men figuratively circling her with crests raised, each staking his territory.

"This close," she sighed regretfully.

This close to accomplishing her goal.

Surely, to ensure a child who was destined to do something great, it'd only take one time to conceive. Although if Jake made love as hot as he did foreplay, she was willing to repeat the exercise over and over and over.

But *noooo*, she'd blown it. Well actually, Andrew had. What timing. What—

Shoot, what if maybe, just as she'd feared at the mall, Elizabeth had sent Andrew here this evening because *he* was the right one? Not that Lilly had any doubt whom she wanted. Jake, hands down. But that didn't mean he was the right one in John and Elizabeth's book.

Damn.

Even if she knew who was supposed to father her child, turns out getting a man naked wasn't as easy as Betsy always made it sound.

Since she didn't know which one was the official, designated *right one*, she quickly decided to go with the hunk she wanted in the most basic, carnal way. She'd come darned close a few minutes ago. Close enough to give her hope that the deed would be done by the end of the night. *Yes!* From here on in, it had to get easier.

And if Jake wanted to clear the path by pulling her stocking out of his pants and one-upping Andrew with an invitation to move in, why would she sabotage that?

She felt herself blush in anticipation of later. If she took time to face facts, she also realized that while she'd known Andrew longer, and he was an okay guy, she actually felt something for Jake she'd never felt for a man before. Besides admiring his dedication to his family and knowing he'd make a great father, she actually *liked* him.

They'd spent eight hours together every day for two weeks in the front seat of a closed-up car. He handled traffic like a master and got her where she needed to go— eventually, because sometimes he seemed to be delaying her by driving in circles. He never once yelled at her to hurry up, shut up, or clean up. He shared all the snacks the neighbors made for him, both with her and the grouchy cat who had him wrapped around his little paw. If she didn't like him, she was sure she could've found something in all that to complain about.

After the last year with her husband, liking was a mighty fine change. Maybe just as important as loving. Brady hadn't stopped having sex with her because he'd found someone else, but because not being able to finish what he started made him angry and resentful. He never asked for help with anything; heaven forbid someone would find out he wasn't the best at everything. If his being unlikable kept Lilly from trying to help him, even if it ate away at their love, well, that was the path he'd chosen.

"Now see here—" Andrew said.

"Good idea," Lilly said, not taking her eyes off Jake. Lord, she could feast all night on this man. "I could use the extra beauty sleep." Her grin probably gave her away.

"Well then." Andrew looked from Lilly to Jake, but he didn't go all pompous on her the way he might have. "I'll just leave this here anyway, so you can celebrate."

He set the bottle of champagne on the island, right where Jake had hoisted her earlier. Lilly hoped she hadn't left a bare-cheek imprint. Andrew paused midstep. Lilly followed his gaze upward and spotted her missing stocking, dangling from an overhead fan blade.

Andrew recovered quickly. "So long, Jake, good to see you again." He shook his hand, bussed Lilly's cheek, whispered, "Be careful, I've heard things about him," and let himself out.

Lilly slowly dragged the stocking free, stretched it between both hands, and turned toward Jake, ready to loop it behind his head and draw him back to the dining room wall. Or the island; she wasn't picky. She just wanted him hot and heavy and between her legs and inside her, *now*.

What a sorry excuse for a best friend I am.

Jake needed to throw something, hit something, he didn't care, he just needed to divert a lot of sexual energy *fast*. He couldn't touch Lilly again without swinging her into his arms and heading for the nearest wall.

One look at what had to be a fierce expression on his face, and she backed off. He could only imagine what she was thinking. Confusion. Rejection?

Lilly covered quickly, turned away, and retaliated by promptly throwing his steak on the hot grill. Even though Jake knew she was hell-bent on burning it—no less than he deserved—he wisely acted as if the situation were just the opposite.

"Wow, you're starting mine, and I know you don't like to cook."

"I can scorch just fine."

"Hm. Okay, I'll take over then."

Lilly threw herself into divvying up the salad bar takings, muttering cryptic comments, ripping open the container. She slammed two plates onto place mats on the island—

Please, no, not the island

She wrenched open the silverware drawer and did the same with utensils.

The look she shot at her phone when it rang was enough to freeze a charging rhino. She stormed over to the built-in desk, picked up the handset, listened a millisecond, then slammed it on the counter. Repeatedly. And then she hung up.

No way he was asking anything about that.

He nuked the potatoes, added her steak to the grill, and tried to sound casual when he said, "Mind if we eat in the atrium?"

Besides a ton of plants, it had some interesting rock formations and a small waterfall, as he remembered. One thing he and Brady had in common—while they both enjoyed the serenity of a garden, they could kill a plant just by looking at it. Lilly was the one with the green thumb.

"It's my favorite place." She sounded as if she objected to sharing.

But then she glanced at the atrium door, the island, and back again. She must've read his mind, because she set everything they needed on a large tray with a great deal less slamming.

He needed to lighten the mood. He needed to tell her how guilty he felt. Maybe then she'd cool whatever this was between them.

"So, did you ever cook for Brady?"

"Once in a while," she said, her voice softening again. "If the chef was off, I occasionally stooped to scrambling eggs on a Sunday morning."

Jake figured he was in trouble again when she lit two candles.

"Boy, not the way Brady told it. He was always raving about your gourmet meals, the dinner parties you gave, some of the dessert recipes you created, things like that."

"Not unless I have amnesia and nobody told me."

He *knew* he was in trouble again when she slipped her arms around him from behind as he watched the steaks. Lord, she felt way too good with her breasts pressed into his back.

"Everything okay now?" she asked.

Remember Brady, he scolded himself. The best friend whose wife he should be looking after, not fucking up against a wall. Life sure would be simpler if she'd stay mad at him just a little longer.

"Look . . ." How to put this delicately? "I know you and Brady had a really hot sex life . . ."

"What?" She raised up on tiptoe, rested her chin on his shoulder, and tipped her head so she could see his face. Her breath was warm against his cheek, and the aroma of hyacinths and red wine commingled, teasing his nose, tempting him to turn his head and see how she tasted.

"I know you must be missing it like crazy—"

"Jake . . ."

He was trying to explain why he had to stop things now, why he couldn't go ahead with what she had in mind, why it wouldn't be fair to her and sure as hell would make Brady roll over in his grave.

"He's gone, I'm here, I was his best friend so I remind you of him. I understand all that."

She pulled away. "I'm glad one of us does."

Jake carried the full tray to the bright Mexican tile-topped table in the atrium, admiring white camellia blossoms along the way, pausing to sniff a particularly large one. "Nice."

"Actually, what you're smelling is fragrant olive and jasmine. But let's not change the subject."

As soon as they took their seats, Lilly refilled their glasses and set the bottle between them.

Good, keep it handy.

"What's really bothering you, Jake? One minute we're—"

"Guilt."

"Excuse me?"

"I want you, Lilly, you know that. You can't help but notice."

"Sometimes. But then—"

"I know, I know, it's my fault. I'm always pulling back."

"Lots of people are afraid to commit—"

He shook his head. "Don't even go there. Look, you have to understand, I loved Brady like a brother. Not like that jerk Andrew, but a good brother. Wanting you, well, it just seems wrong. Disloyal."

"But he's—"

"I went to the funeral, remember?"

She sighed and put her fork down, resting her hands in her lap as she chewed her lip, debating. "Maybe I should explain something."

"I doubt it."

"Jake." The softness in her tone caught his attention the way knocking him over the head wouldn't. "My marriage . . . wasn't working."

"Oh please," he scoffed.

"Really. Brady and I barely touched each other the last year we were married, much less had sex. And before that, well, compared to what you and I were just doing, it wasn't hot at all."

"Sex on the counter while there's a dinner party in the dining room isn't *hot*?"

She snickered. "Let me guess. More stories?"

"Yeah."

"Don't you think somebody would've heard us?"

He gulped. Brady'd never said she was a screamer.

"Don't you think we would've been missed?"

"He, uh, he said it was a quickie between courses."

She grinned mischievously and said, "You think I'm into quickies?" reminding him that while they'd been going at it pretty hot, it certainly hadn't looked like it was going to be over fast enough to set any world records. "During a dinner party. Right."

Pensive, Jake toyed with the stem of his glass. "So, if you didn't have sex on the counter between courses . . ."

"No sex on the counter, period."

"The chair in his office?"

"Doesn't even sound doable. More wine?"

"You were on top." He covered his glass with his hand. He needed to stay very, very sober this evening.

"I knew he was jealous of you, but *sheesh*."

"Of me? No way."

"Think about it. You were smarter, more independent. You could move to Silicon Valley; he was under his father's thumb. He was jealous of how your whole family gets along, you know, as if you like each other. You have so much he wanted."

"I never knew he felt that way."

"I had no idea he was so creative."

"Ah, well, sex in a chair's not all that creative."

"I meant the stories."

"Oh."

"I promise you, you have nothing to feel guilty about." That said, she started eating again. He followed suit, hoping she'd let him work this through in his own mind. Though he was a little curious. She must have noticed, because she said, "What else?"

She had the cutest way of closing her eyes and savoring the first bites of every meal, as if she'd been living off TV dinners for the past year. He'd get a big head about his cooking, but she did the same thing at McDonald's and Taco Bell.

"You really like food, don't you?"

"Tastes like heaven. Come on, what other stories did he tell you?"

"Hm, let me think."

"You're stalling."

"I like my food hot."

"I've got all night."

He didn't, though. He couldn't help it, he still felt guilty. He still wanted to hit something. "You don't really want more sex stories, do you?"

"*More?*" At first she sounded appalled, but then she grinned devilishly. "Yes, more. Where else did I supposedly get seriously naked with my husband?"

"In an elevator at one of the convention hotels."

"A little public for my taste. Where else?"

"In an airplane. You know, the Mile High Club."

On that one, she just grinned and shrugged.

"You didn't."

"Hey, I own a plane, and we weren't always incompatible."

Asking wouldn't cool anyone off, so he switched focus. "He bragged about your decorating this house in one day to look like a sultan's palace."

"It was just one room, and he hired a color-blind decorator."

He lit into his food again, then just had to ask. "What's a sultan's palace look like?"

"I'm not sure, but apparently he thought it should look like the inside of a velvet tent full of floor cushions and scarf-covered lamps. Along with a lot of beads and tassels and fringe and incense burners."

"Oh I gotta see that." He regretted it as soon as he said it, because he was afraid it'd look like a great place to have sex. Damn, what if it was her bedroom?

As sure as anything he'd ever known, Jake understood that Brady'd told him those stories to brand Lilly as his wife, to keep them apart. He should honor that wish. He was *obligated* to honor it.

"How about now?" she suggested.

Was that her bare foot running up his leg? Well shit, of course it was; every topic seemed to lead straight back to sex.

"Some other time. I've gotta meet some buddies in— Shoot," he said, jumping to his feet. "I'm gonna be late unless I leave now."

"*Now?*" She looked shell-shocked, surging to her feet beside him. "But . . . what about, you know, *before*?"

"Momentary lapse in judgment. If you put the steak in a baggie, I can eat it while I drive."

She stabbed his steak with her fork and jabbed the whole juicy lot against his chest.

"Find your own goddam baggie."

Jake slammed an eighteen-pound bowling ball down lane six, sending all ten pins flying, some over onto lane seven. Since he didn't know the guys on lane seven, they were understandably pissed off. Seems their guy was working on a three hundred game and didn't need his concentration broken.

Well, too frickin' bad. He was working on his frickin' *life* here, and he needed to throw things.

"Hey, man, let's not break the equipment," Mike said.

Driving away from Lilly's, Jake had had two choices

of where to go: out with his college roommate for a typical evening (for his roommate) of clubbing and mixed
drinks, or meet up with the guys he used to lay stone with
for a typical evening (for them) of bowling and beer. He'd
opted for throwing heavy balls at shapely pins that
couldn't fight back.

"Just because you had a fight with your lady—".

"She's not mine." He powered another ball down the
lane.

"Hey, it was my turn."

"Oh. Well, you can have my strike then."

"Fine by me, but I think the other team's gonna object."

It was league night. When Jake had shown up, Kevin
said, "Great, I can go home and help Kathie with the
kids," and left, leaving him to sub on Mike's team.

"Sorry, guys," he told the opposing team. "Next round
of beer's on me, okay?"

He should be so lucky to appease Lilly as easily.

Mike sat on the molded plastic seat next to him, leaned
back, and crossed his ankles. "She's mad, huh?"

Without a word, Jake unzipped his sweatshirt and
bared his stained shirt.

"What? Your washer's broken?"

"Funny. It's my dinner. And she's not my lady, she's
Brady Marquette's widow."

"Ooh, some fox, buddy." Mike laughed lasciviously.

Jake debated on throwing *him* at the pins, but that'd
solve nothing. Might make him feel better, though. No,
better not.

He scowled at Mike and hoped he'd take the hint. Then
he explained his dilemma, skipping the steamy sex appe-
tizer in Lilly's kitchen. He could still taste her and was in

grave danger of going seriously insane wondering what color her garter belt was, and her thong, and whether they matched, and if they matched her bra and—*damn!*—how she looked in all of it. She'd look better than fine, he knew, but he wanted a real live show, not an imaginary picture.

For Mike, though, he simply distilled all that down to the responsibility he felt to look after her.

"Why?" Mike asked.

"Remember when Angie left me?"

"Without a word—oh yeah, I remember." Mike shook his head. "That was a helluva binge you went on."

"You don't know the half of it." Jake leaned close, elbows on knees, not wanting to share this with everyone. "I started drinking on the job. One night everybody went home but me. I don't know where I was, probably passed out in the basement or something. Anyway, when I woke up, I started breaking things."

"Yeah, so?"

"You know, vandalism."

That caught Mike's attention. He mirrored Jake's position and whispered gruffly, "You mean the Reynolds job?"

Jake shrugged. "I don't know. Maybe. I don't remember it too clear."

"Holy cow, that was a lot of damage. We all thought it was a vendetta against Reynolds or something."

"Nah, just me. It was Brady who found me and locked me in a trailer for a week and dried me out. And kept me from losing my job. And then made it possible to start up the tech business. So you can see why I owe him not to screw around with his wife."

Mike leaned back and folded his arms across his chest. "Wouldn't bother me—" Jake's glare stopped him cold. "Ooh, some predicament, buddy. But I got the perfect solution."

Yes! Jake knew coming here would help. "Tell me. Whatever it is, I'll do it."

"Buy me another beer?"

"You figure this out, a whole case is yours."

"You're gonna love this. It's so simple. Hey, guys, isn't this simple? Jake here doesn't know what to do about the woman moving into his place." That caught everyone's attention, and both teams drew near. Mike clapped him on the shoulder and said, very seriously, "I have the perfect solution for you, buddy, and I wouldn't do this for anyone but you, you understand?"

Jake swallowed, waiting for the grand solution.

"You move into my place, buddy. You'll be safe there." Mike made him wait for it, then grinned. "And I'll move into yours."

Jake growled, jumped up, shoved his way through the guys, grabbed the first ball on the return, and slammed it down lane six. Strike, big deal.

"Is she hot?" he overheard someone ask Mike.

"Hell yes."

"Hey then, count me in."

"Me too."

Jake power shot another ball at the pins on the next lane over. No one dared object.

John strolled through heaven's White Garden, a place he often went for peace and solitude. The white roses were perfect, never blasted or wilted. Millions of them scaled trellises to the top, then cascaded freely off them, like waterfalls of silk petals.

Elizabeth bustled through the arched gate, glancing neither right nor left as she followed the shortest path toward him.

"I didn't know you liked the garden," he said with a beatific smile.

She glanced around, as if seeing it for the first time. "Oh. Pretty. Do you have a minute?"

John admired a perpetually dew-dropped bud, then nodded, giving her permission to wreck his interlude.

"What do you call it when someone *over*masters a lesson?" she asked.

"Perhaps you should explain who and what."

"It's Jake. If he was here to master loyalty, he's overdone it. I mean, Lilly's practically thrown her naked body on top of the man, and all he can think about is how disloyal it is to want his best friend's widow. So what do we do when someone learns something too well?"

"Ah, but that's part of the lesson. If someone overdoes something, then they really haven't learned it after all."

"So there's nothing we can do?"

"I'm afraid not."

"I was afraid you were going to say that."

When Elizabeth neither continued nor left, John said, "Was there something else?"

"No. Well, yeah. I still have a nagging feeling that I forgot to tell Lilly something, but I just can't put my finger on it."

"Perhaps you should join your peer group. Networking's quite helpful for working through problems that are difficult to define."

Lilly called Betsy and got her machine. In case the cute paramedic was staying over, Lilly resisted the impulse to scream bloody murder into the phone for fear he wouldn't understand she just needed to vent and would instead call 9-1-1 and give them her phone number, which would lead to sirens screaming to her front door and do *nothing* to alleviate all the frustration she'd built up in the last two weeks.

When Jake offered to let her move in with him and followed it up with that crack about being able to sleep later, she thought he was hinting at long sexy nights to come when they'd *need* to sleep in just to keep from exhausting themselves.

Anyway, that's what she had in mind. With their first course on the granite island still scorching her skin everywhere they'd touched, everywhere he'd kissed, everywhere she'd known he would be in another two minutes, well, she darned near drooled at the offer.

But when he bolted during dinner, she figured that he figured she was just another stray, like Mooch, who needed a warm place to sleep. Really sleep.

So she'd been widowed only five months. Didn't bother Andrew. Shouldn't bother Jake. After all, she'd explained that the end of their marriage had been seventeen months ago, not five.

Seventeen celibate months.

Geez, what was a woman supposed to do to get some

passion in her life? Short of putting on her sexy new clothes and strutting a street corner downtown, which really wouldn't be passion at all, just sex, and probably not even as good as she'd had with Brady in the beginning. No sense going there.

Nope, Jake was the guy for her. You couldn't help but admire a guy who loved frizzy cats and messy kids and put his life on hold to pay back his family. She couldn't help but love a man who valued loyalty and friendship and family above all else. Having similar values herself, she wanted to give him the money Brady'd diverted because it was the right thing to do.

So, how to repay him. Actually, this was easy if she failed her mission—and after self-indulgently desiring that antique-cushion-cut diamond the other day, she had reason to be concerned that John and Elizabeth would give up on her and yank her back. That, or she wouldn't get pregnant in time, which also was a distinct possibility, the way things *weren't* going.

In the office, she flipped through Brady's address book, looking for his insurance agent's number. Might as well find out how much it'd take to buy a three-million-dollar policy on herself.

The bracelet zapped her, not that she needed the reminder. She knew if she so much as reached for her checkbook, she'd be on the floor.

"Yeah, yeah, stuff it," she said to Elizabeth, as the agent's phone rang. "I'll find a way."

And she did. Betsy could pay the premium; Jake could be the beneficiary. All Lilly had to do was pass the physical, which wasn't a problem. If she failed her mission and died again soon, Jake would be set. It felt good to utilize a loophole without getting zapped into unconsciousness.

On the other hand, if she did everything correctly and passed the Transition tests and didn't die, well, she didn't know how she'd pay Jake back if that was the case. But one solution already had presented itself. Maybe another would, too.

Sunday evening was moving day. Jake made the offer; Lilly was taking him up on it. He arrived in a mellow mood fifteen minutes after Betsy, giving Lilly two cars to pack with belongings.

"Sorry I'm late. Sometimes my nephews' hockey games don't start on time."

Knowing that being visibly angry with him over deserting her the night before wasn't going to charm him out of his pants, she followed his lead.

"You go often?"

"Oh sure. They're not old enough yet to be embarrassed by all the screaming we grown-ups do. We're conditioning them now so we can keep going later, you know?"

"Yeah, my nanny used to tell me stories about people like you." She rolled her eyes to cover her envy.

He saw right through her. "I'll take you sometime, show you how the other half lives."

"Deal."

He got down to business then, joking about how she could condense all her possessions down to two carloads of clothes and boxes.

It wasn't as if she'd need any of her current wardrobe

past spring. If she got pregnant on time—soon—nothing she owned would fit beyond then. If she didn't, she'd be called back before Easter.

So other than what she could use over the next couple months, Lilly put everything into storage in a corner of her basement to go through later. None of it had any monetary value. It was just what accumulates in clothes closets, linen closets, bathroom drawers, dresser drawers, junk drawers—everything that piles up in the everyday course of life. Old makeup, wrong shade lipsticks, too many combs, too tight underpants, uncomfortable bras, photo albums, snapshots of friends, mementos from vacations. She should've thrown most of it away, but she'd never been good at parting with possessions. Like money, they were her cushion for a rainy day.

Everything of value, mostly jewelry, she took with her. She'd have to sell it or donate it, because it was worth quite a bit, and she'd keep her bargain.

"What about Brady's library?" Jake asked.

"Fully furnished means books, I guess."

"Not Brady's books."

"You're being proprietary again."

"Hey, that's a fine collection he put together. I know what some of those books cost separately. They must be worth even more together."

Brady'd devoured books like some people did junk food; classics, autobiographies, art tomes, scholarly works, it didn't matter. If one was to his liking and originated in a different language, he had to have it. If he could find a first edition, he added it to his collection. Jake was right; the collection couldn't stay. She'd have it appraised and sell it, but she wasn't telling him that.

After flipping through a few of Brady's photo albums, Lilly wanted something similar for her children. She had a few pictures her nanny had taken and some from boarding school. She put those together with ones of herself out of Brady's albums, then boxed the remainder up for his family.

She wanted to take an hour for her last walk through the house, but her recent attitude adjustment provided a little enlightenment on that issue. She told the lovebirds and koi good-bye, made sure there were detailed notes so the professors could take over their care, then locked the door and looked ahead.

Jake's parents' house had five bedrooms on the second floor. Looking into each one closely as she made her choice, Lilly spotted a crucifix, a white-beaded rosary coiled on a dresser, a dried palm leaf tucked behind a framed picture of the guardian angel, and a Bible. Mr. If-I-can't-see-it-then-it-doesn't-exist appeared to be in the minority in this family.

She took the bedroom across the hall from Jake's because its lace-canopied four-poster bed looked cheery and feminine. Her clothes filled that closet, and when she spread out into the closets in two other rooms, he didn't seem to mind.

On their last trip from the car, she and Betsy carried flight bags up the stairs.

"Can you do me a favor?" Lilly asked.

Betsy groaned. "As long as it doesn't involve carrying all this back out."

"I need you to keep it a secret."

Betsy seemed to discern the seriousness of her request, because she slowed down and paid attention.

"Would you buy something if I asked you to?" Lilly asked.

"A vibrator?"

Lilly groaned. "You have a one-track mind, you know that?"

"And this is bad, why?"

"I'm serious."

"So am I." Betsy lowered her voice to a conspiratorial whisper. "You want me to buy you one where *he* won't know about it?"

"*Bet*sy, listen." Lilly explained about the insurance policy and listing Jake as beneficiary.

"But why don't you just—?"

"I can't, okay?"

"No but—"

"*Please.*"

Betsy sighed. "Okay."

"I'll write a letter so Jake pays you the premium back."

"Whatever."

Lilly hugged her. "Thanks, girlfriend. Now, get my camera out of that bag, would you? I want Jake to take a picture of the two of us together."

"Sure. Hey," she said when the phone rang. "Jake's outside, you think we should get it?"

"I don't know."

"You live here now."

"Yeah, but nobody knows that yet."

A couple more rings, though, and Lilly trotted across the hall and picked up the extension in Jake's room. Even on a weekend, it could be one of the businesses he consulted for or an important networking connection getting back to him.

"Hello?"

"Sorry, I must have the wrong—Ooh, is this Lilly *Marquette?*"

Shoot, how much did he want others to know? Her "yeah" was slow and tentative.

"Hmph. I forgot you were moving in today. Have Jake call me. This is Jessica, his sister." No *Can't wait to meet you.*

On the other hand, no *Where the hell's my brother's three million dollars?* either.

"Sure."

The phone rang again before Lilly got out the bedroom door, probably a product of the well-organized Murdoch grapevine. Knowing she probably was going to get interrogated by one of Jake's sisters, she nevertheless picked up the receiver.

Her hello didn't get an immediate response, and she was just about to hang up when she heard it.

"Get out," a voice rasped, bitterly enough to make Lilly shiver. No way this was a sister. "You don't belong there."

12

"I cannot believe this!" Up in Transition, Elizabeth was fit to be tied. She was pacing in tight little agitated turns, but it wasn't helping.

"Need some assistance?" John asked when he appeared.

She'd never get her own division if she kept running to him for help.

Perusing his electronic clipboard, John murmured, "Hm, I see. Money issue. Second man."

"Can she not catch a break?"

"It's just like I always say; people don't know what they really want until they're forced to think it through." John was his usual cool and calm self as he pushed a few buttons, examining new information. "Hm, seems there's a few minutes missing here."

It wasn't as if Elizabeth didn't have a few friends in high places who'd cover for her, though she didn't want to press her luck too often.

"Wait a minute," John said, looking surprised. "What's this threatening phone call?"

"My point exactly." Elizabeth wanted to stamp her foot and yell, but it just wasn't dignified. "I have half a mind to go back, uh, go down there and—"

"Oh, no no no," John said. "Mustn't do that. Rule number twelve-oh—"

"I need a clipboard." Fretting and pacing wasn't getting her anywhere, so she quickly matched her demeanor to John's, adopting silence and a calm, angelic outward appearance.

"Now, Elizabeth, if we gave a clipboard to every angel who thought she was cut out for this job—"

"Please, just let me borrow yours." She stopped short of batting her eyelashes, because of course that wouldn't work on John.

"I'm afraid not."

"Five minutes, that's all I ask." She smiled oh, so sweetly. "Five minutes to look into what's going on down there and why. Please, John. Just five minutes to find out who made the phone call."

"No."

"But how else can I help Lilly? You know she deserves it."

"Does she?"

"Oh, John," she coaxed softly, "that's not fair. Why can't we help her? Just a little."

"The rules have served us well. Stick to the plan and keep mentoring her with the bracelet a while longer. Things will work out if they're meant to."

"But wouldn't it help to find out who made the phone call? And what her plan is?"

"Even if you did, you couldn't tell Lilly."

Elizabeth wanted so badly to chew her fingernails, a habit she'd broken generations ago, but it would send the wrong message. "But if I knew something else, something important, perhaps I could warn her—you know, with the bracelet."

"Stick to the rules, and you'll be fine."

A simple, "Alarm, seven o'clock," before retiring alerted the computer to wake Lilly on time Monday morning.

She hadn't lost any sleep over the nasty phone call. Maybe her own heavy breather had made her immune, but she just didn't think somebody would be threatening her over Jake after only eighteen days. Had to be a wrong number. She dropped off quickly to Enya and woke up to Native American flutes.

Jillian, a.k.a. Murdoch sister number three, stopped by after dropping her kids at school. She came in the back door, scowled at Lilly, and Jake dragged her off to another room. After that, she smiled tightly and said she came to borrow a purse. Lilly might've bought that except Jillian dashed upstairs and darted from room to room until she discovered which one Lilly'd moved into. She left without anything except news, and Jake's devilish twinkle.

"Sorry about that," he said.

"Either she has a split personality or you read her the riot act."

He grinned unabashedly. "My family's a little mad at you."

"Nah, it's more than that. I'm the woman who's moved into your house. They want to check me out." *See what room I'm sleeping in.* "It must be great to have siblings care about you that much."

He cocked his head and studied her curiously, but only said, "Yeah. It is."

By eight-thirty, they were in the taxi, windows rolled up tight against another cold front, headed to North County so Lilly could look over a crisis intervention center that had received high praise.

In spite of her asking for anonymity lately, the grapevine had been buzzing. She barely had to say, "Hi, I'm Lilly Marquette—" and people fell all over themselves to show her the highlights of how their organization or awareness program or foundation was helping others.

News crews were on hand twice. After that, she warned prospective recipients that if the media showed up, she wouldn't. They just slowed her down, and it was hard enough giving so much money away, she didn't need to smile about it and answer stupid questions about why she was doing it, like "Does it have anything to do with being poor yourself after your father's business failed?"

As if her father would want to be reminded.

"Does it have anything to do with your uncle leaving his airplane to you when you really needed it?"

How did people get that kind of information?

The downside of living with Jake was that the car hadn't lost its overnight chill before she joined him. Mooch tried to climb in his lap for warmth, and when Jake pushed him off, he decided Lilly's lap would do. She would've pushed him off, too, but he was toasty, so she let him stay. As a reward, he treated her to a rare purr, which she had to admit made her feel abundantly warm and cozy.

At the first turn, a lady's wristwatch slid along the dash from Jake's side to hers. She caught it as it went airborne. "Somebody leave this?"

"I did some work on it over the weekend for Rachel. She's one of my regulars."

"A gizmo, as Susannah calls it."

"Yeah. I couldn't finish it until my fingers healed, so it's late. If she doesn't call me soon, I want to drop it off at Shaw's Garden. She works there. You don't mind, do you?"

"I haven't been there in ages. I wouldn't mind walking through the Linnean House while you do that."

"Missing your atrium already?"

"I have—well, I *had* an extremely rare *Camellia chrysantha* that blooms later than the rest."

"So stop by and see it."

"I'd rather not go back. The Linnean House should have one." She held up the watch. "You mind if I wear it until then? I forgot mine this morning, and that way it won't fly off and get broken."

"Go ahead."

Admiring Jake's hands as he drove, Lilly didn't know how he maneuvered such large, strong fingers into intricate work at *any* time. While they'd be an advantage hoisting stones at custom home sites, which is probably where he'd developed them, they'd only be a hindrance working on a ladies' watch.

She buckled the brown leather band snugly on her wrist. It wasn't her usual style, a bit on the bulky side, but since it was covered by her coat sleeve most of the time and she was just wearing it to be functional, who cared?

"How do you work with something so small?"

"Expensive tools." Jake merged onto the highway, then studied her, his eyebrows drawn together with concern. "You look tired. Wasn't the bed comfortable?"

"It was fine, thanks."

Rather than move his stuff out of the hall bathroom, he'd given her sole run of the one in his parents' master suite. There were more automatic features in there for his mother, like a motion-detector light that worked after dark—red, so it wouldn't interfere with night vision when she exited. The sink faucets operated on a sensor, same as the kitchen. She'd needed a crash course in how to work the shower, as it had a row of controls where she had only to pass her hand over one higher or lower to change the temperature accordingly. Very user-friendly for an older woman with arthritic fingers.

Lilly hoped their son would be as thoughtful, not just toward her, but toward women in general.

Our son—now that had a nice ring to it, ever so much nicer than *my baby*.

"You have trouble adjusting the temperature for sleeping?"

"No, it was fine. Just"—she sighed—"busy dreams. Not bad, you know? Just confusing. Like it's me, and it's Cloud Nine, and it blows up, but then things get confusing. Sometimes I'm not even caught in the building, I'm standing out on the lot with you and Betsy, watching it burn. Sometimes the paramedics take me to the hospital. Sometimes I stand up and walk away."

With you, she thought, but no sense scaring him with a

commitment issue yet, just in case he wasn't the type. Since he'd never married, he must be.

"Sometimes I'm flying through a perfectly beautiful sky, then for no reason I lose control of the plane. Not mine; a different one. Can't get my feet on the pedals, or the stick's frozen. You know, classic lack-of-control stuff. So it's not the room, or the temperature, or the bed. It's me."

She lifted the most recent dessert pan off the dash. Mooch grumbled at the disturbance.

"Those aren't the usual," Jake warned.

"Tired of Orgasms?"

His smile was brief, but genuine. "I did something for Tom. You know, the guy I filled in for the day you and I met. Susannah's spread the word that I can be had for chocolate."

Oh, if only that were true.

"They're brownies with cherries in them, I think."

Lilly groaned appreciatively, especially since they'd already been cut and all she had to do was lift one out and start in on it.

"I don't think I even want to know the name."

Jake's grin was wicked with possibilities. "His wife said if we like them, we can name them."

We. His neighbors already thought of Jake and her as a *we*?

"Oh God, this is so good."

"Is that your breakfast, or should we stop somewhere?"

"Stop somewhere."

"You know, I've never met a woman who eats like you do."

"You mean because I don't count calories?"

"Calories, hell." He shook his head in amazement. "You don't even count meals."

"But everything tastes so good."

She silently debated whether everyone who got a second chance experienced the same thing. Halfway through the second brownie, her cell phone rang.

"Lilly, Andrew. Hey listen, I just got off the phone with Neidermeyer." Neidermeyer was her broker. "He says you've been moving a lot of money lately, and I was just wondering how you'd feel about investing some back into the business?" In other words, Quit giving it away.

Anyone who watched the news knew she'd been moving something, somewhere, but Neidermeyer knew how much, and it sounded as if he'd shared. So much for confidentiality.

Lilly bit her tongue to keep from telling Andrew exactly how she felt about his intruding in her financial affairs. Marquettes were firm believers in *It's not what you know, it's who you know.* Just wait'll she got a hold of Neidermeyer!

"Tell you what, Drew, I'll think about it."

"Because we can see you get a really good return on your capital, probably better than anything you're getting now."

"Let me think about it, okay?"

"If you'd like to get together sometime, I can show you some numbers."

"Drew!"

Startled, Mooch flew off her lap and cleared the back of the seat without even grazing it. Lilly'd grown pretty fond of the tumble-dried cat. Being deprived of his warm snuggle just irritated her that much more.

"Let me think about it."

"Oh." Andrew sounded surprised, as if he hadn't thought of *that*. "Okay. How about I pick you up at five to sign the contract on the house, and you can let me know then?"

"Fine." Irritated as hell, Lilly snapped the flip phone shut. "Change of plans."

Jake was grinning, probably pleased that she was pissed at a guy he didn't like. "Well, I know where we're *not* going."

"Right. I want a new broker. Andrew and my current one are a little too close, if you catch my drift."

"Mm, meddling, huh?"

"Oh"—she laughed with resentment—"so beyond meddling."

"If that's how you feel, how's your estate planning?"

"Done." Didn't matter anyway, it would all be gone in a few months. But if she didn't meet her deadline, the bulk of her money wouldn't go where it would do the most good. "Now that you mention it, I should have my attorney rewrite my trust. My parents don't want my money. Betsy's fine." Technically, she wouldn't *have* to because the deal would be broken, but since Transition, she'd found she actually liked helping people who really needed it. "I'll set aside three million for you, too."

His head nearly swiveled off in surprise. "No!"

"The road, Jake. *Watch the road!*"

He swerved back into his lane. "It's not that I don't appreciate the thought, but I can just see you getting blown up again. I'd be the prime suspect."

"Don't be silly. You're already the prime suspect."

"Me? Why?"

"Revenge, of course. For Brady screwing you out of the money in the first place."

"I'm sure he had his reasons."

"That's awful big of you. I'd be pissed."

"Well, he saved my life, and I'm not."

It never ceased to amaze Jake what loads of money could accomplish. He'd witnessed it often enough with Brady.

"You need it yesterday, Jake? No problem." And whatever he needed and hadn't been able to get through normal channels was overnighted to him.

"The airlines are booked and you need to go to Santa Barbara? No problem." *Pfft*—one ticket, waiting at the counter.

Now Lilly had the same one-button power. At least she didn't flaunt it, she saved it for when she really needed it—ha! A brief visit with a new broker who Lilly was sure had no business with the Marquettes, and *pfft*—millions moved to a new firm. A brief phone call with her attorney, and *voilà*—her appointment was in one hour to review an updated trust. By lunchtime, she was done, except for returning later to sign the final copy.

He didn't dwell on his own circumstances as a former, wrongfully removed beneficiary. And then he realized two things.

One, if Brady had consulted him, Jake would've agreed, even encouraged him to change the beneficiary on his policy. As much as he loved Lilly, she was Brady's wife, and it would've been all Jake could ever give her.

Two—and this really hurt—for anyone to inherit

Lilly's wealth, she'd have to die. She almost had. That undoubtedly weighed on her mind and was the impetus for making these changes so quickly.

Say she made him beneficiary of her trust—she had no obligation to, but just suppose, because now that the topic had come up, it was dragging his thoughts in this very morbid direction. So say it took her death for him to dig out of debt. Then forget it. Not even accidentally. No one's value to another person should boil down to money.

Although a lot of organizations probably would disagree with him, especially recently. Lilly had given away millions of dollars, and not just for people, but animals, too. On Mooch's behalf, she'd given a hefty sum to the no-kill animal shelter, because even though he hadn't gone through the shelter and been rehabbed, he'd been homeless. In spite of his prickliness, he was okay to have around. He certainly deserved a chance at life. It'd be nice, though, if he quit leaving dead mice parts on the floor of the taxi. Jake was having a helluva time making sure they were out of there every morning before Lilly got in.

His day was filled with exactly what he'd been afraid of—wondering what Lilly had on under that dress and what color it was. Sheer torture. Whatever it was was probably red; Lilly loved red. Was her bra as sexy as the rest of her lingerie? Would he be able to see her nipples through it?

"Hey, watch the curb," she warned.

It was stupid, really. He hadn't been so obsessed with what a woman wore since high school. He hadn't hit a curb in just about as long. Thank goodness it was five o'clock and they were nearly done.

"Here's the last one on the list for today," he said, par-alleling the curb with care. "Sorry we missed Shaw's Garden." He'd planned on photographing the rare yellow camellia for her, but they'd run late and didn't even have time to drop off the watch.

"*Damn*," she said, groaning.

He leaned forward and peered through Lilly's window. "Yeah, awfully dark, isn't it?"

"Doesn't matter."

"What? You never want to quit."

Mooch moaned long and low—anywhere else and it'd be a strong case that someone was trying to murder him. He climbed onto Lilly's lap, shoved his way under the circle of her arms, and lay with his belly flat on her chest.

Lucky damn cat.

With the top of Mooch's head nestled beneath Lilly's chin, he commenced nuzzling her. And purring? He sounded like an outboard motor. Commingled with the moaning, a very stressed outboard motor.

"Jake."

Lilly's whisper was thready and flat, and just thinking that something could be wrong with her scared the day-light out of him.

"Your cat's demented."

"Huh. I've never seen him do that, not even for ice cream. So, you want me to check the door and see if any-one's still here?"

"*Ow.*"

"Mooch!"

"It's not the cat. Don't yell at him."

What else—"Your arm?"

"Yes," she said through gritted teeth. "Start driving."

Her face was pinched with pain, so even though Jake's gut contracted, even though he'd gladly take her place if he could, he didn't question her, just floored the gas and aimed the taxi for the nearest hospital.

Don't worry, Brady, I'm keeping an eye on her for you.

"I *knew* we should've had it checked out sooner. Damn, I should've made you go see a doctor."

"It's not your fault." A quarter mile away, like night and day, Lilly sighed in relief and said, "You can slow down now."

In fact, she looked pretty content to have Mooch making up to her, darned near purring along with him when he rubbed his head under her chin.

"Mm, I didn't know cats were so soft."

If Mooch weren't a cat, he'd be in big trouble. A quarter mile farther, he wiggled free and curled up next to Lilly's hip. No moaning. No purring.

"What was that all about?"

"Got me. It's as if he knew I was hurting. Maybe it was a bad charity or something, because I wasn't even *thinking* anything against the rules."

"You shouldn't still be having pains in your arm after two weeks."

"It's okay, it's gone."

"Yeah, *now*."

She glanced around, noting their route. "So help me, if you pull into a hospital, I'm pulling out my pepper spray."

He braked to the speed limit and turned for home, but he wasn't ready to give in completely. "You should see a doctor."

"No."

"Then at least fill me in so if I have to call 9-1-1 for

you someday, I won't have to stand there and answer their questions like a jackass: How often does she have these pains? *I don't know.* How severe are they? *I don't know.* On a scale of one to ten—"

"All right, already." She covered a smile with her hand, unsuccessfully, and looked anywhere but at him.

"Come on," he coaxed.

"You're not going to like the explanation."

"How do you know until you tell me?"

"I know you."

He scoffed at that ridiculous assumption. "Just because we spend hours together every day doesn't mean you know me."

"Wanna bet?"

"Sure. If you're right, you can have the next pan of Chocolate Orgasms all to yourself."

She gave that some thought, but not much. "Not good enough."

"Okay then, what do you want?"

"I want—and keep in mind I'm only doing this for your child—"

"I don't have a child."

"You will someday." It was her turn to study him. "And on his behalf, if I win, I want you to open your mind and read a book, cover to cover."

"That's it? Read a book?"

"Get real. It has to be on one of those subjects you consider shit. You know, tarot, channeling, numerology, astrology, one of those." When he didn't answer, she grinned impishly, her eyes dancing. "See? Know you pretty well, don't I? Still wanna bet?"

He sat back at a red light, crossed his arms over his chest and thought, *Why the hell not?* It wasn't as if he could lose.

"Fine. When *I* win, you'll get that arm x-rayed."

He enjoyed watching her think, her scarlet-colored lips looking very kissable as her mouth tugged this way and that, keeping time with thoughts ping-ponging back and forth inside her head.

"If you win, and"—she laughed—"believe me, *that's* not gonna happen, I'll let a doctor check me out using any test that doesn't require removal of this bracelet."

She pointed at it so there'd be no misunderstanding, but the most significant thing Jake noticed was that she never said *my* bracelet. It was always *this* or *the* bracelet, or *it*, devoid of any possessiveness on her part. Whenever a charm disappeared, she didn't say she lost a charm, she said, *another one fell off*. So far she was missing two. She claimed that was because she'd given two million dollars away, but he wasn't buying that.

"Deal."

He stuck out his hand, and they shook on it, and it was a very good thing they hadn't been touching when they'd made the deal or who knows what he would've agreed to? Probably something really stupid, like reading a whole set of metaphysical encyclopedias. One book would be bad enough—*if* he had to read one, which he knew he wouldn't.

He moved forward with the bumper-to-bumper traffic as the light changed. "So. Give."

"You were right at the salon. It has to do with giving away money."

"Nuh-uh, you've been giving away millions, I don't buy that."

After a deep sigh, she chose her words with care. "Remember me telling you about John and Elizabeth?"

He groaned. "Not angels again."

"Well, I'm not sure if they're angels, exactly. But anyway, they gave me this bracelet, and when I even *think* of giving money to anyone who doesn't need it—from a charity standpoint, mind you—it zaps me."

He stared at her until someone honked, then he eased forward again. "You're telling me that you think it's coming from the bracelet?" And she was still wearing it? "Maybe it's not angels, you ever think of that? Maybe it's something totally explainable like, say, a *static charge*."

"Mm, I wish."

"Then all you have to do is take it off."

She tried to hide another jolt, but he could tell from the tiny squeak that escaped her lips that she'd just gotten another shock.

"There, see, no mention of money, and you got zapped again, didn't you? I rest my case."

"Elizabeth warned me not to take it off."

"Right. I can see I'm going to have to test it to prove my point."

She snickered.

"What? Afraid to let me put a meter on it and prove there's no current in that thing?"

"Not if, when I *think* about giving money away and your meter registers a charge, you admit I'm right."

"We'll do it as soon as we get home."

They were about five minutes away. This was too easy; he should've asked for her to see a doctor *and* the next pan of fudge to himself.

"What's with the streetlights?" she asked on the final block, a dead-end street.

"The neighbors don't like them on all night, so they just come on when a car drives by."

She twisted around and looked out the back. "They turn off right away?"

"As long as it's one of us. If it's a stranger's car, they stay on about ten minutes."

"You have *every* neighbor's car programmed?"

"It's just a little—Hey, who drives a Jaguar?"

Lilly grimaced as Jake pulled into his driveway. "Oh my gosh, I forgot. I told Andrew he could pick me up at five. Guess he's been here longer than ten minutes, huh?"

If he nodded at all, it was tersely, because after Friday night, Jake wasn't feeling too tolerant about Andrew's intentions. No way that guy thought of himself as Lilly's brother-in-law. A bottle of champagne to celebrate an intrafamily sale? Get real.

"Donna's attorney drew up a contract on the house. I'm supposed to go over there and sign off."

"I would've driven you."

"Be glad for the break. Have some wine, some dinner, wind down. I'll be back later. You want me to pick up a movie?"

"No need, I can get any movie anyone's broadcasting." Then when they were both standing in the cold, he caught her attention across the roof of the taxi. "You sure you want to go with him? I mean, you were pretty mad this morning."

"I know." She fairly danced with glee. "He's going to be so pissed off next time he talks to my broker."

"So should you be going with him?"

"Relax, he's my brother-in-law, not some psychopath. Look," she said with obvious reluctance. "I have to go now. Donna's expecting me."

The streetlight stayed on as Andrew pulled the low-slung, dark Jag into the drive to pick her up. Inside, Lilly held her hand up in a resigned wave, then she was gone.

Jake had been coming home alone to this house for months. It had never felt so lonely as it did now without Lilly.

"Lilly dear, it's so good to see you."

Donna was only slightly taller than Lilly, but seemed more so due to the unnaturally erect way she carried herself. Lucky for her, she looked good in black, because that's all she'd worn since shortly after Brady's death.

She hugged Lilly on the wide threshold of the Marquette mansion, then ushered her into the broad, marble-floored foyer. Two years ago, Lilly had raided her own atrium and given Donna and Frank the huge potted palms that now graced the entry and stretched up to the second floor.

"Sorry we're late," Andrew said.

"I never count on anyone being on time during rush hour." Donna was always gracious. "Here, I'll take your coats. Oh, Lilly dear, are you losing weight? You're so thin. Now I'm not criticizing, dear, I'm just concerned, you know that, don't you? You really should move in here with Frank and me. We'd love to have you, and Antoine always complains that his talents are wasted cooking for just the two of us."

Her chef prepared meals to die for. In spite of that, Donna maintained a lovely figure, highlighted tonight in a silk pantsuit and pearls. This was a woman who spared no expense in keeping herself up. When she'd thought she detected the beginnings of a dowager's hump—Lilly rolled her eyes just remembering the crisis—she quickly hired a personal trainer who came in three times a week. Now she wasn't only ramrod straight, she was strong, too.

"Why, he'd have the weight back on you in no time."

"That's sweet of you," Lilly demurred, "especially since I've gained five pounds recently." Between the fudge and brownies and fast food, she was lucky it was only five.

She liked Donna, she really did. She'd visit more often if her mother-in-law would quit her constant harping about how it "wasn't safe for an attractive, single woman to spend every night alone in that big old house."

Get over it.

"Well, you'd never guess you put on so much as an ounce, would you, Andrew?"

"Lilly looks just fine to me, Mother. Wonderful, in fact."

"Yes, she does. Maybe red has a slimming effect on some people. Come in by the fire, you two, and warm up. I have drinks waiting."

Donna passed their coats to the maid, then led the way to the study, where she handed Lilly a glass of white wine and had one herself. Andrew poured his usual Scotch, neat.

Lilly relaxed in the chair closest to the hearth and wondered why she hadn't been spoiling herself with fires lately. Since she'd met John and Elizabeth, chocolate tasted richer, wine was like nectar, Jake's touch promised all the passion she could ever hope for, and all together, that made her wonder how much better a darkened room with a crackling fire could be than before. Would it somehow seem warmer, more romantic? Ooh, yeah, she had to get Jake in front of a fire some night.

Donna perched on the chair across from her, while Andrew seemed comfortable on his feet.

"So Lilly, dear, tell me what you've been doing to keep yourself busy lately. I've had so many calls about your philanthropic activity. Lord knows, Brady had a kind heart, but he never would have done what you're doing. Whatever made you decide to start taking all these charities under your wing?"

Speaking of wing . . .

Lilly was pretty sure Donna would have her committed if her explanation contained any part of a trip to heaven and a bargain with angels, so she shuddered dramatically and said, "I made a promise that if I lived through that explosion, I'd help others. But that's not the only reason. I really *feel* that I've had so much in my life, it's the right thing to do, sharing, you know, with people who need it." Better head Donna off at the pass, so she threw in, "I'm very careful about not donating to questionable organizations."

"I see. I'd like you to consider investing in the business." Meaning Marquette pockets.

"Andrew mentioned something about that. I'm considering it." At her mother-in-law's steely look, Lilly softened the blow with another lie. "It's a very generous offer. I'm not saying I won't eventually."

"I see."

Better change the subject. "Is Frank here?"

"No, dear, something came up at the office, and he won't be able to join us. Andrew tells me that Jake fellow invited you to move in with him, now that I've agreed to buy the house?"

Lilly didn't like the way Donna said "that Jake fellow," as if his and Brady's fifteen-year friendship meant nothing; but since she wasn't here for an argument, she let it slide and pulled her pen from her purse.

"Speaking of which, how about we get the formalities out of the way so we can enjoy the evening?"

Donna smiled broadly. "I think that's a splendid idea." She slipped on a pair of half glasses and started to sign the contract lying on the small table by her chair, until Drew leaned over her shoulder.

"I'm sure that should be notarized, Mother."

Not to mention read by me, Lilly thought.

"Oh you know, you're absolutely right." Donna patted her motionless hair and gave the matter some thought. "Frank sent his secretary by to pick something up a little while ago. She's a notary, and I believe she's still up in my office. We'll just run these up there and have her do it. Come along, Lilly."

Reluctant to leave the fire, Lilly opened her mouth to demur, but then Andrew shot her a *Let's not upset Mother because we both have to have dinner with her yet* look. In complete agreement, she set her glass on the delicate side table and followed in Donna's wake.

"Thank you," Andrew whispered, falling in step beside her.

Lilly tripped over nothing and leaned on him, surprised to find herself woozy.

"I'll make an excuse right after dinner," he said, "so you won't get trapped here all evening."

"We'd better eat soon. I think the wine's going to my head."

"You all right? Lilly?"

She thought Donna said, "Uh-oh, I must have given her too much," but she'd only had half a glass, maybe less.

Andrew seemed concerned, though. "*What?*"

"She looks awful. Quick, put her in there before the secretary sees her."

"I'll be okay, really—Hey!"

At the top of the stairs, Andrew grabbed Lilly by the arm and shoved her through the first open door. It slammed behind her. And locked.

Startled, it took Lilly a moment to realize Andrew wasn't teasing, wasn't standing on the other side of the door cracking a joke, wasn't opening the door and explaining that he'd thrown her in here for her own good because of something weird and totally unexpected, like the ceiling in the hallway was caving in and he didn't want her to get crushed.

"Drew?" No reply. "Andrew! This isn't funny!"

She rattled the knob and shook the door, and when that accomplished nothing, she kicked it. Unfortunately, with all the heightened senses she had since coming back, pain wasn't excluded, and her toes throbbed so badly that it was hard to stay on her feet.

"Donna!"

"Hush, I'm afraid I'm going to need a little more of your time, dear. Drew, go show the secretary the back way out, will you?"

"Let me out of here!"

"Now, dear, you've been spending money very foolishly." Donna maintained a calm tone even as Lilly assaulted the door again, though this time with the flat side of her fists. "Your broker says you emptied your accounts today."

Lilly screeched and screamed and pounded and kicked. Antoine would hear her. The maid would hear her. The secretary would hear her.

"And you've been spending far too much time with that pervert." Donna's prim voice was only slightly muffled by the door. "The last woman who got involved with him died, did you know that? Oh, he made it look good— the police never even questioned him—but where do you think he got the money to go into business with Brady? You're a Marquette, Lilly. You have to think of your reputation. You have to look out for gold diggers."

What was she thinking? If the cook, maid or anyone else was still in this house, it'd only be out of true loyalty. In which case, she was screwed.

Wait—What had Donna said about Jake?

"I've been trying to convince you any way I could to move in with Frank and me. I called you every week so you'd understand how vulnerable you are, but you're just so darned stubborn."

Suddenly understanding the late-night phone calls, Lilly backed away from the door.

What would Donna and Andrew tell Jake when she didn't go home tonight? Would they make up some story about how she didn't want to see him anymore?

God, Jake, don't believe them.

Lilly quickly found herself sitting in the middle of the carpet, and not very straight either. She didn't remember sitting down.

What the heck?

Her head felt very heavy, and it was hard to focus with the walls swimming in circles.

Was this it? The end?

Before she could appeal to Elizabeth for more time, the room turned black.

13

Jake didn't take Lilly's advice; he skipped the wine. He wanted to keep a clear head so that if Andrew was too tired to bring Lilly home, he could drive over and get her.

Damn, he should have offered. He should have said something before she walked down his driveway and dipped into the low-slung Jag.

He should have his head examined.

He'd been so focused on how he was going to hook a meter up to her bracelet as soon as they got home. How he'd explain everything so it'd be crystal clear and Lilly wouldn't doubt the results, because he sure as hell didn't want to read any blasted metaphysics book.

Maybe she'd call and want a ride home. He carried the cordless phone everywhere in the house with him, just in case. When it finally rang, he nearly stabbed his finger right through the TALK button.

"Hey, Jake, how ya doin'?"

"Gary, hi." Gary was one of his former Silicon Valley

employees, and Jake needed this call right now about as much as he needed a hole in the head. But networking meant business, and business meant paying his dad and uncle back. It also meant hiring back people like Gary, who had families to support and bills to pay, people he'd hated letting go, but had no choice. It also meant earning Lilly's respect.

"Hey, listen," Gary said, "I got your message, and I'll get back to you on that later. But I have a minute now and I just wanted to tell you, you know the guy that bought your house?"

For a song.

"Yeah."

"He's having a party next weekend. Lotsa bigwigs, buddy. I'll schmooze all night."

Jake had to laugh, in spite of himself. Gary schmoozing was about as hard to imagine as catching fish with cat bait. "Get 'em drunk first."

"That's my plan, right after I show off everything you put into the house. I'll call later and let you know how it goes. I just wanted you to be jealous, so you'd move back out here and hire me again."

"Sounds like a plan. I'm working on some leads from this end, too. Stay in touch."

At eight-thirty, he gave in to what he'd wanted to do since the moment Lilly'd left; he called the Marquettes' house. He got their machine. He called Lilly's cell phone and got her voice mail, which was odd because she always had her phone handy. But it was a big house; maybe her purse was in another room. It was early still. He'd try again later.

At eight-forty-five, he put his phone on call forwarding and walked over to Noreen's to hook up an RBD: Random

Barking Dog. The neighbors loved his RBDs, especially the women. Susannah's was a golden retriever. Mickey and Glen went for two yappy miniature schnauzers—go figure. Noreen was getting her very own Doberman pinscher, whose bark was spiced with some very convincing rumbling growls. He'd formatted them so there was no repeat pattern to pick up on. Susannah even had a sub woofer to imitate the sound of a large dog thumping against the door.

It wasn't high-tech, but it kept him busy and made the neighbors happy. And you never knew when someone with connections would see it and want to talk to him.

Noreen had been a stay-at-home mom back when that was the norm, and now she was a stay-at-home grandmother who babysat half a dozen of her grandchildren while her own kids pursued careers. She was pleasantly round, always smiling, and didn't worry about keeping up with fashion.

When she heard Jake had forgotten to eat supper, she *tsk-tsk*ed, warmed over a casserole, and insisted he fill his stomach before she'd let him work. The portion hadn't been modest, but conversation was pleasant, it took his mind off Lilly for ten minutes, and his plate was clean before he knew it.

Installing an RBD was too simple; it allowed him time to think. To worry. And then to castigate himself, because Lilly was undoubtedly fine. Donna'd look out for her. Brady always said Donna doted on Lilly.

Then again, Brady'd said a lot of things that weren't true.

Would Lilly be impressed if Andrew pulled out all the stops—like champagne corks—and made a play for her?

"Jake, phone call. It's your dad."

He was installing a sensor at the front door when Noreen handed him the cordless. He propped it between his shoulder and ear and continued to work. "Hey, Dad."

"I hope you're getting paid."

He didn't mean it like it sounded, he didn't even mean money, but he'd cautioned Jake about refusing some form of payment and making the neighbors feel uncomfortably indebted. Susannah was the only one Jake had been stubborn about, and that was because she'd been looking out for him since he'd been in diapers.

"Noreen makes a killer casserole." He tossed her a wink, making her blush girlishly. "I'm moving in with her when you get home."

"Oh you." Noreen waved him off and left the room.

"Good for you," his dad said. "Now that the contracts're all signed, your mother and I were wondering what you're doing about Lilly Marquette."

He wondered how to break the news to his dad. "You're not gonna believe this."

"Try me."

"Well, I think you'd like her. Mom, too. No, I know you would. She's a really good person, with this really big heart. She didn't know beans about the insurance money until I told her. Turns out Brady changed the beneficiary. I've also found out for myself that a lot of what Brady told me about her just isn't true," he said. "You're awful quiet. Aren't you going to say anything?"

"I thought you were rattling on just fine." His dad sounded amused. "I knew you were taken with her the day she married Brady."

"You did?" Jake couldn't have been more surprised if the house had suddenly fallen on him.

"Oh hell yes. You came home from California for the wedding the same as you always were—you know, cheerful, controlled, glad to see us, looking forward to a week of your mother's cooking. Then you put on your tux and went to the wedding. The next morning, you were a changed man." His dad's voice grew lower. "You had this horrified look on your face, and you were throwing clothes into your bag willy-nilly while you called the airline and demanded they save you a seat on the next flight out. You wouldn't talk about it. You were so upset, you forgot to kiss your mother good-bye."

Geez.

"Julie explained later."

Of course. His sister had worked for the Marquettes back then. She'd been at the wedding. *Shit*, he'd probably made a spectacle of himself.

"Don't worry, son, I know what you're thinking. Julie's just real intuitive that way."

"Must've gotten it from you."

"My radar must be off. I thought you were over her when you came home this time."

"Me too."

"So if she really is such a good person, what's the problem?"

Jake sighed. "The problem is she's my best friend's widow."

"So? You love her, right?"

"Yes," he said without hesitation.

"Son, Brady's gone. He loved you like a brother. If this

is what you really want, he'd want you to be happy, don't you think?"

"But—"

"Wouldn't you, if the shoe were on the other foot?"

"But—" Sure, it made sense coming from his dad, who had more distance and could be more logical about it. "Gotta go, Dad." He had to go get Lilly.

"You think the feeling's mutual?"

Jake laughed, remembering Friday evening on Lilly's granite island, his heart lighter even as parts south grew heavier. "Oh yeah. She's been after me since the day she came into the store."

He raced through the rest of the installation, eager to see if Lilly was home yet. At ten, as he stepped through his back door, it was obvious she wasn't. He grabbed the taxi keys off the hook and headed straight for Lilly.

Lilly lay sprawled on her back on the floor for a long while, knowing she was still alive, thinking the bracelet had finally zapped her into unconsciousness, how could Jake possibly deny any heavenly connection now, and what book would he choose to read to pay up on their bet? She doubted it'd be tarot or channeling, since he was strongly biased against those two.

As she slowly became more lucid, she realized all was not right. Jake never would've dumped her on the floor of Donna's third-story attic office. After a while, and she had no conception of time, she remembered Drew had driven her here, they'd talked to Donna and—

Oh yeah, now she remembered. Even though she'd been moved, she was still at the Marquettes'. Brady's old bedroom was on the floor below her. But not Brady, of course. She might feel weak and powerless and muddled, but at least her memory was unimpeded.

Had Brady known *all* of his immediate family were less than the fine, upstanding people they appeared to be? He knew about his father, of course; he'd laughed about how Frank always got what he wanted, one way or another.

Was her father-in-law behind this? Did he think Donna and Andrew could handle her and get the job done? Whatever the job was. She figured she was about to find out when she heard a key slip into the lock.

"Lilly, you awake yet?"

She lay very still, listening to Andrew's soft footsteps across the attic floor, trying to determine whether he'd paused long enough to lock the door behind him. She didn't think so. Surreptitiously, she slipped her feet out of her shoes; maybe without heels she'd be able to dart past him.

Did Jake wonder what she was doing this evening, whether she was enjoying dinner with her former in-laws? Did he miss her?

"I know you're awake, I can tell by your breathing. Here, drink this, you'll feel better."

Drew knelt beside her, lifted her a little until she was semireclined against him, and held her woozy head. His hand was warm on her cheek, and she had all she could do not to spit in his face. Liquid poured into her mouth before she could refuse, but there was no way she was swallowing anything in this house ever again. That she did spit out, and *oh dear*, it sprayed all over Andrew's face.

He whipped a handkerchief out of his jacket and

dabbed his skin. "Come on, it'll help you wake up." He tipped the glass to her lips again.

She knocked it out of his hand.

"Sorry about your drink. I had no idea Mother was going to do that."

"Right."

"Seems like it's wearing off anyway."

"What time is it?"

"Nine-thirty, give or take."

"I don't suppose it'll do any good to say I want to go home now."

"'Fraid not. Mother wants to talk to you first."

Lilly's eyebrows would've arched in response to such an outrageous proposition, but her face felt heavy, so she doubted anything moved at all.

Donna entered the office in her normal brisk pace. "Ah, Lilly dear, you're awake. Goodness, I had no idea you were so *sensitive*, dear. Help her sit up, Andrew. Over by the desk."

Andrew shifted position and slipped his hands beneath Lilly's arms.

"I'm not—Leave me alone," Lilly said. "Oh God, my head's spinning, Drew, I have to sit down. No, not the chair."

She was so woozy, she'd fall off it, which'd hurt like hell whether or not she broke any bones. Andrew aimed her for it anyway, but her knees buckled—she didn't do anything to resist that, *so there*—and she ended up on the floor next to the chair, draping her arms and head across the needlepoint seat.

She closed her eyes, hoping that if she couldn't see the

room waver, it wouldn't, but that didn't work. If things didn't settle down soon, she was going to be sick. Oh, and on the nice Oriental rug, too. Shucks.

"You were only supposed to get a little mellow," Donna said, "so I could explain things to you, reason with you. You're much too close to the situation to see it for what it really is. It's not good to spend so much time with that Jake fellow. You're under his control. Giving away all of Brady's money doesn't make sense, dear. You'll see that when you're away from that man for a while. When you think things through."

"So—what? You're going to keep me here?"

"Just until I convince you. I wouldn't do anything to hurt you, you know that. This will be for your own good, you'll see."

Lilly snorted, at which she thought Donna frowned, but her facial features were still too distorted to tell. Didn't matter. Lilly had already shifted her murky focus to planning a break for the door. That's *if* Andrew didn't reach out, brush her with his pinky, and knock her flat on her face.

"You'll be yourself again soon."

"I am myself." Giddy, Lilly laughed at that. "What the heck did you give me?"

"Oh," Donna said, annoyed. "I can see it's too soon for this discussion."

Lilly spotted a pen on the desk. Hm, nice pointy end. Not a bad weapon. It looked even better when Donna leaned in, very close, very vulnerable. Was it possible to stab it all the way through her hand and plunge it into the wood desktop, anchoring her there? God, she hoped so. Maybe later, when it quit moving.

Lilly wasn't sure how many minutes passed between the time they left her alone and when Elizabeth showed up. In her present condition, how could she even be sure Elizabeth was really there?

"Yes, I'm definitely here."

"Did Brady know what a stinker his mother is?"

"Oh, I think so."

"Jake's family is nice, though, right? A good place to raise our son?"

When Elizabeth smiled, there was a glow about her. "Yes, they're very nice."

"Are you here to help me?"

"I can only talk to you to keep you awake. I'm afraid you'll have to get out of here on your own."

Lilly was ready to jump into action right then.

Okay, *jump* might have been a little strong, as she immediately found herself on the floor on her butt again. She held her breath, waiting to see if Donna and Andrew had heard the thump, if they'd come back in and make another go at it. But they didn't. They'd probably gone all the way back downstairs and wouldn't hear her moving around. Time to search for a way out.

"Elizabeth?"

She was gone.

Lilly checked the door first. Securely locked. Hinges on the outside. Solid wood. She even checked whether it was old enough to have the type of lock where she could push the key out the other side and reel it in on a piece of paper; it was, but the key wasn't in it.

There was no phone plugged into the jack, no alarm control pad—no surprise there, but Lilly looked anyway. She opened the curtains and flicked the desk lamp on and off, three short, three long, though she couldn't remember which letter was which in Morse code, so she could be sending OSO for all she knew. And who knew if anyone would see it, if anyone would call the police, or if a neighbor would just call Donna and say something funny was going on up in her attic.

Better quit. Better find something better.

Hmm, she couldn't call the police, but if she could make smoke, the alarm system would summon the fire department. Then she could hang out the window and scream her head off.

Jake sped through the dark streets to the Marquette mansion. He had no reason to think anything was wrong, not really. But he worried just the same.

He powered up his notebook computer, networked to the receiver mounted on the shelf behind the rear seat, and picked up the signal from the watch Lilly had donned that morning. Rachel had it made for her feminine side; sometimes she got hassled when she was out in drag at night. She thought a record could be useful.

Jake wouldn't track Lilly or listen in under normal circumstances, but he knew the Marquette men were shady characters. With Lilly still not answering her phone, the worst-case scenario might be the very one he'd encounter, so he began an immediate download.

Meanwhile, he dialed the Marquettes' number on his cell phone. This time, to his relief, Donna answered.

"I'd like to talk to Lilly," he said.

"She's not here right now. Who's calling?"

"Jake Murdoch."

"Oh. Jake." Definitely a chill there. "Drew drove Lilly

back to her house right after dinner. She remembered something in a closet that she thought he'd like. You know, something of Brady's."

Hair on the back of his neck stood up. Suspicious— call it experience, not intuition—he scanned the data scrolling across his screen.

Went back to her house, my ass. According to the GPS chip in the watch, Donna was lying through her teeth.

"I see." Not wanting to alert Donna that he was on to her, he said he'd try Lilly's phone and hung up.

His CATS (Converting Audio to Text Software) program began typing rapidly across the screen. He chose to read text rather than listen to old audio, because even with CATS' language limitations and negotiating his way around other cars out on the road, he could skim it faster. Real-time conversation was too slow, filled with pauses and social niceties. He read nothing pertinent during the time she'd been in the Jag and jumped ahead to her arrival at the mansion.

Sorry we're late

He skimmed ahead and stuck a bud in his ear so he could listen to current audio as he neared his target. All he heard was a shrill shriek—could be an electronic malfunction, could be an alarm. He discarded the bud to give his ear a break and went back to old text to pick up a clue.

That's sweet of you to say especially since I've gained five pounds recently

If so, it was going to all the right places. He started sweating just thinking about those places.

I'm with you Mother Lilly looks just find to me wonderful in fact

Jerk.

I'd like you to consider investing in the business

Reading had its limitations, too; he couldn't always tell who was speaking. Andrew? Donna? Hopefully not Frank. Frank was meaner'n a snake under a pile of bricks.

After an *uh-oh*, there was a bunch of gibberish, then, *I'll be okay really hay.*

Junk typed on the screen spastically, random letters, which could only mean a lot of noise that the program thought should be words, but weren't. He checked and found current audio still shrieking.

Drew Andrew this isn't funny More spastic typing. *Donna*

Then more again. The receiver in the watch wasn't able to pick up whatever was being said until *let me out of hear*

Shit! He'd parked half a block away so they wouldn't see the taxi, which stuck out like a sore thumb. He almost jumped out of the car at that point and ran and broke their door down, but when you had a system like this, you used it to its full capability. No sense going in blind.

It'll help you wake up

What the hell had they done?

Sorry about your drink I had no idea Mother was going to do that

Right

Jake felt a tremendous sense of relief to see Lilly was talking again.

Nine thirty give or take

He checked his watch. Damn, almost an hour ago. Anything could've happened since then.

Oh God my heads spinning drew

Surely this was grounds to murder the bastard, right af-ter he tortured him. If anything'd happened to Lilly—

He'd told his dad he felt guilty wanting his best friend's wife. He'd been willing to buy into the theory that Brady wouldn't mind because that's what he hoped. Now he knew beyond all doubt that what Brady would've wanted didn't matter. Time didn't matter either, whether he'd been gone five days, five months, or five years. But Lilly did. Holding her again, telling her how much he loved her, spending the rest of his life with her—that's what mattered.

This will be for your own good you'll see

Well, of course.

There was little text after that, a couple of *shit*s, and then Lilly was talking to herself again, or more correctly, she was talking to her invisible friend Elizabeth.

He inserted the bud again. He could barely hear Lilly with the shrieking, but it was enough to assure him that she was more lucid, up and moving around. Deep groans sounded like heavy furniture scooting across a wood floor. For a change, he wished she'd talk to herself some more, and louder, so he'd know what she was doing. Too bad he hadn't told her that morning just what kind of changes he'd made to Rachel's watch.

"There!"

Finally. She sounded upbeat, holding her own, giving him time to reach her.

He'd storm the Marquettes' front door, but it was un-doubtedly steel and impenetrable.

Maybe he could scale the side of the house. He scanned backward to check text—yep, he knew where Donna's office was. He could climb through a second-story window and work his way up to it. *That* door was breakable.

A sharp noise blasted through his ear bud. A gunshot? "Son of a bitch."

He sprang out of the car and took off without looking back to see if he'd even closed the door, wondering as he ran if he'd be too late.

Time for 9-1-1 after all. Halfway to the house, he reached for his cell phone, checked his belt, checked his coat pocket, checked his jeans pocket, but *damn* he'd either dropped it or left it in the taxi.

Another blast came directly from the mansion looming ahead.

"Son of a bitch!"

He raced onward, thinking, *Please don't let me lose her.*

14

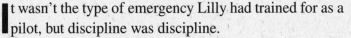

It wasn't the type of emergency Lilly had trained for as a pilot, but discipline was discipline.

She pushed a heavy desk up against the doorframe, then knotted a drapery tieback around the knob, over the desktop, and wedged it into a drawer, effectively locking Andrew out, which really ticked him off. She couldn't make out a lot of what he was yelling through the door, thanks to the screeching smoke alarm, but she wasn't waiting around for an interpretation. Nice of them, though, to lock her in an office with a metal waste can, plenty of paper, and a handy lighter. Too bad she hadn't searched through the trash first; she would've pulled out the aerosol cans before they exploded and scared her half to death.

She ripped curtains off the attic windows and knotted them together to fashion a makeshift rope.

Next she looted the attic's crawl-in storage space. Each minute she spent preparing her escape would be another minute for her drugged, shaky muscles to regain strength. Normal would be nice, but she wasn't in a position to be picky. She threw pillows and blankets and old clothes and anything else soft she could find out onto the roof a story below, to cushion her fall if the hastily constructed rope didn't hold. Even with drugs in her system, her toes still hurt; a hard landing would immobilize her.

Andrew landed a couple good smacks on the door with something large and heavy.

I'm outta here. Good-bye, thanks for a wonderful evening, don't bother walking me to the door, I'll take the window.

A soft heaping pile waited on the second-story roof below, spilling off it, as it wasn't much wider than a ledge. Falling definitely wasn't part of her plan.

Unlike the morning at Cloud Nine, this time Lilly saw Jake running to her rescue, charging into the yard like a man possessed, his entire focus on reaching the front door. She leaned out the office window and yelled to him. He pulled up short, looking both relieved that she was okay and fearful that she wouldn't be for long.

He seemed to divine her plan, as he threw both arms up in a commanding, *Don't move* gesture and bellowed, "Stay there! I'm coming up!"

"No!"

No way she was putting his life at risk again. At the dildo shop, he was a stranger who'd taken a chance; this time, he was someone she cared for, and she had a say in how everything played out. The last thing she needed or wanted was Jake getting hurt again on her behalf.

"Don't. I think Drew's got a weapon."

That didn't worry her nearly as much as what Jake

would do to Andrew. Assault would get him locked up for a while, and her timetable didn't have room for that. The fact that she couldn't get pregnant while he was held over didn't bother her except that meant she wouldn't be able to stay with him permanently. Forever was looking pretty good. She'd almost given up on forever.

She'd get out onto the roof. From there, she'd crawl along the ledge and find a sturdy drainpipe or tree to climb down, at least stay out of the way until the fire department arrived. Let Andrew and Donna explain why the only fire was a little bitty smoky one in a metal wastebasket.

She tossed her red heels out the window, and they bounced on the lawn. They were new, strappy, and sexy, and she still needed them to get Jake into bed. Next she peeled out of her stockings and swung one leg over the windowsill.

Jake yelled, "Stay there! Give me two minutes, just *stay there.*"

It was impossible to argue with someone who disappeared.

Too bad the faulty furnace had been at Cloud Nine instead of here. Donna deserved to have her precious house burn to the ground. A couple second- and third-degree burns would be justified. Something really painful but not life-threatening.

Finally, the shrieking alarm shut off. She didn't know if Donna figured out how to silence it or what. Didn't matter. What mattered was that she could hear Andrew banging on the hinges, loosening them.

Lilly glanced downward, measuring the distance to climb, the width of the ledge, the depth of the landing pile. She checked the rope—the curtains were anchored around the leg of a chair pressed against the wall—pulling and tugging on it to make sure it'd hold her weight. Even if the chair lifted off the floor, it wouldn't fit through the window, so she felt okay about things on that end. Actually climbing down a bunch of knotted curtains was another matter entirely, but they only had to keep her from tumbling two stories into the thorny pyracanthas.

Leaning backward, she scrunched her other leg through the window, then wondered how she was supposed to hold on for dear life, turn around, *and* grab the curtains. She'd just eased onto her stomach and started to slide off when she heard boots thumping across the lower roof.

"Lilly!"

Her heart melted at the sound of Jake's voice, her knight-on-a-white-steed to the rescue.

"*Don't move.*"

"You better not have hurt yourself coming up here."

Strong hands grasped her ankles. "I'm fine. Slide on down here, easy, I'll catch you."

"The ledge isn't wide enough for both of us."

"Don't argue." He tugged at her ankles.

She wiggled and slithered the rest of herself over the sill, feeling his hands slide up her legs, then her body, as she descended inside the circle of his strong arms. On the skinny ledge, Jake turned her and hugged her and nearly smothered her against his chest.

She didn't care whether she could breathe. If he held her this way forever, if she felt this cherished forever, then all would be well.

Fire trucks roared up in front of the mansion. Lilly and Jake watched together, remembering a similar scene.

"We have to quit meeting like this." His breath was hot on her ear, and he made her laugh.

"Promise."

"Come on." He took her hand and drew her carefully along the roof. "Don't look down."

She loved the way his voice was all rough and edgy and gave her goose bumps.

A subconscious sense of self-preservation forced her into a low crouch as she followed him, hand in hand, their steps slow because there was precious little moonlight on that side of the house to illuminate the way. They moved steadily onward until they reached the back of the house and the first-story covered porch that would provide a route down.

"Sit on the edge. I'll lower you." He never took his hands from her, touching her arms as he steered her, her body as she approached the copper gutter. Never had she felt so protected, so safe.

Peering over the edge as he inched her forward, she noted the more gently sloped roof below—*far* below, because the house was built with very high ceilings.

"What?" he said when she paused.

"How on earth did you get up here from there?"

"Guys with brains work out, too, you know. Chin-ups, push-ups, the whole works. Now sit."

She dangled her legs over the edge, feeling cold copper against the backs of her thighs.

"Now just like you did up in the window, turn over onto your stomach, and I'll lower you down."

"Unless your arms telescope, I think we're in trouble."

"Shit, yours don't do that?" He crouched on the roof behind her, still touching her at all times with his strong hands. "C'mon, honey, you can do it."

She peered past her toes. "Is a smooth landing too much to hope for?"

"You ever crashed a landing yet?"

"No. Well, there was that one tiny incident when I was fifteen and overshot the end of the runway a little."

"And to think I was considering flying with you. C'mon, don't look down. Just turn around and flip over."

Cautiously, she eased into position.

"Okay. Grab hold of this." At least he'd been thinking ahead; he'd picked up one of the blankets she'd tossed out, and she hadn't even noticed.

When he told her to slip off her perch, she trusted him completely.

Under cover of darkness, Jake and Lilly stood together beneath the widespread branches of an ancient oak tree, arguing Lilly's options, which was the last thing Jake wanted to be doing right now. She wanted to march up to Donna and Andrew and punch out their lights. While Jake was somewhat in favor of this, he had something better in mind, if she'd just stop pacing—actually, stumbling over tree roots—and hear him out.

"See if I sell my house to her *now*."

"Hey, listen—"

"I'll donate it to the university myself, so there. As long as they give the rent to a needy cause—"

"Listen." He grabbed her by the shoulders and held her

directly in front of him so she'd have to focus on what he had to say.

Still, she clenched her jaw and swore. "I can take Donna, I know I can."

"You know, you're cute when you're mad."

She shifted from foot to foot, her hands tightly fisted. "She may work out, but she's older'n me."

Only one way Jake could think of to shut her up, only one way he wanted to. He framed her face between his hands and kissed her, just like that—no warning, no leading up to it, no giving her a chance to back off, just get it done.

It worked. Lilly froze in place, her gaze locked with his like a deer caught in headlights. She licked her lips, tasting where his had just been. For once she was speechless, couldn't even manage a smile.

"Come on. Follow my lead." He squeezed her hand to impart a little confidence, then kissed her knuckles.

In the front yard, Donna and Andrew were huddled with a fireman and a police officer, explaining that Lilly had a drug problem and didn't really mean to set off a false alarm, but you know how these things are, it happened anyway. They'd been trying to help her through this on their own, "family, you know," but they could see now that she needed to be checked into a resident program, and what could they do to make this whole thing disappear?

"I'd like to make two Marquettes disappear."

Though Jake appreciated the sentiment, he said, "Hush," squeezing her hand where it nestled in his. "Let 'em talk."

"But—"

"Trust me."

"Fine, you listen to them, but I'm getting my purse before they steal my checkbook."

It crossed his mind to take Andrew aside and tell him about the transmitter in the watch Lilly was wearing, to offer to make the evidence disappear for a rather large contribution to the Murdoch-got-screwed fund.

But he chose the other path, the one that would get Lilly's side on record and substantiated so if anything else happened to her—and it damned well better not!—Marquettes would be the primary suspects. Once they knew that, she'd be safe. Nothing was more important to him than her safety.

He didn't wonder how or when he'd started to feel that way, because it was a combination of things she'd done and said over the past two weeks, things he'd never expected out of her: free day care for working teenage mothers, increased publicity for hotline numbers, literacy programs and adult basic education, scholarships to his alma mater, help for stray dogs and stray kids, and even something as simple and personal as a fudge treaty with Susannah.

"They're lying through their teeth," she said when she returned.

"Yeah, I know." He grinned. "Give 'em time, they'll bury themselves."

The little regard Donna and Andrew had for Lilly made Jake sick to his stomach, but Lilly's recounting to the authorities, backed up by an audio and text demonstration of the watch and software, went a long way toward making him feel better. The best part was that most of that technology had been developed with none other than Brady's money. *Ha!*

Getting Lilly home and safely in bed would finish the job. *His* bed would be nice.

And what of respect for his dead friend now?—his conscience prodded now that the adrenaline rush was over.

Well, he was pretty sure after rescuing Lilly twice that even Brady couldn't object. Rationalization?—maybe. She was a helluva kisser.

Finally thinking clearly?—more likely.

Not giving a damn anymore?—definitely. Brady was dead, Jake was here, and Lilly was going to be his. Period. Forever, if she'd have him.

After Angie, after being pulled off the path of self-destruction, he hadn't dared to share his heart with anyone else. Now—Well, now he was thinking he just might have a future with Lilly.

He only wanted what was best for her. He was it.

Lilly picked up her shoes. Jake draped his arm around her shoulders and steered her to the taxi.

Speeding homeward, safely by his side, Lilly said, "I don't know what you're smiling about. They'll still find a way to come out on top, just wait and see."

"You prefer to be on top?"

"Well of course!"

He grinned, thinking of the night ahead. "Fine by me."

Jake kept his free hand on Lilly as they sped home. Not only did she enjoy his touch on her bare leg, her arm, her hand, anywhere he could reach, she was breathless with every minute of it.

He kept asking if she was okay; she kept gasping that she was fine. She considered begging him to pull over to the curb and climb into the backseat with her.

"Jake." She was surprised to hear her voice shake.

"The hospital? Is it your arm again? Are you hurt? I'll get you there—"

"You do, and I won't sleep with you."

"Well, screw the hospital." His grasp on her hand softened. His thumb rubbed lazy circles on her thigh.

Finally, they were on the same page, and she drew confidence from that knowledge. It would take more than drugs for her to miss Jake's intentions.

Finally, she'd be able to complete two goals: step one of getting pregnant was getting him in bed, and they were almost there.

But it was the other goal giving her goose bumps and quickening her pulse: she was about to experience the passion she'd longed for, the all-consuming heat that could make up for seventeen months of abstinence and years of ho-hum sex. About that, she had no doubt. If she was this turned on while he was driving, imagine how she was going to feel when they got right down to it.

It seemed like forever before they pulled into the driveway.

"It's pretty rocky here. You might want to put on your shoes."

When she opened her door, the overhead light showed how dirty she'd gotten the bottoms of her feet. "Nah, it'll ruin them."

Jake solved that quickly, bending down and draping her across his shoulders, uttering a very put on, he-man growl as he straightened up again, making her laugh so hard she had to pee.

"I've wanted to do this ever since I carried you out of the store."

"Ah, so you *are* perverted."

His bare hand grasped her naked leg. "You know, garter belts are a lot more fun when you have stockings attached."

"I can slip some on," she said wickedly, figuring she owed him any way he wanted her.

"Sweetheart, the next thing on you is gonna be me."

A burning flame raced through her from head to toe, then returned to center and burned there, waiting for him to make good on his promise.

Dear Lord, if talk got her this hot, she wasn't going to make it through the night.

As he thumbed open the back door, she slid to her feet and reached around from behind, blindly working on his zipper, ripping it down, dragging the coat from his shoulders. She tossed it toward a kitchen chair, neither knowing nor caring where it landed.

"Wait."

"In your dreams, buster."

He pulled her around him and grinned against her lips as she kissed him. "Oh, I think this could be better than my dreams, but . . ."

Whether he said more, she couldn't say. She certainly didn't hear anything. When he fanned those strong, stone-laying hands of his up alongside her face, holding her, making it impossible for her to continue blazing a path from his lips to his chest to points farther south, she had to go still—well, all except her fingers—and listen.

"Lilly, I want you to be, no, I *need* to know you're sure about this."

"Does *take your clothes off before I rip them off* do it for you?"

"You were drugged."

"It wore off."

She pulled his shirt free from his jeans, liberating his skin to her touch. He felt *sooo* good. Ten times better than chocolate tasted. No, a hundred.

If he hadn't had such a good hold on her, she would've had his shirt over his head before he knew it, but as it was, she couldn't raise it any higher than his nipples. Which, as it turned out, made perfectly good targets for her fingers, and she rubbed and tweaked and generally drove herself more nuts than she appeared to be doing to him.

"I wouldn't want you to wake up in the morning and regret this."

"For Pete's sake, Jake, I've been after you for two weeks." She made short work of his buckle, button, and that zipper.

In a raspy voice now, he murmured against her hair, his breath hot on her scalp. "It's important that . . . that I know . . . hell, I don't know, but I'm sure it was something."

She breathed against his lips, lifting herself up, her skirt hiking itself around her hips as she wrapped her legs around him, pulling herself in tightly to where his jeans were spread open and he had only briefs to protect his erection.

"See how strong I am, Jake? Feel how tight I can hold you?"

His murmur was unintelligible.

"Feel me move against you?"

"Shit, my jeans're falling down."

"Good."

"No, you don't understand."

"I think *you* don't understand."

"If they fall down, I won't be able to get us up the stairs."

She took a long, long moment sliding down him, teasing him naughtily on the way, wiggling against him, feeling her own moistness before she let go and yanked his jeans up.

He jumped. "Uh, careful."

"Okay, big guy, get us upstairs."

He scooped her up, right back where she'd just been, sliding his large hands under her skirt and cupping her bare butt as her thighs locked his jeans safely in place.

"Hot damn, another thong," he whispered raggedly. "Hold on tight."

"Oh I intend to."

His devastating grin indicated he was back in control, sure of himself, sure of her, certain he was going to give her the ride of her life.

They fell onto his bed together. Clothes flew every direction until they were both naked, and no matter how hard she tried to roll them over and get beneath him—because for this first time, she wanted him to be in control, really needed him to give her all the passion she'd dreamed of—he held her on top where his hands were free to roam, driving her slowly, madly insane with need.

Turns out his hands were highly accomplished with a lot more than laying stone and building gizmos. They were doing a fantastic job laying her and building her toward a shattering climax.

"Oh God, Jake, *now*."

He shifted then, finally rolling to one side. Just when she thought *finally*, she realized he was reaching toward the nightstand.

Shit. She didn't need this. She was about to burst, swollen and wet with need, aching for him to push inside her, and he was maintaining a comparatively clear head, fumbling for the drawer. No way she was letting him get a condom.

"*Oh God, Jake*," she gasped loudly, then louder again because it seemed to interfere with him grasping anything he didn't already have his hands on—*her*. He moaned in response, which made her hotter and she thought she was going to come too early. She wanted it to be with him.

Catching him off guard, she grasped his shoulders and rolled the both of them over, away from the drawer.

"Lilly." He started to say something, but then his mouth was all over her, tasting her, kissing her. His fingers dipped low between their bodies and played her intimately until she was mindless and breathless and boneless and desperate to feel him inside her.

"Now, Jake," she whispered. "Please."

It was the desperate *please* that did it. There was no nudging this or grasping that or pausing anywhere. She was ready, and he took her in one swift movement. The dense thickness of him touched every sensitive spot inside and out and sent her flying over the edge, begging him to come with her as he pounded into her again and again.

He wouldn't have to ask how it was for her. Hell, the neighbors probably knew, even the geriatric ones who took their hearing aids off at night. He gave her more than she'd bargained for, one orgasm after another until she thought she'd pass out.

When they finally lay still, arms and legs and sheets all tangled together while they caught their breath and let their heartbeats slow, he chuckled low and deep near her ear.

"Remind me never to take you to a motel."

"Yeah, like that'd ever happen."

"You wouldn't go to a motel with me?"

"Shoot, I'm not letting you out of this bed until you're too old to do it again."

He sighed and laughed and rolled to the side, taking her with him, pillowing her head on his shoulder. "Don't worry. I'm not going anywhere."

She prayed that she wouldn't be either, that she'd make her deadline.

15

What an incredible night.

Jake meant what he'd said when he told Lilly he wasn't going anywhere. He'd promised her breakfast in bed, and it sure as hell wasn't going to be burned, so he kept a close eye on the bacon grilling in the Foreman and thick slices of French toast browning in a large skillet.

Man, could that woman make love.

Now normally, being a guy, he wouldn't use that term in relation to sharing a bed with a woman he'd spoken to less than twenty-one days out of his entire life. It would've been something more basic like screw or fuck. But it hadn't been basic screwing to him—love did that—and he was pretty sure it hadn't been to Lilly, either.

She seemed to have a one-track mind recently, bent on getting him in the sack for what he'd thought would be a simple quickie—for her. Being with her could never be simple for him. Once there, though, he sensed something totally different on her part, a real connection.

Not only had she been making love last night, but mad, *passionate* love. Missionary, on top, doggy style, positions that probably didn't have names and variations on the ones that did. She'd been a woman possessed, insatiable—in a good way—and *determined*.

She'd been shy about making noise until he whispered how much it turned him on, which it did, then forget volume control. She hadn't been shy about demanding what she needed—hell, what guy wouldn't love that?

Her actions as much as told him he didn't need condoms, so she was obviously in charge of birth control, which was a good thing, because he had a lot of lean years ahead, getting his business started up again. Given time, he'd pull in enough money to support her.

Well, except for her charity habit. He didn't mind her giving her money away—it was hers—but he had plans for his, so there'd be no joint bank account.

She strolled into the kitchen then, wearing his favorites—a red thong and garter belt, a lacy bra cut so low it was probably illegal in forty states, a pair of stockings, and *oh yeah*, those strappy high heels.

"You have a thing for red, don't you?"

She shot him a saucy grin. "I have a thing for you."

"Really? I'm glad you told me, because, you know, I wasn't sure last night. All that moaning, it could mean anything."

He turned the toast, his hands itching to get back on her breasts again. He'd promised her breakfast, though. But then she swooped up behind him, lifted his unbuttoned shirt, and rubbed her barely covered breasts against his back.

"We'd better do it again, then," she said. "You let me know which part you don't understand, and I'll explain it. In detail."

To hell with food. With his body leaping to attention, he slammed off the burner and unsnapped his jeans. If she expected him to keep up this pace—not that that was a complaint, because it wasn't—eventually they'd have to raid his trunk. He had a nice selection of new toys they could try out together.

"What's that?"

He followed her curious gaze to the multimeter he'd left on the table. It was small, not much larger than a pack of cigarettes, and he'd brought it upstairs to test her charm bracelet, but later. Much later.

"That, sweetheart, is how I'm going to prove there's nothing heavenly about your bracelet."

"So you say."

"So I do."

Abruptly, she pulled a chair out from the table and sat down.

"*Now?*" he asked with disbelief, and she said, "So there's nothing between us."

On his way to another chair, he trailed his fingers along her bra strap, over her shoulder, and down to the lacy cup. "*Nothing* sounds great."

"Later, I promise. Now, what do I do?"

He patted the table. "Rest your arm here, sweet cheeks."

"Keep up that sexy talk, and more'll be cooking in this kitchen than breakfast."

"Countertop sounds interesting. Hold still." He hooked leads to clips, and clips to her bracelet. His fingers were bumbling and uncooperative with a greater desire to be unhooking something else.

"Hey, I'm not the one dropping parts."

"Watch here." He tapped the readout. "If there's any actual—as opposed to static, mind you—if any actual electricity runs through the bracelet, you'll see the needle move. See? Deader'n a doornail."

She snickered. "You call this scientific?"

"You have a better idea?"

"Yeah, watch the meter. Go on, I don't want you to miss this. Now ask me to write you a check for three million dollars."

He shook his head. "It doesn't matter—"

"Ask me."

"Lilly, I'm trying to tell you—"

"Afraid I'm right?"

He sighed. It'd be simpler to give in and get this over with so he could get it on with her again. "Okay, write me a check for three million dollars."

"Demand it."

He said it again, the roughness in his tone belied by trying very hard not to laugh at himself.

"Okay." She sounded surprised when nothing registered. "Since I'm all connected here, you go get my checkbook and a pen. *There*! Oh, you weren't looking."

He'd seen the spike out of the corner of his eye, but it had to be a fluke, so he didn't admit it. "Where's your purse?"

"Oh. Hm." She glanced around the room. "Must still be in the car."

"Don't move."

Not that he thought she would. He was pretty sure she was as eager as he to get this behind them. Then they could get on the counter or go upstairs or do it anywhere she wanted. He ran for the car, nearly tripping over the cat as it made a beeline for the kitchen.

Upon Jake's return, Lilly flipped open the checkbook and dated the top check.

"Watch that meter. If I get all the way through this, you're going to win a whole lot more than a measly bet."

"Lilly," he said softly. "I don't want your money. It doesn't matter. Even if you'd asked Brady to change the policy—"

"Which I didn't."

"—you're not the kind of woman who'd take—"

"Damn straight. But I feel I owe you some—"

Lilly'd barely begun writing his name when the meter spiked to the top, and the charge catapulted her right out of her chair. She would've sprawled on the floor if he hadn't reached out and grabbed her, albeit awkwardly.

No way!

Jake began analyzing, hypothesizing why it had happened and why the needle still vacillated about midway. But it was hard to concentrate with Lilly straddling one thigh in next to nothing, begging him to tear up the check, and the cat clawing him above the knee in a frantic attempt to join her.

He sent Mooch flying, then tapped the multimeter, turning it this way and that, examining it. "But—"

"*Now.*"

"Oh." He ripped the check in half, not because he believed in any angel crap, but because he hated the strain and irritation in Lilly's voice, and he'd do anything to stop her from being hurt—even though this couldn't possibly be the cause. No way.

Still, meters didn't lie.

She sagged in relief against his chest, her head tucked up against his neck in a pose of complete trust. With each shred of the check, he discarded one theory after another.

Mooch took a retaliatory bite out of his ankle and glared up at him. Relishing the feel of Lilly's soft hair against his cheek, Jake muttered, "Wasn't me who hurt her."

Though he was at a loss to say exactly whose fault it was.

With Lilly's heat straddling his leg and her breasts spilling out of the low-cut lace right in front of him, right below his mouth, his concentration was irrevocably broken. He groaned as he said, "Oh, this is so not fair."

"Not convinced?" Her lips brushed softly against his neck.

"Only that something other than static's going on, but I need time to figure out what."

"And you want to do that *now*?" She wiggled on his thigh.

At the moment, rational breakthroughs were impossible. Shoving the equipment aside, Jake surged to his feet and sat Lilly on the table, missing her grip on his thigh already. "Obviously I didn't do my job last night."

She chuckled deliciously as he towered over her. "You mean it gets better?"

"I don't know about better. But I remember you begging me to fuck your brains out, and it appears to me that you're still thinking."

"I didn't!" Her lustful laugh was laced with invitation.

"Oh yes." He bent her backward until she was spread on

the table before him, the narrowness of her thong barely concealing her from him. "You most certainly did."

"Well then, big guy." She dipped her thumbs into the top band and V'd it downward, out of his way, revealing the nest of curls he hadn't seen in oh, twenty minutes or so. "Better get to it."

An hour later, Jake poked at the French toast in the cold skillet, wondering if it was salvageable. He turned the burner back on to give breakfast another try.

Lilly was still upstairs, singing bawdy love songs in the shower, and he was tempted to turn the stove off and go see what else she came up with, but the phone rang.

Andrew opened with a smooth, "Congratulations on taking round two."

"Go to hell."

"Don't you want to know what round one was?"

"Go fuck yourself, Marquette."

Andrew laughed. "Oops, can't say over the phone. You probably have *three million* ways of bugging it. Father warned Brady not to put money into your little side business. It wasn't right."

Brady'd understood his family better than Jake thought, whereas he'd just underestimated them.

"Oh," Andrew continued, "you know that three million dollar life insurance policy Lilly's buying?"

He didn't.

"Don't count on it either."

Wow was Lilly's opinion of the passionate night she'd wanted and received. *Double wow*—she'd gotten a morning of it, too. If she died right now, in this shower, she couldn't say she hadn't had the best time of any woman ever.

She felt boneless.

She ached deliciously in all the right places.

She couldn't stop singing.

When Jake had shared the shower with her earlier, she'd teased him with lusty, improvised lyrics like *I could have spread my legs* and *Get me to the bed on time*. When she belted out *Murdoch is a girl's best friend*, he grinned mischievously and said he'd heard that vibrators were a girl's best friend. Then he was off to salvage their breakfast.

And as sure as she was standing under the most delicious spray of pulsating hot water, her night hadn't been just about sex. Jake was too tender, too playful, too powerful, and far too generous to be just about sex. He didn't have to say it; she could see it in his eyes, feel it in every touch of his skin against hers, hear it in every word he murmured, every query as to what she liked and how she wanted it.

Now that she'd finally gotten him in bed and knew he'd be back for more, she needed to bone up on increasing her chances of conception. Not only did she want that baby, she wanted Jake, every night and every day, forever.

She enjoyed the shower until she ran out of hot water, thinking mostly of Jake, grateful that he was an adventurous and generous lover. Afterward, she sprinkled in a few plans for her day and the week ahead: giving money away and disposing of more personal assets, like her wedding and engagement rings. Nothing that would interfere with their nights.

"Hungry?" Jake asked when she strolled into his room, wrapped in one navy towel, blotting her hair with another.

He was lounging on the bed, his dark blue robe belted

so loosely that it didn't even cover his smooth chest, and he was halfway through a heap of French toast, smothered in syrup and heavily dusted with powdered sugar.

"It's not as good as the first or second time I cooked it"—he winked—"but it's passable."

"Couldn't wait for me, huh?"

"Are you kidding? You're insatiable. Eating while you're in the shower's the only chance I get to fortify myself. I have to keep up my energy, you know. Here, sit down, have some."

She crawled onto the bed and opened her mouth as he aimed a forkful her way.

"Oh my gosh, you think that's not good?" She caught a dribble of syrup running down her chin and sucked it off her finger. "No wonder you're such a great lover. Are you a perfectionist at everything?"

"I'm great, huh?"

The light in his eyes danced, and she hoped he wasn't going to demand a list of his many ways. "Shut up, you know you are. I told you so often enough."

"Ninety times, at least."

"Maybe if you count by tens."

"Here, have another bite. Not to spoil the mood or anything, but Andrew called while you were in the shower."

She couldn't talk with her mouth full, so she squeaked something that sounded like *What'd he want?*

"He says you're buying life insurance."

She threw her hands up in the air. "That does it. I need a new agent, too."

"I'll take that as a yes. This doesn't have anything to do with paying me back, does it?"

"Jake, I meant it when I said I'd find a way. And if some-

thing happens to me before I do, then that base is covered."
She grabbed his hand, steering more food her way.

"Boy, you really worked up an appetite, didn't you?"

"Mm-hm."

He set the plate aside and kissed away her pretty pout.
"Listen, before we get sidetracked . . . After talking to Andrew, I know who—not how or when, but *who*—changed
the beneficiary. If anybody owes me anything, it's the
Marquettes."

"Can we prove it?"

He snorted. "Frank Marquette has never been caught at
anything yet." He took her hands in his. "While we're on
the topic of money, there's something I know Brady'd
want me to pass on to you, about investing money back
into the family business."

"As if."

"I know, but I can't stop thinking about it, just in
case. The reason he and I went into business together
was because he eventually wanted to distance himself
from the rest of his family. I'm sure he wanted to protect you."

"We both knew they're manipulative."

"Now there's an understatement." He cocked his head
and studied her intently. "He really loved you, you know.
And for good reason." His thumb absently traced circles
on the back of her hand, holding the connection between
them even as Lilly felt the topic shift. "Can I tell you
something?"

"Maybe." If it was anything like *we need to slow down*—
maybe caring for her was scaring him—she'd better be
ovulating, like *now*.

"I don't want to scare you . . ."

Too late.

"I know we met years ago, but we've really only known each other a few weeks."

Just under, by her count. She held her breath, hoping this wasn't *We're moving too fast* or *We should take a break.* She wanted a baby, yes, but more than that, she wanted the whole package. She wanted Jake, marriage, happily ever after; her limited window of opportunity made her impatient.

"And I don't expect you to feel the same way yet," he said, "but it's all the time I need. Lilly, I love you." He caressed her hand between both of his, squeezed it, drew it to his lips. He nuzzled her knuckles, keeping a little space between them while he pinned her with his gaze and finished what he'd begun. "It's fast, I know—a real whirlwind—but there's not a single doubt in my heart."

She couldn't believe her ears. Oh, she'd felt it last night; she knew he was in love with her. She just didn't know *he* knew it.

"That's great! Jake, I lo—"

He pressed his fingers against her lips, cutting off her reply. "No, don't. You don't have to say it just because I did. This is a long-standing tradition in my family, love at first sight. I expected it. Damn, I probably should've been more romantic and sprinkled camellia petals on the sheets and lit candles, right?" He grinned crookedly, then. "But as much as you enjoy food, French toast and powdered sugar was probably better."

She mumbled, "But, Jake," against his fingertips.

"Wait, there's more. You should know I've loved you since the day we met."

She tugged his hand away from her mouth. "But I *want* to— Oh."

"Yeah. Your wedding day." He shook his head ruefully. "Don't think that didn't make me feel like a heel, falling for my best friend's bride."

So many things made sense now; the anger, the running away, the guilt. "That's why you left town so fast."

"Yes."

"And stayed away." She groaned, not sure he hadn't delivered the bomb yet. "You're not going to tell me we can't do this anymore, are you? I couldn't stand it if you do."

"No." The teasing light she was so used to returned to his eyes. "I held out as long as I could, though. And even if you don't love me yet, you'll catch up."

"You're not going to believe me, are you? I love you, you think it's too fast, and therefore you're not going to believe me." He, who had so much trouble with beliefs.

"It hasn't been as long for you."

"Ah. And you're a 'hard data' kind of guy."

"True."

She framed his face with her hands this time, said, "Then analyze this," and placed her lips on his, softly, tenderly pledging her love in a language she hoped he could connect with. Tumbling him onto his back, they shared a long, lascivious kiss that surely spoke to all his senses, inside and out, and told him she, too, had no doubts. She segued into planting slow, feather-light kisses over his chin, down his neck, down his chest.

"Would you do something for me?" He gasped as she pushed his robe aside and flicked her tongue over a nipple.

"Something wicked, I hope."

"Look, uh . . ." He seemed to have trouble forming a coherent thought as she worked her way lower. "While I appreciate the thought, you know, about the *ah*—About the insurance, the fact is, there's only one way I could collect. You'd have to—" He cleared his throat. "And uh—Geez, wait, just let me say—"

Struggling for words, he pulled her on top of him, into the circle of his arms, where he framed her face with his big hands in the tender, protective way she'd come to identify with him and only him, the way she loved him to touch her. He looked her straight in the eyes, making her feel like the only woman in his universe, as if the house could fall down around their ears and he wouldn't even notice as long as she was right there in front of him.

"I lost you once before when you married Brady, but I understood that I was too late then. Now I don't know what I'd do without you."

"You won't have to find out. Jake, I love you. I'm here to stay. That'll be your hard data. Every morning when you wake up and see me sleeping beside you, you'll know. I promise." She sat up on him, unwrapped her towel slowly, and tossed it aside. "Now, where was I?"

Lilly made a stab at cooking the next meal for Jake. She wasn't quite sure where this domestic streak had come from, but if there was anyone she wanted to cook for, it was he. She'd opened a can of broth, dumped in rice and frozen vegetables, and was watching carefully to keep the soup from boiling over when Elizabeth suddenly appeared in the middle of the kitchen.

"*Holy mother of*—Swear to me you'll never show up when we're making love."

"Mm, sorry," Elizabeth said with a sly grin. "I'm pretty sure swearing is against the rules."

Lilly winced, equally sure she'd messed up there. "I'm *trying* to clean up my act." She rooted through a cabinet, found a jar of dried basil, sniffed it, then dumped a spoonful into the soup.

"Your attempt has been less than stellar."

"But you're not here about that."

Elizabeth's grin disappeared.

"What? Shit, you're not here to take me back. You can't be. I'm doing everything you said—"

"Yes, well, about that. I had so much to tell you, and I had a feeling I'd forgotten something very important."

"Oh no. No no no, we had a deal. You gave me the rules. I agreed. Quit pacing, goddammit, and talk to me."

Elizabeth pulled a chair out from the table, and way too quietly said, "You'd better sit down."

Lilly backed against the counter. "I'm not going."

"Well, yes, eventually you are."

"Eventually." Lilly sighed with relief. "Minus the five years you just scared me out of. I'm in love with Jake. That's good, right? I can marry him and have the family I've always—*What?*"

Elizabeth, still pacing, had her face buried in her hands and was shaking her head slowly. Regretfully.

Feeling cold, as if all the blood suddenly drained out of her body, Lilly closed her eyes and whispered, "Just tell me."

"Remember how I said you'd died too early?"

Lilly nodded.

Elizabeth faced her then and took a deep breath. "You weren't supposed to die before your next birthday. But, Lilly, I never meant you to believe you'd live *past* your next birthday either. I just didn't think to say it."

16

Lilly sank to the kitchen floor, her back against the wall. Literally and proverbially. She was alone.

Grant me serenity.

She'd blown that concept all to hell, and no, she wasn't concerned about a little more cussing at this point—what difference did it make now?

How had this happened? It had all seemed so easy in Transition. Go back, get pregnant, get poor—well, that last part hadn't seemed easy, but then it wasn't the part weighing on her mind right now, either.

She was still going to die.

No matter that she really wanted babies to love and raise and do a better job of it than her mother had. To hug and cuddle and do PTA and carpooling, attend Little League and soccer games, go trick-or-treating, the whole nine yards. To watch her firstborn grow into a man, strong and caring like his father.

But *nooo*, she had to give birth and abandon her infant

practically in the same day. Maybe even the same day, for all she knew. She hadn't asked.

God, grant me courage to deal with this.

Besides being unfair to her son, this was so beyond unfair to Jake that she didn't even have a word for it. He'd be a single father. Not that he wouldn't have lots of support—he was on the phone with at least one sister every day—but he'd refuse to be anything but a hands-on dad, when what he needed was the time to reestablish himself and his business.

She'd been on the losing end when Brady had died, and before that, when she'd miscarried. She knew how hard it was to be left behind to grieve. Jake didn't deserve such pain, such sorrow.

This was just too awful. Lilly heard Jake in his basement office, heard his chair squeak as he moved. She wanted to run to him, curl up on his lap, tuck her head beneath his chin, and let him make it all better, but he couldn't. She needed space, time to be alone with her thoughts and see if it was possible to make peace with this. Time to figure out what to do about it. She postponed most of her appointments for that day, hoping Jake would jump at the opportunity to be on his own and go somewhere.

No such luck, so she had him drop her at the mall.

"What're you doing?" she asked, when he pulled into a slot.

"Parking."

"But I'll be here for hours. I'll call you when I'm done."

"Lilly, it might help to talk."

It didn't surprise her that he knew something was

amiss, but it wouldn't help her to discuss it until she had a better handle on it. It certainly wouldn't help him. "I'm meeting Betsy."

"I like Betsy."

No way she could be objective with Jake beside her; she needed time alone. *Grant me wisdom.*

"We'll be doing girl stuff, Jake."

"Oh." Then a more enlightened, "Ohhh."

Though his brow puckered, he didn't ask what kind of girl things two grown women did in a public mall. Growing up with sisters apparently had bestowed some wisdom about when to keep his mouth shut. And so he dropped her at the mall entrance, promising to return in a few hours, sooner if she called.

She wasn't meeting Betsy, of course, because she really did need to be by herself. Lunch at Bread Company; totally alone in a crowd. Strolling both levels of the mall; completely ignored by everyone, even when she became so engrossed in her thoughts that she stopped walking and shoppers had to split into smaller groups to ripple around her. Especially when she kept sniffling and wiping tears away.

Dying wouldn't be so peaceful this time; it would hurt too bad to leave Jake. But the real kicker was: If it hurt this bad to leave him, think how he'd feel.

There should be a *grant me strength* part to that prayer.

He hadn't asked for her to come back into his life, sleep with him, fill him with hope and thoughts of the future. He didn't deserve to have his heart bruised and battered.

If she was this vested in Jake's feelings after a matter of weeks, she couldn't even imagine how she was going to feel about leaving her son after being connected twenty-four/ seven for nine months. When her nanny had asked what her favorite toy was, she'd said her dolls because they were her babies and they needed her. When one of her boarding school teachers asked what she wanted to be when she grew up, she said a mommy. What an innocent she'd been.

Bringing any baby into the Marquette family would have been a mistake, especially one who was supposed to do great things. Why give the little guy a rocky start?

But Jake's family—now there was a bunch of people who looked out for each other, stayed in touch daily. They obviously liked each other a lot, and each other's kids, too. All the family photos, in the house, on the dash, provided a silent window into his world, which was just where she would've liked to raise her babies. Mommy and children get-togethers instead of nannies. Cousins in the same class instead of boarding school. Touch football on the lawn on Thanksgiving.

But it wasn't to be. She couldn't change what she'd agreed to; she had to take control of the time she had left. If she was lucky, she'd met the goal that would allow her to stay another nine months, because she *so* wanted all that time with Jake. She needed it, too, to prepare him for the inevitable. He needed it, even if he didn't know it. But just in case, before she left the mall, she bought everything she needed to know on timing ovulation.

If she was going to go through with this and bring her son into a world without being there to guide him through the pitfalls, was it possible to eliminate some of them *now*? To shape his future *before* his birth? Jake was about as perfect as a man came, except for his annoying habit of writing off everything that didn't have a basis in scientific fact.

Considering what had transpired with John and Elizabeth to conceive him in the first place, that was just wrong.

Lilly took the only route she had. She purchased the book Jake was going to read to pay off his bet and begin to open his mind. Hopefully. This book this month, another one next month, and who knew? Maybe, by the time she was called back, he'd come around.

Jake finally had reason to be grateful that he'd grown up at the mercy of all his sisters' mysterious moods; otherwise, he wouldn't have a clue what was up with Lilly when he picked her up at the mall.

"Feel better?"

"I'm fine," she said. No teasing retort about how he could feel her and see for himself. No sassy bounce in her step. When her cell phone rang as they headed into the city, she checked caller ID and slammed the phone onto the seat. "Ha! Like I want to talk to Donna?"

"You, uh, given any thought to filing charges against the Marquettes?"

"Life's too short. It's not worth the headache."

He wisely thought if he wanted to know more about that, he'd have a better chance of getting an answer later when she was more herself.

He tagged along on the one appointment she hadn't canceled. He had no pressing business at the moment—just waiting on a call back, and he had his cell phone handy at all times. In half an hour, they were in and out of an organization that helped low-income parents with high utility bills. Lilly was a hundred thousand dollars lighter.

"I see you quit closing your eyes when you sign checks."

"Yeah." An infectious smile played at the corners of

her mouth as they returned to the car. "I pretend it's Donna's money. And Drew's."

"Good one."

When they were home a while, and she'd mellowed him up with a glass of wine, Lilly cuddled up beside him on the sofa and handed him a numerology book.

"I knew you wouldn't pick one out, so I did it for you."

"Oh gee, you shouldn't have."

"No problem." Her voice sparkled with mischief. "I told the clerk that you're very scientific and analytical, so he recommended this."

Jake flipped through the pages, pausing to peruse a couple. There were actually *rules* to this crap. He'd think twice before making any more bets with her.

"Scientific and analytical, huh?"

"Well, it was that or palmistry, and I didn't think you had enough hands around to make a fair study of it. But names, everybody knows lots of names. Family, friends, people you went to school with. Geez, Jake, don't look like it's your last meal or something. I'm not saying you have to believe *everything*. Just open that big sexy brain of yours to other possibilities, okay?"

"You think brains are sexy, huh?" He was intrigued. His sisters had taken him aside and explained the brains-and-brawn concept the week he'd started high school.

"Some girls go for brawn," Julie had said.

"Some go for brains," Jessica added.

"And since you've been blessed with a double dose of both, little brother, you're going to be beating them off with a stick."

"Cool," he said, more than ready for his share.

"But our girlfriends go to that high school, too."

"Treat them right—all of them—or you'll answer to us."

With four sisters, he'd learned fast, and those lessons put him in a good position now as Lilly tapped her index finger on the text, and said, "Just think of it as entertainment."

He could tell it was important to her, and since he didn't want to set off any female land mines, he humored her with a nod, albeit a grave one.

Lilly dashed outdoors most evenings to help Susannah take advantage of the nice weather and clear last year's growth out of her flower gardens, which really seemed to refresh her mood. He read the damned book. He even experimented with names and numbers during the hours she spent doing her philanthropy thing.

"Any validity to numerology?" she asked after donating money to a program to keep kids in school.

Just the opportunity he'd been waiting for. He whipped the taxi over to the curb, plucked the hissing cat off Lilly's lap, and tossed her the book. "I marked some of the pages."

"So you can go back and read them, I hope."

"To share. Read what it says about me. I followed all the rules, used my middle name. Go on, read. Page fifty."

"You're baiting me, aren't you?" She flipped through pages dotted with sticky notes, found the passage he'd nearly obliterated with scores of questions and exclamation points, and spent a minute reading.

"See?"

"I see engineers take the same penmanship class as doctors."

Oh, she couldn't distract him that easily. "Admit it, doesn't sound like me, does it?"

" 'You have a keen sense of perfection. You like to analyze and examine things from all angles.' What part of that isn't you?"

"It says I meditate. I don't meditate. And there's more, read on."

" 'You love libraries.' Hm, who was so protective of Brady's collection?"

"Skip that part."

" 'You're intellectual, scientific, dedicated, loyal, honest—' "

He roared with frustration and snatched the book out of her hands, ignoring her bubbling laughter. " 'The world is better off because of your meticulous attention to detail.' Give me a break." He tossed it back onto her lap.

She shrugged, a silent *Who's to say?*

"It's crap."

"Maybe you need to do someone you can be more objective about."

"I'd like to do you," he said with a wicked grin.

"Don't try to change the subject. How about one of your neighbors?"

"I don't know any of their middle names and I damn well am not going to ask."

"Brady, then."

He processed that. "Can *you* be objective about him?"

"I think so."

He reached for the book, but she shielded it with her body and turned toward her door.

"You're driving, I think I'll do a little reading between stops. Ooh, this looks interesting. 'You're disciplined and focused—' "

"If you quit, I'll do some work over at Susannah's tonight."

" 'You're thrifty, responsible, and orderly.' "

"Then you'll have a pan of Chocolate Orgasms by morning."

"All to myself." It wasn't a question.

"All to yourself."

Resigned to her fate—what was the use of fighting it? Elizabeth had all the power—Lilly was determined to think positively, to move forward. She couldn't believe she hadn't ovulated yet, but maybe the stress of getting blown up had thrown her system way out of whack. At least that's what her GYN said when Lilly'd called her. Surely it would happen any day. Surely her time here wouldn't run out so soon.

She still missed the solace of puttering about in her atrium, but it helped a lot to take advantage of the early-spring weather and labor in Susannah's garden. They were clearing it and laying border bricks to expand into a new area.

Lilly'd been right about Jake's being a sucker for women in distress. All Susannah had to do was pick up a brick and look as if it hurt her back, and he'd started lugging the rest of them over from the stockpile beside his garage.

Tsk, poor guy got so hot working in the sun, he had to peel off his shirt.

The only way she could keep her hands off him until they were alone was by working herself half to death. It was nothing less than a darned shame to let all that testosterone—

"Lilly, sugar, those are my daffodils," Susannah complained.

"Oh, sorry, I was, uh . . ."

"Distracted, yes, I know. If I were forty years younger,

I'd be distracted, too." Susannah shook her head. "Land sakes, what am I saying? Five years."

Lilly sighed wistfully. "There's just something about a man in boots and jeans and nothing else."

Had to be the way Jake's muscles rippled and bulged as he stacked bricks in his arms.

He dropped another load at their feet, handy to where they were digging them in all nice and neat. Lilly suspected he knew exactly what he was doing to her because he could use a wheelbarrow if he wanted to. There was one in the garage, she'd pointed out, but he claimed he needed the exercise.

Yeah, right. As if she hadn't heard the weights clacking up and down in the gym every other morning.

"Hey, Jake, how about taking some pictures?"

He tossed her a flirtatious wink. "What kind of pictures?"

"You know, for the album." Now that she knew she wasn't going to be here to raise her son, it was doubly important to leave a record of who she was.

"You're doing an album?" Susannah asked.

"Yeah, I want my son to be able to look back someday, and say, 'So that's what Mom was like. Not afraid to get her hands dirty.' "

"Well I declare, sugar, are you expectin'? Now, stop—Jake, don't let her lift even one of those bricks."

Obviously *son* sounded too definite. Conscious of Jake's careful scrutiny, Lilly rushed to cover her blunder. She waved her hand dismissively. "Relax. I just mean someday, you know? So Jake, how about it?"

She'd wanted some photos for the baby-to-be; in the meantime, she wouldn't mind a few of the hot and sweaty father-to-be.

Jake eased closer under the guise of plucking dead flowers out of her hair. "You sure?"

Lilly understood what he meant. She'd chased him until she caught him, she'd made sure he didn't use condoms, and now she was going to out-and-out lie to him? And then die? Elizabeth had warned her that telling the whole truth about coming back never worked out, but Jake had a right to know. He was the one who had to plan his future around a child.

The *zap*'s meaning was loud and clear.

Under any other circumstances she'd roast in hell for this. But the angels not only approved, one of them was actually guiding her through it, so it couldn't be wrong. Her child was destined to be born, unless she messed up. He was destined to do something great, they'd said.

She nodded at Jake and smiled, trying for a triple play: to reassure him, lift the mood, and change the subject. She tipped her chin up and looked him right in his beautiful dark blue trusting eyes.

"You'd be the first one I'd tell."

Her ploy must have worked, because he said, "You know you're wearing as many dead flowers as you fed the compost pile?" and tweaked her chin playfully.

"I'll, uh, go get my camera." She stumbled backward because she was staring at his mouth instead of where she was going.

"Careful." And then he snapped his fingers as if he'd just thought of something crucial. "Oh hey, I'll go with you. I have a digital camera; you'll be able to see the shots right away."

There was a new one, not *come see my pictures*, but *come see my camera*.

They walked side by side across the lawn. His ploy, she quickly learned, was to continue the conversation away from Susannah.

"I'm not against having kids." Taking her hand in his, he caressed it with the pad of his thumb.

See? she thought to Elizabeth. *He wouldn't mind. Let me tell him.*

"But I'll admit, now's not a good time. I need to dig myself out of this hole I'm in first. Get my family out of debt."

If she'd had any illusions that he wouldn't mind, they'd just been irrevocably erased.

"I hope you understand."

"Sure," she said.

"It's just that you sounded pretty definite back there. You know, the son thing."

She pasted on her most reassuring smile, and he let her enter the house first. "I'm sure I'll have one someday."

"Huh. Sounded more definite than that."

"There's just some things a woman knows, Jake."

"Don't go getting all cryptic on me now. Let me guess. John? No, wait, must be Elizabeth. Geez, you should've bought me a book on angels, not numerology."

"I can still get—"

"No!"

His hasty reply reassured her that she'd been correct in not pushing the angel issue—yet. "How about using what you've learned to help me pick out a name?"

"Only one problem, sweetheart. I don't recognize it as truth."

She smiled up at him. "But you'll help me anyway because you're a more enlightened guy now."

"I'll help you anyway"—he retrieved his camera from a closet—"because if *you* start reading that book, you'll see new meaning in every address we go to."

"Ooh, I hadn't thought of that. You think I can tell a good charity from a bad one by its address?"

"Do I? No. Would you think so? Probably."

She stuck her tongue out at him. He kissed her quickly, trying to capture it.

"You know," he rumbled against her lips, his hands lifting the hem of her T-shirt, "there's just something about a woman in dead flowers and jeans and nothing else."

Lilly winced, her cheeks flaming hot with embarrassment. "I can't believe you heard that."

"I'd claim I'm psychic, but you'd never believe it."

"With good reason." She ducked out of his arms. "Come on, I want a picture with Susannah."

He held the camera at arm's length, snapped one of himself, and winked at her.

"Just for you. Oh wait, I know, I'll get one with a stack of bricks on this side." He indicated the left side of his chest, still bare, smudged with dirt. He dogged her steps back to the garden, teasing her with images of bricks against his bare chest. "They'll contrast nicely with my 'nothing else,' don't you think?"

"I hope I don't go all limp and drop one on your foot."

Susannah shrieked when she saw the first picture of herself on Jake's little screen. "Well goodness, sugar, you just erase that right now," she said, swatting his biceps.

"I'll take another."

"You most certainly will not." To be sure, she stomped

away. "It's time for my shower now, so I'll just leave you two to your fun."

Lilly prolonged their time in the yard—in view of anyone walking a dog—by posing alongside the brick mowing strip she'd dug in, next to the bluebird nest box she'd cleaned out, with the taxi, in the taxi, and wherever else she could think of to tease Jake a little longer simply because they both enjoyed it.

"Now get on the hood," Jake directed.

"Cheesecake's not very original."

"Yeah, but I'll like looking at it. You got a bikini?"

"Oops, getting late. Time for my shower."

He sighed pitifully. "I'll just go upload these to the computer so you can pick the ones you want later."

His put-upon, glum tone didn't fool her for a minute. Sure enough, she was rinsing shampoo out of her hair when he poked his head inside the shower door and rumbled a very male, "Mm-mm, now that's an even better picture."

"No!"

Her right hand shot out to ward him off or block herself from his viewfinder, she wasn't sure which because it was all reflex. With the other, she desperately swiped water off her face so she could open her eyes and see what the heck he was up to.

"Unless your camera's waterproof, I wouldn't recommend trying it."

"Hell, woman, who needs a camera? When it comes to you, I've got a photographic memory."

"Good, then you don't need to be in here." That'd never fool him; she didn't sound very firm, even to herself.

"Well, *need* is another issue entirely." His tone was husky and deep and full of exactly that as he shucked his jeans, stepped into the tub, and closed the door. "You soap my back, I'll soap yours."

She reached for the towel draped over the frame. He clamped a hand on it, letting her dry her eyes but nothing else. Then he reached out the door.

"I'm serious about the camera."

"This is better. Trust me."

Uh-oh.

"Knowing how insatiable you are and how many loads of bricks I carted across the yard, I thought reinforcements were in order." At which point, his hand came back with two toys. "Lifelike? Or plain ol' plastic?"

"Ah, raided the trunk, I see."

She studied them, then him, chewing on the inside of her cheek as she debated.

"Batteries in place, ready to go." He waggled them to increase temptation, as if she needed more than him standing there in front of her, dark eyes twinkling, his body nude and aroused.

"Lifelike won't intimidate you?" she asked.

"Are you kidding?"

He exchanged the rejected one for the bar of soap, slicked his chest with it, then turned her around and pressed himself against her back, drawing lazy circles on her skin with his body. His sexy whisper rumbled in her ear.

"Real life guys don't need batteries, babe."

Feeling him against her just about did her right then.

He ran the bar of soap leisurely over her breasts, taking his time before he set it aside. He cupped her then, supporting the weight of her breasts as his very talented fingers tugged her sensitive nipples into hard pebbles.

She had no idea where the vibrator had gone, but if he didn't get to it soon, they wouldn't be testing it this time around.

Stretching her arms up and back gave her fingers free run of his wet hair. Circling her hips against him brought him to a full erection against her cheeks as warm water cascaded over them, energizing every square inch of her skin. She felt free and decadent, as if she'd gone native under a gentle outdoor waterfall. Cherished, knowing she was in the arms of her other half.

"Ready?" he murmured, and she was pleased to note the unsteadiness in his voice.

A low hum tickled her breast then, and after a startled laugh of surprise, she let her head fall back onto his chest, let him show her the way. Whatever he wanted to do was fine by her. She knew it'd be great, just like everything else they'd done together.

Ever so slowly, he inched the thrumming toy down over her soap-slicked body, fluttering it here, pressing it there, testing her reaction, her pleasure, until she parted her legs and it finally nestled where she wanted him.

"I want you, Jake," she gasped. She tried to turn and face him, but he held her where she was. "*Now.*"

"Oh, you're gonna get me"—he chuckled deeply against her neck—"in a few minutes."

He didn't get one second longer than that because Lilly was desperate for more, much more, her whole body consumed with a burning desire that only he could fulfill.

"Please, Jake."

"Please what?"

"I have to have you."

"I'm right here, sweetheart." His erection slipped between her legs.

Finally.

When he withdrew, she tugged at his scalp, his hair, and cried out in frustration. And yet he teased her again.

"Inside me," she insisted.

His hands got busy and eased something else inside. "Like this?"

Ohhhh.

Taking his time, he let her adjust to the size, the feel, the humming pressure. He was in control, and for once she recognized the immense power that enabled him to focus solely on her wants and needs, mentally processing what she liked and when she needed more.

Her muscles convulsed, contracting with strength that surprised her. Her knees weakened with her climax, and she knew if she didn't get Jake soon, she'd be too wrung out, too boneless to get him inside her, to experience his very male, gotta-have-you-now intensity that always took her over the edge.

He eased up, and she did a little focusing of her own. She took stock of the hard, slippery tub, then twisted within the protective circle of his arms and climbed him until she could lower herself onto him in one smooth, earth-shattering motion. He braced her against the wall and moved inside her, flesh against flesh. She thrust rhythmically against him until they peaked together, waves of ecstasy throbbing through her until both of them were sated.

Drained.

Unable to think.

She didn't know where he finally found the strength—

because she was draped bonelessly over him, head resting on his shoulder, gasping for air—but he was able to lower them both to the floor of the tub. There, locked chest to chest, water spraying over their heads and pooling around their bodies, their heartbeats gradually slowed, their breathing grew easier and deeper, and their bodies finally cooled down.

"Damn, woman, you are incredible."

She laughed in delight and rained kisses all over his face, skimming his eyelids and nose and lips and cheeks and a rough five o'clock shadow.

"God, I wish I'd found you first," she said. "And I don't mean just the sex. Spending time with you has been like being with my best friend."

"Even when we argue?"

She grinned. "Especially when we *banter*."

"Is that what we do?"

"Yes, like when I say I'm famished and are you going to feed me now?"

"I gotta teach you that it's fun to cook—it's the only way I'm gonna get any rest."

"Yeah, like that."

He lifted her off his lap—oh man, how she loved the way he could do that. It just proved how big and strong he was, *manly* as Betsy would say. Lilly's feminine side swelled with pride that she'd made him hers.

When he picked up the vibrator and said, "I'll leave this with you," she laughed and said, "Are you kidding? I'd just have to hunt you down and have my way with you again."

17

Just because Lilly'd had her eyes opened didn't mean it didn't suck.

Spring was here, the time of new beginnings. Cold days were few. Daffodils and tulips and hyacinths replaced crocuses. Bluebirds flitted around with grass in their beaks, refilling their nest boxes in the avian version of love and future.

So far she'd found no chink in Jake's protective armor; tarot, channeling, heaven, angels, and numerology were all pretty much anathema to him. There was nothing in his bedroom or taxi—his domains—that spoke of belief of any kind. No cross or St. Christopher medal. No rabbit's foot or four-leaf clover. No crystal or totem. If he couldn't see it, hear it, and prove it, it didn't exist.

If there was to be any hope that he'd accept her fate—and his—more easily, she had to turn up the pressure.

What would Jake tell their son to cushion the pain of losing his mother when he was so tiny and helpless? It was small consolation that motherless with the Murdochs had to be worlds better than what she'd had—knowing her own parents were too disinterested and too disconnected from her to provide the nurturing she'd always craved. She'd been alone; her son would have aunts, uncles, cousins, and someday maybe even siblings.

Lilly's last stop of the day was at the children's club, after school so the facility wouldn't be empty, but brimming with life. Mooch rode in tucked under Jake's arm like a football, which he seemed to find quite satisfactory.

"You're here!" Ollie beamed and rounded his desk. "Boy, have I got news for you."

Lilly mirrored his excitement when she said, "What?"

"I can't wait to show you. The pet center's barely started, but we have a space. Come on, this way. Oh, here's Reggie. Reggie, this is Mrs. Marquette, remember? She's the lady who's making the pet center possible."

Reggie ducked his head and very, very quietly said, "Hi," then shyly peeked through lowered eyes to gauge her reaction.

Not wanting to overwhelm him, Lilly smiled warmly, calmly, when what she really felt was the urge to throw her arms around the little boy and say, "Good job!"

Instead she held out her hand and said, "Hi, Reggie. Can you show me where it is?"

No one was more surprised than she when he took her hand. "We're gonna get two kittens," he said with slightly more volume. He looked longingly at Mooch, then craned his neck up at Jake. "He won't be jealous, will he?"

"He'll be just fine, sport. Just fine."

They spent extra time in the bare room set aside to be the pet center. Already there were crayon drawings posted on the unfinished drywall, depicting a plethora of pets.

"That's a bunny," Reggie said, pointing at a purple out-line with two large upright ears.

"Did you draw this?" Lilly asked softly, bending down in order to hear Reggie better, but not so close as to send him skittering away.

He stared at her for a moment, then nodded.

"Well, it's very good. Who did the others?"

"Kids."

"Do you know what they are?"

He proceeded to name off hamsters, gerbils, puppies, goldfish, and colorful birds that existed only in some child's mind. She and Jake stayed until it was time for Reggie to run and meet his grandmother.

"You did that," Jake said on the way out the front door, taking Lilly's hand in his.

"I'm only one cog in the wheel." She shrugged off his praise, though it felt good to know—no, to *see*—that her money was making a difference. "And it might not last."

"Everybody has to start somewhere."

To avoid rush hour, she and Jake ate dinner at An-gelo's, a nice little Italian hole-in-the-wall on the Hill, a place Lilly never would've discovered on her own. Not many other people did, either, and they lingered over lasagna and wine until Jake's cell phone rang.

"Yeah, okay. Uh-huh, usual place? See you in an hour. Remind me to give you your watch." He snapped his phone shut and said, "One of my regulars."

"Do we have to leave right away?"

"Actually, we've got a little time to kill. What would you like to do?"

She kicked off her heels, leaned back in her chair, and wiggled her feet onto his lap. "I want another dessert."

"I hope you're not expecting me to rub your feet while you're eating."

"I'll rub yours later."

"My feet don't hurt."

"I wasn't talking feet."

"Well all right then." He gave Lilly a really good foot massage under the table until time to leave. She looked forward to paying him back after his last time call.

She'd met a few of his regulars, no one remarkable, so she was pretty surprised when they were driving down the street later with Rachel in the backseat, and Rachel suddenly stripped her dress over her head. Lilly snapped straight forward, eyes on the road.

The only clue she had that Jake had noticed was a cheeky little grin aimed her direction. Otherwise he and Rachel carried on a pretty normal conversation, Lilly thought, until she started listening closer.

In reply to Jake's query about the kids, Rachel said, "Oh, they're fine. My wife's taking them to Florida for spring break."

"You can't go?"

"Not with one of my crew out on maternity leave and the other ready to drop any day. That's okay, though. With the kids out of the house, Rachel gets to play more."

As the two of them shared a chuckle, out of the corner of her eye, Lilly caught a wig coming off, so she turned her head just far enough to make sure Rachel was decent. And then farther.

"Lilly, meet Ron," Jake said.

Ron was using a wet wipe to clean off makeup with one hand as he stuck his other over the seat for a handshake.

"Hi, how are you? Hope you don't mind me changing

back here, but I have to be back in male mode before I get home. I haven't told the kids yet."

"Ah," Lilly said, realizing the voice should have been her first clue. After leaving Ron at his BMW, she said, "So that's who left the underpants behind."

"Nah, not those big white things. Rachel's into silky, sexy string bikinis and thongs."

"And you know this, how?"

"We were in the same fraternity. Ron and I."

"For transvestites?"

"No!" The shocked look on his face was priceless. "Oh, ha-ha, very funny. And he's a cross-dresser, not a transvestite."

"There's a difference?"

"Sure. Well, maybe it's a geographical thing, I don't know. But he says most cross-dressers are heterosexual."

"Still sounds like a liberal bunch of guys you went to college with."

"They didn't know. Man, somebody raided Ron's dresser once and found all those panties—" He laughed to himself, shaking his head in admiration, absentmindedly rubbing Mooch behind the ears. "He had us all convinced they were trophies. I believed him until I picked up Rachel a few months ago and recognized her. Him. Oh damn, she forgot her watch."

"You could've warned me."

"And miss the look on your face when you found out I *am* open-minded?"

"It's not the same thing. You can see and hear Ron. Or Rachel. Whomever. I want you to open your mind to the possibility of things you *can't* see and hear."

He snorted. "Yeah, like that's gonna happen."

* * *

On Wednesday morning Lilly was tidying the kitchen, already dressed in a slim skirt and tailored blouse, just about ready to leave, when the door flew open. A young woman ran in—had to be a Murdoch sister from the dark hair and navy eyes. She was wearing a flannel shirt, jeans, bouncy ponytail, and an attitude.

"I'm Jodie." No smile was forthcoming. "I just stopped by for Mom's Jell-O mold."

Lilly smiled to herself, understanding Jake's sisters' curiosity. He was their baby brother, and every day when one of them touched base via cell phone, she was right there.

Jodie winced. "Or was I supposed to pick up a purse?"

Lilly grinned, glad Jodie was the nervous one. "That's what Jillian came for."

"Ooh. Caught." She didn't seem upset about it, either, as she brushed her long bangs aside and anchored one fist to her hip. "Well then, I might as well say it. Jake says we can't give you a hard time, that you didn't have anything to do with his business folding."

"That's right, but—"

"Well. You might not have taken it, but then . . . you're still the one who *has* the money, aren't you?"

"Look, I understand." She really did. She'd like to know if Jodie was more open-minded than Jake, so she put on a kettle of water, hoping to defuse the situation and get to know her a little better. "You want to talk about it over a cup of tea?"

"No."

She set out two mugs anyway. "I know this probably doesn't mean much because you don't really know me, but I promise Jake'll have it all back, every dime, in a few months."

Jodie cocked her head and studied Lilly, much the same as Jake would. "He shouldn't have to wait."

"I know. And if I were you, I'd be just as protective."

"*Hmpf.*" Jodie opened a cabinet, borrowed the first bowl she laid her hands on, then banged out of the kitchen, head high.

Out the window over the sink, Lilly watched Jodie gun her pickup truck down the drive and said, "Boy, I wish I had a sister like that."

Lilly found Jake keyboarding away as if there were no tomorrow. He was in his office, which basically was just a desk and a tall halogen lamp in a corner of the basement.

"Ready when you are," she said.

The man could type like there was no tomorrow. "Hey, good news. I'm online with Gary right now, in Silicon Valley. He used to work for me."

"Something important?"

"Something big, don't know when I'll be done."

No "Do you mind?"

No "Take the car and go without me."

In fact, no more attention whatsoever. Already, he was off in another world. Lilly understood how important it was to him to pay off the family loan to the Marquettes. Her mission wouldn't be any worse off for waiting a few hours.

The robotic vacuum was rolling its way through the first level of the house, so Lilly moved the schefflera to a better light situation and shook off its dead leaves. Jake's robot didn't just do a random pattern, it also zeroed in on debris.

She lined up a new insurance agent by phone and made sure that project was under way. When the debt was paid, Jake's sisters would forgive her. Maybe they'd even think of her fondly when they held her son.

An hour flew by with other calls, setting her schedule for another week to come, researching more programs. There were so many, and they weren't getting any help with her stuck at home all day, so she looked in on Jake again to see if he had reached a stopping point.

"Hey, Jake . . ."

He said, "Mm," but she knew it was automatic, and he didn't really hear her.

"I need your keys."

When he unsnapped them from his belt and handed them over without question or complaint, she knew he was somewhere far, far away. She could leave with the taxi—her appointments were in familiar areas of the county—but he wouldn't like it.

"Jake!" He finally looked up at her and blinked, so she pointed at the monitor and asked, "What's so interesting?"

"Oh, uh, I'm waiting for Gary to do his thing, and while I'm waiting on him, I thought, since we were talking yesterday about believing in things we can't see, I'd knock out a program."

"For?" It was a cue for him to finish the thought, which he did. But she didn't like the answer.

"For analyzing the data from the multimeter next time I hook it up to your bracelet."

"Nuh-uh. Those zaps hurt. That last one in the kitchen? It's the very last one I ever expect to get, thank you very much."

"It's the only way you'll convince me."

"Hm." She might have to reconsider. "Wavelengths and stuff?"

He shrugged, meaning *whatever*, so she didn't have to suffer through the long version. He also did a double take and snatched his keys back, then tugged her fingers to his lips and kissed them tenderly—if a bit absently in a cute, professorial sort of way.

Within seconds, he was back on the computer and totally oblivious when Lilly leaned close and said, "Unless you know the wavelength of an angel, it won't work."

Around midnight, Jake realized the entire day had flown by. Gary reported that he'd schmoozed his way through the party all right. In fact he'd been in the right place at the right time, and upon hearing raves over Jake's automated home system, had bulldozed his way right past handing out business cards to setting up appointments for the following week.

With luck, the online marathon would result in upgrades that would knock the socks off even the most jaded Silicon Valley techies, the ones who thought they were already ahead of the curve. Ha! If they only knew.

With luck, he could be back in business within the month.

Was it too soon to propose to Lilly? He loved her, even if he didn't always understand her. He wanted her with him this time. He'd wanted her last time, too, but this time she was his to ask. Big difference.

Lilly by his side, the opportunity to make big bucks and pay off his debts just around the corner—yes sir, things were looking up.

He didn't remember eating, but there was a paper plate

in front of him, so Lilly must have managed something. He was hungry now, but he'd agreed to a two-hour break so he and Gary could catch some z's, not eat. Sustenance could come later.

He found Lilly in bed, or he should say all over the bed. She was sprawled diagonally across the queen-sized mattress, leaving no room for him. Not that that would stop him. He stripped off his clothes, picked the largest empty spot he could find, and eased right in, dragging her bodily up alongside him until they both fit. By then she was awake, and he didn't get his two hours.

Nor did he mind.

When Lilly awoke to an empty bed on Thursday, she donned one of Jake's business shirts, buttoned two buttons, and headed straight for the basement. As expected, she found him online, clicking away on the keyboard.

"Gary again?"

"Big. Really big. If I move to the Bay Area, will you go with me?"

"Just try leaving without me."

"Great." The clicking never even slowed.

"You want breakfast?"

He grunted, which probably would tick off most women, but he'd spent so much time driving her around, doing what she needed to do, that she didn't begrudge him his time now.

With the long shirttails skimming her thighs, Lilly darted around the kitchen, setting out bacon, eggs, and butter. Jake never seemed to hate cooking. Maybe she should give it a go—just this once. Otherwise they were going to starve, because she didn't know any places nearby that delivered breakfast.

She preheated the Foreman for the bacon while she did

what she enjoyed in a kitchen, setting out plates and utensils and cups and everything else two starving people needed. She managed to close a drawer on a finger, which slowed her down quite a bit because the excessive pain— counterpoint to the extreme pleasures she got from food and sex—necessitated a few minutes of icing.

"Well, good mornin', sugar."

She whirled around to find Susannah standing just inside the back door, grinning at Lilly's partially buttoned shirt with approval.

"I know it's warmed up a bit, but you'll still catch a chill dressed like that."

Lilly's fingers flew upward, poking buttons through what she hoped were corresponding holes. "I, uh, wasn't expecting anyone."

"Yes, I see that. Oh, don't mind me, hon. I'm just dropping off some mail that was left in my box by mistake."

"Excuse me," Lilly said. "I'll go put some clothes on."

"Oh now, don't you bother. I've known Jake since the day he was born, and it does this old woman a world of good to see that his heart's finally healed. I was worried about him, don't you know? All broken up after Angie walked out. This was before you married Brady, so I don't suppose you knew her. Sweet girl, that one. Poor as a church mouse. Misguided notions of love, but her intentions were good, I suppose."

It was none of Lilly's business, really. She shouldn't ask. "Why'd she leave him?"

"Well, she felt she had to, I guess. She probably thought it was only fair, though if she had asked any one of us, we would have told her better. Oh my, Jake was a wreck after she left. Drinking and staying out all night. Why, sometimes he wouldn't come home for days on end. His poor mother didn't know what to do with him. Even his father was at a loss, and you'd think men would know about what other men go through at a time like that, wouldn't you?"

"But—"

"Brady Marquette was your husband, wasn't he?"

"Yes."

"I don't have much nice to say about that family. But if it hadn't been for Brady, I'm not sure Jake would be here today. I think the drinking would have done him in before too long. Drying him out and sending him to the West Coast was the best thing for him, and then—

"Oh my, listen to me going on and you standing there missing your husband. Well, sugar, I guess one way to look at it is that Brady saved Jake's life—for you." She looked rather pleased at that rosy conclusion.

"Susannah . . ."

"Yes, sugar?"

"Why did Angie leave Jake?"

"Why, don't you know?"

Struck mute, Lilly shook her head, somehow knowing this was going to change her life.

Saddened, Susannah sank into a chair, as if the weight of the world were upon her in having to break this to Jake's new love. "In her mind, I think she felt she didn't have much choice in the matter. Oh, we didn't know this at the time, you see, but Angie's mother ran into the Murdochs later, and she told them. Angie thought leaving sooner would be easier on Jake than later—so he would remember her the way she was."

"Susannah—"

"You see, she knew she was dying."

18

"**B**etsy, if you're there, pick up."

Cell phone in hand, Lilly sped along county streets in Jake's taxi. To hell with her appointments. She was no longer interested in Christian Women for Emergency Relief or a program to promote diversity awareness. She'd thrown on jeans and an old T-shirt, and forgotten to comb her hair. So what?

Taking back streets, feeling as if she were driving a big yellow target, she nervously avoided traffic in hopes that nothing bad would happen to the taxi. Geez, give her an airplane over a car any day.

She hadn't asked for the keys; didn't have to this time. She'd found them on Jake's dresser. So now she was a car thief. If John recalled her today, would she get into heaven?

Who the hell cares?

She had more important matters troubling her. More important than wondering what that gross crunch was on the mat beneath her sandals. More important than Mooch curled up on the passenger seat, twitching his tail, blinking at her in a very feline message to deal with it, both the crunch and her messed-up life.

So . . . Angie had left Jake, and he'd gone off the deep end. He loved her now. When it was time for her to die, whether today or tomorrow or in a few months, it'd hit him just as hard, maybe more so. She was afraid he'd self-destruct all over again. This time Brady wouldn't be around to rescue him. If he survived physically, he'd be twice-burned. Other women might regard him as high risk, or he might be afraid to commit himself ever again, either of which meant he'd never have the kids he so deserved.

Did she have nine months left to prepare him, to break down his system of nonbelief in *any*thing, to show him that there was a world beyond what he could analyze? Or merely a few days?

She needed to know, needed to prepare for the inevitable, but there was one factor she couldn't work her mind around. Was she pregnant yet? How much time did she have?

If she was, should she leave now so she wouldn't fuel Jake's love with her presence day after day, every day? But leaving was what Angie had done, and look where that had gotten him. Damned if she did, damned if she didn't.

If she wasn't, she couldn't leave him yet, because John would rescind her earthly privileges and she'd die again right away, and Jake—the stubborn, opinionated, close-minded jackass—so wasn't ready.

Knowing whether she was pregnant would clue her in

to her next step. When the time came, she'd have to give Jake the only safety valve she had any control over. She'd have to make *him* leave *her*.

In the drugstore, she circumvented the feminine aisle twice. One of the ladies from her tennis club was there. Lilly didn't need tongues to start wagging over why she was looking at home pregnancy tests just months after burying her husband. News like that would end up on her mother's doorstep, even in Death Valley.

She speed dialed Betsy again. "Pick up, it's an emergency."

"What's wrong?"

"I'm standing here in the store looking at about a dozen pregnancy tests. Which one do I buy?"

"Are you late?"

"How would I know?"

"Oh yeah, I forgot. Well, could you have gotten pregnant in the last week?"

"Yes."

"Then it's a waste of money."

"What?" She whined without shame. "Why?"

"Well, *someone* forgot their high school biology."

"You're assuming I learned it in the first place."

"And you and Brady never . . ."

"I always thought when the time was right, it'd happen."

Betsy sighed, but she also took pity on her. "Okay, listen up, here goes. Unless they have quicker tests than I know about, it takes a week for a fertilized egg to reach your uterus, and *then* your body starts producing whatever it is that the test detects. Not before. So you could be pregnant and still get a negative."

"Shit, I'm screwed."

Betsy chuckled. "So I gathered."

Lilly groaned, wondering whether to hang up on her best friend. "Hold on, I've got another call. Jake's probably wondering where his taxi is." She clicked over, eager to hear him, as always, in spite of the fact that he'd undoubtedly read her the riot act. "Hello?"

"Lilly, dear."

"Donna," she said without a hint of warmth. She'd rather get yelled at.

"Have you decided to come home yet?"

Lilly snickered. "Get real."

"In light of the situation, we feel it's our responsibility to protect your assets."

"Well, it's not. Forget it."

Lilly started to click back to Betsy, until Donna said, "So we're taking steps," which made the hair on the back of her neck stand up.

"Meaning what?"

"Meaning we'll put pressure on Jake until you come home."

"Tell you what, Donna." Lilly took a moment, as if really putting thought into a compromise. "I'll come home on my birthday."

"At the rate you're giving money away? I don't think so, dear."

"Well, it's that or nothing."

"I thought you might say that. Look out the window."

She glanced out at the parking lot. There was a guy behind the wheel of Jake's taxi, waving at her. "Hey!" she shouted, to no avail. She would've run after him, but he was already pulling into the street. "Donna, that's not Jake's taxi, it's his uncle's."

"It's part of the collateral on the loan, dear."

"Which you can't just repossess when you feel like it."

"Well, we'll leave that up to the courts to settle. You know how long that can take. If you won't come home, at least stop giving money away. Don't make me take the next step."

Late that night, a furious Jake finally tracked the taxi to a chain-link fenced lot behind an abandoned service station in a seedy neighborhood.

"Look at the bright side." Lilly was worlds perkier than she had been of late, trying to ease the situation. "It's a good thing you forgot to give Rachel her watch, or we'd never have found it."

"I'm still mad at you."

Though it didn't temper his undying love for her. He couldn't imagine ever not wanting to do what was best for Lilly.

She lapsed into silence, which would last all of five minutes before she took another stab at winning him over with her sweet talking ways. She'd been like that ever since she'd called him away from the computer. Lucky for him, one of the Murdoch Masons pickups was in the garage for the winter.

He'd donned his dad's *Don't mess with masons, we mortar our victims* T-shirt as a warning. But she ignored the hint.

Not that she was coming on to him, because nothing could be further from the truth. She'd securely stowed the come-hither looks. In his experience, women didn't pass up using pretty smiles and gentle nudges to gain forgiveness, especially when their quarry was as mad as he, but Lilly certainly wasn't lowering herself.

"What the hell was so important at the store that you couldn't wait five minutes for me to get off the computer?"

"Ha!"

"Okay, ten minutes."

He was just beginning to think she'd chosen to be quiet after all, when she said, "Girl stuff. You sure it's safe to be here?"

"Stay close to me."

He should have his head examined for issuing the invitation when he didn't want her there in the first place, but he needed a second driver.

For a defunct station, there were a lot of vehicles, maybe a dozen. The yellow taxi stood out like a sore thumb. They crouched near the fence.

"I sure hope you're gonna pipe down and be useful," he whispered.

"What can I do?"

"Pick the lock on that gate."

She laughed lightly, then said, "Oh, you were serious," when he didn't join her.

"Well, as an alternative, can you hot-wire the car?"

"Uh, no, I always left that to the chauffeur."

"Lucky you."

"Are you trying to make me feel useless?"

"That'd be the plan, yes."

He crept around the perimeter, searching for an easy way in, keeping his eyes open for evidence of a guard dog. "Well shit! Look what they did to my car."

"What?"

"They wrecked it."

"Eww, it looks worse than I thought."

At that, he stopped dead in his tracks and turned, and Lilly ran smack into his chest. Would've felt good, too, if he weren't having a bad day.

"You *knew* it was wrecked?"

"Well . . ." She shifted from foot to foot. "I wasn't sure. I heard this funny crash kind of noise about a block away from where he, you know, repossessed it."

"Stole it."

"Yeah that. I heard this huge bang and I saw a lot of commotion, people jumping out of their cars, running out of stores, that sort of thing. But I couldn't see who it was. So I didn't know for sure. And I didn't want to tell you it was wrecked and then find out I'd worried you for nothing."

"Oh man, if he killed somebody with my uncle's taxi—"

"Relax. I'm sure there would've been an ambulance if he'd hurt anybody, and there wasn't. Not even by the time you arrived."

"You saying I was slow?"

"I'm saying you took so long, that by the time you arrived, a victim could've been reincarnated."

"No such thing."

She huffed and crossed her arms over her chest. "Sometimes you make me so mad, I hope I turn into an angel right before your eyes."

"You're pretty much a devil right now."

"You wish," she said, and he caught her grin under the one unbroken lightbulb in a square block.

"Stop that. Let's get in there and see if it's driveable."

"I thought you didn't have a key."

"Sure I do."

"But you said—"

"I just wanted you to see how much trouble you caused."

"And the lock on the gate? I know you don't have a key to that."

"Piece of cake."

"Don't tell me. You have some illegal, high-tech opener." He said nothing. "So what're we waiting for?"

"Oh, uh, checking things out takes time."

"What d'you think?"

"I think it looks like he hit a telephone pole."

"Hm."

"*Did* he?"

Lilly shrugged, her head tipping toward one shoulder. It was little movements like that that were so endearing and made it difficult to stay mad at her.

"Better get your lock gizmo."

Jake fetched what he needed from the pickup, feeling Lilly's gaze resting on his back like a curious kid checking over Santa's shoulder.

"That's it?" she said.

"What?—it's a work truck. A bolt cutter's a tool."

She snickered, and while he was absolutely positive she didn't mean it to be sexy, it surely was. He was having a devil of a time staying mad at her, when he'd be perfectly justified in doing so.

"Let's go," he growled.

They were through the gate in seconds. Still no sign of

a dog, so maybe Mooch hadn't gone far. As Jake strode over to the taxi, he could see he wouldn't be driving off with it. He didn't have to open the hood to know the radiator'd been smashed into a sieve.

He stared at it for a minute, then opened the trunk and handed Lilly a trash bag. "Bag up our stuff; otherwise we'll never see it again. The merchandise, too. I'll look for Mooch."

He hunted for half an hour. Then he and Lilly sat side by side for another half hour, hoping Mooch would return to the familiar car, but he didn't.

"I hate to say it, but this isn't getting us anywhere." It hurt to give up, but what was the point of sitting there all night? "We could be home making lost and found signs or something."

"It's all my fault," Lilly said for the hundredth time as she climbed into the truck and slumped in her seat, brushing nonstop tears off her cheeks.

Jake drove away slowly, looking for eye shine under every bush, behind every barrel. "You say Donna had some guy take the car to make me mad and drive us apart so you'd come into line with her plans? Is that right?"

"That's what she said on the phone. Right before, 'Don't make me take the next step.'"

"What a bitch." He tugged at Lilly's hand until she scooted across the seat, then he held her close, relishing how she eventually sighed and softened against him. "We'll advertise under Lost and Found."

"We can call the animal hospitals, too. Shoot, I feel so bad."

"I know. Me too."

He dipped his head and nuzzled the top of hers, and she pulled back, *just like that*, and said, "We need to talk."

A frisson of fear leaped on top of his misery—and he'd thought things couldn't get worse. "You're breaking up with me?"

"No!"

"Then *geez*, don't say that." He covered his pounding heart with his hand.

"You really thought I was breaking up with you?"

"Ye-es. What's a guy supposed to think when a woman starts the 'We need to talk' speech?"

She bucked up with a sniffle, and grinned. "Heard that a lot, have you?"

"Once is all it takes. So what's up?"

"I can deal with Donna picking on me. But having her cause you trouble . . ." She shifted away slightly, though the emotional distance was immeasurable. "I mean one day I'm independent and you're going along fine, and then *bam*, all of a sudden, I'm living in your house, riding in your car, and Donna's making your life a living hell."

"C'mere." He hugged her back to him as he drove, tucking her beneath his arm where she could rest her head on his chest.

"Maybe if I get my own place, she'll let up on you."

"No." Maybe if he pounded Andrew into the ground, they'd think twice before making Lilly feel this bad again. "We'll deal with it. Together."

Two days later, Jake was slumped at Susannah's kitchen table, absently toying with the saltshaker while he waited for her to get ready. She was perched on the chair across from him, arranging a stack of coupons to correspond with the food aisles in Dierbergs.

He'd tried throwing himself into his work to forget his problems. Now that he'd seen his CATS program in action, up close and personal, he knew what else it needed to take it to the top, that one extra step that always put his work above everyone else's.

He converted his own wristwatch and picked a code word that didn't fit in everyday speech, not his anyway: Angel. There wasn't an undercover cop in the country who wouldn't give up his own mother for one just like it.

Eventually, Susannah couldn't stand his brooding anymore. "What's the matter, sugar?"

"Take your pick."

"Still mooning over that stray cat?"

"He wasn't just a—" Jake took a breath and composed himself. "He was *my* stray cat."

"And you miss him."

"I even miss the little mouse parts he left in the taxi."

"Ugh." Susannah grimaced, but just as quickly put on a bright face and said, "There now, see? He's a hunter, he won't starve."

"We've been to all the shelters. I call them every day. Put up flyers with his picture. Called an ad into the newspaper. I don't know what else to do."

"Sounds like you've done all you can, sugar."

"Hasn't been enough."

"Mooch is smart. He found you once, maybe he can do it again."

"Why the hell didn't I put a tracking device in his collar?"

"So *that's* what you're beating yourself up over."

"Yeah."

He spilled some salt, and while making circles in it with the bottom of the shaker, he debated whether to tell her the rest. Might as well.

"I don't get women."

"Jake Murdoch, shame on you. Lilly's living in your house this very minute. Why would you want others?"

He blinked, decoding that. "I mean I don't *get* women."

"Oh. Did you and Lilly have a fight?"

"She'd have to perk up to fight."

Susannah patted his shoulder, which didn't console him at all. "She misses Mooch."

"She thinks I can't forgive her for losing him."

"Is she right?"

"No, of course not." Although he might blame her just a little for taking the taxi in the first place. "Did she tell you they had a special connection? Whenever her arm hurt, he'd be all over her, getting as close as he could. She didn't mean for the car to get stolen. I know it wasn't her fault."

"Have you told her that?"

"Only a hundred times a day."

Susannah's hands stilled. "She really loved that cat. Why, when we were clearing the garden, he'd come nosing around—you know how cats just love to help, poking into everything you're trying to do. Oh, Lilly got such a kick out of playing with him." She laughed, reminiscing. "She'd wiggle little branches underneath the dry leaves. He'd pounce on them. My, I never had so much fun working in the garden before."

"She talks about moving out."

"Oh. Oh my." She put her hand on his, making him stop with the saltshaker. "Well, let's think about this. It hasn't been that long since she buried her husband, right? Maybe things are moving too fast. Maybe grieving for Mooch now reminds her all over again of how she lost her husband. It was pretty sudden, wasn't it?"

He nodded.

"And there was that explosion in the store; she came pretty close to death there, too. Why, I'm sure all of it's been so overwhelming, just all piling up on her, like."

"I didn't think of that."

First Brady, then her own near-death experience. She hadn't dealt with that well at all, talking to angels—*ha*! Now Mooch was gone. Jake remembered how devastated he'd been over Angie, and that was before he knew she'd died. Damn. What Lilly must be going through if this renewed even a smidgen of her grief over Brady. He sat up straighter, working this out in his own mind, analyzing it, getting a handle on it so he could fix it.

"I remember the first time I said something about death—I don't know, how she'd catch her death without a coat on, something like that. All the joy just went out of her, like turning out a light. Geez, poor thing, it's probably all catching up to her at once. I need to help her through this."

Susannah bounced to her feet. "Good boy."

He laughed ruefully. "But what do I do? It's not like I can suggest she go see someone about it. I mean, I tried that for her arm. She'd have my head."

"You can be supportive."

"That's a chick word."

"So?"

"Guys have a different vocabulary."

Susannah chuckled. "Oh, I see. Well, think romance."

"I do wonderful romance."

"I don't mean sex."

He blinked. "I love her. I can't be romantic without sex."

"Lord, sugar, this could take all day." Susannah slipped a cardigan on over her blouse. "Come on, take me shopping, and I'll explain the difference."

Lilly checked her saliva in the small ovulation predictor; still no ferning. Was the damned thing defective or what? She threw it into a bathroom drawer and slammed it.

She could already be pregnant. Considering how important that was, she reasoned she ought to just intuitively know. But she didn't. She was running out of patience and frazzled from worrying about running out of time. This was one thing she had to get right.

And when she got back to heaven? She was giving them a piece of her mind about how come they could send her back and manage long-distance electric shock therapy, but not a two-way phone connection? *Gimme a break.*

Please.

If she failed, would she go through Transition again where she could complain, or directly to the back of that horrendous line? If the latter, she wouldn't get the opportunity to tell anybody anything for a long, long time.

Lilly stared at the two photos Jake had snapped of himself, all bare-chested and sweaty. *Yum.* Nothing sexier than a man with brains *and* brawn. Tucked into the frame of the dresser mirror, they never failed to bring a smile to her heart and a stupid grin to her face. What a ham.

In spite of his pain over losing Mooch, he'd turned up the charm on her. Fresh daffodils and hyacinths on her dresser every morning, so they were her first sight of the day. Sure, they were right out of his mother's garden and he didn't have to go far or put much thought into it. But he did. A pretty crystal vase. A peachy floral bow. Gentle curls of ribbon artistically scattered around the base, echoing the colors of spring.

She'd seen no prior evidence of this side of him, so she figured he was getting tips somewhere. And that wasn't all. Either he was banking on chocolate as an aphrodisiac or he'd been talking to Betsy, because suddenly there was homemade Snickers pie for dessert and a bite-sized Snickers bar on her pillow every night. Then came the Easter M&M's sprinkled in her lingerie drawer.

He hadn't confined this to the bedroom, either. New honeysuckle-scented candles lined the edge of the bath-tub. A pretty bottle of bath oil sported a new floral ribbon to match the one on the vase, so she was pretty sure these little touches didn't come from the store.

More candles on the breakfast table.

"Power out?" she asked without thinking.

"It's not romantic if the power's out."

Boy, did she feel stupid.

Not as stupid as Angie, though. What on earth had been going through her mind to leave Jake? He would have stuck with her to the very end.

Falling in love really screwed with a person's mind.

It hurt to see Jake hurting. He wasn't sleeping well since Mooch went missing. She watched him pace the backyard at night, heard him calling the cat's name softly in hopes he was nearby and just needed a little more help getting to the right house.

He called the shelters every day. He drove by and checked each one every day. Many of the small cities that comprised St. Louis County had their own animal control departments, and he checked all of them, too.

Clearly Jake wasn't the giving-up or leaving kind of guy. He should run as far from her as he could get, as fast as he could go.

Yep, falling in love *really* screwed with a person's mind.

The first day of spring came and went. The succession of blooming bulbs and flowering trees reminded her that the third anniversary of her wedding was just around the corner. Of course she wouldn't celebrate it, but she couldn't just forget it either. It had happened, she'd been in love and happy for a while, and it had made her who she was today.

It was also the day she'd met Jake. Now there was a strange thing to think about. If she were going to live for years to come, every anniversary would evoke both sad and happy memories. Talk about a mixed bag. Fortunately, Jake would only remember the date as a good one, the one on which they'd met.

Spring also meant that Lilly's shortened biological clock was rapidly ticking down. Suppose she wasn't pregnant. If she didn't ovulate soon, she wasn't going to make it until her next birthday, and there were loose ends that needed to be tied up. The least she could do was buy

Jake's uncle a new car, a good one with lots of bells and whistles, leather seats, and a quality CD player.

Zap.

"Go away."

Something large and sedate, definitely not yellow. With the right vehicle, he could be a limo driver. She reached for her cell phone.

Zap!

"Stop it. I am so frickin' mad at you guys. I'm keeping my promise. You don't have to sit up there with your finger on the button."

Determined, she ran to the kitchen and yanked open the drawer where Jake's mother kept her supply of tools. Hammer, no. Screwdriver, no. Pliers . . .

"Need help?"

She started, and then laughed at herself when she realized it was Jake. As if John would sneak up behind her. "I'm trying to find a tool to break this bracelet." Only a little zap; they didn't believe her.

"It, uh, goes nice with what you're wearing."

She was in jeans and a T-shirt, and what difference did that make anyway? "I'm not trying to accessorize, I just want it off."

Za-ap! She would've cursed at that one, but it took her breath away. Elizabeth was taking her more seriously now.

Desperate, Lilly grabbed one chain with the pair of pliers, jammed it all the way on to the part that cut wire, and pressed hard. The link gave a little.

Her knees buckled, her heart really did stop—none of that romantic bullshit—and she crumpled to the floor like a wet dishrag. On the way down, she caught a flash of bright light, a whispered warning.

One was all it took to understand who was in charge. "Lilly!"

"I'm all right, I'm okay," she said automatically as Jake scooped her up, not really sure whether she was, but she felt blissfully alive in his arms again.

No way this bracelet was coming off if it meant instant recall. No way she'd leave before the last possible moment.

"It was just a mistake," she said. "I'm sorry."

"I'm not mad at you, sweetheart."

"I'm uh—" Now how should she put this? "I was talking to, you know . . ."

Lilly felt Jake's chest expand against her body as he took a deep breath. A very deep breath. Long, steady pressure that made her oh, so aware of him.

"You okay?" she asked in a strained whisper.

"Shut up, I'm counting."

"Counting?"

"You know, as in 'to ten.' Only in your case, I may need to go all the way to ten thousand."

She grinned at his put-upon tone. "You're saying I'm a pain in the neck?"

"Farther south. Now that you've mopped up the floor with your butt, are you going to change into a skirt and give money away?"

"I'm thinking if people want my money, they won't mind if I wear jeans."

"I know I don't." He fondled her rear as he set her on her feet.

"I'm going to make a call first." She gazed at the pliers wistfully, then tossed them back into the drawer. "See you in about fifteen minutes?"

Her attorney suggested she buy a car that would hold its value better than average—*"Yes, a Mercedes would be fine"*—then donate it to a charitable organization that would in turn lease it back to Jake's uncle at a very low rate.

No more zaps, neither during that call nor the ones to buy and insure the largest, glossiest black Mercedes currently available in St. Louis.

"So there." Feeling she'd one-upped Elizabeth and John, she slammed out the back door in victory.

She found Jake in a chair on the back porch, one ankle propped on the other knee, the numerology book spread open across both. Neat columns of letters and numbers covered at least one page of graph paper.

The young mother who lived on the other side was pushing her son on a tire swing, and Lilly sat on the armrest to watch. She leaned against Jake's broad shoulder and spiraled her finger through a lock of his hair simply because he liked it, and she liked touching him. She couldn't dwell on what she'd miss. She had to ignore the pain, had to be content with knowing that he and her son would enjoy simple things like sitting on the porch, or swinging on a sunny day.

"You still talking to them?" he said.

"Who?"

"John and Elizabeth."

Taken aback that he not only was acknowledging their presence, but had remembered their names, she slipped her arm around his shoulders and smiled with great pleasure.

"So, you're starting to believe?"

"Oh hell no. I'm just making conversation."

Thinking he was coming around had lifted her mood,

and she wasn't letting it get away. "Well, maybe you shouldn't mention them unless you believe in them."

He muttered something that could've been, "Like that'll be a problem."

"What?"

"I said I'm having a problem."

She squinted at him suspiciously. "With what?"

He tapped the eraser end of the pencil on the paper. "According to this, I need a full birth name for this to work—" He shuddered.

Touched that he was not only honoring their bet, but also working on her request for a boy's name, she tempered her grin. Couldn't stop her tongue, though, when he shuddered so adorably.

"What's the matter? Afraid lightning'll strike?"

"That'd mean I believe in this crap," he said, grinning triumphantly. "May I continue?"

"Please."

"According to the rules—and no, I'm not buying into this stuff—you need a full name to work with. You know, a *last* name?" He let that hang there between them.

"Oh."

Since Elizabeth had delivered the bad news, marriage was a topic Lilly no longer wanted to entertain. As a matter of fact, she was downright *afraid* to go there, for Jake's sake. He'd already lost one fiancée. If he lost another—or worse, a wife—the poor man might think he was jinxed.

"Hm, I hadn't thought about that." She moved to the chair across from him, so she could see him better, propping her feet up next to his thigh so they were still touching.

If she got pregnant, would he insist on marrying her?

When he learned she'd used him just to get pregnant because two angels told her to—oh boy, that was rich—would he even want to? Geez, Elizabeth and John should come with warning labels. Next time, she wasn't agreeing so fast.

"Lilly? I don't want to pressure you"—he grinned sexily—"at least not until I have camellia petals and candles on hand. But if this son you're wanting to name is *my* son, he won't be named Marquette."

Shit, she couldn't let him think about proposing, because she didn't want to turn him into a widower. She'd have to turn him down, and how would that help her goal?

"Oh, right. I should go back to my maiden name, shouldn't I? I think I'd like that."

Jake paused a moment, mulling over her neat sidestep. It probably wasn't the answer he'd been leading toward, but she wasn't giving him an opening if she could help it. He scratched out Marquette and, neatly spacing letters as before, he printed Carpenter.

"You remember?" she murmured, inordinately pleased.

"About you, darlin'? Everything." He gazed into her eyes the way he always did, strong, intent, sucking her in like a vortex, and she was relieved when he said, "Ready to go?"

"I'm waiting on a new car for your uncle."

"Is it yellow? He won't like it unless it's yellow."

"It's black."

"He won't like it."

"I don't think Mercedes come in yellow."

His eyebrows arched, but he held his tongue. She should have held hers.

"I thought he could be a limo driver."

"He doesn't like limo drivers. He likes the freedom of throwing puny tips back at people. That'd kill a limo business."

She blinked. "Maybe if he's a very good limo driver, he won't get puny tips."

Grinning broadly, as if he knew a secret, Jake chuckled. "I'll leave it to you to explain that to him. Right after you convince him that accepting an, oh I don't know, hundred-thousand-dollar-plus car doesn't come with strings."

She chewed her lip.

"There's more?"

She nodded apologetically.

"Let's see. You've never met my uncle, but you buy him a nonyellow Mercedes—granted, a rather nice one, I'm not faulting you there—and you presume to think he could be a limo driver. That right so far?"

"You don't have to make it sound like an evil plot. There are no strings attached."

"Huh. I just figured you out."

She waited quietly, but not eagerly.

"You have a death wish."

"Oh c'mon, if he doesn't like it, he can trade it in for a whole fleet of ugly yellow taxis. My attorney arranged a nonbinding lease arrangement."

"Which he can't afford."

"At a hundred dollars a month."

He grinned with boyish capitulation then. "Oh, so you do know my uncle. He'll love it. Think we'll be done by six tonight?"

"I don't see why not."

"Good. Bring something tropical to change into."

She sat up straighter, waiting for more, an explanation, a punch line, *something*, but it never came. "Why?"

"You'll see. Just do it." He winked, leaned toward her, and whispered enticingly, "I'll bring the camera."

She fanned herself. Damn Elizabeth for making the hottest guy on the planet fall in love with her and then not let her keep him.

"I don't have anything tropical."

"Then come naked."

19

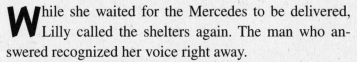

While she waited for the Mercedes to be delivered, Lilly called the shelters again. The man who answered recognized her voice right away.

"He's not here," he said, weary with strained patience. "You only have to call once a day."

"I know."

"Let me guess. You and that fella're gonna keep calling every hour anyway."

"Pretty much."

He sighed, said, "Okay," and hung up.

Jake's sisters organized their own continual, rotating search of the smaller shelters. Their unsolicited sibling support was so far out of the realm of Lilly's experience that she experienced the warmth of a deep, emotional hug every time she thought about it. Maybe she should hold a family lottery to name her son. Better wait until she was pregnant, though, or they might think she was a conniving slut and come after her with a full arsenal of sisterly offenses.

Because Jake was being so good about the numerology thing and she didn't want him to set it aside, Lilly ran off dozens more LOST CAT flyers so he wouldn't have to. Every dime he made went right into the bank, yet he was offering a generous reward to whoever brought Mooch home.

As devoted to the cat as he was, Jake not only hadn't let up on his newly attentive behavior toward Lilly, he segued it right into the just-delivered Mercedes. After thirty minutes of driving around and stapling flyers to telephone poles, she finally gave in and rolled her window down.

"It's not that I don't like the hyacinths, but . . ."

"They don't go with the new leather smell, do they?"

"My throat's starting to hurt."

"Well, where're we going next?"

She checked the sticky note, which he wouldn't let her attach to the dash, so she'd stuck it high up on the windshield instead. "Library headquarters."

"That's no good."

"What?"

"For the flowers. What say we drive into the city and find a woman who looks like she'd appreciate them?"

"By way of the Humane Society?"

"You read my mind."

In Union Station, Jake started looking for women who looked as if they wouldn't hit him if he approached them with flowers. By the time he'd given away two, Lilly'd made four little girls smile with delight. She'd just turned to tell him she was finished when he snapped a picture of her and the children. She hadn't planned it, but it'd make a nice addition to the album.

When Jake's phone rang just outside the pound, Lilly went in alone. Upon her return, she slouched in her seat. "He's not there."

"We'll check the others." Jake squeezed her hand, which helped a little bit. Mostly it was his deep rumble, though, that reached out and shared the burden.

He also sounded a little brighter than ten minutes ago, and Lilly did a double take. "You look, I don't know, stunned."

"That was the FBI on the phone."

"Oh please tell me, I beg you, that they're going after my in-laws."

"Better."

"They're calling in hit men?" *Yes!*

"Somehow I doubt it, but listen. I was pretty excited. It might've been the ATF or NSA, I don't know. Some government initials. Doesn't matter. It was an agent who heard how I integrated CATS with GPS in Rachel's dress watch, and he wants me to put a presentation together."

"All *right*." It was about time he received some good news. "Wait, does doing that make you as happy as the home control stuff?"

"Close enough."

Then she gave him the high five he deserved.

He started the car. "APA next?"

"Yes."

As the sun dipped below the horizon at six o'clock, Jake parked the Mercedes outside a gate set way back on the east parking lot of Shaw's Garden.

"Nobody's around. You can change in the car while I get the cooler out of the trunk."

"Huh?"

"Remember I said to dress tropical?"

"For here? Why?"

"You'll see."

"It looks deserted."

"It's after hours."

"Then how're we getting inside?"

"Piece of cake."

"No, uh-uh, if you pull a bolt cutter out of that trunk, I'm turning this car around and leaving your ass here."

He waggled a key. "Ron thinks you're cute, by the way."

"Hm, I'm not sure how to take that." Lilly wasn't sure she wanted to trespass, but she'd yet to see a yellow camellia this spring. And they weren't actually breaking in.

"Hey, Ron's got great taste in women. Where're the clothes you're changing into?"

"I'm just going to stay in my jeans."

"Huh. Okay. Let's leave our phones here. You take the key, I'll get the cooler."

It must've been heavy, because carrying it defined the muscles in Jake's arms so nicely that Lilly almost missed the fact that he'd donned a really gaudy Hawaiian shirt. Inside the gate, she strolled beside him toward the Linnean House, her favorite spot in the gardens. It was here she'd first fallen in love with camellias and why she'd planted them in her own atrium.

The Linnean's reputation had it as the oldest continually operated greenhouse west of the Mississippi River, but it was scarcely the typical boring glass structure expected of a greenhouse. It was built of brick, for one thing, with soaring arched windows, a slate-and-glass roof, and a cute mermaid fountain by the double doors in the long wall.

The quaint romantic atmosphere was exponentially heightened by this clandestine, after-hours dinner and knowing that Jake had chosen it because of what it would mean to her. Small tea candles surrounded the fountain. Wall sconces were turned down low behind the camellias. Double doors onto the perennial garden stood wide open, with the rose garden just beyond.

Even the yellow camellia couldn't hold her attention when soft instrumentals floated from hidden speakers, filling the house. Lilly recognized "We've Only Just Begun" and "Love Is a Many-Splendored Thing," among others. She didn't need to identify the rest to know she was in the presence of a master.

Jake carried a bench over from the entrance and set it beside the fountain, then bowed theatrically.

"M'lady."

"Boy, you're pouring it on pretty thick."

"You ain't seen nothing yet."

It tickled her, this new, extraromantic side of him, so much so that she had let him run with it for days now. Was it her imagination, or did his voice rumble more than normal, raising his sexy quotient to an immeasurable peak?

Nor was he relying on that alone. He'd raided his mother's good crystal and filled two glasses with dry white wine. Lilly plucked a bunch of grapes out of the cooler to munch on while Jake went all out setting up a silver tray with a doily, cheese cubes, hunks of salami, and crusty Italian bread.

"Good thing I'm not into health food."

"I would've brought granola and tofu."

"Ugh."

"See, I know what I'm doing."

She didn't doubt that for a minute. As designated driver, Jake had little wine. Lilly sipped her way through a glass as they dined, listened to music, strolled through the moonlit gardens and talked about anything and everything. The hours flew by until they eventually packed up together, and yet they lingered.

"I'm flying to San Jose in the morning." He sounded as regretful as Lilly felt upon hearing the news. "I hate to leave."

"I'll check for Mooch every day. Every shelter, I promise."

"It's not Mooch I hate leaving."

She knew that beyond any doubt.

"I'd invite you along, but we'd never see each other. Gary's set up a meeting for tomorrow, and then we'll have to go back to his place and work out whatever needs working out. I'll get finished sooner alone."

"What about your other presentation? You know, for the government agency you can't remember?" She suspected he just wasn't supposed to say.

"I can do both."

She thought about the consequences if she ovulated while he was gone. "If I miss you really bad, can I fly out to see you?"

"Sure." He cocked his head, eyes twinkling as merrily as if she'd just offered to strip down right there. He held his hand out to her. "Dance?"

His warm smile and soothing voice tugged her closer, but she prolonged the moment.

"Come on, you can't resist."

"And why's that?"

"According to what I read, today's a lucky number day and I'll get whatever I go after. If you don't dance with me, I can only conclude that the principles behind numerology are bogus."

"Nice try"—she didn't even try to hide her amusement—"but you're too scientific to base a conclusion on one test."

He shook his head slowly, mocking how the weight of the world might rest on this one decision. "Sure doesn't bode well for numerology."

Then, with a devastating grin, he turned his hand palm up and crooked his fingers, beckoning her. Lilly shivered, knowing well what those fingers could do.

She felt the draw, the strong magnetic pull Jake had whenever he gazed at her as if she were the only woman in existence. She had no doubt a thousand naked women could walk by right then, and he wouldn't even notice.

That alone might have been enough to draw her slowly into his arms for the next dance, but when the first notes of "I Will Always Love You" began, Lilly rushed to their haven. Jake had no way of knowing how appropriate those lyrics were. He probably wouldn't even make the connection after she'd gone.

But Lilly knew. She didn't want him to see the tears that slipped free and ran down her cheeks, so she melted against his body, rested her head on his chest, and followed him in a slow dance by the trickling fountain.

She wanted more of this. She wanted to throw things and cuss and demand a heavenly hearing, but nothing would come of it. Why ruin what little time she had to spend with Jake? She wanted him to remember her as happy and glowing with love.

They danced slowly, covering little ground, totally absorbed in each other.

In a crazy way—and Jake wasn't sure he'd ever admit this to anyone else because it was so antiguy—he had had fun all week with the no-sex aspect of being romantic. Looking on the whole thing as a game, he'd given it his all. He'd expanded on Susannah's ideas, built on them, developed his own, and fine-tuned each one with Lilly in mind.

He'd given her time to grieve, to sulk, to come to terms with life as it was. To realize that just because Brady and Mooch had left her suddenly, it didn't mean he would. To understand that just because she'd had a couple brushes with death herself, it didn't mean she should withdraw and prepare for the worst.

It was never far from his mind that they had an anniversary coming up. Lots of couples celebrated the day they met. His parents did, as well as his sisters and their husbands. Somehow, in his family anyway, meeting your mate held more significance than the day you got hitched. It came first, made the second possible, and therefore was more important. A true landmark, a turning point in two lives that then proceeded as one.

He was very cognizant of the fact that Lilly's and his anniversary was also Lilly's and Brady's wedding anniversary. One was inextricably woven with the other.

How could he celebrate the most important day of their lives without reminding her of Brady and death and separation?

He had better odds concentrating on romance.

He had to hand it to Susannah. If not for her counsel, he would've thought he'd already reached his goal many times this week. He would've stripped Lilly naked and kissed her all over until she begged for more. Surprised her in the shower and taken her up against the wall. Spread her on the table and shown her just how alive she was. He'd given her all the time he could bear.

He wined and dined and slow danced her at the Linnean House until well after ten o'clock. Thanks to a timer delay and remote control, he took dozens of photos of them together, which he'd print tonight and leave around for Lilly to find in the days to come, while he was out of town, working toward a future that would be so much richer just for having her in it.

He kissed her senseless every fifteen minutes, giving her a preview of the night ahead.

"Guess we'd better go," he said finally, before he forgot himself and unsnapped her jeans.

He locked up and tossed the keys back inside the gate for Ron to pick up in the morning, and the gardens were left as pristine as they'd found them.

The ride home was punctuated with long, quiet pauses while he traced lazy circles on the back of her hand, anticipating where he'd be tracing more, in less than an hour. She sighed contentedly, and he kissed her fingers.

"One of our phones is blinking." She flipped open the one with the red light.

"Yours or mine?"

"That's odd. It's a 9-1-1 from your house."

Every outside light was on when Jake barreled into the driveway, both on his house and next door. Susannah met them as they flew out of the Mercedes.

"It's Mooch," she said.

He's back! Jake thought, in spite of Susannah's tone being brisk, urgent, and not at all reassuring. At least Mooch was home.

"I know he's here, sugar, but he won't come to me. I think he might be hurt."

"Okay." He squeezed Lilly's hand, sharing the moment for good or bad. "Then we all need to calm down and be reassuring."

Susannah wrung her hands. "I can't. So I'll just go inside. Call me."

"Turn off your spotlights."

"I'll get yours," Lilly said.

She left the yellow light on by the back door, something Mooch would be familiar with. Hoping he'd be lured by the sound of dry food pouring into his bowl, she filled it with a great deal of noise, then sat on the porch steps and waited.

Jake strolled the backyard, calling softly.

"Maybe he's afraid of the Mercedes," Lilly said, and he backed the unfamiliar car out to the curb.

As Jake strolled back up the drive, he heard a quiet, tentative meow from behind the holly bushes. There were way too many sharp leaves to go in after the cat, so he sat on the driveway and waited.

"Come on, big guy," he crooned. "I've been missing you. Lilly's here, too." He didn't think about what he said, just kept throwing out soft, reassuring verbiage.

Mooch finally ventured out in a low, wary crouch, glancing this way and that, evaluating whether this was a good move. Eventually he decided it was, because he climbed onto Jake's waiting lap and found himself engulfed in a firm hug that no amount of claws discouraged.

"I've got him!" he called to Lilly, who ran around the corner.

"Is he okay?"

"It looked like he might be limping, and there's something on my fingers."

"Blood?"

"I think a better question is his or mine? Let's get him inside."

Side by side, they checked him out on the floor of the laundry room, where they could close the door and not have to chase him through the house if he wiggled free. He kept up a long, drawn-out yowl, just in case they had any question as to how undignified this was for him.

"He's lost weight," Jake said. "I can feel his ribs too much."

"There's blood caked on his right paw."

"See a cut?"

"No, not yet."

"Let's give him a bath."

"You can't bathe a cat."

"Sure you can. Though"—he winked—"it might take both of us."

"And a set of steel gloves."

"Nah. Fill the sink with water."

"Yeah, what've you got to lose? Your arms are already clawed up."

"You never considered nursing school, did you?"

She sniffed. "I know something about first aid."

"Yeah, what?"

"You need peroxide and Polysporin."

"Wow, bill me in the morning."

A slow smile spread across her face, warming him to the core. "Nah, advice is free, as long as you take it."

"And if I don't?"

She rose first. "Then you pay the price."

He was willing to find out what the price was. Later. "Mind filling the sink now?"

"Oh. Sure." She activated the sensor.

"You have time to change into a white T-shirt."

"Very funny."

"Okay, don't say I didn't warn you."

He rose beside her and had all he could do to hold on to Mooch, who probably was wondering why the hell he'd come home for this. "Check the temperature on the inside of your wrist."

"That's for baby formula."

"Huh. Then what do you do for a baby's bath?"

Strange how Lilly's face fell as she stuck her elbow in the rising water, as if she were sad. Who could be sad with Mooch back? But when Jake got no more sass from her, he knew she was. They both turned quiet and thoughtful, until the water started flying. Besides, who could listen to Mooch's moaning and not laugh?

Twenty minutes later, they were all soaked to the skin.

Mooch, the lucky one, got a quick blow-dry. Every time the cat moaned his disgust with the whole procedure, Jake felt bad for him, so after he was dry, he tried his best to cuddle the fur ball. At the same time, Lilly was applying Polysporin to the worst of his claw marks.

"Ow."

"Baby."

"Not you. He just clawed my thigh."

"Watch how I'm doing this then, because you're doing your own thigh."

After that, they piled into Jake's bed and curled up together, the cat snuggled between them. He purred.

Jake sighed contentedly.

So did Lilly.

Then Mooch wanted the hell out of there and squirmed free, though he dug in the blanket and nested near their feet.

Lilly scooted closer to Jake, curling up against him where Mooch had been, fitting her head beneath his chin.

Jake's heart leaped into his throat as Lilly came to him. This was *so* much better than snuggling the cat.

"He's dumber'n I thought," she murmured, her breath tickling his neck.

Did making love to Lilly require ousting the cat?

Jake pulled her on top of him. Didn't hurt to remind her how strong he was, how thoroughly he could love her.

She sighed deeply against his chest then. Her whole body went lax.

It was going to be long time until morning.

20

First thing in the morning, nothing to eat, nothing to drink. Swish, swish, swish. Get a saliva sample. The procedure had become so routine for Lilly that she barely gave it any thought. It was just another step before washing her face.

"You look awful." The mirror covered the whole area above the double-bowled vanity, so it was impossible to ignore her image. "Really awful."

Last night had been blissful, with her head pillowed somewhere on Jake's body—his shoulder, his chest, sometimes his arm, depending on how she'd moved about, because she hadn't slept restfully.

But the dreams! As a natural method for a person to work things out in her mind while she was asleep, it wasn't working. It was normal to relive a traumatic experience in dreams, but surely not for that experience to morph so much that, as she woke up each day, she wasn't a hundred percent sure where she'd be. She'd resorted to testing her senses before she opened her eyes, concentrating first on touch to make sure she was in a bed, not on a parking lot. Then hearing, grateful for Jake's deep breathing, not a crackling building and sirens. Then smelling, always reassured when smoke didn't burn her nose. Only then did she open her eyes.

Dreams of being poor came less often, of being pregnant more often, but that was only normal, given how the focus of her life had shifted.

The last thing Lilly did before leaving the bathroom neat as a pin was check the predictor for the telltale fern pattern she was supposed to see as her estrogen level increased. Instead of throwing it in the drawer and slamming it, she stared at it.

Was that—?

Could that be what the manufacturer called a fern?

She yanked open every drawer in the room, searching for the instruction sheet with the side-by-side diagrams that she needed for comparison, and finally found it in the box in the first drawer she'd already searched three times.

She took a deep breath. Could it finally be time? Would she get the full nine months? Hands shaking, she held the slide next to the diagrams.

"Lights, on!" she ordered, afraid to look away.

So many emotions ran through her simultaneously that she couldn't function. Her mouth was open, but she didn't yell. Maybe she squeaked her euphoric "Yes!"

Her muscles quivered, yet she couldn't move, couldn't run to Jake's bedroom and jump in bed with him. Her knees shook, and she had to lean against the wall.

As for breathing, forget that until she grew light-headed and finally gasped for air.

Heart pounding, she caught her reflection in the mirror again. Quick!—finger comb hair, massage that one crease on her cheek. Maybe it'd go away before she jumped in bed looking like a scarfaced Halloween ghoul and scared Jake out of the mood. Brush teeth. Strip off her T-shirt.

Not bad. But she had a slinky teddy that'd be better. Having him unsnap the crotch was half the fun.

As her heart soared with delight, her very soul swelled with a hearty dose of peace and satisfaction. It was about to happen. She was about to get pregnant. She'd get her extra months with Jake. In that time, she'd find a way to prepare him for what was to come. She'd badger him until he believed in something, *anything*, until she knew he'd accepted it, so she'd know he'd be okay after she left. There was so much good he could do, he and their son.

"Oh my God, I can't believe this!" she whispered for herself alone. And hugged herself, blissfully alive, ready for the next level. A quick scan of the information sheet said that to get pregnant, sex was advised within the next thirty-six hours.

Well, okay!

Finally, all systems go, cleared for take off. Lilly ran down the hall to her room and yanked a teddy—red, of course—out of the dresser. She was all thumbs and clumsy feet and nearly fell on her butt getting into it, but she managed. The silk skimmed her skin, all smooth and sexy and begging to be torn off. What else could she do to make this a morning to remember?

Hey, the vibrator had been his idea. It was her turn. She raced down to the basement, where Jake had stored the undamaged stock from Cloud Nine. The first item she grabbed happened to be a tiny spray bottle.

"To enhance pleasure, spray one time on tongue prior to oral activity," she read off the label, laughing at how it was worded, as if not saying oral sex cleaned it up for marketing. "Guaranteed to give your man ecstasy. He'll think he's on fire."

"Yeah, we'll see." Of course, it was one of the items Jake had salvaged from the store, so it must be pretty good. "Well, here goes."

She uncapped it, spritzed once on her way upstairs, thought it was too light to be effective—since it was new, it wasn't primed properly—and spritzed again. Yeah, definitely more mist on the second go-round. Kind of warm and tangy. No time to read what was in it. She was uncertain how this was going to enhance Jake's pleasure, but discovery would be fun.

"Oh Ja-ake," she sang out in the hall.

No, too perky.

She lowered her voice, trying for smoky and sexy, slipped one red strap off her shoulder and slinked into his room. "Ohhh, Jake."

Not only was he no longer sprawled across the mattress on his back, it got worse. Right smack on the neatly made bed sat a dark blue carry-on suitcase. Open. Half-full. Jake—already dressed, except for a shirt, the rat—was sorting through a dresser drawer. When he noticed her, he did a double take, and clean socks drifted from his hands to the floor.

His stunned reaction did wonders for Lilly's confidence. She strutted her stuff across the room and leaned back against a bedpost. Tipping her head back, she ran her fingers slowly down her neck, then her chest, until they settled in the V between her breasts. She cocked one knee just so and hoped to heaven she projected sexy, not stupid.

From the sensuous gleam in Jake's eyes, she figured she was on the right track, getting him hot. Beads of sweat actually popped out on his bare chest.

Which is why it was so totally unexpected when he stared at her with longing in those beautiful bedroom eyes, and said, "Now? But I've got a flight to catch."

Jake yearned to pluck Lilly right off that bedpost, toss her on her back, and show her how excited he was. He had a lot to show.

Instead, what rushed out of his mouth before he could get his words right was, "I overslept. I have to leave, like, ten minutes ago." He had a meeting, damn it, one crucial to wiping out his family's debt.

"Oh," Lilly said, but she didn't look dissuaded.

In fact, just the opposite. She slowly slid her hands up the bedpost, stretching her arms overhead. Red silk inched up her thigh, tightening where it was anchored between her legs, which just threatened to anchor his gaze there, too, except that he wanted to see all of her. If she started stripping, he was in big trouble.

"I, uh—" He had to clear his throat so he didn't sound like a puberty-struck teenager. "I don't know if I can get a later flight."

Okay, he saw something flicker across her face. He liked to think it was acknowledgment that today was very important, not just to him, but to several people.

"How long will you be gone?" Smoky and sensual, her words seduced every cell of his body.

He shrugged; not eloquent, maybe, but words were

damned near impossible right now. "Three days, maybe four. No, three. I'll keep it to three."

"I don't think I can wait that long." As she arched her back, her breasts thrust toward him, begging for his hands to touch her. *Just one touch.*

"Go throw some clothes on."

"W-what?"

"I'll help you pack. If we get pulled over for speeding, you pay the ticket."

"But—"

He plucked her off the bedpost then, careful not to let his hands stray from her face. Well, okay, he could grasp her shoulders or hold her by her arms, but that was it. "Look, I love you, you know that, don't you?"

She nodded, but worry lines puckered her forehead.

"If it was just me, I'd be naked by now—trust me on that—but sweetheart, I don't bail on anybody I love. I won't bail on my family, and I certainly won't ever bail on you. But my folks worked their whole lives to get where they are. They've risked it all for me. Let's face it, financial solvency lasts a lifetime. Sex lasts five minutes."

She grinned then.

So did he. "Yeah, I know, but that's all I'd be able to give you right now."

"Maybe that's all I need."

"Sweetheart"—he laughed gently—"that's never been all you need."

He kissed her deeply, thoroughly, until he knew her knees were mush because she was getting shorter—either that, or aiming for the bed. He tore himself away, one of the hardest things he'd ever had to do.

"Go get dressed. I'll throw some of your clothes in my bag, you won't need much."

"But . . . but there might not be an open seat on the plane."

"Then you'll be on the next one." He gave her a gentle push toward the hall, noticing little dots of moisture on her upper lip that he wanted to suck off. Later. "Let's go, we're wasting time. The sooner we get there, the sooner you get laid."

Lilly flashed him a saucy wink and took off running ahead of him. She was in dark jeans and a red T-shirt in seconds, but due to the long layover scheduled in Phoenix, he'd be thinking about her in that teddy for the next six hours and thirty-seven minutes. Longer if he counted driving time.

No way, wasn't possible to survive that.

Mile High Club, here I come. He wouldn't mind becoming a member.

"If you're gonna zap me over the price of a ticket, do it now," she muttered.

"I'm not—Oh, them."

She glanced upward. "Good, glad we got that straight."

Was he prepared to live the rest of his life with this peculiarity of hers?

Lilly slipped into strappy red heels—his favorites, the ones that raised her ass several inches to a much handier level.

Yeah, guess I am.

"Is it getting hot in here?" She brushed her hair back off her face.

"Nope, you're just burning up for me, babe."

Surprisingly, she didn't have a comeback for that corny line. Hopefully she'd be struck just as mute when he mentioned his plans for club membership. Could they get into the same bathroom without attracting attention?

He grabbed panties and bras out of her drawer, and what was that flash of red? Tights? He grabbed those, too. Adding a couple T-shirts, he flew back across the hall to stow it all in his suitcase, shouting instructions as he went.

"If you need anything out of the bathroom besides your toothbrush, go get it."

"Oh my God—*no*." Lilly charged down the hall, screaming.

Man, if she'd just gotten her period, she wasn't going to be the only one.

He zipped the suitcase, ran downstairs, threw it into the car, and ran back inside to hurry things along. He found Lilly bent over at the kitchen sink, moaning, crying, her face under the faucet.

"What's the matter?"

"Ibburns," she burbled under the flow of water.

"This isn't one of those angel moments, is it?"

When she tilted her head and glanced up at him, his heart seized. Her eyes were red and watery. Her face was splotchy beneath the sheen of water running off her chin. Her lips—

"Ohmygod ohmygod ohmygod—"

"What—" He peered closer. "What'd you do to your lips?"

Swollen, they appeared tight and uncomfortable. An allergic reaction to her lipstick?

Geez, why now?

She stuck her face back under the cold water. But she also held out a small, familiar bottle.

"You didn't."

Her nod consisted of tight little jerks, and Jake saw his meeting slipping away from him.

"Not water," he said, pulling her away from the flow. "That makes it worse."

"Can't."

When he let go to fetch a better remedy, she ducked back under the faucet and he had to pull her away again.

"I know it burns," he crooned, trying to sound comforting, but from the copious amount of tears streaming down her face, he wasn't having that effect. Dabbing at her cheeks with a towel, he grasped her chin and held it so she'd have to focus on him, so she wouldn't go back to the water, which just spread that stuff everywhere no one wanted it to go. He tore off a piece of bread and held it in front of her mouth. "Eat this."

"I need ice!"

There, he had it in. "No ice. Chew." He stuffed in another chunk. "Keep chewing. Swallow. Here's more. Better yet?"

"No. It's hot, I need water."

"Trust me, you need bread. Geez, I can't believe you used that stuff."

"I did it for you."

"Yeah, think how well that'd be going right now." As if chewing would've helped him.

"More bread."

He knew she was recovering when she snickered. "What?" he asked.

"Just picturing you with a hot dog bun wrapped around—"

"I doubt it works that way. It hurts just thinking about it. And if you still think it's funny, just imagine where the burning might have spread *to*."

She clenched her thighs tightly. "Eww."

"Exactly." He tossed the bottle into the trash and risked a hug. "From now on, let's vote on everything we try before we try it, okay?"

"Sure," she said, leaning back and puckering up.

"Forget that."

"Aw, c'mon, it doesn't hurt anymore."

"Want a glass of water?"

"Mm, maybe I'll wait."

"Yeah, maybe I will, too."

"Can we still make the flight?"

He checked the wall clock. "It'll be close."

Twenty minutes later, they were caught in highway traffic as it slowed to a crawl.

"It might be an accident." It was Lilly's fault, they both knew it, but Jake was kind enough not to say so.

"Might be everyone rubbernecking a flat tire, too. Either way, we're not going to make it."

Moments later, all lanes were blocked. Jake slumped against his door, undoubtedly feeling the weight of the world on him at this moment. His parents. His uncle. Maybe others; things like this always had repercussions that trickled down.

"It's my fault. I'm sorry."

He started to argue, but she forestalled him by raising her hand. "I'm the one who used the spray. I'm the one who took extra minutes. If we'd left when you were ready, maybe we could've been in front of this."

If he hadn't come to her rescue with the bread, patiently feeding her morsels until the fire in her mouth was extinguished, he'd be miles ahead. Boy, she'd never try anything like that again. If she'd gotten her tongue as far as him, he wouldn't be walking, much less driving.

"How can they sell something like that?"

"Trust me, most people don't have that reaction. You must be really sensitive."

Yeah, thanks a lot, Elizabeth. "What if I'd gotten it in my eyes?"

"Then we'd be on our way to the hospital."

She squeezed his hand, aiming to comfort him. "Hey, there's no reason for you to miss your meeting over this. What time was your arrival?"

"Twelve-thirty." The look she tossed him must have said *Then what's the rush?* because he shrugged and said, "Hey, all I could get was a connection through Phoenix."

"Piece of cake." She speed dialed the hangar and made arrangements to use her own plane.

"I thought you sold it."

"Not yet. It's ours for three days. If you need more time than that, I'll have to fly it back alone."

"All *right*." When the cell phone rang, he amended that to, "Don't answer it. They're calling back to change their minds."

"It's your phone." She handed it to him.

After a minute of conversation, all he said was an ominous, quiet, "Shit," that gave her the shivers.

He flipped the phone shut and said nothing. He didn't

have to. His lips were tight with anger. The pulse in his neck jumped at an alarming rate.

"What?" she asked, watching him work the inside of his cheek. She had to know.

Finally, he spoke, his voice terse and low. "Marquettes strike again. My dad just received a notice of foreclosure."

"The house?" The home he'd been reared in, decorated and tended lovingly by his mother.

He nodded, twice, then shook his head with thoughts left unsaid.

"But your dad built it." The home his sisters and their families filled on holidays and birthdays.

"And my grandfather. My uncles. Some of my cousins."

Jake called the bank and confirmed that the check had been sent automatically, as it was every month.

"Then there's a record of it," she said.

"But no proof they ever received it, of course."

"That does it," Lilly snapped. "Take the next exit."

He waved a hand around uselessly. "We're not moving."

"There's a shoulder."

"I can't—"

"For heaven's sake, it's not as if you're going to lose your taxi license. We're in a Mercedes. No cop racing to an accident is going to pull you over for driving on the shoulder."

He muttered something under his breath, then nosed the car to the right. Crossing the shoulder altogether, he headed down the hill to the access road. "Pray there're no bottles hidden in the grass."

"*You* want me to *pray*?"

"Hey, you seem to think you've got connections."

"I wouldn't count on them for this. Go right."

"The airport—"

"Can wait. We're going to pay a little visit to the Marquettes."

"We're going to leave it to my dad's attorney."

"Maybe. *After* I have my say."

"Yeah, like that'll make them change their minds."

"Look, if we don't handle this before you get to California, are you going to be able to concentrate on what you have to do there?"

"It's my problem, not yours."

Lilly held up her cell phone. "Either drive me over to Donna's, or I'll call a taxi and get there myself. If I have to, I'll jump out of this car."

The tiniest grin tugged at the corner of his mouth. "Wait'll I get to the bottom."

When he didn't turn right away, Lilly sighed with purpose, holding the back of her hand up to her forehead as if checking her temperature. "Darn, I think that spray has residual effects. I shouldn't fly today, I might be under the influence."

"Damn, you're pigheaded." He rolled his eyes, but he turned right onto the access road.

"Yeah, you love that about me."

His grin widened. "Yeah, I do. I can't wait to see you give Donna a piece of your mind."

"It's time."

Unaccustomed to John's upbeat tone, Elizabeth frowned and cautiously said, "What?"

"It's time to set Lilly free."

Elizabeth bubbled with joy and confidence. "You mean—"

"No more help. No more shocks. It's time to see if our little bird can fly on her own."

"She'll do just fine, I know it. Oh, John, you'll be so proud of her."

"I didn't approve of your bracelet idea when I first saw it, but now I believe it might have merit. If this works, if Lilly's finally learned her lesson, how would you like to try it on a few more people?"

"Oh yes! I could help so many souls."

"But if Lilly fails—"

She cringed inwardly. "She won't, you'll see. I hardly ever zap her anymore."

"See that you don't, not under any circumstances. From here on, the bracelet will be a lifeline only. Let's see if she's truly learned anything."

21

Jake trotted up the broad, brick-edged steps of the Marquette mansion a half step behind Lilly.

She was hell-bent on reading the riot act to her former mother-in-law. Jake favored the attorney route himself, but he'd enjoy watching Lilly throw her weight around. He always enjoyed watching Lilly do anything, but if it involved one-upping a Marquette, all the better.

In fact, he was looking forward to it so much that he almost missed appreciating the determined sway of her hips as she ascended all ten steps. Almost, but not quite. And since he knew she had on a slinky red teddy under her jeans, he was eager to get this over with quickly.

But when no one answered the doorbell after two rings, he grew restless about missing his meeting in Silicon Valley. "Let's go, she's not here."

"Oh yes she is." Lilly stabbed the bell again. "The investment club meets here every other Friday for lunch, and I guarantee Donna's inside making sure everything's perfect. We couldn't pick a better day, actually." She grinned. "Don't be surprised if I have to mess up some stuff to force her hand."

"What kind of stuff?"

"Oh, whatever I can get my hands on."

"You don't throw china, do you?"

Lilly's grin blossomed into a full smile, lighting up her face with impish determination. "If you're squeamish, you'd better wait out here."

He chuckled that thought aside. "Wouldn't miss it. But look, we're the last people she's going to open the door for."

"The last thing you need is this nagging at you while you're trying to create new technology."

She plucked a key from her purse, much to his surprise.

"Do they know you have that?"

"Well, they did."

"Geez, if I were Donna and drugged somebody, I would've at least had my locks changed."

"Lucky for us, she's not as smart as you." Once inside, Lilly swung the door wide, then hauled back and slammed it. "That ought to bring someone. If not"—she raised her voice—"I'll start in on more fragile stuff."

"Uh, when you're breaking china, keep in mind that today's not a good day to get arrested, okay?"

"Is that a numerology thing?"

He snorted. "Please. Or hey, how about that lamp on the table? It's simple, but it'll still make quite a racket."

"It's a Galle. Don't let Donna hear you call it simple."

He took a second look at the squatty red-and-amber table lamp, which looked ridiculously small, almost lost, in the huge foyer. "Old? Or expensive?"

"Yes, and yes."

"So you don't really know."

"Are you kidding? I touched the table once and got the full lecture. It's over a hundred years old. She paid sixty grand for it."

He choked at the thought. In fact, it pissed him off. How many more people could Lilly help with that amount of money? He was about to say just that when he noticed her circling the foyer, idly fondling the trunks of the two soaring palm trees as if they were her lost children.

"Hey, Jake, you know anybody with room for these?"

He glanced up to their full height, closing in on the second-story ceiling. "Are you kidding? Even if I did— No, you wouldn't actually break in here some night."

"It's not breaking in if I have a key."

"Still."

She grinned wickedly, and he could practically see the wheels turning to a plan that he wanted no part of.

"Stop that. I'm not going to help you." He resisted an impulse to kiss her grin away, but just barely.

"Well, she owes me."

"That's beside the point. We're not breaking or stealing anything."

"Let's call it repossession."

"She's probably listening to you and calling the police."

"Then I guess I'd better move this along." Lilly punched the intercom button and said, "Donna, I know you're here. I'm in the foyer and I want to talk."

That sounded like a war declaration. Jake braced himself, feet slightly apart, arms crossed over his chest. He strove to appear formidable, the better to dissuade Donna from throwing the first punch at Lilly. Taking time to put the bitch in her place would slow him down too much.

Then, utilizing CATS's latest feature, which he'd developed for just this sort of occasion, he activated the software remotely with the key word. "I sure as hell hope you brought an *angel* with you."

"If that's your way of sweet-talking me, it won't work."

"How about throwing you over my shoulder?"

"Ooh"—she winked up at him—"later."

He didn't get to throw out a sexy retort that'd put Lilly's body on full alert, because Donna strode into the foyer from the back of the house, nothing tentative in her step, nothing soft about her all-black garb. She faked surprise and pleasure to see Lilly. Him, she ignored.

"Why, Lilly dear, when did you get here? I must have been in the greenhouse arranging the centerpieces for lunch—today's the meeting, you know—and I guess I didn't hear the bell."

"Then how did you know I rang it?"

Way to go, Lilly!

Donna's smile faded. To make a point, she checked her watch. "I haven't much time."

"That's fine, I only have a minute. I'd like you to drop the foreclosure on Mr. Murdoch's house."

"Why certainly, let me get the papers. I'll just be a minute." Stiff-backed, she disappeared into the study.

Stunned, Lilly whispered, "Well, that was easy," to Jake.

"Careful, it doesn't take long to dial 9-1-1."

Donna returned with a typewritten statement, which she handed to Lilly. "Just sign at the bottom. Then I'll call Frank with the good news, and we'll take care of all of your accounts."

Lilly barely glanced at it with disbelief before crumpling it into a ball. "A power of attorney?"

Jake added his two cents with a derision-laden snort. "Just so there's no misunderstanding, I'm here for a receipt."

Donna's nose wrinkled at the indignity of acknowledging him. "For what?"

"The monthly mortgage check."

"I didn't receive one."

"Funny, but I already called the bank, and they confirmed mailing it to you."

She admitted to nothing, and Lilly lobbed the crumpled ball at her feet. "The receipt?"

Donna held her silence. Jake remembered her doing this from time to time with Brady, who'd referred to it as her collection technique. She was so used to people gushing to fill quiet gaps that she usually got her way with it.

Well, not with him!

Maybe she wouldn't agree to drop the foreclosure, but he had a backup plan. He never understood accusing someone of a heinous crime without a tape recorder. He'd gone one better and improved the CATS program, when activated, to instantly copy a transcript to the detective who'd first expressed interest in the software. It was transmitting from his basement office as they spoke. Steered in the right direction, Donna would tighten her own noose.

"How can you live with yourself, Donna, drugging Lilly the way you did?"

Knowing the program's one weakness was voice recognition, he made it a point to identify her by name. He'd add diagnostic voice wave patterns on the next go-round.

"I'm afraid I don't have another copy." Donna picked up the POA and smoothed it on the foyer table, then handed it back to Lilly. "I'm sure a few wrinkles won't matter."

"It was you, wasn't it, Donna?" he prodded.

"Otherwise, I'm afraid Mr. Murdoch will drop dead from the stress, and then poor Mrs. Murdoch will be spending what should have been her golden years in one of her children's back bedrooms."

Jake kept at her. "I doubt you could make Andrew do it. He's kind of headstrong. He'd be hard for you to control, I guess."

Donna sniffed, but otherwise ignored him.

Okay, so he wasn't a natural born detective, but in the right hands, CATS could be a dynamite tool.

"You owe me, and you know it," Lilly snapped. "Now give Jake—"

"Really? I owe you? Oh, you must mean when you took those drugs and set off the alarm, and I covered for you?"

"I was thinking more along the lines of my never having told Frank why you're really wearing black."

Say what? Jake was all ears now.

"I'm mourning my son."

"Right." Lilly rolled her eyes.

"Don't go getting all high-and-mighty with me," Donna sneered. "I'm not the one cohabitating with my dead husband's partner less than six months after his death. If that doesn't scream conspiracy, I don't know what does."

"How about still mourning your sister's dead husband?

The same one you visited every Tuesday night for the last ten years?"

Donna gasped.

Jake glided away so if anything started, Lilly'd have plenty room to get in a few good punches before he pulled them apart.

Instead, she kept her cool as she slowly advanced on Donna, indirectly, like a cat playing a mouse to the end.

"Wasn't it convenient that Brady and Uncle Quentin died so close together? Everyone thinks you're grieving over your son, but I know better. Now, I see two options here. I can stay until lunch, and we can play this out in front of your investment group. In fact, I'll bet your sister's coming today. Mm, that could be awkward. Or you can give Jake his receipt. But I'm telling you, do it soon—"

Donna bristled.

"—or find a way to write off the whole damned mortgage."

Donna sniffed her displeasure. "I suppose, this one time, if I receive another check, I could overlook its lateness. It must be right now, though."

"I don't carry a checkbook," Jake said.

Lilly's hand dived into her purse. "I do. You can put a stop on the first check and pay me back next week."

"What're we waiting for then? Let's get it done." Relieved that he hadn't sidetracked her checkbook today of all days, Jake clapped his hands together, signifying that all discussion was over and he was ready to leave for the airport.

Lilly flipped open her checkbook. "You know, Jake,

just so this doesn't happen again, like month after month"—she needled Donna with a momentary glare—"how about paying the whole thing off now?"

"I knew it!" Donna went theatric, throwing her hands up in the air. "You have absolutely no concept of how to handle money."

"Oh, so if I do it, it's stupid, but if you do it, it's a good investment?"

Against a strong desire to see Lilly kick the living shit out of Donna, Jake stepped between them. No sense wasting time on a catfight now that they'd reached an agreement. Besides, if they didn't get out of there soon, they could have breakage. China was one thing; an irreplaceable sixty-thousand-dollar lamp was quite another.

"It's not up to me," he said to Lilly, putting himself between her and the lamp, "and it's not that I don't appreciate the offer, but it's never a good idea to mix love and money."

The lines around Lilly's mouth softened, as if she'd just blown him a mental kiss. He almost forgot where they were, and his body was certainly leaping ahead to Lilly in a red teddy, so much so that he had trouble following her logic.

"I'm lending it to your dad, not you. And I've never met him, so there, no mixing. Besides, I've seen your work. You'll have enough rolling in soon to pay him back, and then he can pay me."

"All the same—"

"So call him. No wait, we're in a hurry." Lilly signed a blank check and tore it out of the book. "Shoot, that's the last one. Well here, fill it out for this month's payment.

I'll write a second one when we get home. If your dad wants it—and knowing the Marquettes, I strongly advise him to take me up on this—he can use it until my birthday. If he doesn't like borrowing from me, he can refinance. Donna, *dear*, you can start writing that receipt now."

One-upping Donna and solving Jake's problem without getting zapped made Lilly feel really positive that things were finally heading in the right direction. There was a flow now, a current that invited her to follow its lead, almost as if John and Elizabeth had stopped fighting her.

She was restless to get in the air. In Silicon Valley, she could get down to the real business at hand and do what needed doing today. And tonight. And tomorrow.

Oh, how I'm going to enjoy this!

"I'd be very careful about accepting a loan from her," Donna warned Jake, the preposterousness of which made Lilly laugh out loud.

Jake didn't bother to keep his distance from Donna as he traded the check for a receipt, and his smile, if you could call it that, was chilling. "She could be the devil's bride, and I'd still choose her over you."

His deep, rumbling delivery gave Lilly goose bumps. She hoped it scared the living daylights out of Donna.

"That would be a very big mistake." Donna, whose view had been out the sidelights of the front entry, strode over to the door and threw it open.

Andrew bounded up the steps.

"Well?" she asked eagerly.

"Good news, Mother."

Jubilant, Donna rounded on Lilly and Jake. "They've agreed to exhume Brady's body!"

Lilly froze on the spot. This was absolutely ludicrous. She couldn't believe what she was hearing. Her gaze darted back and forth between mother and son, waiting for one of them to laugh and say, "Ha, fooled you." But they didn't. When she found the strength to speak, she hoped she didn't squeak.

"Whatever for?"

Donna circled her, taking her time now, strutting in victory. "Everyone knows, dear, that you're quite accomplished with plants, so I called in an expert from the university. He's examined your atrium thoroughly. He's confirmed that you were growing toxic plants that could easily mimic a massive heart attack in a healthy young man."

Lilly was so appalled, so angry, she could barely see straight. But she couldn't let Donna know she'd gotten to her. She wouldn't give her the satisfaction.

"Yet," Lilly said with a cool smile, "you're the one with a history of drugging people."

"I hadn't seen my son for a week before he was struck down."

Could this bitch really poison her own son?

Had it been long-term?

Was that the underlying cause of Brady's physical problems?

Oh God, Brady, I never suspected.

Had he? But then, who suspects his mother of poisoning him?

"Why?"

"I'm sure they'll ask you that, dear."

It was difficult to keep her head, but Lilly'd had calmness drilled into her endlessly during flight training. She fell back on it now, knowing it was the only way to win. "Good, then. I need to know if you murdered him. And if you did, I'll be sure to let your sister know everything I know. Tell me, do you know who Andrew's real father is?"

Head held high, Lilly breezed by Donna toward the door, silently vowing to get even if Brady's death turned out to be anything other than a congenital condition. If John and Elizabeth didn't like it, they could just deal with it. They'd neither said a word about how she was supposed to handle life outside of conceiving a baby and giving away money, nor were they using the bracelet to send warning zaps now.

Maybe she should have broken something, but a hundred-year-old lamp was irreplaceable, and she couldn't do it. Not even to Donna.

Maybe she shouldn't have tossed such a smug look at Andrew as she stepped out onto the front porch. It was a mask anyway; inside she was seething over the possibility that Brady's family relationships might have been weighing heavily on his mind the last year of their marriage, and she hadn't known.

Maybe she should have waited for Jake to get through his pithy statement to Donna and catch up before she started down the steps. Lilly was in the right, but she also understood the Marquettes' power. Even in the wrong, they could cause her a lot of grief. If they had her picked up on some trumped-up charge on the way to the airport, it would touch off a series of events that'd end her days here very soon. Too soon.

Maybe she should have held on to the railing, so that when Andrew stuck out his foot at the very last second, she wouldn't have tumbled head over heels down the steps.

Her right arm hit on the edge of a brick and snapped with a loud crack.

God, that hurt.

The pain was predictably magnified. Intense. She swore a rather inventive blue streak while Jake scooped her into his strong arms, buckled her into the Mercedes, and zoomed out of range of the Marquettes.

Ohgodohgodohgod.

She'd give up all the great sensations she'd had over the past month if this blinding pain would just stop. Silk sliding over her skin. Hyacinths in her bedroom. Irene's Chocolate Orgasms. Passionate, all-night sex. Even Snickers bars.

"Oh God, Jake." And this was the worst reality: "I can't fly."

"You're not gonna yell at me about the emergency room this time, are you?"

"Only if they don't give me drugs."

"At the rate you're yelling, I'm sure—"

"Shit, you'll miss your meeting." She cradled her right arm against her chest and doubled over until the shoulder strap of her seat belt locked.

"It's not important."

"Yes it is."

"Well okay, it is, but forget it anyway. Why would I want to do business with people who wouldn't understand that you need help right now?"

"For your family."

A couple blocks away, he pulled over to the curb. *Shit, he'd changed his mind?*

"Damn, I've never seen anything swell so fast. I don't

want to scare you, sweetheart, but this is bad. Really bad. That bracelet's going to cut off your circulation if I don't do something."

She inched the bracelet down to where her wrist normally tapered. Every touch, every movement, hurt like hell. The chains were growing tighter right before her eyes.

Jake jumped out of the car. Lilly squeezed her eyes shut, tried to control her breathing and get a handle on the pain, but it was too intense. She couldn't concentrate, but she didn't give up trying.

The car barely rocked as Jake slid back in. "How's it now?"

"Please tell me you were buying drugs."

"Where? It's all residential here."

"Hey, at this point—*geez, it hurts!*—I'm not picky, okay?" She wouldn't know how to buy drugs from anyone, but guys automatically knew that kind of stuff, didn't they? He'd been self-destructive once.

When Jake touched her arm, she nearly went through the roof.

"Whoa, easy. Does it really hurt that bad?"

With her good arm, she dug her fingers into his thigh and squeezed. "Does that hurt?"

"Keep your eyes closed. Take a deep breath."

She tried, she really did. She was just about to tell him it wasn't helping when she felt a little tug at her bracelet and heard a snip. Almost before the sound registered, Lilly's arms and legs grew heavy. For the first time in her life, it took strength to drag oxygen into her lungs.

"*No,*" she wailed, staring at her bracelet now, at the one chain that dangled, cut clean through.

Whatever you do, don't take it off.

Lilly knew exactly what was happening. She remembered the long, long line waiting for her outside the pearly gates.

"Shit, if it's going to hurt this bad the whole time, just go ahead and send me to hell now."

"I—"

"I'm not talking to you."

"Yeah, I kind of figured that. I thought you had an in with these angels."

"I worked so hard to keep my end of the bargain. I'm *so close.*"

"Hold still, hon. I've got one more cut to make."

She shuddered with the effort it took to speak. "You can't."

Oh God, she was getting weaker, and she wasn't done here yet. A part deep inside her yearned to mourn the son she'd never have, was insistent that she do so. A larger part regretted that she hadn't had time to prepare Jake to face her death and not implode.

"I need time to tell him," she said, hoping Elizabeth could hear her. "I need time to make him understand." At the moment, Jake was patiently studying her, but that could be short-lived. "Your family needs you to stay strong."

"You talking to me now?"

"Yes!"

"Hey, just wanted to clarify things."

"Shut up and listen, would you?" It took several gasps to collect enough strength to go on. "Your family needs you. People need your technology. It'd be wrong if you do like you did last time . . . you know, if you self-destruct?"

If he didn't listen, if she had to make him hate her to accomplish this, she would. Whatever it took, even the naked truth, because she loved him.

"It's cutting off the blood to your hand, Lilly. You'll lose it."

It hurt like hell, too, but what difference did a hand make? If the bracelet went, so would her life. Angie's departure had set the pattern. Upon Lilly's death, she had no doubt Jake would repeat it.

Dear, sweet Jake. He was so important to so many people. She was out of time, she understood that. No more bargaining room there.

Elizabeth, are you listening? I promise, if you let me get through to Jake, if he comes to accept my leaving or if I have to make him hate me so it won't hurt so much, then no matter what, I won't bitch about the dreaded line.

"Lilly? You ready?"

"*No.*"

"Don't be stupid, it'll be too tight by the time we get to the emergency room."

Lilly's head lolled against the head rest. "You can't let them. Jake, please, whatever you do, don't . . . don't let them cut it off." It was an effort, but she covered the remaining chain with her left hand. No more sneak attacks. No one'd be able to get to it without her knowing it. She didn't have the strength to beg; her eyes would have to do it for her. "I'm not strong enough to stop anybody . . ."

"It has to go."

". . . but you are."

"No way. You're crazy with pain. I know what's best."

"Jake, please, you have to believe what I know is true."

If he didn't stop them, she knew that the next cut would end her last breath.

Visibly upset, he raked his hand through his hair. "No."

He was *so* not ready for this.

"If you don't open your mind—If you don't stop them—I'll die."

22

t's not possible!
  Jake felt Lilly's life, the very light of her, fade. Right before his eyes, like a bulb on a rheostat, her spirit just dialed down and stayed there, close to flickering out.

All over a broken arm? He thought not. Everything else looked fine; she must be bleeding internally. Her whole body sagged in the passenger seat, melting into the leather as if becoming one with it. He raced the Mercedes through the streets toward the nearest hospital, driving like a man possessed, holding his hand on the horn through every intersection and supporting Lilly in an upright position in between.

"Where does it hurt? Lilly! Talk to me."

"It's John and Elizabeth."

Her conviction defied argument.

Though he'd been in love with her from the first time they'd met at the church, it was nothing compared to the depth of his feelings now. He'd die to save her, if he could.

He'd die if she deserted him.

She winced at every bump in the road. As much as it hurt him to see her in pain, he couldn't slow for every pothole. Too much was at stake. He turned a corner to find, too late, that he'd ventured onto a street with a huge Allied moving van blocking the way. Without hesitation, he eased over the opposite curb and drove along the sidewalk.

"I love you. Lilly, can you hear me? Stay with me, sweetheart. I love you."

Eyelids drooping, she rolled her head toward him and studied him through lowered lashes. "You shouldn't."

"What? Why not? No, never mind, it doesn't matter. I do and I can't stop just because you said so. You ready to give in yet? If you are, I'll stop and cut that off."

"If you do, I'll die."

"How can you believe that?"

"Look at me. How can you not? I can tell you now."

"What?"

"Everything. Why I came back."

"Back?" He didn't want to tell her she was incoherent, saying crazy things. He needed to keep her calm. Let her ramble.

"From heaven. After the dildo shop blew up."

She spoke quietly, and in order to hear her better, Jake leaned toward her as he drove. Sometimes there were long pauses between phrases, so long he thought she'd passed out. But then she'd start up again. Always on the same train of thought, so her brain was hanging in there.

"They wouldn't let me into heaven because I needed to learn things. Like charity. So I had to come back and give away all my money."

"You have a bunch left."

"I failed. I'll be early again. I swear, I won't mind as long as you'll be okay, but they're going to make me stand in line."

Okay, so she wasn't completely lucid.

"We're here. Hang on, they'll fix you up."

He slid the Mercedes to a crooked stop outside the ER, scooped her up, left both doors open, probably left the car running, and ran inside, yelling for help.

One look at Lilly, face pale, lips blue, and she was triaged right into an exam room. A nurse tried to push Jake out, but she was no match for him. He watched everything the staff did, answered every question he could because Lilly was barely able to speak. Half an hour ago, she'd been fighting mad, ready to tear her mother-in-law's heart out and hack off part of Andrew.

Had he been so wrong to cut the chain? He knew it had to be done. How could he know it would effect her like this? Except for this one thing, she was the most sensible, levelheaded woman he knew. Her belief that her life was tied to that bracelet was so strong.

He'd believed in other powers once, long ago. He'd trusted them. But now he only trusted himself, and he knew what was best for Lilly.

Was that how Angie had felt about him when she'd learned she was dying? That she was in the best position to make a life-altering decision for him?

She'd been wrong. Could it be possible that he was as well?

"That bracelet has to come off."

Jake's head snapped up as the nurse spoke. She was all business, with short salt-and-pepper hair and a bounce in her step as she bustled about the room. Lilly should pay attention to this gal.

"Right away."

Lilly managed to say, "No," and with a look, reminded Jake that she was counting on him.

For what? To refuse treatment that would save her? He pinned his hopes on the nurse. "There's gotta be something else—"

"Why didn't you just finish the job?"

"She's convinced she'll die if it's cut."

"Just give me drugs," Lilly begged.

"With that break? Oh yeah, you're gonna get drugs all right. And you're gonna get out of that bracelet."

"It can't come off."

Uncertainty gripped him in the gut. He felt ill equipped to argue this reasonably and make Lilly come out the winner.

"Come on, Lilly, help me out here. You want to lose your whole arm?"

"Hey, they said I couldn't take the bracelet off. They didn't mention the arm."

The nurse shook her head at Lilly's weak attempt at humor. "You convince her. I'll be right back."

Alone together, Jake pulled a chair up to the exam table and squeezed Lilly's good hand between his. If he could just take some of her pain away. If he could just give her some of his strength. "I'll tell them to go ahead anyway. I'll tell them we're married and you're nuts, and I'll give them permission to treat you."

Her eyes fluttered open, and she seemed to summon strength from deep within because she was very convincing when she said, "I'm not worth it."

"Bullshit."

"I tricked you . . . into sleeping with me. I needed . . . to have a baby."

"If this is some crazy scheme of yours to scare me off, you can just forget it. I love you; get over it. Now let me do what's best for you."

"No."

"God, I'm begging you."

Blue lips twitched in a semblance of a smile. "You're praying?"

"Get real." He'd tease her, distract her, or get her mad enough to fight, it didn't matter which, as long as one of them worked. "Dear John just doesn't have the right ring to it."

He could do better; for Lilly, he *had* to do better.

Her eyes drifted shut. Her face was pasty white. He needed a solution, fast, and her belief was so strong, how could he fight it?

It was impossible.

She owned his heart, and because she believed this with all hers, his was won over, too. He knew, as sure as if John and Elizabeth came down here themselves and stood right in front of him and told him so, if the bracelet came off, Lilly would simply stop breathing and die.

Accepting it made his path clearer.

"Okay, you got me." He sighed deeply. "I believe it. So what do we do now?"

"Nothing."

"Maybe I should pray or something, right?"

"Just accept it. I came back for a reason. My time's up."

She opened her eyes again, but they were heavy-lidded. The gold sparks were gone, leaving her irises a dull brown. But even though her body was so weak, her incredible inner strength radiated throughout the room and touched him.

"You're at peace with this?"

She nodded. "I hope I didn't make you hate me."

"Never."

He squeezed her hand and pulled it to his lips and held it there. He didn't realize his cheek was wet until she lifted one finger and traced the track. Barely a breath later, weakness overcame her again, and her eyes shut. He feared it was forever and he wanted to throw something, anything, and yell and kick a hole in the wall. But then he felt her fingers move against his, the gentlest hint of pressure.

"Lilly."

"Hm?"

"This accepting thing's pretty hard. I'm a guy. Guys need to *do* things, active things. You know, to make it better. To fix it."

"You could make a promise."

"Anything."

"Don't self-destruct again."

"What're you talking about?"

"After Angie left—The drinking."

Jake took a deep breath. "In case you can't tell with your eyes almost shut like that, I'm letting you know right now I'm counting to ten thousand again."

"I don't have that much time." Another twitch of her lips. "Promise me."

"Sure."

"Too easy."

"Okay. I promise, if the angels come and get you, I won't go off the deep end. I'll rejoice."

"Liar."

"Look, what can I tell you? Six months ago, I lost my best friend, my business, my home, and racked up more debt than most people do in ten lifetimes. And then I came back to St. Louis to start over. Now what about that sounds like 'victim' to you?"

One eyebrow arched, as if she acknowledged that what he said was true. "But you closed your mind. So promise me . . . anyway."

"I promise." *God, let her breathe easier, please!*

And she seemed to, then. "Sorry about your meeting."

"There'll be others."

"You should go."

"I'm not leaving you. Not now, not ever."

"Everything'll be okay. I promise. There's more . . . than enough . . . to pay your dad back."

"Would you forget that? I swear, you've always got money on your mind."

"Oops."

It was too difficult for her to breathe, let alone explain the crooked little grin lifting the corner of her mouth, so he didn't press the issue. He didn't say anything else that required she struggle to answer. Instead, he kissed her knuckles, enclosed her hand tightly in both of his, and shut his eyes.

"Dear John."

Asshole. Who do you think you are, torturing Lilly like this?

"You, too, Elizabeth. Damn, I'm supposed to pray to you guys while you're doing this to her?"

"Maybe you should pick somebody else . . . to pray to."

"Like who?"

"Shoot, a prayer like that . . . might as well use a rabbit's foot."

She was losing it again.

Whoever's listening, please, save her.

Once he started, it was difficult to stop. He spent long minutes making promises out the wazoo about how he'd live his life and how well he'd treat people and how he'd, maybe, start going to church again.

The chain he'd cut was the one with the oval charms, and he saw them in his mind's eye, one by one.

Serenity—not damn likely he was going to be feeling any of that today. Maybe not ever again if Lilly didn't give in and let them take care of her broken arm.

Courage—he was in grave need of this if he was going to follow her wishes and refuse treatment.

Wisdom—how did that go? Grant me wisdom to know the difference?

"This is a test, right, John? Elizabeth? You're testing me for some reason?"

If only he knew which answer would get him the passing grade. But Lilly said he didn't even have to pray. He just had to accept that there were things beyond what he could see and hear and prove. That her leaving somehow made sense.

He was still struggling with that when he realized someone else was in the room.

"There, piece of cake."

Lilly's hand went limp in his. Barely audible, she whispered, "Remember. It's okay."

Jake's eyes flew open as a skinny, freckle-faced guy set a pair of cutters aside, along with the severed bracelet.

"You weren't supposed to—*Oh Jesus*. Didn't they tell you?"

With her last breath, Lilly whispered, "There's no light. It's so cold."

23

Lilly wanted to tell whoever was moving her to stop it. The swaying nauseated her. But just as in a dream, while she struggled to vocalize something that seemed so important, so life-and-death pivotal, no matter how hard she tried, no words came out.

Cold seeped inside her, chilling her to the core, the kind of frigid where you shiver until your lips are numb and your teeth chatter.

Her face was wet. No surprise there; she had a lot to cry about. Her failure was so obvious, John and Elizabeth probably had banned her from Transition. Knowing she'd better have an explanation ready when she got wherever she was going this time, Lilly pondered what she'd learned over the past few weeks.

It *was* better to give than to receive—especially from the perspective of the hereafter. While money secured creature comforts, it was relationships and love that saved a person's soul. Comforts were fleeting; the others everlasting.

Think twice before chasing money.

Beware of a mother-in-law who always used *dear* as a form of address, mourned her dead lover right under her husband's and sister's noses, worked out after sixty, and made it a practice for everyone in the family to trade house keys.

Stay out of anyplace you don't want your name linked with in headlines like *Dildo shop detonates, one dead.* She owed her mom an apology for that one.

Marry the right man first.

Well shoot, anybody could pass those on a written test. But how did one remember the lessons and take them on to the next life? She hadn't before, and she probably wouldn't again. She really needed a one-on-one chat with someone in the know.

"Elizabeth!"

Lilly wasn't surprised when she didn't receive an answer. No one had to tell her she'd really screwed up her last chance. John surely knew she had a list of suggestions as long as her arm and therefore had assigned her a *Go directly to the end of the longest line* card.

Do not visit Transition.

Do not talk to Elizabeth.

"Elizabeth . . ."

The deep, sexy rumble reached inside Lilly, chasing away the chill, warming every cell of her body. Hearing it again comforted her so much that she began to think they'd let her into heaven after all. Regardless, she wanted to curl up and crawl inside Jake and stay there forever, but she had to settle for turning her head and nuzzling her cheek against his . . . his what? She couldn't tell.

"Elizabeth . . . Is that you?"

"Could be." Betsy said.

Betsy? Why is she here?

Okay, now she was really confused. Betsy hadn't been at the hospital and she sure as heck shouldn't be here.

"She calls me that when she's really, really mad at me. You know, like for getting her blown up. Hey, Lilly, can you hear me?"

A rhythmic sound grew louder, and Lilly struggled harder to open her eyes. It sounded like approaching footsteps, not squeaky ones on a hospital floor, but crunchy ones.

What on earth?

Strong arms cradled her, shifting her to a different position.

"I'm sure you're not supposed to move her."

Didn't seem so bad now.

"Well I can't just leave her lying there. She'll go into shock, if she isn't already."

Lilly couldn't see him yet, but there was no mistake. Only one man possessed that deep, sexy rumble. Only one man ever made her heart race and her toes curl.

But Jake wasn't supposed to be here; this was her journey.

Shoot, if he'd pulled a Romeo and Juliet in the ER and ended up in the same line, she'd spend the rest of eternity giving him hell for being so stupid.

Unlike her first energy-field trip to heaven, Lilly was still receiving sensory input. The cold was bad enough, but now her nose burned, too—inside, the same as it had after the fire at Cloud Nine.

Damn, this didn't mean—No, not hell.

They wouldn't.

Would they?

She might not have done everything John and Elizabeth had wanted, but she'd done a lot. She'd given away millions; she'd helped a lot of people in need. She'd ensured that Jake could pay off all his debts and get down to what he knew best. After all, what he did helped people, even if it was in a different way than John had asked for. Progress counted. She didn't deserve standing in an endless line with a bunch of miserable strangers who spoke in unknown dialects. She would've thought John and Elizabeth knew she understood now that money was a funny thing: Receiving it brought food, shelter, and luxury on earth; charity brought eternal salvation.

But no matter what, she remembered her vow. Jake had promised; she wouldn't complain about dying early or about the line.

Something cold rubbed across her cheeks and forehead. It was a gentle touch, but uncomfortably icy. She wanted it to stop. She fought her way out of the tunnel, out of the darkness, finally opening her eyes to daylight and a big surprise.

Huge, fluffy snowflakes filled the sky, thick wet ones that floated downward and coated everything with a fresh white coat. Well, everything except Cloud Nine, which was blackened and burning. The yellow taxi was nearby, still with two red, heart-shaped balloons dancing above the antenna.

This wasn't heaven, hell, Transition, or anything in between.

Hallelujah!

"I'm back," she rasped. Her throat was raw from heat and smoke, but so what? "I'm back!"

She inhaled deeply, smelling unpleasant burning things, but still, she was alive and breathing. As she pushed the hand of snow away from her face, her heart lifted and soared with the knowledge that she wasn't dead and on her way to the back of an endless line.

She lifted her head off a broad, T-shirt-covered shoulder and stared right into the dark blue bedroom eyes of—*Yes! Thank you, God*—Jake.

Her heart leaped right into a no-hands cartwheel. "Jake."

"Hey, that's right. Hold still," he cautioned, gently rubbing snow across her forehead. "You'll be okay if you don't move."

"Would you quit with the snowbath?"

"Let me get the soot off. You might be bleeding underneath."

It sure felt like heaven, the way his voice rumbled through his chest and into her body, humming with sexual electricity and expectation and the memory of his touch.

As her awareness level increased, she discovered she was sitting on his lap. Too bad they had this thick fur coat between them. She wouldn't mind losing it, but shrugging out of it would mean pulling herself out of his arms, and no way she was going there.

She stared at him, drinking him in, grateful to see no face or tongue piercings.

"What?" he asked suspiciously.

"I was afraid you'd gone and done something stupid."

She closed her eyes briefly and murmured, "Thank you, John. Thank you, Elizabeth."

Betsy *tsk*ed. "She's not making sense. I'm calling 9-1-1 again."

"Give me a break. I *died*."

Betsy studied Lilly, snuggled all deep and safe and cozy in Jake's willing arms. "Girl, if you're dead, I wanna be dead, too."

"Don't worry. You get the paramedic."

Betsy scanned the parking lot, empty except for a few non-EMS spectators, said, "There she goes again," and punched three digits into her cell phone.

"Well, geez, give him a minute to get here."

Jake cocked his head, just so, studying her. Oh yeah, that was the same—the feeling she got when he looked at her as if she were the only woman around. If he could market that, he'd be so filthy rich—

Not that that was what she wanted anymore, no no no.

"She looks all right to me."

She wanted to listen to his deep sexy rumble for the rest of her life.

That raised a question or two, like just how long *was* the rest of her life? Her head spun with the concept. The past month seemed so real. Had it all been a dream? A premonition?

"Was I dreaming?"

"Don't know." Jake's arms tightened around her. "The mind's a funny thing. Sometimes it doesn't see what's right there. Sometimes it sees what we can't."

Betsy plopped down next to Jake's hip, and said, "That's quite a philosophy."

"It's brand-new. I'm trying it out." He barely looked at

her, and certainly not with the undivided attention he gave Lilly.

"You should have seen him charge in after you, Lill. My God, Jake, that was so brave. All those flames, all that thick, black smoke." She took Lilly's hand in hers. "I don't know how he found you in there. It was awful. But when he carried you out—"

Betsy became very emotional then and paused to wipe away tears and soot, and to compose herself. Lilly was grateful her best friend was alive and well, but really, she could do without the distraction. Where the heck was a cute paramedic when you needed one?

"Your fur coat was burning, but he put it out."

"Oh my God."

His hands. Lilly pulled hers free and turned Jake's over to check the damage.

"They're clean," he said. "Not that it'd make any difference to your coat now."

"I don't care if they're clean. You're hurt."

"Nah."

"They're red."

"Huh. Just from the snow I was using to put out your hair, and the coat, I guess. Damn, look at your limo."

She glanced over his shoulder. Not only was her formerly immaculate black Mercedes totaled, the insurance photos were going to get a lot of attention due to the rainbow of panties and bras littering the top, and its new, vibrating hood ornament.

"My driver—is he okay?"

"Fine," Betsy said. "The repairman's helping him nurse a broken arm, but otherwise he's okay."

A news van pulled into the lot then, and Lilly just

knew what they were going to highlight. Might as well take out an ad that told everyone in the city where she'd been today.

Sirens wailed in the distance. If things unfolded the same as before, she and Jake would be hustled off to the ER and different treatment rooms. Then it wouldn't have been a dream, but some kind of sick precognition, and she wasn't interested. She didn't want to be separated from him, not even temporarily.

"Wait, whoa," he said, holding on to her hand. "What're you doing?"

"I want to get up."

"No no no, wait for the paramedics."

"I'm okay. I just want to go home." Was that déjà vu she was feeling? Were those the very words she'd spoken before? She couldn't go through this again. She couldn't lose him again. For her own peace of mind, she had to break what might be a cycle.

"Sounds like they're almost here. Please, go to the hospital and get checked out."

"Don't worry, I won't sue for getting blown up."

"I'm sure the owner'll take great comfort in that," he said dryly.

It took a couple tries to get to her feet. Jake didn't stop her again, but rose with her, steadying her until her head quit spinning.

"You must be freezing," she said.

"I'm all right." He picked up his jacket, the leather scarred with burns. Shit, this was too spooky.

"You sure that's out?"

He held it against his body while he patted it down, and of all the stupid things, she envied that jacket.

"How about giving me a ride home in your taxi?" That'd be different. Change was good.

Jake put himself in her space, dipping his head to be more on her level. "You sure you're okay?"

"You have no idea."

"That's why I'm asking."

She grinned. "I'm fine."

He patted his jeans pockets. "Okay then, let me get the keys. No sense in you freezing. You can start it up and get warm while I handle whatever I have to do here. The store belongs to a buddy of mine, and I need to make sure he's on his way."

Yes. Her path was changing already. Of course she didn't want to change it completely.

After searching his jeans, Jake checked the jacket and finally found the keys. He stroked the rabbit's foot dangling from the ring.

"Good luck charm?" she asked hopefully.

"It's weird. I found this on the floor earlier, and all of a sudden, I had an urge to put it on here."

"So, you're not normally into good luck charms."

"I am now."

Maybe that's all that counts.

He detached the foot and slipped it into his jeans pocket. When he withdrew his hand, several dollar bills came with it. They unfolded, separated, and fluttered to the snow.

Lilly simply stared at them.

Jake bent down and snagged a couple as a breeze came up. Betsy picked one up, then scowled at Lilly. "Well? You could help, you know."

Gingerly, Lilly put just the toe of her boot on the nearest one.

Betsy curled her fingers and lightly knocked on Lilly's head. "Hello? Who are you and what have you done with my best friend?"

Lilly laughed and pushed her away, and Betsy retaliated by scooping up a snowball.

A quick succession of emergency vehicles—fire, police, EMS—pulled into the lot, adding their own brand of noise and confusion to the scene.

"I meant it, Betsy. You get the cute one. I get to go home."

"What cute—? Oh, I see what you mean. Sure you're all right?" Betsy dropped her snowball and walked away without waiting for an answer.

Jake tugged the bill from beneath Lilly's boot. "Thanks. Go sit in the taxi. I'll send one of them over to check you out."

"I want to go—"

"I know, I know, but it wouldn't hurt to get a second opinion."

"I'm *not* going to the hospital." She plucked the keys from his hand and marched to the taxi, prepared to warm up and figure out how to stick around Jake without scaring him off.

Hm, he'd saved her life. A dinner, at least, would be a nice way to say thank you. A couple bottles of wine. Some good music. A nice fire—the regular kind—for the two of them to cuddle in front of.

She didn't even get the key in the ignition. As she slid behind the wheel, her gaze strayed around the interior, and she felt—What? Instantly disappointed?

The dash wasn't laminated with photos.

No touch football, music recitals, synchronized swimming, or a small boy crying in a pink snowsuit.

No tassels hanging from the rearview mirror.

No half-eaten pan of fudge.

Her heart sank. Maybe it was lame, but she needed something. After all, knowing Jake's name wasn't proof of anything. There'd been other customers in the store; maybe one of them had called him by name. Instead of starting the car, she searched it, throwing all four doors open, covering every square inch of carpet and seat, desperate for a sign, any sign that she'd been there before, that she and Jake belonged together forever.

"Everything okay?"

She whirled around to say—What? She had no idea. If she told Jake what she'd experienced and why she was searching the taxi, he'd have that husky paramedic standing next to him strapping her onto a stretcher so fast, her head would spin.

"Yeah, fine." She said it too brightly, but they didn't know her, not really; they wouldn't notice. "Just, uh, airing it out."

"The taxi's fine; it's your coat that stinks. This is Martin. He wants to check you out."

Resolved to get this over with as quickly as possible, she smiled nicely at the young paramedic and followed almost all his directions while she kept an eye and ear tuned to Jake.

He rushed through everything so fast with the officers, they'd probably end up labeling the explosion as suspicious and put his name at the top of a short list of suspected arsonists. She liked to think he was in a hurry to get back to her.

Would he accept her dinner invitation? Would it be from a sense of obligation? How would she know?

"You done with me?" he asked the police

"Yeah, yeah, we got your number, right? And the owner's on his way?"

"Five minutes, no more."

"Okay, you're done."

While he stopped to fill a shopping bag with stray merchandise littering the parking lot, Lilly ditched her coat so she could climb around better and continued her search. There just *had* to be something familiar in here. Proof that this Jake was *her* Jake.

"I think this is yours."

"Uh . . ." She turned her head, but kept one hand on the floor, as if marking the spot, and found Jake holding her purse. "Thanks." She tossed it onto the front seat.

"We can go when you're done there, doing, uh, whatever you're doing."

"Okay."

"What *are* you doing?"

She covered embarrassment with a laugh as she straightened up. "I lost an earring. I was hoping it fell off in here when I got in, you know, a few minutes ago, but I guess not."

They both stared at the parking lot. The storm was over, leaving a good eight inches of snow over everything.

"Maybe when it melts," she said.

"Doubt it. You ready to go?"

He closed the back door on his side and slid behind the wheel with his shopping bag. Lilly walked around to the passenger side and took another look on the floor in back, searching, searching, searching. The car rocked as Jake twisted in his seat. She could feel his gaze heavy on her, but she wasn't ready to give up yet.

"Hey," he said, "your phone's ringing."

"Ignore it."

"Could be important."

"Ignore it."

"Can't. I hate a ringing phone. Hello? Yeah, this is Lilly's phone." He listened briefly, then leaned over the seat back. "He says he's your broker."

"It's a test, just hang up."

"He says it's a once-in-a-lifetime deal. Now or never, you're in or you're out. Sounds big." Jake waggled the phone her direction.

"Seriously, just hang up." She gave up on the backseat and closed it up.

"Sure?"

"Oh yeah. I've already had my once-in-a-lifetime deal."

"Okay, it's your money."

As he flipped the phone shut, she got in beside him and buckled up. Just to be safe, she turned the phone off and tossed it into the back. "I suppose you're thinking I'm acting strange."

"Actually, I was just wondering . . ."

"What?"

"Shoot, I hope this doesn't come off sounding sleazy, sitting in front of a sex shop and asking you out, but would you like to join me for a drink? We could toast being alive."

Lilly smiled slowly. So, she wouldn't have to ask him first. "I'd love to."

"You would?" Besides his sexy rumble, he cocked his head and gave her a grin to die for.

"Yeah." She nodded and went one better. "And then how about dinner at my place?"

"Deal." His voice rumbled, his eyes twinkled, and she was going to have a hell of a time remembering she was no longer on deadline. It was hours between now and dinner, time she could put to good use letting him get to know her.

He pulled a roll of bills out of his pocket, said, "Excuse me," and indicated he wanted to put it in the glove box without bashing her knee.

She leaned her legs toward the door, and he stowed the money. If she'd blinked, she might have missed the sparkle. "What's that?"

"What?"

"Something shiny fell out."

She nearly cracked her head on the dash in her haste to snatch the small golden charm off the floor mat before it got lost. She turned the oval over.

"Huh. What's that?"

Serenity. "Oh. My. God."

"What? It's just a cheap charm that fell off somebody's bracelet."

"But no, it was in the glove box."

"Mm, nope, I clean it out every night. Look, see, there's another one by your foot."

As Lilly picked up the shiny asymmetrical star, the sun popped out and made the off-center rhinestone glitter. Hot on the trail now, she threw open the door so she could maneuver easier and ducked down to the floor. She turned up several stars that hadn't been there before, some with rhinestones, some plain.

"You like jewelry a lot, huh?"

Elizabeth's bracelet. Lilly ran her hands over the mat, along the carpet, across the seat, with a passion borne of determination. She hoped Jake didn't think she'd lost her mind, but she had to see—"I wonder if they're all here."

"You think there's more?"

"Should be *Courage* and *Wisdom.*"

"Let's be brave and smart and get to the bar, okay? It's cold out here."

"Ha-ha."

"Hey, it's the best I can do when my teeth are starting to chatter."

Awed by her find, Lilly slowly took her seat, the charms clutched to her chest. "It was real. I can't believe it, it was real."

"Look at you, you're shaking." Jake flipped the fan speed higher.

"Oh my God, Elizabeth, thank you so much." She spouted tears and had to brush them away.

"Uh, Betsy's not here. And she thinks you only call her that when you're mad at her."

Jake leaned across Lilly and pulled the door shut, and when his arm brushed against her breasts, she figured, Forget the charms. She had her sign. Now she had the rest of the day. With luck, she could parlay it into the rest of their lives.

Jake was studying her, waiting for something. She didn't say anything for a moment as she waged an internal debate. To tell him or not? To risk scaring him off now, or see where she stood right from the get-go?

"Elizabeth's an angel. I talk to her sometimes."

"I see."

"Do you think you'd have a problem with that?"

He looked at Cloud Nine, the fire under control, the building a disaster, then turned his attention back to her. "Yesterday maybe. Today"—he shook his head—"nope. As long as you're talking to her, tell her I said thanks, too."

"Or you could."

"Ah." His smile lit a fire in her belly. "This is a test, right? I talk to your angel, and we get to spend the afternoon together?"

She couldn't help grinning. "Maybe longer."

He looked heavenward and shouted, "Thank you, Elizabeth!"

Well, that certainly was clear.

"Good enough?" he asked.

"Oh yeah."

"Then let's go celebrate. My Sister's Place sound okay? It's a family bar. We take turns running it."

"Four girls and you?"

He looked at her curiously. "You've been there?"

She shrugged it off. "Lucky guess. Sounds great."

She took his hand in hers, noting that while she didn't have the heightened senses she'd had before, he still felt pretty darned good. His hand swallowed hers, their fingers intertwining. Was it too soon to scoot across the seat and lay one on him?

"How'd you like to give some money away?"

She cleared her throat so she wouldn't squeak. "Excuse me?"

"Ten percent of everything we net at the bar goes to charity. In light of what happened here, I'm making an executive decision to increase it today."

Slowly, confidently, she smiled. "Make it twenty, and I'll match you dime for dime."

"Twenty it is." He put the car in gear and headed out of the lot, the deep snow sparkling in the sunlight. "Jodie and Jillian are on today. They'll probably give you the third degree. You know, are you married? Engaged? Do you have kids? Do you like kids? That kind of thing."

"Bet they won't be as transparent."

"Oh heck no, women're better at that sort of thing."

"Well, as long as you admit it, no, no, no, and yes, a lot. You?"

"Ditto."

"Boy, if we keep covering ground this fast, we'll be engaged by midnight." The thought gave her goose bumps, and he didn't jump out of the car, so apparently he didn't scare easily.

He squeezed her hand, as if he'd felt it, too.

"What's in the bag?" she asked.

He glanced at the sack beneath their joined hands. "Oh, stuff I picked up off the lot, mostly from the holiday rack. The owner said to pick up what I could and get rid of it. Maybe my sisters'll want something. Or you. Go ahead, poke around and see if anything's interesting. You like red?"

"I do now."

Reluctant to release Jake's hand, selfishly wanting all the contact she could have, Lilly reached over with her free hand and maneuvered the bag to where she could peek into it. She wasn't nearly as uncomfortable sifting through crotchless panties as she'd been—what?—an hour ago? Latching on to a sheer red leg, she pulled a stocking free.

He sat up straighter. A dead woman couldn't miss the spark in his eyes.

"Ah, so you're the scarlet stocking type, huh?" he said, his tone laced with all the hope she could wish for.

"I am now."

"Is it your size?"

"Doesn't matter. I'm not planning on wearing it."

"No?" He sounded disappointed. "What then?"

"I'll show you when I know you better."

He glanced at his watch. "Is after dinner too soon? I mean, after all, if we're going to be engaged by midnight . . ."

Lilly smiled comfortably, knowing she didn't have a clue how to apply a stocking rope, but if there was ever a man she wanted to try, Jake was right there beside her. "How do you feel about being tied to the bedposts?"

Jake's answer was clear and simple. He stepped on the gas and said, "Screw dinner."